D0290255

WITHDRAWN

WINNETKA-NORTHFIELD
PUBLIC LIBRARY DISTRICT
WINNETKA, IL 60093
847-446-7220

WITHDRAWN

In the Fall They Come Back

In the Fall They Come Back

A Novel

Robert Bausch

BLOOMSBURY

NEW YORK · LONDON · OXFORD · NEW DELHI · SYDNEY

Bloomsbury USA
An imprint of Bloomsbury Publishing Plc

1385 Broadway	50 Bedford Square
New York	London
NY 10018	WC1B 3DP
USA	UK

www.bloomsbury.com

BLOOMSBURY and the Diana logo are trademarks of Bloomsbury
Publishing Plc

First published 2017

© Robert Bausch, 2017

All rights reserved. No part of this publication may be reproduced or transmitted
in any form or by any means, electronic or mechanical, including photocopying,
recording, or any information storage or retrieval system, without prior permission
in writing from the publishers.

No responsibility for loss caused to any individual or organization acting on or
refraining from action as a result of the material in this publication can be accepted
by Bloomsbury or the author.

ISBN: HB: 978-1-63286-400-0
         ePub: 978-1-63286-402-4

LIBRARY OF CONGRESS CATALOGING-IN-PUBLICATION DATA IS AVAILABLE.

2 4 6 8 10 9 7 5 3 1

Typeset by Westchester Publishing Services
Printed and bound in the U.S.A. by Berryville Graphics Inc., Berryville, Virginia

To find out more about our authors and books visit www.bloomsbury.com. Here
you will find extracts, author interviews, details of forthcoming events and the
option to sign up for our newsletters.

Bloomsbury books may be purchased for business or promotional use. For
information on bulk purchases please contact Macmillan Corporate and Premium
Sales Department at specialmarkets@macmillan.com.

Once again for Denny—be with me darling, early and late . . .

*In memory of Skip Franzen. He was my brother
in every sense of the word; solid as stone; never given to needless worry.
Courageous, calm in any storm. When it counted most,
no one was ever a better friend . . .*

What follows is based on a true story . . .

I

A High Old Time

In the fall of 1985, shortly after I got out of graduate school, I had the good fortune to land a teaching job at a small private school in Virginia called Glenn Acres. I went around telling everyone I was going to begin my professional life as an English teacher, although teaching was not, as the Catholics like to say about young men destined for the priesthood, my vocation. It was an emergency job—something I fell into so I would have some income and I could save up for bigger and better things. My plan was to work for two or three years and then go to law school. I scored a 160 out of a possible 180 on the LSAT, so I knew I would get in almost anywhere I could afford to go.

And I was right about that. As I write this, I am in my twentieth year of practicing law for the Federal Government—in their antitrust division. My two years as a teacher seem long ago and far away now.

What happened to me in those two short years may have been a consequence of some fault in the understanding between teacher and student, but it changed the world for me in ways I'm still contemplating. This is not a story about teaching. Nor is it about education, or school, although most of what happened started in a school. This is a story about caring a little too much; or maybe about not caring enough. I really don't know which. The only thing I know for certain is that I wish a lot of it did not happen.

My girlfriend Annie believed all the trouble began with Leslie Warren in the fall term, during my last year. Leslie lodged a complaint against me early that year, and Annie thought the complaint, however untrue, got me so bound up with the injustice of it that my "Christ complex" emerged and I spent the entire year trying to right all the injustices in the world. I admit Leslie's complaint hurt me; it was so deeply disturbing on so many levels that I lost the ability to comprehend loveliness for a while. But I worked with her—with the most beautiful young woman I will probably ever know—and when I think now, even now, how much Leslie came to mean to me—I can scarcely get my breath. What happened to her—what became of us, really—is the one thing I can't get myself to accept. Even after all this time.

When I first saw Leslie she was strolling across the school parking lot, carrying her books against her breast, her fine hair, almost the color of corn silk, swaying in the fall breezes. A perfect September day, at the beginning of things, and she looked like autumn—like the blossoming harvest of gold and amber, in sunlight.

I hoped she was a teacher, but I soon found out she was a junior, hoping to finally get the credits she needed to graduate from high school. She was everybody's worst nightmare, I heard—she was not in my class that first year, so I counted myself fortunate, in a way. But in other ways, I longed for just the opportunity to catch sight of her. I am not talking about lust either—just a kind of aesthetic pleasure. You can't help but admire something so perfectly structured. She had high cheekbones, a sleek but soft jaw that curved exactly right around dark red lips. Her eyes were light blue under naturally dark brown, exquisitely arched brows, and dark, curled eyelashes. I had never looked upon such a face. You didn't notice her body—although it was lithe, and shaped well enough. I know the way I'm talking about her only furthers the notion that I was in love with her, but in truth, I wasn't. Or at least, I wasn't in love with her in the way you might be thinking. She was only seventeen when I first saw her and it was hard not to discount all the rumors about everybody's nightmare. She was so perfect I wondered how she could be so completely wild and cross, full of such bitter trouble that nobody wanted anything to do with her. Not having her in any of my classes that first year did not keep me from getting to know her anyway; maybe I even understood her a little bit.

The truth is I don't think my trouble started in the second year, or with Leslie's eventual complaint about me. I think it may have started with little George Meeker, in my first year, before I'd ever spoken with Leslie Warren. If I had not been drawn so completely into George's predicament, perhaps I wouldn't have been so deeply involved in the events of that second year—the last year as it turned out.

I said I wished a lot of it did not happen, but I think mostly I did what my accidental profession called me to. I know that sounds noble, and as if I'm really going to end up talking about my work as a teacher after all, but really I'm not. To say this story is about teaching is exactly the same as saying *The Adventures of Huckleberry Finn* is about the Mississippi River.

After a few months of teaching, I wondered how anybody could be a teacher for his whole life. It turned out to be really hard work. I had to deal with as many as twenty to twenty-five students per class, five classes a day, five days a week. That could be as many as one hundred and twenty-five different personalities every day. I had to teach them how to write—how to think on the page, express themselves honestly and correctly, day in and day out. Do you have any idea how many pages and pages of student writing you'd have to read and evaluate just to teach one simple idea? If each student is hard-working enough to produce only two pages of writing per day, that's 1,250 pages a week. Of student writing. And they all had to write about something that mattered, not just to them but to the rest of the world. (How could one escape the burden of teaching values?)

You're teaching them writing, so what else do you do with them? You can have them read, but then they have to write about what they've read, so you have to read that too. And what do you have them read? Every choice is a step into the moral arena. Every assignment you make gives you the feeling that you're standing at the base of Hoover Dam, and you're about to pull the plug that will unleash a deluge. But you have to do it because that's your job. I did it for two whole years. I think I was actually getting pretty good at it until all the real trouble started. I don't want to bore you with details, but I developed ways to get around the various writing requirements that gave me time to actually do some good work with individuals—with the students who cared about what they were learning.

When I first saw Glenn Acres I thought I was in the wrong place. It was a big ranch house—one level that sprawled over most of a quarter of an acre at the top of a long, sloping hill that ran all the way down to a four-lane highway. (I learned later that in fact it was a converted ranch house, with several extensions built on. Just after the Korean War the owner sold it to Mrs. Creighton, the headmistress, and her husband, and they remodeled the inside with rooms and bulletin boards and blackboards, bookshelves, a drinking fountain, and just about everything you need in a school except a gymnasium.) When I first saw it, I was sure it was somebody's house. I was almost afraid to knock on the back door. I had to knock several times, each time more and more loudly. Mrs. Creighton, a red-haired, middle-aged woman with a mop in her hand, finally opened the door. I was immediately aware of a palpable odor in the room. It was an odd mixture of Mr. Clean, lemons, and dog shit.

"Yes," she said.

I thought she was a housewife and I'd interrupted her morning routine. "I'm sorry," I said. "I must have made a wrong turn or something."

"You here for the interview?"

"Well," I stammered. "I came from . . . I'm Ben Jameson. Is this Glenn Acres Preparatory School?"

"Come on in," she said. "I'm Mrs. Creighton." She was not tall. Her hair was piled into a great bun on the back of her head. She had a long face, at one time certainly beautiful. She wore bay leaf-shaped glasses on the tip of her nose, and a gold chain ran down each side of her face and then back up over her shoulder. She was wearing high-heeled shoes and gray slacks; a red blouse that hung too loosely down the front and back. She used the mop in her hand to push a bucket full of the offending cleaning fluids in front of her to make room for me. "My goodness you're tall. Don't bump your head."

I leaned down and stepped into the room, but I'm not that tall; only a quarter inch over six feet.

"I've been cleaning up after North," she said. Then she gave a short laugh. "The dog. He messed again."

In the corner, ravenously renewing his supply of bulk for the next day's deposit, was a great oversized lounge chair sort of brown-and-white dog, his tail wagging in sweeping approval. Next to him, watching almost jealously was another dog that looked exactly the same, except he was wheezing from the effort and taking a break from his bowl.

"That's North Carolina eating over there," Mrs. Creighton said. "And the older one there watching him is South Carolina." She stared at them smiling, proud of their names. Then she looked at me and said, "Of course the kids all call them 'North and South,' or just 'Blue' and 'Gray.' The civil war, you know." She was smiling as she said this, so I gave a short laugh, but then she stopped smiling.

"Blue and gray," I said. "That's funny."

"Just come around here to my office."

I followed her, my eyes burning and watering, and my nerves at just the right pitch, so that the slightest suggestion of anything untoward would throw me into a panic. I am the type of fellow whose hands don't shake, whose voice does not tremble in moments of crisis. What happens to me is I sometimes begin to sweat profusely. I have made small rooms more humid all by myself.

It was a relief to get out of the close, warm, caustic air where the dogs sprawled on the gray stones. (It was, I later learned, the "Math room.") Mrs. Creighton led me past a great, long picture window, through a door at the back of the room and out into a small hallway. She turned and smiled and I noticed that her teeth were shaped in such a way that from the wrong angle, or with just a quick look, one might think her two front teeth were missing. But they were there, hanging back a little from the others, tending a little toward the bridge of her nose, and very definitely healthy and white. The glasses balanced on the tip of her nose, and she gestured for me to follow her. "Just back here is my office." She said this with pride, and I felt compelled to remark that the wallpaper was very pleasant to look at, and I liked the pictures on the wall.

"Oh, those," she said. "They came with the house. I never took them down. So did the wallpaper."

"Nice desk," I said.

She pointed to a chair next to the desk. "Sit down."

The room was dimly lit. Only one window, shaded by the oak tree outside, let in any natural light, and she had a desk lamp that focused a weak neon beam on the blotter under it. The window was half open, but the air was still humid, too warm, and inert. One of the panes in the window was cracked from one corner to the next.

Mrs. Creighton struggled to get seated, and when she was settled in her chair—a high-backed, dark brown leather thing with wheels and puffy squares stitched into the leather—she wheeled it up to the desk and began studying some papers piled in front of her.

"Well," she said. "You're mister . . ." she paused, looking at me.

"Jameson," I said. "We spoke on the phone."

"Mr. Jameson." She sounded so pleased to see me, as if she'd been waiting a very long time for this exact moment. I liked her face. She reminded me of my mother a little—honest, directly open and without guile. In spite of the odd shape of her teeth, she was not afraid to smile. "Yes, Missssterrr, Jameson." Her eyes fell to the surface of the desk, scanning the piles of paper again.

I waited, sweat gathering on my brow and running down the side of my face. She shifted a few of the papers, then found what she was looking for. "Ah, here it is." She adjusted her glasses and studied my application for a while. Her hands were gnarled and ravaged by arthritis, but she still painted her nails. She glanced up from the form and said, "You've graduated just this year?"

"Yes ma'am."

"Uh, huh." She went back to the form. I felt my stomach move, then heard it growl. It sounded like one of the dogs.

"You like young people?"

"Yes ma'am."

"Well you should. You're a young person yourself."

"I look younger than I am."

"How old," she went back to the form, looking for it.

I told her I was twenty-five.

She laughed. "You're a very young man indeed."

"Yes ma'am."

"Just say yes," she said, looking into my eyes again. She had to frown a bit to keep her glasses in the right place on her nose.

I wasn't sure I heard her right. "What?"

"And don't say 'what.' Say 'pardon.' That's so much more . . ." she paused, looking now out the window. She turned back to me, "Proper. That's not the word I want is it?"

"Polite?"

"No. So much more—well. I like it better." She smiled and the glasses slid a bit down her nose. She pushed them back with her index finger.

I wasn't sure what to say next. It was quiet for a moment.

"What *were* we talking about." She put her hand up to her chin, frowned again—really scowling this time. I thought I would not like to be in the scope of that look for having disappointed her. I watched her as politely as I could with sweat trickling down the sides of my face. "Let's see," she said, smiling again. She looked closely at the form once more, holding onto the frames of her glasses. It didn't appear that she was actually reading anything on it. "You've never taught before."

"No ma'am."

She did not glance up at me, but it stopped her. "You don't have to call me ma'am."

"Sorry."

"You got your BA in history?"

"Yes."

"And your MA in English?"

"Yes."

Now she looked at me. "Why?"

"I don't know." I could see she didn't like that answer. "Well no. I do know, it's just that I'm not sure why."

She tilted her head back, looking at me through the thick lenses, so that it looked as if she was actually looking down her nose at me. She waited for me to finish.

"I was thinking I might go to law school later."

"Really."

"It's an idea I was tossing around. But not right away. Maybe five years down the road or so."

"You think you can teach writing?"

"I think so."

"What makes you think so."

"I learned how to do it in school. If I can learn it anybody can." I figured modesty might impress her a bit.

She said, "Being a good learner doesn't guarantee that you'll be a good teacher."

"I know. Of course."

"I've known a lot of very bad teachers."

"I guess I've been lucky," I said. "I've only had one or two."

"What didn't you like about them?"

I thought about this for a minute. I could see what she was after and I wanted to say just the right thing. "I don't think they cared about their students."

It was quiet for a while. Now she seemed to be reading my application very carefully, still a slight frown on her face. "Mrs. Gallant, our usual English teacher, had to leave us. Her husband is in the military." She put my application down. "But that's not why she had to leave. She was a very good teacher and the students loved her, but she was not prepared to do the one thing I absolutely require."

This didn't seem to call for an answer. I met her gaze though, and realized she was watching me closely.

"We've had to be very vigilant with our students the last few years," she said. "Drugs and alcohol you know."

I nodded as though I did know, but again said nothing. I'd smoked a lot of dope and knew I might very soon have to lie.

"Our students must keep journals in English class. Do you mind having them do that?"

"No."

"And they must be told that if they fold a page over in their journals, no one will read what they've written there."

"Certainly."

"But you must read everything they write on those folded pages. You think you can do that?"

"Well . . . I guess if . . ."

"Mrs. Gallant couldn't do it. She refused, she said, on moral grounds."

"I could do it," I said. "It's not a question of morals, really." I would have said anything just then. I knew I was very close to getting the job. I did not know or consider the consequences of such a breach of faith. My main worry was that she would not believe me. "I see nothing wrong with being vigilant," I said.

"Children in school have no rights we need worry about. I want to get that issue settled right away. There are drugs, and very bad things in schools these days and we can't afford not to pay attention to everything. That is the first thing I want you to agree to."

"Oh, I agree. Yes." I think I smiled. Inside I was fairly singing, *I got the job. I got the job.*

"You also will have a bus route to follow in the morning."

"Bus route?"

"If you teach here, you will also be assigned a bus route. You will drive one of the school buses to pick up students in the morning and take them home in the afternoon. The school day begins at eight sharp, and your bus route has to start at 6:15. You would have to take over Mrs. Gallant's route—which looks like the perfect match for you, since it begins only a few blocks from where you live."

I tried to smile, to cover the shock that must have blanched my face.

"Don't worry," she said. "The buses are all automatic transmission and very manageable. You'll drive one to and from work. Keep it at home."

"I've never driven a bus." I didn't want to think about where I'd park one.

"It's not hard." She hummed a little to herself, then she said, "Well, there's a text you can use if you want. It's a few years old." She pushed her chair back and leaned over to a bookcase behind her. She came up with a book called *Adventures in Literature*. It was old, with threadbare binding and a torn spine. "The ones in the English room are in much better shape than this," she said, almost to herself, looking at the book in her hands as if she just discovered its condition. She put the book down on the desk and looked at me. "Well I just love literature so much, don't you?"

"Yes."

"It's just grand to teach it, isn't it?"

"Yes ma . . ." I caught myself. "Yes it is."

"Well," she waved her hand toward the big room we'd just passed through. "That's the English room. There's lots of books in there so you'll have others to decide about—if you don't want to use this one. Just pick one that you know there'll be enough of them for your classes."

We fell quiet for a while again. I was afraid to ask about it, but I wondered what my salary would be. As if she could read my thoughts, Mrs. Creighton said, "We are a private school, Mr. Jameson. So you know we can't pay you what the county . . ."

"Oh, I understand."

". . . would pay." She looked at me. "The starting salary is $15,500 for the nine months. The gas for your bus will be paid too, of course."

"That's fine." I had been making less than $10,000 driving a cab part-time, so I was very happy about the salary.

She invited me to a faculty meeting that afternoon. "I think we're going to get along just fine," she said. "Yes, we are going to have a high old time."

That's exactly what she said: "A high old time." I get tears in my eyes now just remembering it.

2

The Best Possible Education

MRS. CREIGHTON WAS married to an accomplished, unsuccessful guitarist. He sold furniture on the side in one of the more prominent discount furniture houses—a place called Maxwell's Silver Hammer. He was a man who tended to the heavy side, balding down the middle of his head, but with enough hair still in front to comb it straight back so that the top of his head looked as though it was lined for sheet music. He was slightly round-faced, with prominent jowls, and a very thin, almost invisible black mustache that he kept clipped at just the exact width of his mouth. He always wore dark suits, a white shirt, and a tie. He did not ever look like a guitarist, but he could do things up and down the neck of one of those things other musicians only dreamed of doing. He could play any kind of guitar— electric, flat box, twelve-string, bass. He had a collection of them in his basement—something I would learn later that year.

Mr. Creighton was also the recruiter for the school. It was he who got people to sign all the papers and who worked to keep enrollments healthy and growing. In other words—and this is how he looked at it—he was the salesman. Outside and inside. He attended juvenile court almost every morning, and that's where he got a lot of his recruits, but he also knocked on doors, and called people on the phone to ask if their children were happy in school. In the afternoons, he was working at Maxwell's selling furniture, but he often asked his clients in that venue if they were interested in providing the best possible education for their young teens. Mr. Creighton believed in the school, and in his wife, but he didn't know a thing about education and he was not very well educated. Gradually I came to notice that Mrs. Creighton frequently made allowances for him in polite conversation, but he was talented, and funny and charming and anyone could see that she loved him totally and without reservation.

Each day before school, the two of them pulled into the parking lot before dawn. Mr. Creighton drove a dark burgundy Cadillac, with a tan leather top. A beautiful car, to people nearing their fifties— or, truth be known in Mr. Creighton's case—their sixties. Sometimes Mrs. Creighton would drive her big, silver Oldsmobile, which was not a bad looking car either. When they rode together, Mrs. Creighton would emerge from the car and step jauntily to the back door of the school. Mr. Creighton always lurked a bit by the car—as if he were waiting for someone else to emerge. Mrs. Creighton would open the door and say, "Oh my." Or "Whew!" in a high-pitched but routine sort of exclamation that let her husband know he should linger by the car a little longer. On warm days he'd go down the walk and retrieve the *Washington Post*, then stand at the back of his Cadillac reading the front page and the sports section, while Mrs. Creighton cleaned up after North. When she was done, he'd go inside with her and they'd sit in her office and have coffee together, chatting about the school, the day's business, prospective students, or the Washington Redskins. At around two, just before the first buses started filling up to take everybody home, Mr. Creighton would get back in his car and drive to Maxwell's.

On my first day I was a little late, maybe five minutes. Not enough for me to worry about it much, I thought. The air was humid and hotly damp—the kind of day that promised unreasonable heat in the early morning, and dangerous pollution levels by noon. It was not yet full sunrise and the sky had a pale luster to it—as though it were lit by kerosene somewhere beyond the horizon. Tree frogs and crickets began their pianissimo finale and millions of stars, little by little, dissolved into the blue. The sky was darkening in the west, and cold-looking, but it was already eighty degrees.

Mrs. Creighton waited for me at the door. On this morning, her husband had taken my bus and gone to pick up my little gang of students.

"Looks like it's going to rain," I said.

"You're late." She was not smiling. It was almost as if she were announcing something awful about the way I looked—she might have said I was bleeding out of my ears in the same tone of voice.

"I'm sorry," I said. "Traffic."

"You have a responsibility to drive your bus and you were to be here at 6:00 A.M. sharp." She told me what Mr. Creighton was doing and I was of course properly horrified. "Now he'll miss his morning coffee, because he's taking care of your business."

"He didn't have to do that," I said. "I'm only a few minutes late."

"You must be on time. We've got children standing on street corners at specific times, and you can't make them wait."

"I'm sorry." I felt awful.

She handed me a map that showed my route. "I should have given this to you yesterday."

I sat down on a picnic bench just outside the door and began studying my bus route. Students began arriving around seven fifteen; most of them gathered under the great oak on the other side of the building—just outside the English room—smoking cigarettes, talking and laughing. The sound of their youthful clamor, the freewheeling uncluttered voices, frightened me a little. Mr. Creighton arrived with my crew around 7:30. He let them all pile out, then drove the bus around to the back of the school. I waved to him as he passed and he smiled, but I don't think he was pleased. Apparently, he didn't like traffic any more than I did.

It started raining just before classes began. I stood behind my desk in front of the room, my books arranged neatly, a notepad resting prominently and at just the right angle on a lectern that was situated just to the right of my desk. Outside, rain poured softly down; a steady enduring shower. I had made some class notes about what I would say. I held the roster in my hand. I could hear the noise outside my room, but I waited patiently for my students to wander in. What came first was North. The great, sad-faced animal came loping in, slowly, from the hallway and stopped in back of the room with a puzzled look—as though he wasn't sure where he was supposed to invade next. His purple tongue lolled to the side of the black lips, and his nose was angled slightly upward, as though he were in a car and had stuck his head out the window to get air.

He was not used to me. I thought he might start growling.

"Hello," I said. "You're not going to leave another deposit in here are you?" I chuckled at myself, still slightly amazed at how nervous I was. I'd worn a gray sports jacket and black loafers with gray socks and black trousers. My shirt was light blue, button-down collar. My girlfriend had sent me out with an admiring smile and a black umbrella. "You look very much like a professor," she said.

"I'm not a professor, Annie. I'm just a high school teacher."

"Just? Isn't a high school teacher just as good as a professor?"

"Well they certainly work harder."

"Have a beautiful day, sweetheart." She smiled, as if she knew something I didn't, and closed the door.

Now, I looked in the eyes of North. I saw a shadow come into view, back beyond the door—a lithe figure that paused and seemed to listen for me. I couldn't make out a face, but I noticed she had her hands up around her chin or her neck, and she seemed to be paralyzed

15

there momentarily, as if my presence in front of the room must have been a shock to her too.

"Hello?" I said.

She stood there for a moment, then moved to her left, stopped, whirled around, and went back out of sight to her right. All I noticed was that she had long, stringy hair that hung in front of her like a bright red waterfall, and she never took her eyes off the floor in front of her. She was bent over at the waist and stayed that way.

The dog walked begrudgingly and warily toward the hallway to his left—the one that led to the Math room. "Good," I said. "Go in there and haunt those folks." Students began filing into the door beyond the Math room and dispersing to the other rooms, dripping water everywhere. My group and a good many sophomores and seniors came barging through the door to my right—what was probably, at one time, the front door of the building. Smoke, and the smell of cigarettes and the warm rain, came in with them. They clamored through to the Math and the History rooms. My students stopped and found seats in front of me.

Even at twenty-five I already knew that really young people—early teens who have just begun to discover their bodies, sex, and the fabulous "other" of their friends—are as self-conscious as human beings ever get. They are not only excruciatingly aware of themselves—of every single smallest flaw in their physical appearance, their voice, their eyes, their carriage and the way they walk, sit, stand, or lean on the wall—they are also certain that no one fails to notice these flaws. They are sure that all people are as conscious of them as they are of themselves, and usually they are so worried about what others may see that they do not notice very much about each other. This is one of the most generous and equitable of all ironies: one has to point out the flaw in somebody before they all latch onto it and begin the torture process of the poor devil whose defect has been singled out.

On my very first day, to prove this point about how little they noticed about each other—and I hoped perhaps to mitigate the potential for viciousness in my first class (the juniors)—immediately after I called the roll, I sent one student (his name was Timothy Bell, but everybody called him "Happy") to Mrs. Creighton's office. Then I told everyone to get out a sheet of paper and write down what Happy was wearing this morning. Almost all of them had difficulty doing that. They did not know. Most of them guessed and of course they guessed wrong. Then I went and got Happy out of the office and told him to have a seat. The entire class was amazed when they saw what he was wearing. "See?" I said. "We don't really observe as we think we are being observed." I have to admit that I got a sense of power to see them looking at me with such awe. I had actually taught them something. I admit it was thrilling to realize the influence I might have. Influence is a kind of power, I suppose; but I was not, nor have I ever been, particularly enthralled by it. I was always proud of the fact that my students learned something valuable beyond participles and prepositions from me. From the beginning I liked how that felt; these young kids sitting in rows, fidgeting and talking in front of me, had so much to learn. Can it be characterized as "power" if one is totally unconscious of it? And can a person be accused of "abusing" his power if he is totally unconscious of it? I mean if you don't really know, if you can't really know that you're exerting any sort of influence, how can you be accused of abusing it?

I've always liked how my students gradually became people to me, even if I couldn't memorize all their names. This was something I was aware of from the beginning, but it always surprised me how normal most people, even very young people, turned out to be once you got to know them a little. I've told people that those two years of teaching were a kind of blur, but that is not entirely true. My memory of it kind of merges and extends—it was a lot of people and a lot of classes and a lot of days and papers and meetings and just going on with my job but it was memorable.

When I had the classroom settled again that first day, and the noise began to subside, I wrote my name on the board. "I want you to call me Ben," I said. "That's who I am. And I'll call you by your name. We are going to get to know each other."

They sat quietly, waiting for me to say something else.

"So, I will only use this class roll until I know you."

Mrs. Creighton came around the corner. "Don't forget to call the roll, Professor Jameson."

"Yes," I said.

She addressed the class, moving in between two rows and toward the exit to the Math room. "Class, this is your new English Professor. Mr. Jameson. He's a recent graduate of George Mason University."

Some of them nodded. I wasn't much older than they were and I was embarrassed to be so new, standing in front of them. I realized I was afraid somebody would notice a flaw in me and point it out to the others and then I would be at their mercy. I did not like the way they looked at Mrs. Creighton. They had this expression of fright, and impatience. As if they knew something bad was going to happen and they just wished it would be now so they could be done with it. One of them, a black student named Daphne, raised her hand.

"Mrs. Creighton? Does we have to call him Mr. Jameson?"

"*Do* we. And yes, you do."

Somebody else said, "He just said he wants us to call him Ben."

Mrs. Creighton regarded me, and I shrugged. It had stopped raining and the world outside now blossomed with light. "It's Mr. Jameson," she said, sternly. Then she smiled, said more gently, "Or Professor Jameson."

"Ben is all right," I said. "I really prefer it."

"You do." She did not look away from me.

"If you don't mind," I said. "I mean . . ."

She smiled, and turned to the class. "You and Professor Jameson will work these kinds of things out." She let her glasses fall from her nose and dangle on the gold chain at her breast. She walked slowly— it almost looked painful—to the front of the room. She approached me, and I noticed the slight odor of jasmine. Her hair was bright in the freshly washed sunlight that now beamed through the window, and I realized she was trying to get close enough to me to whisper. I kept my eyes on the class but leaned toward her.

"Why did you want me to see Happy?" she said under her breath. She did not let her lips move much at all.

"Oh, that was just an experiment. I'm sorry. I should have told you I was going to do that, but I didn't know I would until just now."

"He's not misbehaving?"

"No. Not at all."

"He was very flummoxed," she said. "And so was I."

I wasn't sure what "flummoxed" meant. "What did he say to you?"

"He just said you told him to come to the office." She was still speaking through her teeth. "Don't send them to me if you can help it. I want my teachers to handle things themselves, okay?" Though she had whispered this, and I'm pretty sure nobody but me heard it, I still felt the blood rush to my face. The class began to squirm a bit and sniff. (I would come to see that somebody always had the sniffles, in every class.)

I looked at Happy. He was a thin, bright-looking boy, with light blond hair that he kept closely cropped to his head. "Happy did you think you were in trouble?"

"I never know what I do wrong," he said. "I'm always doing it though." The students laughed. Mrs. Creighton smiled broadly and regarded the class. Then she winked at me, walked to the side door, and went into the Math room. I heard her say, "Good morning." I was very happy that she forgot I had been late that day. I was once again aware of my good fortune—even if North's morning offering was still slightly tainting the air.

I learned to wake up much earlier than necessary, and to leave my apartment in plenty of time to arrive where I was supposed to be, when I was supposed to be there. In the beginning, I actually looked forward to driving the bus. It wasn't that big, but it gave me power I'd never dreamed was possible in traffic. When I stopped, everybody had to stop. When I got going again, everybody could be on their way. And it wasn't bad driving it to and from work. I always had company, and it was easy to park the thing in the back of the parking lot at our apartment complex. The landlord didn't even give me any guff about it. She seemed glad to have it there, and impressed that I was a teacher. But maybe I only projected that attitude onto her. I was impressed, I can tell you. It is a powerful feeling sometimes.

3

Small Miracles

EXCEPT FOR WHAT happened with little George Meeker, my first year in the classroom went rather smoothly. In fact, I think it's fair to say I had more trouble outside the classroom than in it. I had students who didn't care and who wanted to fail, so of course I failed them. I got through mostly though without having to do that too often. I'd call parents and talk to them, I'd arrange conferences with them, and generally take the time that the job required to keep everybody on track.

I wouldn't vouch for how much anybody learned about writing. They learned one hell of a lot about the world, eventually, but you can't really teach writing by talking about it, any more than you can teach somebody how to ride a bike that way. You've got to put a person on a bike and run alongside of him until he gets the idea, and if you want to teach writing you have to make your students write. So I had them writing every day. As I'd promised, they each had to keep a daily journal. I also had them writing book reports, business letters, and personal narratives about what happened to them over the summer, or about what they wanted to do over the holidays, or during spring break. I had them write about abortion, and gun control, and civil rights, and capital punishment. I had them describing what Rocky Road ice cream tastes like; or a raw potato; or pasta with meat sauce. Describe, analyze, compare and contrast, define . . . write, write, write. I also told them that I would not read any page that was folded over in their journals. It was not a promise, so I didn't think I would feel too bad if I did what Mrs. Creighton demanded of me.

In any case, I soon realized it was impossible to read every page of the journals with so many students. So I learned to just briefly skim through, speed reading the pages without really concentrating on much of anything. Every now and then I'd write in the margin, "Thank you for sharing." Or, "This is good," or, "Well done," or "It's good to be honest." Stuff I almost never had to explain, and could be applied next to almost any text. Sometimes I didn't read the journals at all; I was so pressed for time I only paged through and wrote my equivocal marginal notes without reading a word. Even doing that took hours. (Remember, I had 120 to 130 journals to read each week.) There were very few folded pages and those I did read, I saw nothing in them that warranted either being folded over or my interest. At least in the beginning.

But I had them writing at least. The problem was, of course, you can't really learn much about writing unless you have a pretty good editor—and I mean both line by line, and overall—and there was no way any human being, even Superman, could keep up with so much writing from so many people over so short a time. I don't want to keep harping on it, but you must understand: to teach writing you have to respond to their writing. What do you do with them while you're taking the time to respond to what they've written? You get them to write something else. But this does something pretty fatal to your energy and your willingness to plug away on the work they've already turned in, because you know as soon as you're done with it, they will have something else to turn in, and while you're working on that, what do you have them do? Write something else, and it goes on and on like that until, I suppose, a teacher finally burns out. I don't know how long it would have taken me. After two years, I was okay, but who knows? I've heard that when a teacher burns out it really is like going down in flames. Talk about the rock up the hill. Compared to an ordinary high school English teacher, Sisyphus had it made.

Still, I got into it sometimes. The problem wasn't always daunting if you got students who were smart and fun to work with. I had students I really treasured. It's only natural, of course. You are drawn to talent because you see results fairly quickly and you feel good about that. You feel as though you're accomplishing something. Also I had students I felt sorry for. George Meeker was one of those. He suffered at the hands of his classmates and of his parents, who gave every indication of a terrible lack of civility and grace. What happened with him is as good an indication as any of what I came to see as my duty, and it was this idea of what my duty was that got me in all the trouble.

Forgive me. I don't want to be glib about this. When the thing that ultimately ruins you has begun, you don't necessarily recognize it at the outset. In fact, you might not notice it at all. The truth is: Nothing on earth, ruinous or otherwise, announces itself the way we'd like it to. Until the last few weeks of my last year, I think you could say my work was at least satisfactory. For some students it was probably outstanding. Perhaps most of the others would easily forget my name and everything we did in our classes. I don't think that's true, but I don't know.

One of the most important people I came to know in those two years was Francis Bible. I met him before I'd taught my first class. He was the oldest teacher at Glenn Acres School, white-haired, tall and craggy, and he insisted on being called "Professor Bible." In a way—in a very good way—he turned out to be a sort of mentor to me. When I first saw him, at the faculty meeting that afternoon the day I was hired, I thought he was Mrs. Creighton's father. He walked up to her and put his hands on both sides of her face and kissed her on the forehead. (She was embarrassed a little I think, because I witnessed it.) Then he turned to me and smiled. "Who is this young man?" He leaned toward me, his great mane of white hair so imposing that I took a step back. He wore a white suit, a thin black tie. His face was broad and round, with jaws that looked puffy and red. His glasses, wire-rimmed and thick, inflated his eyes, and his heavy white brows crowded around the lenses like ornamental weeds. He was tall and paunchy, with bulky shoulders and arms that bulged under his tight-fitting white suit jacket.

"This is our new English teacher," Mrs. Creighton said. Then she nodded at Bible and told me who he was.

I shook his hand, told him I was happy to meet him. I said it was a very interesting last name.

"It just means *book*," he said. "You've certainly met folks named Bookman, Booker, and so on. Yes?"

"I guess so," I said.

"It's Greek. *Bible*." He still held onto my hand. "I'm not from Greece."

I looked down at my hand and he let go of it. "I teach social studies and history here," he said.

I nodded approval.

"And a little bit of life," he whispered.

"Yes sir."

"Engaging," he said loudly. His voice boomed in the hallway where we were standing. Mrs. Creighton frowned at him as he turned to her. "An engaging young man; I wonder if he smokes."

Mrs. Creighton's frown only deepened. She did not approve, but she was not really frustrated with him. It was clear that she revered him in a way; that she was only waiting for him to quiet and settle down so she could get started with the meeting.

Bible turned to me. "Do you smoke, lad?"

"Sometimes."

"If I ask you for a cigarette then certainly give me one."

"I will, if I have one."

"Let's hope you do. I'll teach you things if you take care of me." He turned back to Mrs. Creighton and said, "Let's get on with our meeting, Julia."

The meeting took place in the Math room, which happened to be the first room I saw when I came for my interview. It had Florida windows that ran from one side of the door all the way around the room to the other side of the building. These windows were wide open, of course, but not just because of the residue of North's morning deposit and ultimate clean up, but also because the weather was blisteringly hot, and the air conditioner wasn't working that day. The other rooms would have been too stuffy, according to Mrs. Creighton, who sat at the front, her glasses again on the tip of her nose. She had changed clothes from this morning. Now she wore a bright white blouse, orange slacks and white sandals, her toenails painted dark red. She had a multicolored light scarf around her neck and draped down the front. She spoke with stentorian exactness to calm everybody down.

"I have lots of things to cover today, people," she said.

I was so happy to be sitting there, employed, at a real faculty meeting. What kept going through my mind was that I was a member of the faculty. Me. Faculty. I couldn't believe it.

I've already described Professor Bible, who sat in the front row, directly in front of Mrs. Creighton. I was off to the side, under one of the open windows. Next to Bible was Doreen Corrigan, the Business, Typing, and part-time Math teacher. She was young, athletic-looking—with white jeans, penny loafers, and a blue button-down shirt. She had light brown hair that she wore very short—a man's cut. A necklace with very small blue stones adorned her neck. Her green eyes were sharp and highly critical of everything she looked upon. She did not have good skin—early and continuing battles with acne had scarred her with red blotches and pockmarks on her neck, jaw, and even her cheeks and around her mouth, but she didn't seem to care about it.

"As I'm sure you've all guessed," Mrs. Creighton said, "we have a new English teacher." She pointed at me and I nodded.

There was a French teacher, who came to teach one class in the morning each day and then left the premises. I think I saw her only once or twice the whole time I was there. Her name escapes me.

On the other side of Doreen Corrigan was the Home Economics teacher, Mrs. Brown, who was massive and quiet. She did not look up. She took notes with a sawed-off pencil that almost disappeared between huge, puffy fingers. The mass of skin under her chin was larger and seemed to weigh more than anything above her jawline. She had jet black hair and dark eyes. If she were willing and able to lose two or three hundred pounds she would be absolutely beautiful. As it was, she looked like a manatee wearing a human mask.

I immediately felt sorry for her.

I tried not to look her way, afraid the look of pity on my face would be perfectly readable, so I concentrated on Professor Bible. He had a tall glass of water on his desk and tipped it a bit to sip from it every few seconds as the meeting progressed. He did not say anything, although he may have been listening. I couldn't tell. When the glass was about half empty, he withdrew a piece of chalk from his breast pocket and placed it in the glass, watched it float to the bottom. Then he set the glass on the edge of his desk and left it there. I kept waiting for him to take another sip out of it—I think I was afraid he would do that, but he didn't. At one point, for no apparent reason, he turned to me and smiled, then sat back in his chair and appeared to concentrate on Mrs. Creighton, who spoke of the "enrollment" success for the year. "We've got full classes across the board," she said.

"And very few convicted felons in this bunch," Bible added.

Mrs. Creighton ignored him.

He whispered to me, "Most of the parents are worse than their children."

Mrs. Creighton said, "Leslie Warren is back with us this year."

The room seemed to shrink a little, as if everyone drew in air at once and brought the walls in closer.

"Again?" Doreen Corrigan said.

"She is determined this time," Mrs. Creighton said. "She has promised to behave herself."

Bible shifted in his seat a little. Then he whispered to me, "She's dangerous. Stay away from her."

He tried to warn me.

Mrs. Creighton talked awhile about how to handle her and in the process explained to me that she wouldn't be in my class until her senior year, if she made it that far. She understood everyone's reluctance to work with her. "But her mother says she is a different girl."

"What's wrong with her?" I asked.

Bible, still whispering only to me said, "She's ruinously beautiful. She's promiscuous. She's into drugs."

"Professor Bible, please," Mrs. Creighton said.

He spoke a little louder. "Just informing our new young teacher."

"He'll learn about her soon enough," Doreen said.

Bible nodded her way, then turned back to me. "Leslie is angry at everyone she meets. She thinks she's smarter and more sophisticated than the 'boobs' at this place."

"I guess I'm glad she's not in my class."

"She won't last the year," Doreen said.

Glenn Acres was a private school. So we were all free to do more with our students than teachers in public schools. We had less to fear from school boards, and even parents. We were not governed by the county, except for fire codes and curriculum requirements. Methods were our own. So I did use some pretty unorthodox methods at times, to "get in amongst them and stir them up" as Professor Bible used to say.

That was the other thing about being a private school. People had to have money to enroll their children at Glenn Acres. Even so, many of the students who came there had been expelled from the public schools, and could not be enrolled anywhere else. These were kids who had gotten into serious trouble with the law and the state had simply given up on them. Their parents had money though, and did not want to allow them to quit school, so they came to Glenn Acres. Also, some of our students were the children of parents who were decidedly upper crust and did not want their children attending a public school. They wanted something better and more challenging. It was definitely a strange mixture. Kids who had been charged with crimes alongside those whose parents were attachés and ambassadors. Washington, D.C., is famous for its odd populace. You might see an actor or talk show host in Hollywood or New York, but in Washington, you could find yourself sitting next to a famous senator or congressman, or a member of the White House staff, or even the king of Burundi. You might end up with children in your classes who were the unruly, undisciplined, spoiled sons and daughters of these people.

Shortly after my first day teaching classes, Professor Bible called me into his classroom. It was just off the hallway, across from Mrs. Creighton's office. I stood in the door, waiting to see what he wanted, and he was planted behind his desk, holding another glass in front of him with a piece of chalk in it. I was feeling pretty good about how the day had gone.

He looked up at me. "Well," he said.

I asked him what he was doing with the chalk.

"I'll show you tomorrow."

I waited, but he sat there, just watching the glass—as though he expected the chalk to suddenly dissolve, or shoot up into the air.

"You wanted me for something?" I said.

"Yes. Yes, yes." He still didn't take his eyes off the glass. "I was wondering if you wanted to sit down here for a minute."

I walked over and sat across from him in a student desk.

"You're new at this," he said.

"I am."

"You have children?"

"No. I'm only twenty-five. I'll be twenty-six in August."

He met my eyes now. "You married?"

"I'm thinking of it. Annie and I—I have a roommate and we're . . ."

"Yes, your generation does things that way."

I had no response to that. I thought he was probably old enough to be my grandfather. I understood his reluctance to accept our way of doing things. He put both hands up and placed them on either side of the glass with the chalk in it.

"I sure am curious about that chalk."

"Special kind. I get it special. Not the cheap stuff they buy here. This is quality chalk."

I said nothing.

"Well let me have a cigarette and then I want to ask you something."

"I don't have cigarettes on me."

He shook his head.

"I'm sorry."

"You have a little fellow in your morning class."

"Which class?"

"Junior—eleventh grade. George Meeker."

"I don't know yet—I haven't got my roster memorized, or . . ."

"He's in your first period class. A little fellow. Wears horn-rimmed glasses."

I nodded. "I think I remember him."

"I had him all last year for history. He won't be in any of my classes this year."

"Is there something wrong with him?"

"There's nothing wrong with him. No, not with him."

I waited.

"I want you to pay close attention to him."

"Why?"

"Look closely at his neck, his eyes, and the back of his hands. Let me know if you see any bruises, or unusual marks."

"Really," I said. "So we've got one of those."

"Is it too hot in here for you?"

"No, sir."

He smiled. "You should go now. But come back tomorrow morning."

I was sort of shocked that he dismissed me so suddenly. He took the glass in his hand and carefully removed the chalk, studied it for a moment, then put it back. "Not soaked enough," he said. Then he seemed surprised to see me still sitting there across from him.

"Come back tomorrow morning," he said gently. "Bring cigarettes please. Marlboros or Camels, either one."

"Okay." I got up and went to the door.

"I'll show you something you won't soon forget," he said.

"Really."

"Tomorrow," he said. "Come back tomorrow."

The next morning, after I had unloaded all my students and parked the bus behind the school, I went to Bible's room with a pack of Camel Lights. When I tried to hand them to him, he stopped me.

"I don't want them."

"I thought you said . . ."

"Oh, I'll have one, today sometime. But I don't want the pack. I can't have the pack. Anyway I'd rather not smoke Lights." He waved his hand, dismissing the idea, then he got up from his desk and went to the chalkboard. He picked up the chalk and began to write, and I could hear the chalk hitting the board, making that sound chalk makes, but nothing appeared. It was as if he were writing with a piece of plastic that sounded like chalk. But he kept writing. Then he stopped and turned around to face me. "There," he said. "You can see what I wanted to show you."

There was nothing on the board. I stared at it, then turned my eyes back to him. "I don't see anything."

"Sure you do."

"No, I don't."

"There's a blackboard there."

"I see that," I said, and as I spoke, I noticed something beginning to appear on the board. Gradually, what he wrote became clear, and it was in chalk. He wrote:

This is invisible chalk. It only becomes visible when the person looking for it begins to realize that he is ready to learn.

"How'd you do that?" I asked. I really was amazed.

"That chalk I showed you yesterday? I soaked it. Took it out last night. It dries hard again, but now it's moist. It has water in it, and you can't see it until it hits the air and dries."

"That's amazing."

"It gets their attention," he said. "And that's what we want, right?"

"Yes, sir."

He smiled. Then he said, "Did you notice little George Meeker this morning?"

"He was fine. He doesn't talk much."

"Sometimes he will."

"What should I do if . . . if he . . ."

"Just let me know. It may not be a problem this year. We turned it over to Protective Services and things seemed to settle down after that." He smiled sort of ruefully, then he said, "Of course, now George won't have anything to do with me."

"Why?"

"Just keep a close eye on him."

"I will."

He handed me the chalk. "You can use it for your classes today."

I thanked him, and he put his hand on my shoulder and guided me to the door. "Don't forget," he said. "A cigarette sometime today. It will taste very good."

I told him I wouldn't forget, and eventually I gave him plenty, but you know I can't remember if I ever went back that day and gave him a cigarette. I might have, but I don't remember it. I had so much fun with the damned chalk that day, just writing on the board and watching it come into view. Of course it amazed every one of my students. They gasped in surprise then laughed. We were a bit noisy, but it got their attention.

I broke a little piece of the chalk off and took it home to show Annie. On the little chalkboard we have in our kitchen I wrote "I love you," and then let her watch it gradually become visible. She thought it was funny. "It won't fade away like it faded in, will it?" she asked.

"No."

"I'm not talking about the chalk," she said.

I laughed. "Never in a million years."

Annie was only five feet two inches tall. I'm almost a foot taller, but I was never as overbearing as the size difference might suggest. In fact, she pretty much told me what to do most of the time and I did it. I convinced myself that I wanted to keep the peace in our house, but the truth was I was a little afraid of her. She was very good-looking—dark black hair, wide, white, straight-toothed smile and large dark eyes—and I could not believe that she had fallen in love with me. No matter how I turned myself in front of the mirror, I thought I looked like an odd amalgam of Mr. Rogers, of children's TV fame, and Abraham Lincoln before the famous beard. At any rate, I was surely not the kind of man who "landed" women like Annie. So I didn't want to stand up to her in a way that might alienate her or clear up her eyesight long enough for her to get a good look at me. The fact that she loved me was miraculous, and that miracle was all I needed to persuade myself that I loved her, too. I thought we were going to have this great life. Among the two or three most disappointing things about all of this is that I came to see that the whole time I was living with Annie, believing I was so happy, I had mistaken gratitude for love.

4

Intimations

WHEN I GOT back home after classes during those first heady weeks, I'd spend the afternoon going over class rolls, studying names, and making notes for the next day. It was early yet, and I didn't know any of my students well enough to have an idea about what I might be able to accomplish with them, but I felt so goddamn lucky. I'd forgotten about law school. I was done with being a student for a while. I believed I could probably keep working at Glenn Acres all the way to the end of the decade. (It's funny how things work out. By 1988 I was already in law school. There were two whole years left in the decade and Glenn Acres was already behind me.) The salary was not great, but it was so much better than what I'd been making; Annie and I actually felt sort of well off. I was so energized and ready to go each day. Thinking about it now, I admit I was also a little ambitious. I wanted to do a reasonably good job—I wanted to be memorable. I don't think anybody wants to be a bad teacher.

As the session wore on, my days got to be incredibly full. I taught one freshman class—ninth graders—two sophomore classes, one junior, and one senior class. There were twenty-eight seniors; forty-eight sophomores (two classes with twenty-four in each), twenty-six juniors, and thirty-one freshmen. My first class met at eight in the morning—the juniors. Then I had sophomores at nine and eleven, and the freshmen at ten and the seniors at one P.M.

I left school at two fifteen every day, drove my students to their homes, and then I'd park the bus in the back lot of my apartment building, walk up to my place, and spend the afternoon grading the work I'd collected during the day. On Fridays, I'd crash on my couch and sleep the whole afternoon, putting off all that work until Sunday night. I fell into that routine, and enjoyed it completely. I didn't think about the future much. I was just too busy.

At first, I tried to be careful when I wrote in the margins of the papers I graded. I didn't want to be like all of the teachers who had commented on my work throughout my years of schooling. I would avoid saying those things that my high school teachers had said to me. Things like: "Did you bother to proofread this drivel?" Or, "Is your mind so small that you have to repeat this construction over and over?" Or, "Did you sleep through all your English classes in middle school?" I would not condescend to my students. I'd avoid comments like, "You should not be in a college preparatory class," or "You should think about getting into the vocational program," or, "You are woefully unprepared for this level of work. See me." (I always hated it when my teachers wrote "see me" on my papers when I was in college. It didn't mean they wanted to help me; it meant they wanted to talk me into dropping the class. One professor, in an advanced astronomy class, actually said to me, "How'd you get in here?")

I hoped to be a different kind of teacher, and I think overall, I was. It is a fair assertion to say that I listened to my students, and tried to draw them out. I encouraged them if I could and gave them hope and belief in what they were doing.

One day after school Annie got home from work pretty late, and I didn't feel like cooking, so we went to Arby's and got roast beef sandwiches. I'd been teaching for a while but we hadn't talked much about it after the first day, so when we were seated at the table and unwrapping our food, I started talking about my day. I mentioned Professor Bible.

She said, "Who's he again?"

"He's the old guy. Hair as white as a wedding gown. Thick, too."

"What's he teach?"

"Social Studies, and History."

She poured a large amount of white horsey and red barbecue sauce on her roast beef, then covered it with the top bun and tried to lift it without letting it leak down the side of her hand and back onto the napkin in front of her. Her face was a study in concentration.

I should tell you a little more about Annie. I've already said she was pretty, and that I was a little afraid of her. She had a way of ruining my sense of well-being just with a look, or with the tone of her voice. Not that I feared physical harm. I was constantly worried about a sudden loss of affection, and she was always capable of disarming me. "Fuck you" was one of her favorite expressions. She used it judiciously— only when she wanted to end discussion, or when she wanted to begin one. When she ended a discussion with "fuck you," it really was the last thing she would say—sometimes for hours. When she began a discussion with "fuck you" it was usually followed by the conditional form of some proposition—to wit, "Fuck you if you think I'm going to the beach this weekend." Or, "Fuck you if you don't want to eat out tonight." Or, "Fuck you if you want to be such a neat freak."

Anyway, that afternoon at Arby's I watched her struggle with her sandwich. She turned her head to take a bite. While she was chewing,

I said, "Professor Bible's just one of those guys, you know? You can tell he's interesting. He knows a lot and he's got a lot of experience. Mrs. Creighton said the kids love him."

"So he's old enough to be harmless."

"I think I might learn a few things from him. He said he would teach me things if I . . ." I stopped. It occurred to me that the proviso that I keep him in cigarettes would probably diminish the promise of what I might learn. "He is just so imposing."

"He might teach you things? He said that?"

I pointed to her chin. "You've got . . ."

"What?" She had a little Statue of Liberty-shaped strip of horsey sauce and red barbecue smeared from the corner of her mouth to her jawline.

"Barbecue sauce," I said.

She wiped the lower half of her face with a napkin. "Why would anybody announce that he will teach you things?"

"That's why I think he's interesting. You know what he said to me when I was leaving today?"

"What?"

"He wanted to know if I was a Marxist. I told him that I was just the English guy, and he laughed. It was a good laugh. I don't think he takes himself too seriously."

"Does anybody even pay attention to Marxists anymore?" Annie wanted to know.

"Reagan does."

"The only Marx he knows is Groucho."

"Well, he's met Gorbachev," I said.

"Gorbachev's not a Marxist."

I took another careful bite of my sandwich. We ate quietly for a while, looking out the window.

"Did you see any bruises or marks today?" she asked. I had told her about George Meeker.

"No. He looked fine." Another perfectly spotless bite of my sandwich. I held it close, over the paper, but I didn't use too much sauce, so it was fairly easy to keep the thing clean.

"Have you gotten to know anybody else on the faculty?" Annie burbled, through a stout mixture of sauce, meat, and bun.

I told her about the others. She was curious about Doreen Corrigan.

"Is she attractive?"

"I think she's a lesbian."

"Really. What makes you think that?"

"She's kind of boyish—you know. Masculine and . . ." I didn't finish the sentence. Annie frowned and her eyes looked slightly out of alignment—as though one of them might lazily wander off in another direction. Horsey sauce dripped down both sides of her mouth. "Jesus Christ," I said. "You look like you've just been devouring a dead skunk or something." I reached across the table with my napkin and wiped the sauce off her mouth. She leaned toward me a little, to let me get all of it. Her hands were still sauce-dipped, and the sandwich was again beginning to fall apart as she tried to negotiate it into position for another bite.

"Damn you make a mess," I said.

She laughed, or seemed to. Her mouth was full, so it was hard to tell. When she was done chewing, she said, "Important dating tip for our children. Never order an Arby's Roast Beef sandwich."

Sometimes I liked it when she made references about our children like that—it meant she saw us together in the future. Other times, I didn't like it so much. It could get to feel like a kind of intimation or hint of pressure to go ahead and do something about our relationship. On this night, it was charming and I smiled. "Never douse your sandwich in a half a gallon of sauce." I held my unsoiled fingers up, and then took another clean bite. "There's a way to do it that's not so messy."

She shook her head and called me a snob.

After a long pause she said, "Why do men always think they know a lesbian when they see one?"

"I didn't say I knew it. I said I thought she might be. The way she dresses and all . . ."

Annie shook her head. "Men," she said.

"So, is it your contention that most gays, male and female, do not have a certain way of carrying themselves and often do not dress in a certain way?"

"Wow. You already sound like a professor. So perfectly pompous."

"I just appear pompous to you because my mouth is clean," I said.

"Fuck you," Annie said, which of course ended the discussion.

When we were finished eating and were walking to the car, I said, "I really like Mrs. Creighton, but I think she's a bit on the ditzy side."

"Why?"

I told her about North and South, the odor in the math room. She already knew how my interview had gone.

"You're going to have a ball in that place," Annie said. She laughed a little too loudly about the dogs and North's morning deposits, but I could tell she wasn't pissed off anymore.

"Mr. Clean really is an awful smell," I said. "I think it might be better if she just used water to clean it up and let everybody get used to the smell of shit in that room."

"Can't she keep the dogs somewhere else?"

"I guess not."

"Does she live there?"

"No. She gets there before dawn every morning."

We drove home in silence. When I unlocked the door to our apartment, Annie went immediately to the bathroom to wash her face. When she came back, she patted me on the shoulder and I took hold of her hand and pulled her into my arms. I wanted to tell her I was sorry. I don't know why but when she was in the bathroom I got this picture of her with the horsey sauce all over her face and I felt profoundly sorry for her. It was the strangest thing. I didn't say anything, though; I just kissed her on the cheek and told her I loved her. We sat on the couch for a while, and then I got up to put on some music. I picked out something by Fauré but before I could turn it on, she said, "So you're an English teacher."

"Yeah. Hard to believe isn't it?"

"Do you know where to start?"

"I'm getting them to write. I'm a writing teacher."

"And reading?"

"Of course."

"Good luck," she said.

I didn't like her tone. "Why do you say it like that?"

"Like what?"

"Like I'm going to be trying to do the impossible?"

"I guess I just remember what it was like being in high school English classes."

"So do I."

She said nothing. I put the record on and then turned the volume down low. When I came back I said, "My classes will be different."

"You think so."

"I know so."

"Well, like I said. 'Good luck.'"

"That's what I love about you," I said. "Your abiding faith in me."

"I have faith in you. It's the students I'm worried about."

5

Before My Helpless Sight

I GOT LOST in the work with my students and their writing those first few months, but I remembered to keep a close eye on George Meeker. It wasn't hard to do that—he really was different. He was short for a junior, almost diminutive; small-boned and thin. His horn-rimmed glasses alone would have made him stand out from the others, but he kept his hair cut close to his skull and he was always dressed in a suit with a white shirt and tie and highly shined shoes. He had keen, deep-set eyes that frequently looked worn—as though he had not slept in a long time—but he was always awake and attentive in my class. He read books in his spare time, so he was one of those students who would get your attention anyway; he could talk about almost anything, and on occasion the others accused him of being a know-it-all. He was also mercilessly teased for his short stature, his shyness, and his name. *Meeker.* What could be more ironic? God has a plan alright and it's not mysterious. I think it is utterly diabolical.

I strived to protect George from the other students, at least in my class, but I could not vouch for what might have been happening to him in other classes, or outside in the break area. George was a little boy in every feature, but he was trying desperately to be a man; to kill the little boy in himself. This spectacle was frequently hard to watch. But he never looked bad or injured. He was good-spirited, and had a lot to say in class. He wrote about ordinary things: fishing with his father, going to the library and checking out books on dinosaurs; the unfairness of late fees for slow readers. He did not withdraw from the fray, as it were, and he stood up to the teasing and harassment of the others. I got to be kind of proud of him in those first few months.

Then one day, Professor Bible stopped by my classroom. I'd just finished my last class and had to get outside to the bus, but he lumbered in and sat down in the chair by my desk. He seemed out of breath.

"Did you talk to George Meeker today?"

"He seemed fine."

"Did he say anything to you about his father."

"Not today. But I can tell you—that boy loves his father."

Bible rubbed his chin, staring at me.

I put the day's pile of papers in my briefcase and closed it. "Lots of grading today."

He had no response.

"Lots of grading every day," I said.

"You bring cigarettes today?"

"No, but I'm prepared." I opened my desk drawer and retrieved a pack of Camel Lights. I'd bought them a week before, and hadn't opened the pack yet.

As I was tearing the cellophane from the pack, Bible said, "I prefer the regular camel filters."

"This is all I've got today."

"Mrs. Creighton told me that George is worried about what's going to happen to him tonight."

"Tonight?" I handed the pack to him. He held it in his hand, studying it. For a moment he seemed confused, and I had a stab of fear that he was showing his age; that I'd have to tell him what he was holding in his hand. But then he opened it and retrieved two cigarettes. One he put in his shirt pocket, the other he let dangle out of his mouth.

"You're not going to light that in here, are you?"

He shook his head. "George's in big trouble. He washed the family car and forgot to turn off the hose yesterday and his basement got a little flooded."

"That would get *me* in trouble."

"His father was out of town yesterday. He comes back tonight."

"George said nothing about it to me," I said.

He handed back the pack of cigarettes and I put them back in the drawer and waited. He just sat there, looking off into space. I really had to get out of there. It was almost two twenty, and my students were probably already waiting on the bus.

"Well," I said. "I should get going."

"Look at him closely tomorrow."

"I will."

"Pay attention."

I had my bag in hand, standing by the desk, and he looked at me now with serious, darkened eyes. It was almost as if the thick brows over his glasses had turned to a darker shade. He said, "That boy's going to need you. Do you understand?"

"I do."

"This is where you learn a few things," he said, rising from the chair. He took a deep breath; then, with the cigarette still dangling from his mouth, he left the room.

The next day I watched George take his assigned seat in front of the picture window, halfway back in the first row of seats. This morning, instead of taking out his notebook and a pen, he stared out the window. I had graded all their papers and I was ready to talk about problems I was seeing repeated by everybody. This would take most of the hour, and then I'd let them go without a writing assignment for one day. (I sometimes just had to design breaks like that for myself, to keep from going mad.)

I think I was demonstrating the singular and plural form of the word "woman." I wrote on the board, "1 man, 1 wo<u>man</u>, 2 men, 2 wo<u>men</u>." As I gave my talk about their writing, George seemed to check himself a bit—sitting back in his seat and furtively glancing down at the front of his shirt, his pants.

I said, "All of you write the word 'women' when you mean one 'woman.' You see how to remember it?"

He looked out the window again. I walked down the aisle toward where he was sitting. I talked about the use of possessives, I think, or some other issue. He did not look at me, but I thought I noticed him take in a little extra air, as though he had stifled a cough or a sneeze. Then I realized he was trying desperately not to cry.

I didn't want to embarrass him, but I was concerned about the reaction if he actually started crying and the others saw him doing that. I stopped midway down the aisle, a few feet away from where he was sitting. Happy Bell, the boy I'd sent to the office back on that first day said, "Hey Mr. Jameson."

I looked at him. "Call me Ben."

"Mr. Ben."

"Just Ben."

"Just Ben."

This led to jeers across the room.

"Settle down," I said.

George slowly turned his head, his chin held high. He would not be cowed. I noticed again how small the boy was—small in size and bone structure; he was almost delicate and very pale. His skin looked like brushed marble. Under his chin, at the top of his throat, he wore a bruise that ran from one side to the other. It looked as though he'd been tilted from a horse by running full speed into a small branch.

"Watch this," Happy said. He produced a Kleenex. All eyes were on him as he stood up, staring at it as though it was alive.

"Sit down now, Happy," I said.

He threw the Kleenex into the air above his head, and it wafted down, slowly in front of his face. He did not lean back or forward. He kept his face exactly straight, and as the tissue passed his nose, he breathed in hard and it stuck there against his face covering his nose and mouth.

The whole room erupted in laughter.

"How'd you do that?" I said.

Happy took the Kleenex off his face and said, "I'll show you." He threw it up again and everybody cheered. This time it didn't move toward him at all and fell to the floor. He picked it up. "Wait a minute." He was in a hurry. The class was still laughing very loud. It echoed off the shelves and books that lined the room. He threw it in the air again, moved a little to get exactly in position in front of its path. When it passed his eyes he inhaled again very fast and it moved gently to his face and stuck there.

"Let me try it," somebody said.

"Settle down now," I said, but I was laughing too.

Mrs. Creighton came in, a look of puzzlement on her face. "What's all the noise in here?"

I didn't know what to tell her.

Happy sat down, the Kleenex wadded tightly in his fist. He tried not to laugh, as did the rest of the class.

"What's so funny?" Mrs. Creighton said. She was not amused, and it astonished me to see how easily her face sank into a kind of visual reproach. She looked as though she were repressing a shout. I just knew her demeanor was a result of something other than the noise in my room and I did not feel like laughing anymore. "Happy was demonstrating a little trick he learned somewhere."

"This is school," Mrs. Creighton said, through tight red lips, so that it almost sounded like she said "skole."

"I'm sorry," I said. "It's my fault."

"If you would please refrain from such loud displays," she said—but she wasn't talking to me, she was addressing the class. Her voice was high-pitched and strained, not loud—almost a quiet scream. "It disturbs the other classes, and disrupts the entire program. This is a small building."

"I really am sorry," I said.

She still did not look at me. It was quiet for a moment. Then she said, "Every one of you knows better."

The students were quiet now, but suppressed laughter adorned every face—eyes averted from Mrs. Creighton, each student about to burst from the effort not to laugh. I looked at George and he seemed to have control of himself. He wasn't laughing, but I could see the struggle against tears had stopped. He did not look at me, but his face appeared calm now.

"Happy," Mrs. Creighton said. "You come with me."

"Mrs. Creighton," I said.

She looked at me, still the stern expression on her face.

"It's my fault. I let him show us the trick."

"Would you like to see it, Mrs. Creighton?" Happy said.

A slight titter arose in the class.

"No, I wouldn't," she said.

Happy started to get up to go with her, but she put her hand on his shoulder and gently put him back in his seat. "I'll let it go this time."

Happy did not look back at her. He stared straight ahead, still clutching the Kleenex in his fist.

"Okay." Mrs. Creighton smiled at me.

I felt insanely reassured. "I really am sorry," I said. "I thought we needed a little levity this morning."

The stern look returned, but now it was attenuated by a kind of busy, preoccupied sort of expression. "We've got to prepare for parent conferences."

"Okay," I said.

"George is out sick today," she said. "Could you leave the assignment for tomorrow for him on my desk—or . . ."

"George is here," I said. "He's right there."

Again there were slight snickers from the class.

She looked over at George and I realized he had sort of frozen himself in place—as if he were waiting for somebody to hurl cold water on him. He stared straight ahead, gripping the front of his desk with both hands.

"George?" Mrs. Creighton said.

He would not look at her. He said, "Ma'am?"

"What are you doing here?"

"I came to school," he said, and his voice broke. "I want to go to school."

"Well your mother called me this morning . . ." Mrs. Creighton stopped.

It got very quiet in the room. Everyone just sort of waited for him to say something. I felt so sorry for him.

"I'm in school today," he said, his voice trembling.

"Are you sick?"

"I'm in school," he whispered.

"George," she said, loudly.

"I'm not sick," he said. Tears welled in his eyes. "I'm in school."

Looking slightly tired, and a little confused, Mrs. Creighton started to turn and leave through the door she had come through, but then she changed her mind and walked rather purposefully to the Math room. The class breathed a sigh of relief, and some of them started laughing quietly again.

"Come on you guys," I said. "Let's get to work."

I decided to forget what I'd planned for the class. Now I didn't want to talk, and I figured the best thing to do was to get them writing something so I could sit and watch them and worry about George in silence.

"Would you like to learn how writers actually write?" I said.

They had their notebooks out, each with pen in hand.

"It's a little like what Happy did with that Kleenex."

Now they were puzzled, but some of them started laughing again, quietly.

"You start with something very light and airy, thrown into the air—an idea, or a thing you remember, or maybe an experience you have to tell about." I strolled around the room and their eyes followed me. George continued to stare straight ahead. I said, "Try this: Everybody take your pen and put it to paper."

"You want us to write something?" Happy said.

"Right now, I want each of you to put the point of your pen on the paper and I'll tell you when to start writing. Okay?"

They did as they were told.

"When I tell you to start, I want you to begin writing, whether or not you have anything to say. In other words, I just want you to start the actual physical activity of writing on the page. But I want you to write words. I want you to write whatever is in your mind—even if it's nothing. If you can't think of something to write, just write, 'my mind is blank, my mind is blank, my mind is blank,' like that, over and over. You'll get tired of writing that. When you get tired of it, write, 'I'm tired of writing this.' Then you might begin to wonder why I'm asking you to do this, so write that. But the key is to just start writing, and don't stop until I tell you to."

"What should we write about?" Happy asked.

"You understand," I said, "I don't want you to stop writing for anything. Not to think of a word, not to correct anything you've written, not to try to remember an event, or how to spell a word, or anything at all. Once you start writing, do not stop until I tell you to."

"But what do we write about?" Happy asked again.

"Write about anything you want."

"I don't want to write at all."

Again, titters of laughter. I realized they had nothing to say yet; they were not angry or challenged or in any way threatened by ideas.

I also knew this was a private school and I could do almost anything I wanted within reason. And then it hit me what I could have them do. "I'll give you something to think about, and you can write about it or not."

He nodded, then set himself, pen in hand. The others, too, got ready. It was almost as if they were now engaged in something very much like a race. They were definitely at the starting line.

"Close your eyes first," I said.

They did so.

"Now concentrate on what I say. And no matter how you feel, only listen. Wait until I tell you to begin. Okay?"

A few of them nodded.

"Listen carefully." I paused for a few seconds, then I went on. "The sun is bright this morning, and it won't rain anytime soon. Don't you like it when the sun makes shadows through the leaves of those oak trees outside our window? Think about how beautiful fall is. I like the cold air, and the benevolent sun."

"What kind of sun?" somebody asked.

"The kind sun. Don't talk. Just listen." I was in front of the room now. "Can you see the shadows in your memory? Open your eyes for a moment and look out the window. See how green the grass is on the sunny side of those shadows, and how deeply green the grass is in the shadows? Really look at it now." They all gazed out the picture window, even George. "Look carefully. You can get up if you want." Some on the far side of the room stood up so they could see. Again I said, "Look how dark green the grass looks in the shadows. Shades of color. A beautiful world. And it's all here for us to see and enjoy because why?"

They were quiet for a long while, some still staring out the window, some looking at me now. Finally, somebody said, "It's nature."

"Well," I said. "Some people think God put it there. President Reagan thinks it was God."

A few of them nodded.

"Do you think God put it there?"

Several of them agreed that God had done so.

I said, "Well some people also wonder, if he made the gorgeous spring and fall, why did he also make tornados and hurricanes. What would be so wonderful about a god like that? Others want to know why we refer to God as a *he*? Would God be a man, really? With hormones and whiskers, biceps and pectorals? And would he really need genitals? What makes him a man? What would make him a woman? What would make him human at all, except humans? Some say if we were all dogs, then God would be a dog. If we were all elephants, then God would be an elephant. The truth is: a lot of people say there is no God."

"Mr. Jameson," Happy said. "I don't appreciate . . ."

"Now," I said. "Everybody start writing now. Happy, whatever you were going to say, put it on the paper. Start writing what's on your mind now and don't stop until I tell you to."

They all began writing furiously. I came to call this little exercise my "God Assignment." It always got students writing. It's just simply true that no one can write very well who doesn't want to write, and who has nothing to say. I gave them something to say.

I went to my desk and sat down. I watched them, the intense look of anger, frustration, and denial in every face; the hard-edged look of a need for rebuttal and defense driving them. (A few agreed there was no God, but they wanted to tell me that as luridly as they could.) All of them went after the idea, in words. All except George. He was sitting there, staring at me, nodding his head. Tears ran down his face. The bruise on his neck looked from a distance like a bandana.

I think that was the beginning of everything.

6

The Learning Curve

AT ELEVEN THAT day I took my lunch to Professor Bible's classroom. He was eating an orange, peeling it at his desk, putting the peels on a paper towel in front of him. He had a hot cup of tea balanced to his right on a pencil box.

"Come on in," he said. "Did you bring your lunch?"

"Just a sandwich," I said. I showed him my lunch bag.

"Want some tea?"

"I'll just sip on my Coke." I pulled up a chair and sat down on the other side of his desk. When I opened the Coke it made a hissing sound, but it didn't overflow. It got his attention, though. He watched me as I removed the cap and set it on his desk in front of me. Then I took out a ham sandwich I'd packed for myself and began to eat. "You saw it?" I said. "The mark on George's neck?"

"I heard about it."

"He's had that mark before?"

"Last year."

"Well," I said. "We have to do something, right?"

"You know," Bible said, leaning back in his chair. "Last year, before I found out about his father's curious methods of discipline, I just thought little George was shy. The quiet type. You know. Then I attributed his reticence to the abuse. After that, it never occurred to me again that maybe he really was the shy type. That his demeanor had nothing whatever to do with the abuse."

"It doesn't?"

"Not a thing."

"How do you know that?"

"It's a very well-researched theory of mine," he said.

"Does Mrs. Creighton know about this?"

"A tested theory."

"Tested? How?"

"I asked George if anything was bothering him." His voice was deep and sonorous—he could have easily gotten a job reading the news. He reached up and removed his glasses. "Did you bring cigarettes?"

I had brought the pack with me. As I handed him a cigarette I repeated my question. "Does Mrs. Creighton know about this?"

He seemed to nod slightly as he talked. "I asked George if there was anything he'd like to change." His face was expressionless, but the big shaggy brows seemed to sink a little. He gently put the cigarette down on the desk mat, next to his pen. He lined them up. In spite of his bulk, his hands were small and delicate. He wore a small blue ring on the pinky finger of his right hand. "Do you know what he said?"

"What?"

"He said, 'no, sir'—real quiet, you know how he does. And I said, 'George, pretend you have the power to change one thing—one big thing in the world, in your life, what would it be?' And he thought about it for a while, really hard. Then he said he wished he could stay up later. He wished his parents would let him stay up later. And I said

I wasn't interested in his daily life, but his life. What would he change about his life? And he thought about it again—really gave it some thought—and then he says, 'I'm afraid to ask girls to go out with me.'"

This made me smile—not because I was amused, but because I recognized that very fear.

"Isn't that the saddest thing?" Bible said. "He's sitting there with a blue bruise on his throat from his father's hand, and all he wants is to stay up later, and have the courage to talk to girls."

"What'd you tell him?"

"I told him about a psychologist I read about. Some guy who was supposed to be brilliant, and successful. People read his books. I couldn't remember the name. Still don't." He waved his hand. "I just know he was famous and he invented a kind of therapy based on his experience. So I told George about how this guy was afraid to ask girls for dates, even as successful as he was."

"Aren't all of us afraid of that?"

"This psychologist was incapable of it. He was a grown man and he couldn't make himself do it. He lived in New York, and he was terribly lonesome. So one day he walks to Central Park, and every girl he sees in the park that he might want to go out with, he stops her and asks her if she'll go out with him; a hundred, two hundred a day. He forced himself to do that, every day."

"Damn."

"You know what happened to his fear?" Bible leaned forward now, studied my face. "He didn't have it any more. And that's what I told George. The guy wasn't afraid of asking girls out anymore because he'd already asked so many of them."

"Did anybody ever say yes to the psychologist?"

"I don't know." He gave a short laugh. "Maybe somebody did." He sat back in his chair and rubbed his eyes.

"Mrs. Creighton knows about George?"

"Mrs. Creighton knows all about it. She's handling it the best she can. This is a private school and George's parents are paying customers." He folded his glasses with one hand, opened them again. "I trust that sounds as cynical as I intend."

I had no response to that.

"I have a headache," he said. "And I'm so very tired."

"I'm sorry," I said, lamely.

He opened his red eyes and regarded me. "Do you know how long I've been doing this sort of thing?"

I didn't know what to say.

Doreen Corrigan came in, smiling. "What are you two powwowing about?"

"Just chatting," I said. At the same time Professor Bible said, "George Meeker."

Doreen's expression changed. "Oh."

"Did you see his neck?" I said.

"I saw it. In Math class." She pointed at Bible. "I told him about it."

"If this has been going on," I said, "Why can't we do something about it?"

"What?" Doreen said. "Call social services?"

"Yes."

"I did that," Bible said. "Last year."

"What happened?"

"Two things," Bible said. Doreen said at the same time, "Nothing." They looked at each other, and then Professor Bible went on. "Two things. George got so angry at me that to this day he won't talk to me. He won't even look at me."

"You're kidding."

"Like you said the other day, that boy really loves his old man."

I shook my head. "Jesus."

"Hell, he doesn't even know he's abused. It's just normal life to him."

"But he is abused."

"He's punished," Doreen said. "He sees it as punishment. He thinks he deserves it when it happens to him. He doesn't even know that other kids don't get treated that way when they're punished."

"Oh of course he does," I said. "How could he not know it?"

"He could be an outcast among them," Bible said. "He could be one of those kids who is so picked on he has no friends; he has no contact with others that would instruct him in the matter."

"Well then I'll tell him."

Doreen laughed. "You think it's that simple. We've all told him."

I felt kind of foolish.

Professor Bible said, "I wanted you to watch him—to see what's going on because maybe you can reach him in some other way. I think he was in school today because he wanted to be in your class."

"Why my class?"

"He wants to write. He's smart. You get them writing."

"What's he saying in that journal of his?" Doreen asked.

"Oh, he writes a lot," I said. He did write a lot, and I had commented in the margin on several pages about how good it was. I'd written, "Thank you for sharing," and "Wonderful insight" next to portions of text that I had not read one word of. I felt something cold filter into my blood. I took the last bite of my sandwich then put the paper it was wrapped in back in the bag. I didn't want to look directly at either one of them. I had nothing more to say, and when they realized that, Bible took another sip of his tea.

Doreen said, "Has he written anything about his 'punishments'?"

"Nothing," I said. I gulped the last of my Coke. Then I looked at Bible. "You said two things happened. But you never said what the second thing was."

"Social services sent a team out to talk to his mother and father, then they talked to George, then they came and talked to Mrs. Creighton and me."

"It was a lot of nothing," Doreen said.

"George was furious. Like I said."

"What about his parents?" I asked.

"I think they were happy to let George handle it," Doreen said.

"What's he saying in his journal about his father?" Bible wanted to know.

He had written a paper about fishing with his father, and I'd seen the word father, underlined, on several pages of the journal. He'd ended one entry with how much he loved his father. I'd seen that. So I said, "Like I said, he seems to love his father very much."

Bible shook his head. He flipped his glasses open and put them back on. "I don't suppose you'd mind letting me read the folded pages in his journal?"

"I can't do that," I said.

"Why not?" Doreen said.

"I don't know. It just feels wrong. I feel bad reading them myself."

"How will he know you let us look at it?"

"I don't care if he'd know it," I said. "I'd know it." No doubt you have already guessed that I was not exactly taking a principled stance over the privacy of my students. I was protecting myself. I had no idea what the journal said, so I was not going to give either of them the chance to read it before I did. "I'll look at it again," I said. "Read it more carefully, now that I know what is going on."

"Have you been reading his journal all along?" Doreen said.

"Of course."

"Cindy Gallant didn't. She barely glanced at them."

"Really," I said.

"She told me half the time she didn't read them at all."

"Why'd she make them keep one?" I asked, pretending not to know.

"Just for busy work, I guess," Doreen said. "To give them something to do while she graded their papers."

"Well," I said, "that's amazing."

"It's not a sin," she said. "It's legitimate. A tennis coach doesn't see every groundstroke her students hit against a wall. It's just for practice."

"That's an interesting way of looking at it," I said, feeling vaguely justified. Then I lied again. "I read them. Every page, except the ones they fold over."

"You really don't read the ones they fold over?" Bible said.

I didn't know if they knew of Mrs. Creighton's requirement. I blurted, "Right."

Bible looked at Doreen and then back at me. "I should think it would be just too tempting to resist."

"So you'd read those pages," Doreen said, laughing slightly.

"Those would be the *only* pages I'd read," he said, and we all laughed at that. I was relieved to see they did not know. Bible reached down and picked up his cigarette.

"Where'd you get that?" Doreen asked.

He pointed at me.

"Can I have one?"

"Sure." I handed her the pack. She took one and then said, "Lunch is almost over," as she went out the door.

"I guess I'll have one too," I said.

Bible leaned back in his chair again, took some matches out of the center drawer of his desk, and lit his cigarette. "Do me a favor," he said.

"Yes, sir?" I was still shocked that he'd lit his cigarette in the classroom.

"Open that window over there." He pointed to a narrow window next to the chalkboard, a few feet from his desk.

I did as he asked and then sat back down in my chair. "Can I have the matches?"

"Oh," he said, looking at me very sternly, a thick cloud of blue smoke around his head. "You're not allowed to smoke in here."

When I dropped George off at his house that day I felt so sorry for him. Other kids jumped from the bus and sprinted home—their hair blowing high in the wind. They scattered the leaves as they made their escape from school, the bus, and me. But George stepped down to the ground as if he were testing the surface of a new planet; as if he were worried about the atmosphere.

"See you tomorrow, George," I said.

"Yeah." He didn't look back.

I drove home wondering what I could do to save him.

7

One Does What One Can

Of course, that night Annie said, "Why do you have to save him?"

"Somebody has to."

"But why you? Why is it your job?" She sat on the couch next to me. She was wearing a towel over her hair and she'd just washed her face, so she wasn't wearing any makeup. "Shouldn't you simply tell Mrs. Creighton what you're thinking and let her handle it?"

"He's my student."

"The county has services for that, right?"

"I think so."

"Of course they do." She put her foot up on the coffee table, then placed a cotton ball in between each toe. While we had this conversation, she carefully painted her toenails bright red. "Fairfax County has some sort of child abuse organization. What is it called, anyway? I've read about it. It's not Child Abuse, it's . . ."

"Did you know that the United States had a society for the prevention of cruelty to animals before it had any kind of child protective services?"

"That's it. Child Protective Services. Call them."

"They already tried that, last year. It didn't work."

"Call them again. Eventually if they get enough people reporting it, they'll do something."

"If I do that, I will make an enemy of the person I'm trying to help."

"What do you mean?"

I told her about Professor Bible and George's reaction to him. "Bible says he can't teach the boy anything now because he is so bitter about it."

"Well then forget about it. He doesn't want help."

"He just doesn't know it."

"Know what?"

"That he needs help."

"I didn't say he didn't need it. I said he doesn't want it."

"He's being viciously abused by his own father. A boy that age."

"What's age got to do with anything?"

"Think how long it must have been going on. George is almost an adult. How long can a person take abuse before . . . ?" I stopped.

"Before what?"

"What does that do to a person? Won't it make George just as violent and maybe dangerous as his father?"

Now she looked at me. "You do realize that this is your Christ complex coming through again."

She knew how I'd react to this. Somehow, she had got the idea that I liked to control things a little bit more than the next person and she'd started calling it my Christ complex. But it was a sore subject with me and she knew it because we'd fought over it before. I don't have any such complex, but any time I tried to get anything to work out better than it appeared it would work out, she brought out the label. This time, all I said was, "That's not fair." I was willing to let it go.

But she said, "You're trying to prevent the—the—the *creation*, if that's the word I want. You're trying to prevent the creation of a criminal."

"What?" I fairly yelled this.

She went back to her toes. "You have to intervene here because of the damage being done to George."

"That's got nothing to do with criminals."

"Well what do you mean then about the damage? Isn't that what you're worried about? A violent childhood, abused children grow up to be violent themselves?"

"I can't talk to you about these things," I said. I got up and went into the kitchen.

"You don't have to get mad," she yelled so I could hear her.

I stuck my head back around the corner. "I can't stand by and watch that little boy get tortured like that. I'm sorry if that bothers you."

"It doesn't bother me. It just means you're sweet."

"Thank you."

"But it's your Christ complex. You have to fix everything."

"I just want to fix this. That's not a complex." I waved my hand in dismissal and went back into the kitchen. I was going to cook dinner that night, but I'd made up my mind to simply make a few sandwiches and forget about a hot meal. The idea of eating well at that moment made me a little sick.

The next day I collected all the journals in my classes. When I got home that afternoon, I began reading through George's entries. His journal was thick—pages wrinkled and curled, so he must have gotten it wet somehow—but the ink was not smeared. As I guessed from merely glancing at the pages, he said nothing of any significance for page after page. He wrote about what kids that age always seem to write about: sports, movies, music, and "hanging out." He probably mentioned more books than the others, but even there he only talked about what he read and what he was going to read. No thinking about the books, or for that matter the sports, movies, and music. He had entries that only listed the songs he liked, or the movies he'd seen. He did not talk about anyone except his father, and what he said about him was not bad. *My father likes to go fishing and sometimes he takes me. We have so much fun.* At one point he wrote, *Dad made toast for me this morning. We played football yesterday. I caught the ball every time almost. He said I was getting good.* Only two pages were folded over and tucked into the binding. I put a check mark on each one, then set the book aside. I went through all the other journals, too—without reading them, mind you. I made marginal comments as always. "You're doing better here." Or, "Practice is beginning to show." Or, the old standby: "Thank you for sharing."

I don't know why I waited until I was done with the others before I went back to George's book. Perhaps I hoped Annie would get home and stop me before I kept my word to Mrs. Creighton and violated it to my students. I did not bother to read the folded pages of any of the others, and I'd gone through 122 journals. (Several students did not have their journals when I collected them. This was a usual boon that I tried very hard not to gleefully react to on days when I collected the journals. I pretended I was very unhappy about it, in fact.) I reasoned that this was a crucial situation; a moral necessity. I had to know what was going on with George's father. It was my duty to read the folded pages. In other words, it was a decision I would have made no matter what Mrs. Creighton expected of me.

I made a hot cup of coffee, sat down on the couch, and opened his journal. The first folded page was filled with very small, very neat writing.

10/12/85

I washed the car yesterday. I thought I would do something constructive like dad always says I should do when I'm home with nothing to do so I washed the car. I did a real good job. It looked very nice in the sun. I even dried it off with a towel. I could see myself it was so shiny. I wanted to take a picture of it so I went into the house and looked for my camera but I couldn't find it anywhere. When I was in the house the phone rang after I had been looking for a long time. After I answered the phone it was mom. She asked me what are you doing and I didn't want to tell her about the car. She was going to the airport to pick up Dad, and she wanted me to eat what she made in the refrigerator. She made me some chicken noodle soup and told me to eat a sandwitch too. I could have a soda if I wanted. She said she and Dad would be home before ten at night but that I should do my homework and be in bed by then. I said I would't wait up and then I went downstairs to do my homework. That's when it happened. I forgot I left the hose on. I fell asleep. I am so stupid. I can't do anything right. I forgot to turn the water off and it leaked into the basement. When I woke up and put my feet down from the couch to get up, they got soaked. The whole floor was covered with water. I'm in big trouble now.

10/13/85

I was punished for letting the water in the house yesterday. My stomach still hurts. Dad made me hold the phone book against my chest and then he hit the book as hard as he could. He kept pounding on it. He hit it so hard this time. I haven't told him about my back. When he hits the book it hurts my stomach, but my back against the bed post too. It drives me back against it. I haven't told him about it. Dad came in last night and said he was sorry. I was crying

10/14/85

The bruise on my neck will go away. Dad says the bruise will go away but I pulled too hard against the cord if I didn't pull so hard on the cord there would be no bruise at all.

Mom noticed it and told me not to go to school. She left for work after she kissed me and said just stay home today. I thought she might cry and I told her I was sorry about the water. She was so angry about the basement because that's our family room. That's what she said to me. That's our family room and look what you've done to it. I wish I wasn't so stupid.

I think I am ruining a lot of things because I'm so stupid. Dad says I am just not a good thinker he says I'm smart in other ways.

I asked every girl in English class to go out with me. Then Math class. Then History. I'm beginning to be good at it. Nobody ever says yes, but I am not afraid of asking anymore. I just go up and say want to go out with me and they say no. Daphne said she wasn't allowed to date yet. A lot of them say that.

I wish I wasn't so stupid. If I was bigger, and stronger and could play sports and if I wasn't so stupid.

When I was done, I put his journal back with the others, then stretched out on the couch to wait for Annie. I figured she'd understand once she saw what George had written. I had to do something. I just had to.

8

Teaching What Matters

I WANTED TO talk to George, first. That would require real delicacy and tact—since I had to pretend I hadn't read his folded pages, and I didn't want him to feel threatened in any way. If anything, I hoped to win his trust. This wasn't any teacherly instinct. I felt sorry for the kid.

He was absent the next day, though. At the end of the class, I went in to talk to Mrs. Creighton. She was sitting at her desk, her glasses balanced on the tip of her nose, writing notes in the margins of a huge checkbook. When I came in, she did not stop what she was doing, she only said, "Yes?" and waited for me to identify myself.

"It's me," I said.

"I know."

"I've got a sort of problem."

Now she met my gaze, staring at me over the top of her glasses.

"It's about George Meeker."

"Yes, he wasn't here today."

"Do you know what's going on with him?"

"He had a dentist's appointment," she said, but tentatively. Almost as if she was asking me if it was true. I could see she knew I was not worried about George's attendance.

"His father," I started.

"I know about that."

"You do."

She said nothing, but she did not look away.

"Isn't there something we can do?"

"Don't talk to George about it. That would ruin everything."

"Ruin everything?"

"I am aware of the problem and I am dealing with it."

"I was talking to Professor Bible about it, and . . ."

"George doesn't trust him."

"I want to avoid . . ."

"You should let me handle it. I'm working with George's parents and I've been in touch with Child Protective Services. There's no danger to the boy. His father is just very strict."

"He hits the boy."

"As some fathers do, but it may not be abusive."

"Of course it is." Now, I had her full attention. I think she was shocked that I contradicted her. "Mrs. Creighton, I've read some things in the folded pages of George's journal. What he tells me—what he says about his father's . . ." I didn't know how to finish that sentence. I finally said, "Beatings. That's what they are. He ties him with a bungee cord to one of the posts on a four poster bed, and then he puts a phone book against the boy's chest and pounds on it with his fists."

"Did George tell you that?"

"He wrote it in his journal."

"But how do you know it's true? How can you know for sure he's not making it up?"

I couldn't believe my ears. "I've seen the bruises on the boy's neck. Haven't you seen them?"

"Yes," she said disgustedly. "I've seen them." She went back to what was on her desk. I stood there with nothing more to say. Finally she said, "You shouldn't keep your children waiting."

"They know where I am."

"Look," she said. "I don't approve of what his father is doing. I said I'm working on this problem." She took her glasses off and let them drop to her chest. "Would you like to talk to George's father?"

"I would," I said, without thinking. No part of my conscious self was involved in the choice of words. My body said it, without me.

Later that day, when I told Bible that I was probably going to have to talk to George's father, he said, "I've talked to him. A big fellow, and quite beastly."

"Really."

"Sells Buicks and Chevrolets; owns a dealership in Fairfax. He's really an engaging and entertaining fellow until he loses his temper."

"Mrs. Creighton says she's scheduling a Parent–Teacher night, so we can do it then. It won't seem like I've asked to speak to him special or anything."

"Let's have a cigarette." He was standing in the doorway of his classroom. Behind him the window was open and I could see he had just finished eating his lunch. His class was outside, as mine was. I had a pack in my pocket. I handed him a Camel Light, and he said, "Have you thought about what you'd say to the boy's old man?"

"No."

"By the time I met him, I'd already called Protective Services on him." He retrieved a lighter from his pocket and lit the cigarette. I watched him draw on it deeply, inhale it, then let it out slowly through his nose and mouth. "You know," he said. "when you only have one or two of these a day, they taste really good. Even these lousy lights."

"So what happened when you turned him in?"

"I didn't turn him in. You can't really turn somebody in over a thing like that. You report your suspicions. That's what I did."

Mrs. Creighton came from her office. "Could you two please take your cigarettes outside?"

"I'm not smoking," I said.

She stared at me over her glasses. Professor Bible had not moved.

"Okay," I said. I moved toward the back door, and Bible came along behind me. He acted as though I was the one with the cigarette. "I'll go outside with you," he said.

Outside he opened his jacket and leaned against one of the picnic tables. A slight breeze lifted his white hair and the sun shone off a bald spot underneath. He did not even glance my way as he smoked. I said, "So what happened when you talked to him?"

"Who?"

"George's father."

"I didn't get a word in edgewise. He said 'how dare you' a few times. But mostly he let me know he was going to raise George the way he saw fit. He used the word *discipline* a lot."

"How'd you keep from decking him."

"Like I said. He's a big fellow. Knows what he wants."

"And that's it? That's all that happened?"

"That's about it. Except George no longer speaks to me." He studied his cigarette—twirling it in his fingers. As it got smaller, his puffs got longer, and deeper. Clouds of smoke drifted around his face and up over his head. When he was finished with it, he dropped the butt at his feet and stepped on it.

How can anyone figure out what makes human beings tick? I hate to ask such an abstract question, but look at it. Countless people have hated their parents and for good reason, but what do you do with a fellow like George Meeker? His father was like a God to him. All he wanted was to win his father's love and approval, and if that meant suffering at his hands—if that meant being tortured like any prisoner of war—that was what he would do. I understood finally why George was always impeccably dressed in a suit and tie, why he always wore his hair clipped neatly, and why he always clacked around in brightly shined wingtip shoes. He wanted to be a man. He saw how charming his father was with other men, he saw that his father's friends did not have to endure his wrath or his torment; so he wanted to kill the child in himself and become a man as quickly as possible. He must have known at some level that if he could just be a man in his father's eyes, he would gain a perfect kind of redemption; he would gain his father's love, and an end to his suffering.

It was awful to watch.

I took Mrs. Creighton's advice for a while. I said nothing to George, intending to wait until I'd spoken to his father, but I started thinking about how I could get him to recognize that what his father was doing to him was cruel, and evil. If I could only do that, perhaps he would come to know that he was being abused, and we wouldn't need anybody's help. I kept asking myself what I could possibly do without confronting him directly about it. And then something happened one day in the junior class that gave me the answer to my question.

We were talking about "heroism." I don't remember what story I'd had them read, but we ended up talking about heroes, and what a hero was. "We're going to address a lot of things in this class," I said. "Questions like, 'what is the nature of the good life,' or 'what is the value of love.' We'll discuss what moral behavior is, and heroism. What is the nature of the hero and what's the difference between a traditional hero and a mere protagonist."

"How do you define a hero?" this one student said. His name was Mark Talbot. He was tall and lean, and wore wire glasses and had read a few things. I liked dealing with him because he was clearly smart. And when he asked me that question, George spoke up. His eyes seemed to come alive and he said, "A hero is a person who leads in spite of danger or suffering."

Happy Bell said, "A brave person who doesn't take any . . ." he stopped and looked at me. He seemed to think a bit about what he wanted to say, then he said, "crap."

"You know," Talbot said. "By that definition, Charles Manson was a hero."

"You're an idiot," Happy said.

"Charles Manson?" I said. I was aware of a look of consternation on some faces, so I explained who Charles Manson was. Most of them knew quite well, though they were not real clear on the crimes he committed. When I talked about the murders of an entire household of people, about the LaBianca's final hours in their own home, I realized George was watching me with bright, almost fiery eyes. Finally I said, "How does Manson fit the definition of hero?"

"He was brave. He didn't take no crap from nobody," Happy said.

"In what way was he brave?" I said.

"I don't know."

I smiled at him—nodded a kind of thank-you—then pressed on. It hadn't hit me yet what this had to do with George and his problem, but I saw he was interested, he was paying attention, and I wanted to get back to the subject of cruelty; of criminal behavior and heroism. "In what way is Charles Manson brave? Anyone?"

Happy smiled across the room at Talbot and then said, "Well, he had the courage to do what most people never dream of doing. He was a leader—he had followers."

I said, "Hitler was a leader and had followers. He did things nobody ever really dreamed of. But is he one of your heroes too?"

I would later find out that Happy was Jewish and I had trapped him far more completely than I knew. At first I was almost afraid he would say, "Yes, Hitler is one of my heroes too," at which point I might have done some things right then and there that I shouldn't— you cannot teach anybody anything in a rage and I knew that would be my response to such a stupid comment. But Happy shrunk a little in his seat, looked slightly insulted. Then he said, "No. Hitler ain't no hero."

"He was to some people," Talbot said.

One of the students in the back, a young girl named Jaime Nichols, said, "Who's Hitler?"

For a moment, I was shocked into silence. I could not believe it. I just could not accept that any human being born after 1945 didn't know who Hitler was, and it made me suddenly quite zealous. I think that's the only word for it. I was not going to tolerate such ignorance, and my respect for history—my belief in a kind of justice, and the true need for historical awareness—lit a fire in me. At that moment I was suddenly aware of something enormous in the back of my mind that would be the engine of everything I did with these kids, and it would be the avenue by which I could take George out of his troubles. I could teach him about his father's cruelty by showing him the cruelty of others, in spades. I know it sounds simple, even juvenile to think I could do something so prosaic and useful, but that's how I felt. George did not know his father was a fiend, but he would learn it because, indirectly, I would teach it to him. When Jaime Nichols asked me who Hitler was, I didn't say anything or show how shocked I was, except for that initial moment of silence.

Talbot did not respond either. He only smirked at me finally and said again, "Hitler was a hero to some people."

"But not to you?" I said.

"No. I don't have any heroes."

"I just don't understand what a hero is then," Jaime Nichols said. She was so small, it was always a shock to hear the resonant, deeply adult quality of her voice. She had short-cut black hair and kind eyes, and I felt sorry for her; sorry for her ignorance. "Happy described the traits of a hero, didn't he?" she asked.

"Not all the traits of a hero," I said.

Talbot turned in his seat. "It's all in the eye of the beholder."

"A lot of things are," I said. "But a lot of things aren't. Isn't there some component of virtue bound up with the idea of a hero?"

"What's that mean?" somebody said.

Happy laughed a little.

"What's so funny?" I asked.

"I don't know. I guess a hero's a hero to anybody who worships him."

"That's a beginning, but it doesn't really define anything," I said.

Mark Talbot said, "I worship Leslie Warren, but that doesn't make her a hero."

"Everybody worships Leslie," Happy said. There was general laughter.

"Well," I said. "Leslie is a beautiful young girl . . ."

The laughter died down. Jaime Nichols said, "I think she's a cold-hearted bitch."

"That's enough of that," I said. "I won't have that."

She smirked and looked out the window.

"Maybe," I said, "For a while there, Hitler was a hero to some. But is heroism really in the eye of the beholder? Use Hitler for your answer. And for God's sake, think about virtue."

"What does any of this have to do with English?" a broad-faced kind of chunky girl in the front row said. Her name was Pamela Green. She had a small, smartly curved mouth and now, because she was puzzled, it looked almost as if she was pouting. She wore her short, light brown hair combed straight down on either side of her face.

"It has everything to do with English," I said. "Literature helps us define the heroes and the villains among us—because it reflects our thinking about those things throughout the ages."

George was now smiling, and I had the cheeky misapprehension that he had learned something from me. It would take a while for me to begin to see the deeply rich measures of George's face. He was like a child in that way more than any other; his face betrayed what he was thinking or feeling exactly. To tell you the truth, I felt a sort of lucky elation—the way you feel when you win at poker, or hit the jackpot on a slot machine. I was being paid to do what I had been doing all day: talking with kids about things that really mattered in the world. It took Mark Talbot to bring me back to earth.

"Heroes save lives and villains take it," he said.

I jumped at this idea. "That's a great way of putting it."

"So Hitler and Manson took lives. Villains."

"Right."

"And an ordinary ambulance driver. Hero."

"Well, no—maybe not . . ." I paused.

"Doctors and lawyers and policemen . . ." He looked around the room slowly after he said this word, then he repeated it. "Policemen, they're all heroes."

"They can be," I said.

"Not to me," Happy said.

"They can be if somebody's trying to kill you and they show up to save your life."

"That's their job," Talbot said.

"Still . . ."

"They get paid to do that. And sometimes they go on strike. The cops in Boston are on strike right now . . ."

"Ok, Mark. I—your point is well taken. It won't be as simple as you made it sound to define what a hero is. But that is why you study literature," I said. "That's why I love it so much."

George was not paying attention anymore. He was writing in his journal, feverishly working over it as I talked. I didn't think he was taking notes, and I had the idea that I would collect the journals that day so I could see what he was writing, but I didn't do it. The thought of all that work made it easy to let it go another day. Besides, I wanted him to have time to finish what he was writing.

"Literature," I said, "is about everything. It's about history, and psychology, and sociology, and philosophy, and art, and anthropology, and music, and biology and zoology, and even mathematics. It's about all things human."

"How can it be about math?" Pamela Green said.

"Read Einstein," I said. "The theory of relativity. That's literature."

They were all looking at me now. Even George stopped writing and stared at me. I felt as though I had just finished an angry, eloquent outburst in which I had won the day in an argument; a kind of triumphant satisfaction, but powerful anticipation as well. I was already thinking about the films I would get about the holocaust and about what I would let them all see: Bodies piled like white sticks; black flies swarming over eye sockets; flesh sucking bone; black shadows hurled into pits or knocked in half by gunfire; and the seedy little corporal who engineered it all.

It's quite possible I was a little nervous, too; a little intimidated by the big series of tomorrows in my path, but all I can remember of that particular day was my belief that I had found a way to do something about George without actively intervening in his life. And it would be educational for everyone. I could not wait to begin it. Intellectually, I'm sure I must have understood that I should not put too much faith in this work, this business of being a teacher who influences his students to conquer iniquity. That day I got them writing about God was a case in point. I had gotten them to write a lot on the subject—some of them angrily—but one real ghastly result from that assignment was that many of them wrote long-winded, boring, simple-minded essays about the savior and God and how unbelievers should suffer.

As excited as I was, the thought of having so many individual personalities waiting for me to do something was unnerving and even, at times, threatening. I wanted so much to believe that I was in the right place, doing the right thing, working out a real future for myself. At some level, perhaps I wanted to sharpen my moral blade for the time when I would face the more advanced students in a college classroom. Even if I went to law school someday, it would serve me. The grandest mistake any person or culture can make is to lose sight of the difference between what is law and what is right.

All of these kinds of things probably went through my mind at one time or another after that day, but the one thing that really got me going was the certain belief that I was about to make a difference in George's life, and teach the rest of them something pretty amazing, too: that evil is real, and sometimes it is human and often looks like it ought to be good. Why else would it attract so many people?

9

Introducing Hitler

THE SCHOOL ONLY had one video machine: a twenty-five-inch color TV strapped to a five-foot stand, with a videotape player on the shelf below it. But nobody ever used it. Bible called it a "new-fangled contraption" and when he wanted to show a film, he used the school's film projector. So I had the video machine to myself. (When I first dug it out of the closet in the back of Mrs. Creighton's office, I could write my name in the dust on it.) I showed videos to every class. Not just documentaries, either. I showed them *The Sorrow and the Pity*, *Night and Fog*, *The Twisted Cross*, but I also let them see *The Diary of Anne Frank*, and *Judgment at Nuremberg*. My subject matter was simple: human cruelty. Nothing else. I didn't get into politics, or political systems; I didn't talk about democracy, or fascism; just human cruelty.

I rented the videotapes from the Fairfax County Library which had an enormous collection. I didn't care how long the films were, either. My classes all took one hour, so I would begin a film and let it go as far as it could in an hour, then at break between classes I'd rewind it and start over. At the end of the day I'd leave it where it was, note the number on the counter, and the next day, at the first class, I'd play it to the end, then rewind to that number and start it there for the next class. My method worked perfectly. I don't think my students missed more than a frame or two of any of the films. And, I have to admit this: I realized while they were watching films, I had pretty much nothing to do. It was a nice way to give myself a break for a solid two or three days each week.

I don't think those kids had any idea what was happening to them. Some of the girls cried and cried. Even a few of the boys got fairly teary when they saw the films of the bodies and the camps. I heard one of the kids talking at break, and I got a bit of a scare when I heard the words, "dirty movie." But how could anybody call any of those films "dirty." If anything on earth could be said to have extreme "redeeming social value," it would be films like that. So I made up my mind not to worry.

I did the holocaust film project for everybody. I wanted all of them to know. But I kept my eye on George, hoping to see some evidence of enlightenment; of new understanding. Surely, I reasoned, he would begin to recognize the cruelty of his own father if he saw how it operated when it was official and government-sponsored. I am not suggesting that George's father was as bad as the Nazis, but only that he was cruel—and that if I made George an expert in methods of human cruelty and madness, he would begin to see that his father was in the same arena: a cruel and brutal bastard.

During the several days that I was showing these films, it rained. Every day. A long, soaking, drippy, sad rain. One day early in that drenched week, just after I had parked my bus in the back and raced to my classroom to keep from getting wet, I saw Leslie Warren hop out of a blue Ford Escort and start up the sloped driveway to the back entrance of the school. She tried to run, carrying a lot of books and notebooks in one hand and holding a newspaper up over her head with the other. Near the top of the driveway she slipped on some wet leaves and fell to her knees hard. She tried to get up, then sank back down again. I ran out to her, skating and skidding up to her myself. It was very hard to be sure-footed on that slick asphalt.

"Are you okay?" I said.

She looked at me. She had a dark bit of leaf on her chin. "Help me up."

I leaned down and took her hand. Her books were scattered at her feet, and mud and black leaves clung to her legs and her skirt. I said, "Did you hurt yourself?" I reached out and gently removed the black leaf from her chin. "You're not cut are you?"

"I'm all right." She brushed the front of her skirt and then she screamed, "Fuck!"

It's possible my feet left the ground.

She started gathering her things and I leaned down to help her. The rain increased and I felt the icy stab of each drop on my back as I picked up her papers. When I handed them to her, she smiled. I touched her arm to steady her and started to try to move us the rest of the way up the hill. It was very slippery, so she held onto me as we walked. When we got to the back door of the school, she stopped and looked at me. "You're new aren't you?"

I nodded, let go of her arm and stepped back a bit. Her voice was smooth—only slightly low-pitched—like sweet, low notes on a piccolo.

"You teach English, right?"

"I do."

"Yeah, I've heard about you." Now she had a wry smile on her face. I was finding it hard to believe anyone could find the nerve to talk to her, much less be sharing gossip.

"I hope you've heard good things."

"I bet you've heard about me too, haven't you?" The look on her face was so expectant, so completely innocent—but she knew what people were saying about her. I tried to avoid letting her see anything in my face, but I said, "No, I haven't heard anything much."

She laughed sweetly, knowingly. "I bet it's all bad."

"Do you think you've been bad?"

"I try my best."

I laughed nervously.

"It was nice of you to help me," she said. "I hope to be in your class next year."

I couldn't take my eyes from her face, and I didn't have the where-withal to say anything. She smiled again, and I nodded again, and then she went on inside.

The rain came and went all that week. It would clear a bit at night, and the wind would pick up a little energy, herd a few leaves across the moonlit parking lots and empty driveways, and then before midnight the moon would vanish and the rain would start up again—pouring for a time, forcefully and with apparent purpose, as though the heavens wanted to rinse the earth clean of anything not cemented to the ground. In the morning it would stop, then begin to drip, mist up, and swiftly turn again to a steady leak from above. I thought the weather was a perfect backdrop to what we were studying, since it made everything appear black-and-white—like the footage we were all watching on the screen—and for more than a week, the sky remained as gray and light as un-brushed steel.

George was in my first period class. And one day, when we were pretty well finished with all the videos I could find on the subject, I began the all-important discussion I had been building up to. It was still cloudy outside, but now it wasn't raining, and periodically, the sun would break through the gray dome and send scattered beams down through the leaves. I started by asking one question: "Why cause other human beings to suffer?"

Of course, the answer I hoped for was, "It must be hate." What I got seemed only slightly off the mark. One student said, "War." Another said, "It's politics." We talked about racism for a while, and then finally, somebody said it: "Hate."

79

I said, "What about love? Can a person love you and still make you suffer on purpose?" I waited awhile, looking at all of them, and then I said, "George?"

His eyes seemed to enlarge and he stared at me for a moment, but not as though he was thinking about how to answer the question. His head was tilted slightly, his hands splayed out in front of him on the desk. His eyes went right through me, really, and weren't seeing me at all.

"George?"

Now he focused on me. "What?"

"What do you think?"

"What was the question again?"

He hadn't even been listening. I repeated the question for him, and this time without hesitation he said, "No."

"No?" I said. What was I supposed to do then? Could I say, "What about what your father does to you?"

Happy said, "Sometimes people do things because they love God. They torture or kill people over it. Right?"

"That's right," I said, and the class went on. I realized the whole experiment led to nothing with George. He sat there, quiet, appearing to listen to what everybody was saying. I made one more stab—a direct attempt to hit the mark, without naming names. I did not look at George as I spoke. "What about parents who beat and abuse their children? Is that hate? Or love?"

George said, "It's anger." He did not turn away from me, and his face was expressionless, but it still broke my heart. "It isn't love or hate. It's just anger. Children need to be managed . . ." he stopped.

"Yes, but . . ."

"They have to be made into good people. It's just discipline."

"But it doesn't have to be abusive," I said. "You don't mean that . . ."

Happy said, "It shouldn't be torture."

"What's any of this got to do with the holocaust?" George said.

"Well, we were talking about cruelty," I said. "Is it cruel for parents to physically harm their children?"

They all agreed it was. Even George. He was smiling now, looking around the room as everybody talked. He didn't know I had focused everything toward him, that he was the impetus for everything we'd done for the past week and a half, and his ignorance of that fact made me see him as even more vulnerable; I think I may have been embarrassed for him. I know I suddenly felt exquisitely sorry for him.

I don't remember if I thought my effort was a failure—it was, after all, only the beginning of what I hoped would be a sort of awakening on George's part—but I am sure it was not a smashing success. Still, what I tried to do for him became sort of emblematic of a trend in my teaching over those two years. It was always personal with me. Most of the time, what I taught was aimed at somebody in particular.

The holocaust project drew praise from Mrs. Creighton and the other teachers. It had certainly given my classes something to talk about, to think and write about. I couldn't wait for Parent–Teacher night. I thought I was doing pretty good, to tell you the truth.

I read almost all of the journals after the first week of the holocaust project.

(George) folded
11/06/85
Sometimes I wish I was dead. I'm so stupid. Those stick figures in the movies, those dead people getting piled into mounds of white skin and bone made me sick to my stomach. I don't like people. I really don't like people.

(Jaime Nichols) folded
11/08/85
those nazis were really mean. They didn't care about anybody at all except themselves i'm glad the united states went over there and beat them. It's a good thing they were stopped and didn't get to come to the united states. So many families killed and in awful ways. I wish I didn't know about all this now. I think Mr. Jameson, if your reading this, and I bet you do read these folded pages too. Their the only pages I would probly read myself if I had to

go through so many journals. I bet your reading this right now and if you are, I'm sorry you decided to show us so much death and destruction and all by those people of the old times in England and Germany. That's what I think, and I don't care if you read it, but I'm going to fold this page over anyway just in case you dont' really read the folded pages. But I know you do. Jaime.

(Mark Talbot) folded

11/08/85

I think Jaime Nichols has a crush on Mr. Jameson. She never takes her eyes off him. She's as dumb as a paper clip. She didn't even know who Hitler was. Leslie Warren likes her sex and especially when she's had a little pot. Last Saturday I took her to the mall and we hung out for a while, got stoned, then we went down to the Presbytarian church and down the basement steps to the little cubby hole there by the back door. I made out with her. I touched her cunt and she smiled and then she was breathing really heavy. So fast and heavy I couldn't keep kissing her. She put her hand in my pants and grabbed my cock and started pulling on it and all. I'm going to really give it to her this weekend. We're going to a party in my friend's house and his parents are out of town. It's going to be sweet. She was begging me to rub her cunt and put my fingers in between the lips of it and all. She was so hot and wet, and breathing and panting so much she started begging me to fuck her. You reading this, teach? Got a hard on? I got you, didn't I?

I hoped Talbot was a liar. I didn't like the idea that he was with Leslie in that way. I felt as though he dishonored her, defaced her. Perhaps he was only trying to trick me into revealing that I was reading the folded entries. Not that I was jealous or anything. I just hated the suggestion that she would lavish her affections on such a sloppy, gangly fellow. I didn't think he was worthy of her. Nor was the behavior he described with such relish.

(Happy Bell) folded

11/8 /85

Mark Talbot's an asshole. He asked me for drugs. I told him to fuck off. He's always trying to do drugs and all. Asking me for ludes and angel dust and stuff. He knows all the words and talks like he knows all about it and he don't know shit. He begged me to give him celophane yellows and blues. Nobody, mr. fuckwad, gives that stuff away no more. Anyway, nobody in this place has the nerve to fuck with that stuff. the drug game is totally bogus in this jaile. All these rich fucks and they can't score a little coke even from their mommy and daddy. Don't worry if your reading this mr. J. I dont do drugs. I'm going to make something of myself.

My eleventh grade class was memorable because of George, I suppose—but Jaime, Mark, and Happy helped it along, too. Most of the dreary entries in the journals of sixteen- and seventeen-year-old children kill brain cells at an alarming rate, and no one should ever be forced to read them. The only interesting entries, predictably, were the ones they did not want me to read, but even those were usually feral and utterly boring. Still, I realized I could keep track of some things I was not supposed to know about—although many of my students never did trust that I would not read the folded pages. I ignored them, did not respond to their suspicions and I suppose for some, I earned a measure of trust over the days and weeks of the school year. I didn't know what to do about the drugs, though. I knew they were testing me with references like that, but I couldn't just ignore them. For a long time, I watched them vigilantly, but eventually they stopped talking about it, and I never did find any drugs to speak of. I think most of my students were pretty smart and some were smart alecks. (One day Happy showed up with a paper lunch bag taped under each eye. I said, "What's that supposed to be?" and he said, "I'm really tired. I haven't slept at all. Do I have bags under my eyes?")

I think George trusted me, at least. But I could not penetrate his innocence; I could not break through his naive belief that his life with his mother and father was normal. Since I couldn't break through to George without, as Bible said, making him "an enemy," I decided I would have to arrange a talk with his parents. I knew that's what Mrs. Creighton would want me to do, but I never got a chance to ask her to arrange it. What happened was that a meeting with George's mother was sort of inadvertently and unwillingly thrust upon me. I was, to put it bluntly, ambushed on Parent–Teacher night.

10

Ambush

I'D NEVER BEEN to Glenn Acres School at night. The ceiling lights were dull and bald, like the lights in a prison, and they made eerie shadows on the walls and on the faces of people. The whole event turned into a long, tedious, impossible sea of faces and names, hands reaching in to shake mine, eyes brimming in really inadequate light. The building was so crowded, it was like a teen party raided by unruly parents, everybody milling around. At one point I was talking to one of my seniors, with her mother and father standing right there, and this little shadow seemed to filter into my space; it was a presence that suddenly appeared in my peripheral vision, right next to me, small and below my belt level, and I turned reflexively to see what it was. I was leaning away, too—as a sort of defense, really, since I thought it might be a large dog or some other animal with significant teeth and a tendency to slobber—and this little gnome-like face, with too much hair around the nose and mouth, stared up at me from the shadows with eyes like small black beetles. It said something that only registered as a deeply troubling snuffle. I jumped back, raised my arms in an instinctive way, and let out this helpless, miniature scream that sounded like, "Eeek."

"This is my grandmother," the student said.

Instantly I tried to smile and pretend the hairy face had not scared the shit out of me. "How do you do," I said, reaching for her little hand.

"What'd he say?" she snarled.

"I'm so sorry," I said. "You startled me."

"Don't worry about it," the student's father said. "She has that effect on lots of folks."

"Don't be cruel, Frank," his wife said.

"She can't hear us."

"*I* can hear you," the wife sneered.

He shook his head, smiling at me as if I should know what he had to put up with, and I nodded my approval. We were definitely on the same page. I wanted the little grandmother to get away from me. She kept kneading this white napkin in her hands, and I was afraid some part of her was dripping.

I met Happy Bell's father next—he grabbed my hand and congratulated me on getting the kids to "pay attention to the important issues"—and then he told me how much Happy liked me. "I think the boy will get a scholarship if he does well enough in your class."

"He's a bright boy," I said. "Very funny."

"Funny. What do you mean funny."

"Humorous. He keeps us all laughing."

"Oh, really."

"But smart too. He's very smart." I had been told by Mrs. Creighton not to alienate anyone with the naked truth about their offspring. She told me people don't want to hear the bad news about their children unless there's real trouble. A kid would have to be a real beast to get any of us to report even slightly disappointing news to his parents. What they want to hear is just the good news: how bright, well-behaved, outstanding, and truly beautiful their own specific child is.

Happy's Dad was not smiling. "I don't want him to be funny."

I didn't know what to say for a space. He seemed to be waiting for me to respond, and he still had a hold of my hand.

"I don't want him to be the class clown, you know what I mean?"

"Sometimes," I said, extracting my hand, "A class clown can be a pretty positive thing. I myself was . . ."

"Not him," he said. "Not my boy. He's going to be serious about his education."

"Yes, of course." I wanted to say, "You named the boy 'Happy,'" but I kept my mouth shut.

"If he does well in your class, he'll have a scholarship. We're working very hard on getting him in to the University of Virginia."

"Good."

"I'm counting on it. We can't afford the tuition to send him to college. This is his one chance. He needs that scholarship, absolutely."

"Well I'm glad to hear you're all working so hard on it."

"Yes, sir," he said, winking at me. "Absolutely got to have it, and he will if he does well in your class."

I smiled. "He has to do well in other classes, too."

He winked again, and moved off, but he raised his arm and pointed his finger at me as he departed. I couldn't tell if it was a sign of affection, or the intimation of a kind of threat. I didn't like the way he winked.

Then I met Mark Talbot's father and mother—both leaned a bit too close, both wore thin wire-framed glasses that made their eyes look like peeled hard-boiled eggs, and both were "certain" that I was doing the right thing.

"About what?" I asked.

"I was worried at first," Mark's mother said. "I must admit, watching movies about Nazis and all that murder and killing—I couldn't figure out what you must be up to."

"I still don't know," the father said. "I don't care. It's gotten him interested in school again, in learning."

"I'm glad," I said.

I saw Leslie Warren walking around with her mother and father. Her mother looked ordinary—blonde hair, fairly chiseled face—but her father was clearly the font of Leslie's preternatural beauty. He had deep-set blue eyes, perfectly quaffed hair. He was tall and slim as a tent pole. Leslie waved to me as she passed and I smiled. It felt like a kind of small triumph that she acknowledged me.

More people came in. Then a few more. Before I knew it, I was sitting on the edge of my desk smiling at folks and touching hands like a politician. I didn't see George, nor, for a long time, did I remember that I wanted to. I was just too busy. Near the end of the evening—just as things were winding down and Mrs. Creighton had thanked the last cadre of parents for coming—I saw George squeeze through two people and start toward me; lurking behind him was a very lean, tall woman with close-cropped hair that seemed plastered to her head like some sort of sudsy shampoo.

"George," I said. "Glad to see you."

"This is my mom." He turned and pointed at her. She wore a brown blouse and black slacks that were creased perfectly down the middle of each leg. She had on flats. Her hair was graying on top, but in those awful lights, it looked almost as if she was going bald in the center of her head. Her eyes were huge, dark, and menacing. She was at least six inches taller than I was.

"Hello," I said.

She did not smile. "I'm Eileen Meeker." She put out her hand and I touched the palm of it with the tips of my fingers before she drew it away. Then she turned to George, who was staring up at her warily— as if he was afraid she might topple over and he'd have to catch her. "Please excuse us Gay-org, would you?" She actually called him *Gay-org.*

"So long," I said as George nodded at me. His mother said something to me, in a low voice, but there was a lot of noise, so I leaned a little closer to hear what she was saying. I only caught the tail end of it.

". . . corrupt and wrong. I'm sorry."

"What?" I said. "I didn't hear you."

She moved closer to me, and that made it necessary for her head to bow a bit, so she could continue to look right into my eyes. From that close distance, if I opened my mouth, she could look down my throat fairly readily. I remember a really strong impulse to back away, but there was no place to go. I was still leaning on my desk. Then I realized she was talking to me very directly and frankly. "Do you believe in God? Do you have any sense of the propriety of what you're doing? Are you even human?"

"I'm sorry," I said. "I didn't hear the first part of what you said."

"The very idea."

I realized she was snapping at me. I felt cornered and sunk. "Excuse me," I said. "Perhaps we should have a private meeting about this."

"I've said all I wanted to say. I've asked Mrs. Creighton to take George out of your class, but apparently you're the only English teacher . . ."

"Mrs. Meeker," I said. "I still don't know what your complaint is."

Her eyes seemed to expand—she was fighting a powerful emotion. "Do you know my son is reading all about Nazi Germany because of you? Do you know he is real interested in Nazis now?"

I didn't know what to say.

"I've caught him drawing swastikas. Making pictures of Nazi soldiers."

"Your son is not a Nazi," I said. "I know him well enough . . ."

"You don't know him."

"Well, but I do know him," I said with as much restraint as I could muster. "I've been communicating with him most of this year and I've been reading his thoughts in his journal . . ."

She leaned further down, so her face was almost exactly above mine. "You don't know him."

I studied her eyes. She did not straighten up; I did not bend any further back. We were like that for only a few seconds, and then I said, a little too loudly, "I know him well enough to notice the bruises around his neck." Her mouth opened but she didn't say anything. Then, feeling the heat rising in my throat and up the back of my neck, I said even louder: "The rather frequent bruises around his neck as a matter of cold fact!" And as I said this, I moved from the desk, toward her, and she backed away until I was leaning in toward her. She blinked. Behind her, I saw Mrs. Creighton coming toward us.

"Are you insane?" Mrs. Meeker said.

"Am I?"

"Well," Mrs. Creighton said as she slipped easily and gracefully between us. "Thank you so much for coming." She tried to reach for Eileen Meeker's hand, but the indignant, regal bully pulled back.

"I'm sorry," I said. "I thought you must know about the . . ."

"Not here," Mrs. Creighton said.

"Where then?"

A man I didn't recognize called across the room, "Mrs. Creighton, thank you so much. It was a wonderful evening." She waved, sort of disconcertingly. Then she looked at me. "This is not the time or the place, young man."

I looked for George. I saw Professor Bible slip through a departing mélange of parents. He strolled over to us with his hands in his suit pockets, his head barely upright. He had a look he always got when he was thinking—his brows crowding his eyes, his mouth slightly open under the white mustache.

Mrs. Meeker was saying she would take George out of the school, that she had never been treated so rudely in her life. "First that old man," she indicated Bible, "and now this, this, this . . ." she pointed at me.

"Young man," I said.

"Mr. Jameson, please!" Mrs. Creighton said.

Bible said, "Excuse me."

Everyone looked at him.

"People are leaving," he said. "The night would appear to be over. Perhaps we can all sit down here and discuss this little problem?" His voice was so smooth, and reassuring, I almost sat down at the instant he suggested it.

"I have nothing to say," Mrs. Meeker said.

"Mrs. Meeker," I said. "I'm sorry if I've offended you. It was not my intention to be rude."

She suddenly looked as if she might actually smile, but then I realized it was the damn rummy light from overhead. There was something absolutely steely in her expression. She did not take her eyes off me as she spoke. "I know your type. I know what this is."

"I really don't know what you think I . . ."

"I know what you people are thinking."

"Please," Mrs. Creighton said.

Professor Bible said, "We only have George's interests at heart. We don't know you and we . . ."

"You have caused me and my family nothing but heartache."

"We haven't understood," Mrs. Creighton said. "Perhaps if we . . ."

"You have no idea. I know people like you. I know." It was almost a shout.

No one said anything. Mrs. Creighton again reached for the woman's hand, she recoiled from it a second time, only now she had a look on her face of one who has been stricken hard with something wet and sloppy. "How dare you?" she said. Then she hollered, "Gay-org?" Her voice went way up there on the "org" part of the name. She sounded almost like an old-fashioned car horn. She called him again: "Gay-org."

George came round the corner timidly. I had the feeling he'd been listening in at the end of things. "Yes, Mom?"

"We are going home," she said, still glaring at us with those steely eyes. "Get my coat, and anything in this building that belongs to you."

"Mo-om."

"Empty your locker."

"I don't have a locker." George's face was sad now. He knew what was up, and he didn't want it.

"We will not be coming back here."

Professor Bible said, "Oh come now. It's not as bad as all that."

"It's every bit as bad as all that."

"Mo-om," George whined.

"Mrs. Meeker. We are only concerned about George," Professor Bible said.

"So am I. I don't want him learning about Nazis."

Bible looked at me. "Is that what this is about?"

"I asked her about the bruises. It's about that too."

"George, do you have your things?" Mrs. Meeker bellowed. "We are going."

"Well go then," I said.

Mrs. Creighton took hold of my arm. "Stop it!" It was the loudest noise in the room, a terrific shout. Her face was as angry as any human face I'd ever seen. I think all of us jumped. No one said anything for a long time. Then Mrs. Creighton said, "We must all calm down, now. Important decisions should be made without passion." Her voice was trembling, but it was amazing how completely she had gotten hold of herself.

George began to sniffle, but he manfully resisted outright crying. Finally, he said, "I want to stay here."

Mrs. Meeker turned, grabbed him by the hand, and dragged him out the door. The three of us watched her go, saw her cross the yard, open the car door, and shove George in the backseat as if she were kidnapping him. Then she slammed the door, walked around behind the car without looking back, got in and drove off.

The next day, Mrs. Creighton wanted to see me right after my eleven o'clock class.

11

The Natural Curse of Private School

AS EXPECTED, GEORGE was not in school, and I figured I was in a lot of trouble. When I walked in the door of Mrs. Creighton's office she said I was about to have that conference with George's father—that in fact he had requested it himself, and he wanted it to be a private conference.

"When?"

"He'll be here today."

"What about my bus route?"

"I'm asking you to come back here after. He wants to meet at five thirty."

"Can't he make it earlier?" I didn't want to drive everybody home, then come back to the school and wait around all afternoon.

"I didn't ask, and I don't think it's a good idea to do so."

I shook my head.

"He's probably coming after work, at the end of his day."

"Well, it's a long time after the end of my day." Even with my bus route I was usually home by three fifteen or so. "He wants a private conference with me."

"Just you."

"Not Professor Bible, or . . ."

"Just you."

"Great."

"You did say you wanted to talk with him." She gestured for me to sit down and I did so. She watched my face and I tried to get comfortable, waiting for whatever else she was going to say. My heart was beating a fairly strident rhythm, and I could not believe how dry my mouth was.

"I liked this thing . . ." she started, then seemed to lapse into puzzled thinking. She gazed around the room, fiddled with some papers on her desk. Then she went on: "This business of teaching them about the holocaust."

I nodded, but said nothing.

"I think it's important to do things across the curriculum."

I knew a "but" was coming.

"And your class has been much attuned to what's happening in Professor Bible's history classes."

"I'm glad."

"I wonder if you didn't go too far though with the younger ones. The tenth graders."

"I got good papers from them too."

"I suppose it was okay for most of the seniors, but I even wonder about . . ." she paused.

"You mean George."

"No, not him particularly."

"It was that class—Jaime Nichols was the one who didn't know who Hitler was. Eleventh grade and she doesn't know—that's how it started."

94

She sat back and put her hand up to her face, ran her fingers over her chin. "You are not going to like what I'm going to say to you next."

"I haven't liked much of anything so far."

She frowned.

"I'm sorry," I said.

"I wonder if you really want to be a teacher."

I said nothing.

"You make your own decisions here, but if you were teaching in the public schools you might already have been fired."

"For what?"

"Impertinence, for one."

I asked her to explain exactly what she meant by that, and when I was "impertinent."

"Don't take that tone with me," she said. Her voice was quiet and calm.

"I'm sorry. I don't mean to sound disrespectful."

"You don't *sound* disrespectful, you are *being* disrespectful." She put both hands on the desk in front of her and leaned toward me. "And if you want to know when you've been impertinent, examine your behavior right now."

"I'm sorry."

"And last night."

"I know I should not have lost my temper." It was quiet for a space, then I said, "I'll be better, I promise." Suddenly I realized I might actually lose my job. She nodded and settled back in her chair. She looked exasperated and I was afraid of what she was going to say next. My heart was beating like a paint mixer.

"I hope you will give me another chance," I said.

She seemed surprised. "What?"

"Don't fire me."

"I'm not going to fire you."

"I'm very glad to hear that." I think she must have noticed the deep breath I took, the way my face relaxed. "You had something to say I wasn't going to like?"

"If you'll let me finish?" She raised her brow and stared at me. At that moment, when I knew she wasn't going to fire me, I had so much affection for her I didn't care what she might say. "Mr. and Mrs. Meeker are not just parents," she went on. "We are not in the same position here as the public schools. Students don't just flock to the door because they live within an arbitrarily set boundary line, and the law says they have to attend our school. This is a *private* school. Do you know what that means? We count on enrollments for our very lives, here."

"I know," I said.

"You don't act like you know. Mrs. Meeker is not just Gay-org's mother, she's a customer, a client. Their money helps keep our doors open and pays your salary. And as in any business, we have to operate on the principle that the customer is always right."

"Even when the customer is clearly wrong?"

"Yes. At least we have to treat the customer as if she is right, and that means we do not flaunt how wrong the customer is, and we don't argue with the customer."

Now, I wasn't feeling so affectionate. I think it's possible I was feeling sorry for her. I know my unreasoning respect was beginning to weaken and it made me sad to realize it. I thought she was above talk like that. But then it hit me that she had tried to prepare me. She said I would not like what she was going to say. Maybe she understood better than I did how corrupt it would sound to be talking about what was essentially concern for money, rather than George's neck.

"I know we have to be courteous," I said. "I wish I had not lost my temper."

"Make sure you don't lose your temper this afternoon. George's father can be very—direct."

96

"I promise," I said. "Do I meet him in here?"

"You can use this office if you want. I won't be here."

"You're not even going to be in the building?"

"He wants to see you alone. I told you that."

"But I thought you'd be . . ."

"I'm leaving you with a key so you can lock up when you're done."

"Can't I ask Bible to join me?"

She gave me a scornful look. "Just be here will you? I'll leave the key right here in the center drawer of this desk. And I'll put the dogs in the Math room as usual."

"Okay."

"And whatever you do, don't forget to turn out the lights and lock up."

"I won't."

"If you think of it, you might let the dogs out for a bit before you lock up the Math room. It might spare me a mess in the morning."

"Should I mention our concern about the bruises on George's neck, or . . ."

"What I want you to do," she said firmly, "Is make sure he doesn't take George out of this school. Do whatever you have to do to keep that from happening."

I didn't know what to say.

"If you and Professor Bible would just leave those things to me, I would take care of them. I was dealing with the situation," she said.

I did not have the courage right then to ask what she was doing about it. All I said was, "Okay."

"I don't think I have to forbid you to mention the abuse, do I?"

"No, ma'am."

Her expression darkened. "I hate to be called *ma'am*."

"I mean, no, you don't."

Now she smiled, began lifting pages from the pile of paper on her desk. Without looking at me, she handed me more tissue so I could wipe the sweat that dripped out of my hair. She may as well have said "run along," so I did.

I needed to talk to Bible before my next class but he wasn't in his room. I went outside and found him standing under the big tree by the basketball court, watching the kids play a hotly contested game of half-court ball. When he saw me approach, he smiled and waved. He was wearing his customary white suit, and black bow tie. His hair was as white as his shirt and flew high in the sunny breezes. It was an absolutely beautiful day for November—bright and clear, with only great puffs of white cloud high in the deep blue dome above us.

"Want a cigarette?" I said.

"You ever play?" he pointed to the court.

"All the time. I still do, in fact."

"Why don't you join them?"

"Nah."

I handed him a cigarette and he pulled out a lighter and lit it.

"Can I talk to you?" I said.

"Sure." He watched the players on the court, puffing his cigarette.

"George Meeker's father is coming to see me."

"I heard."

"I'm pretty nervous about it."

"He's a pretty scary guy."

"You think he's going to try and knock me around?"

"When's he coming?"

"Five thirty this evening. I have to come back here and wait for him."

"You'll be by yourself?"

"Yeah."

"She did that to me last year."

"Really."

"I think that's the way she wants it."

"What happened?"

"Well, that's when I confronted him. And when George began to hate me. He had George with him."

"Oh, I hope he doesn't do that to me."

One of the boys missed a pass and the ball bounced into the grass at Bible's feet. He picked it up and threw it back on the court. He was still watching the game, his face turned from me, but he said, "I'll stick around if you want."

"I'd appreciate that. But Mrs. Creighton said I should meet him alone."

"I'll be in my classroom; I won't horn in on the conference." He puffed on the cigarette. Then he turned to me. "Don't worry about it, young man. It will be all right."

Bible was so big in my mind, so capable and venerable. I believed him.

12

Imminent Threats of
Varying Degrees

GEORGE'S FATHER WAS huge. Probably in his early to late forties. He was not much taller than George, but he was massive from the waist up, incredibly broad in the chest, with arms the size of small dogs. He wore a dark sports jacket, tan loafers, and a wide leather belt. His hair was dark brown, piled high in the middle and tapered down to just skin on the sides by his ears. His face was stony, with crevices like the surface of Mt. Rushmore, minus the four presidents. He had a small, very thin, short mustache that stuck straight out under his nose, as though electric current would not let the bristles lie down. His eyes seemed always darkened by the heavy brow—so all of his expressions were shaded with irritation. Even pleasure would register as a kind of pain, or frustration. Displeasure looked like murder was in the offing. And he was clearly displeased with me.

He did not knock on the door. I was sitting at Mrs. Creighton's desk, wondering if I had heard a car outside in the parking lot, and the door in the hallway simply opened and closed. While my heart seemed to scatter and scurry in my chest, I heard someone removing his coat, and then he came around the corner and stood in the doorway. Seated at the desk, I could scarcely get to my feet fast enough. I stuttered, "Y-y-you must be Mr. Meeker."

He had a pair of tan gloves in his hand. He smacked them in his palm and came to the desk. "Mr. Jameson."

"Sit down," I said. I tried to see past him, across the hall to Bible's room. His door was closed and I couldn't tell if he knew Mr. Meeker had arrived.

Mr. Meeker reached across the desk and offered his hand. I shook it, noticing the grip was nothing to write home about. We both sat back down. "What can I do for you?" I said.

He smiled and said, "You have some complaint, I'm told."

"I have a complaint."

"That's what I was told."

"I thought you wanted to see me because . . ."

"I was told you," he pointed at me on the word *you* and paused there for a fraction of a second, "have a complaint."

"What were you told?"

"What's your complaint?"

"Well, it's not a complaint really."

"Really."

"Certain concerns . . ."

"What concerns, sir?" He raised his voice a little. "You have made allegations against me and my family."

"I don't know what you're referring to," I said, calmly. "I don't even know exactly what it is you're asking."

He sat there looking at me. Finally he said, "Are you denying that you accused my wife?"

"Accused her of what?" I immediately regretted letting that question out. He was going to have to address the abuse, the very thing I had been told to avoid.

He dodged the question. "You think you can tell my wife how to raise our son?"

"No."

"You think it's your job to insult her?" His voice was a little louder.

"There's no need to raise your voice." I remembered what Mrs. Creighton expected of me, and I did everything I could to rein in both my fear and my temper. He did piss me off.

In a calmer voice, but still fairly piercing, he said, "What right have you to speak to my wife as you did last night."

"I am sorry she misunderstood me."

"She did not misunderstand."

"She was angry when she got here and she said a few things . . ."

"Are you going to argue with me?" Now he was indignant, his voice almost quiet in its malevolence and disbelief.

"No, sir. I'm just trying to explain . . ."

"You don't have to explain anything."

"I just want to say . . ."

"My wife and I know what kind of person we're dealing with." He stopped, leaned toward me, as though he were going to let me in on a little secret. "We know your type."

"What type, sir?" I really wanted to know.

He sat back and folded his arms. "Liberal."

"Really now. Is that supposed to offend me?" I couldn't help my tone. Conservatives always think they're really hoisting you up on the scaffold whenever they call you a liberal. I took it as a compliment. (Just as every conservative I've ever known takes it as a compliment when I call him a "conservative," and what I mean when I call somebody a conservative is that he is a tight-assed, lily-white, deeply religious, highly hypocritical, racist Visigoth on a black horse, moseying up a barren trail, with a statue of God in the saddle with him, and the New Deal, help for the poor, civil rights, and the environment a burning village in the background.)

Mr. Meeker went on. "I want you to apologize to me and my wife, or we are taking George out of this—this—school." He hated saying the word, "school."

"Wellsir," I said—one word, like that. "I already apologized to your wife, and I'm saying to you now, that I am sorry." It was hard to get air for the last word in that sentence. But I did it. He was not amused, pleased, or satisfied.

"I want a formal apology."

"I will put it in writing. I'm terribly sorry for the way I spoke to Mrs. Meeker."

"Not just that."

"And if I did anything to offend you, sir."

"I want you to apologize for what you suggested to my wife about me and my son."

Well, now we were back in the real world. We were right there where I did not want to be, the place I'd hoped to avoid. I studied the desk in front of me, the way my thin, white hands seemed to tremble above the papers there. I let my fingers touch down, gently. "Sir," I said. "I really like George."

He seemed to snort a little.

"I think he's smart, and in his own way a wonderful child."

"What do you mean 'in his own way'?"

"He's unique. Not like the others."

"What do you mean?"

"He's so—so mature. Yes, that's it. George is really already a young man, and he's devoted to you."

He nodded, as if I wasn't telling him anything he didn't already know.

"Perhaps his imagination runs away with him at times . . ." This was a bald lie. I didn't think for a minute that George had imagined those bruises, and although he had never mentioned his father's abuse, he had written about it—written about it so analytically he may as well have been describing his favorite flavor of ice cream—in his private journal entries, but I couldn't tell his father that. All I had was the bruises, and how could I mention those, knowing how Mrs. Creighton wanted this meeting to go? I know. I am not unmindful of the fact that, from a certain point of view, it might be construed as fairly certain that I didn't bring up the bruises because I was mortally afraid for my life. I've thought of that.

At any rate, I was in enough trouble for mentioning George's imagination. Mr. Meeker took it up like it was a fire hose and the building was on fire.

"What did he say to you?"

"Oh, nothing directly . . ."

"What has he been saying?"

"Nothing."

"What are you getting at?" He raised his voice again.

"Sir, if you would just calm down."

"What did that little bastard say to you?"

"The little bastard didn't say anything to me!" Now I was loud. It took him back. He glared at me in silence. More quietly (and desperately) I said, "And he's not a little bastard to me, sir." He almost rose from his chair. I felt my heart tremble. To forestall his rage, I said, "I have always liked George. George is a good guy—he's a good student." Remembering it now, I think my voice sounded pathetic. I felt pathetic.

Mr. Meeker settled in his chair again. For a brief moment I think his face might have looked sad, but then he said in a quiet, almost confessional voice, "He's a weak little failure is what he is."

I must have blanched. I know I shook my head.

"Does that shock you?" Mr. Meeker said.

I didn't know what to say to that. Either way, I'd insult him. If I said it didn't shock me, I'd be admitting that I thought he was a prick and nothing he said would shock me. If I said it did shock me, I'd be admitting that I thought he was a prick because of what he said. So I muttered, "Does George know how you feel?"

"He's a little girl. He's not even . . ." Mr. Meeker stopped. He seemed to consider something and seconds ticked by. All I saw now was this man struggling with his emotions. I was actually trying to imagine how I would ask him about the bruises. I'd completely forgotten Mrs. Creighton, the purpose of this meeting; I don't think I remembered that I was a teacher. It's possible I remembered that I shouldn't bring it up, but in the softening of his face—in his apparent sadness—I saw an opening. I felt, for the first time since he walked in the door, as though I was in a position of power. Finally I couldn't help myself. I just blurted it out. "Do you sometimes hit George with your fists?"

He didn't answer, but he slowly nodded his head.

"Hard?"

He looked at me. "As hard as I can."

"Mr. Meeker," I said, slowly. "I wonder if you know how much damage . . ."

"He'll be tough. He'll be able to take it. He'll be a man when I'm finished with him."

"And how will he feel about you?"

"I'm treating him like a man."

"And that's how you treat other men?"

"What?"

"How do you think he'll feel about you?"

"He'll respect me."

"He'll hate you."

Now he stood up. "Who the fuck do you think you are? You're not much older than George."

I remained seated behind the desk. The feeling of power was gone and I figured the desk would be a nice barrier between me and Mr. Meeker's tan loafers. "Mr. Meeker, please," I said. I could not have finished the sentence anyway—I didn't know what I wanted him to do, unless it was to get the hell out of there—but he interrupted me.

"Get up."

"Mr. Meeker, there's no need to . . ."

"Get out of that chair."

I reached over and picked up the telephone. He stood there while I dialed two numbers.

"Who are you calling?"

"If you don't sit down and get control of yourself, I'm going to finish calling the police."

"You are."

"Sir, I've dialed two of the three numbers I need. If you don't sit down, I'm dialing number three." It was a lie, but he believed it. He moved a bit, as though he might leave, but then he simply sat down, adjusted himself and crossed his legs. I put the phone back in its cradle. "I will apologize to you and your wife in writing. But I want you to do something for me."

He waited, silent, sort of brooding there across from me. He might have been trying to decide if he wanted to kick my ass anyway, and deal with the police later. I was trying to figure out how to say what I wanted to say as delicately as possible.

"You own a business in town, right?"

"I want that letter," he said.

"You'll have it. I'll write it today."

He nodded, still fighting himself.

"You own a dealership of some kind?"

"Chevrolet, Pontiac, Oldsmobile." His eyes remained dull and uninterested. He was waiting there for something.

"You have salesmen working for you?"

"Yes."

"Lots of them?"

"No."

"How many?"

"Four."

"Don't take this wrong, but how do you keep them interested?"

"Interested?" He uncrossed his legs, and leaned a bit toward me, curious.

"You know. What do you do to motivate them?"

"We have incentives."

"What kind of incentives?"

"What's it to you?"

"I just want to know."

"When do I get the letter?"

I shook my head. "I'll write it today."

He started to get up.

"About those incentives?"

Now he looked at me, frowning. "What?"

"You said you have incentives in your business, for the salesmen . . ."

"Bonuses, better demos, cherry floor time, that sort of thing," he said impatiently. He stood and started toward the door. Then he stopped and looked back at me. "Believe me, I know how to motivate people. Sometimes I take the entire sales staff and their families out to dinner at a very expensive restaurant."

"That works?"

"Sure."

"You ever beat the crap out of one of your salesmen, put bruises all over him?"

With a great flash of scorn and anger he said, "Fuck you," and started around the desk.

"Now wait a minute," I said, reaching for the phone again. Remembering this event now, I think I am always going to be very proud of the way I'd worked the conversation around to what he was actually doing to George, but at the moment I was terrified again. I backed against the wall, and tried to dial the phone with the same hand that held the receiver in it. With the other hand I tried to block Mr. Meeker's approach. But he just batted it out of the way and took hold of the front of my shirt.

"Mr. Meeker, listen to me, listen to me."

He had to reach up to grab my shirt by the collar, and we were both behind the desk, so anybody looking at us from the door might have thought that Mr. Meeker had lifted me up and was holding me in the air against the wall. That's how short he was.

"I'm tired of listening to you," he said.

"Please let go of me."

"Not before I teach you a little lesson, teacher."

Just then, Professor Bible came into the room. I was against the wall, and Meeker still had the front of my shirt and Bible said, "Did you call the police?" in a very calm voice.

Meeker looked at him.

Bible leaned down as though he were trying to look out the window to his right, behind Meeker. "Isn't that a police car out there?"

Meeker let go of me and patted his jacket down in front, then walked to the window.

"Oh no," Bible said. "That's just a cab. I thought it was a cop."

Meeker turned to him, flustered. "You're—you're—aren't you . . ."

"Professor Bible."

"Oh yes."

"Sorry to interrupt your beating," Bible said. "But it's a lovely day out there, isn't it? Not the kind of day for blood, what do you think?"

Meeker looked at me, then back to Bible. "Couple of wise guys."

"Sir," I said. "I really was trying to make a point here."

"You were." He remained over by the window. Bible stood in the doorframe and I was still against the wall behind Mrs. Creighton's desk.

"If you could just think for a minute about what you're trying to do . . ."

Professor Bible came further into the room. He towered over Meeker and was almost as broad, but he was paunchy in the middle and stooped forward a bit in his posture. His head was every bit as large as Meeker's, but his age was apparent. He had small sores on his broad, pale forehead, and his white hair stood up on top of his head like wild pampas grass. He gestured to the chair Mr. Meeker had been sitting in. "Mind if I sit down?"

"Go ahead," I said. Meeker met my gaze, then dropped his eyes to the floor.

"Don't you want George to be a successful man?" I said.

He wouldn't look at me, would not even acknowledge that he'd heard what I said. Bible said, "I'm sure he does. Every father does."

"Why not try to motivate him like your salesmen? Incentives instead of punishment?"

"I don't need to be taking advice from you," Meeker said. "You're just a kid yourself."

"Sir, please listen to me," I said. "Our only interest is your son's welfare."

"Yeah, well," Meeker said. He started to withdraw, but then he stopped. "You write that letter. If I don't have that letter in my hands by this time tomorrow, I'm going to take George out of this school and sue you bastards for every penny I paid to this place."

I nodded. Bible said nothing.

"Tomorrow," Meeker said again.

"Should I just send it home with George?"

"What?"

"Will he be here tomorrow?"

"He'll be here."

"I'll put it in a sealed envelope," I said.

Meeker waved his hand and went out into the hall. I heard him slam the back door.

Professor Bible said, "Nothing anybody can do with a man like that."

"We got to do something," I said.

The next day it rained again. This time a steady, cold, damp drizzle that went right to your soul. No coat was capable against it. If you went outside, you shuddered in it, unable to keep warm. It made the air in the building, even the warm air, feel cold and bleakly damp. George waited for me at the end of his driveway when I picked up my gang. He got on the bus without saying anything. He wore a light blue raincoat, clearly not warm enough, and held his arms wrapped tightly around his body to keep warm. When he got up to the top step, he put his hand on the railing to balance himself and one of the boys in the first row of seats covered his hand and held it there.

"Don't," George said.

"Hey date monster," the other boy said. His name was Nicholas. He was one of those California types that the girls love: a dark thicket of hair, tan skin, muscular and tall.

"Don't," George said again.

"Leave him alone," I said.

"How many girls you ask out now, Georgie?" Nicholas asked. He let go George's hand. "This little date monster has hit on every girl in the ninth, tenth, and eleventh grade."

"His mommy calls him Gay-Org," one of the other boys said. The whole bus erupted in laughter. George seemed to grow shorter, as he found his way to the back and sat down. People were starting to enjoy the idea of having a "Gay-Org" to pick on. All of them stared at him.

I drove the bus to three other stops, hoping we'd pick up somebody who might distract the vipers in our little group—my bus was small, only room for thirty seats. It was, in the common parlance of the game, a "short bus." But it was all Glenn Acres could afford. (They had three of them, and Mr. Creighton spent much of his time during the day, when he wasn't selling furniture, keeping them running. They were pretty old buses.) Our short bus was not for "special students," as it so often is in the big public schools. Still, these kids were special in their own way.

They were not very special in the method and means of their crowd mentality, however. They had found a weak link and they were all happy to pick at it. I knew I couldn't do much to forestall their torment because that would only further alienate George, and it wouldn't do me any good with the other students either. They were all singing in unison, "Cheer up, Gay-Org, the girls won't all say no," to the tune of the funeral march. Still, I ended up yelling at them to be quiet, and I did say, "You'd think you could find something more worthwhile to occupy your time." A few of them snickered, but it got them off George temporarily, and before long I was pulling into the driveway at school.

Gay-Org. Why would his mother use that name so loudly at Parents' night? Why would she insist on using a name for her son that would guarantee him pain and isolation, not to mention utter humiliation in the face of every one of his peers? Some philosopher once said there are people who would not be capable of love if they did not know that it existed. I think a lot of people know it exists and they're still not capable of it.

13

Feints and Stratagems

So concerned about George's troubles at home, I completely missed what was going on right under my nose. He was tortured in school as well—not physically, but mentally. I began to watch for it, looking for an opening to take some sort of effective action. I felt so impotent against his father and mother.

I wrote the letter Mr. Meeker asked for. In the first draft, I said what I really wanted to say:

November 16, 1985

Dear Mr. and Mrs. Meeker:

I am profoundly sorry for interfering in your wonderfully efficient scheme to destroy your son's sense of well-being, and utterly ruin his personality. Lessons on cruelty are so hard to come by these days, what with all these folks on television and in the movies talking about love and all. This is a cold, hard world, and what better preparation for your son than introducing him to brutality as soon as possible. I know you will completely demolish any possibility that George will begin the ugly path toward sensitivity and compassion. My only concern is that we find a way to persecute him here at the school as well, so we can insure that he won't trust anybody, at all, ever. Perhaps you two, who have demonstrated such worthy skills along these lines, could suggest ways we can make George suffer here. Would you prefer that only the adults here smack him and beat him up, or could we enlist the help of some of the older students? We have several seniors that I'm quite sure could smash him in the chest every bit as hard as you do, Mr. Meeker, and we could always have one of the older girls watch him do it so it would be like having his mother there, approving. I'm open to suggestions.

> *Sincerely,*
> *Ben Jameson*

I had fun writing it, and when I showed it to Professor Bible, he begged me to send it to the Meekers. But I knew I couldn't.

For one thing, I didn't want to do that to Mrs. Creighton. I promised her I would try to smooth things over, and that was what I was determined to do. I would not let the torture go on—I was still committed to getting George to recognize what dizzying assholes his mother and father were, but I couldn't just go at them the way I wanted to without causing them to withdraw their boy from the school. If that happened there would be no way I could keep my eye on him.

What I wanted to do, all the time, was tie George's mother and father to a bedpost with a bungee cord and make them hold a phone book against their chests while I beat the living shit out of them. That's what I wanted to do.

In the final draft of the letter, I wrote:

Dear Mr. and Mrs. Meeker:

I am profoundly sorry that I offended you. I was misguided in my attempts to interfere in your family's methods of dealing with discipline and for suggesting that I might know better what is best for your son. I am sorry that I implied any abusive situation exists, although I am certain if abuse were taking place, agencies of the state are better equipped to deal with it than I am. Please forgive me for being so impertinent. I am new at my job and perhaps a little too enthusiastic about my duties toward my students. I take their welfare very seriously, so I hope you will forgive me for overreacting to injuries I noticed on George. As I am sure you will agree, it is George's well-being and overall health and development that should govern all we do.

> *Sincerely,*
>
> *Ben Jameson*

I hated myself for writing it, and even more for giving it to Mrs. Creighton the next day. But I didn't hate myself for long. I was in for quite a surprise.

When I handed Mrs. Creighton the letter, she smiled slightly, her eyes blinking in a slow sort of knowing way, as if she could understand more about me by this little capitulation than I might want or allow. I smiled back.

"We'll keep at it," she said. "Don't you doubt it."

"Meanwhile," I said, but I didn't finish the thought. She knew, and I knew, George would continue to suffer.

"Do me a favor," she said, holding my letter on the edge of her desk so I could see it without getting up. She pointed her pencil at the penultimate sentence. "End this sentence with the word 'overreacting.'" Her voice was so soft it sounded like seduction. "Don't mention the injuries."

I took the letter back to my classroom and did what she asked. When I had the new, tamer version, I brought it back. She was typing, but when I came in she lifted a piece of paper from her desk and handed it to me. "Here," she said. "Read mine."

Well, she sure surprised me. This is what her letter said:

Dear Mr. and Mrs. Meeker:

Enclosed please find Mr. Jameson's apology for his inexcusable behavior on Parent–Teacher night. I assure you, he has made amends with me and he will be a much more professional and restrained teacher and colleague from now on. I hope he will perform to our standards in the future and that we will have no more brash judgments or rude behavior.

One of the reasons I cannot have my faculty making such allegations against parents who have enrolled students in this school is that such activity is irresponsible. As I told Mr. Jameson only this morning, reckless accusations like that make this school subject to libel, and rightfully so. I asked Mr. Jameson to consider what might happen to your business, Mr. Meeker, if such scandalous accusations were ever made public.

I looked at her. "This is pretty strong." I didn't know what to make of the last paragraph. I wanted to ask her if she intended to threaten the Meekers, but then she lifted another sheet of paper from the typewriter in front of her. "Here's the second page."

Mr. Jameson was very wrong to confront Mrs. Meeker on Parent–Teacher night and that is why he is apologizing. But he is the second teacher to notice significant and troublesome abrasions on George's person—especially about the neck and upper body. Also, two other teachers, Mrs. Gallant last year, and Miss Corrigan of our current faculty, have questioned me concerning George's overall welfare. If there is one more incident like this, or any noticeable injury of any kind, I will enlist all the power and influence at my command to insure this situation is as well-publicized as any Labor Day sale you've ever had, Mr. Meeker. As I'm sure you know, people with even modest sensitivity would not want to do business with one who brutalizes a child. If you wish to withdraw George from this school, there will be no refund of tuition this year. Also, if you withdraw him, please be assured that we will do everything in our power to insure that all of his records, including these various issues concerning his physical welfare, are speedily forwarded to his new school.

Sincerely,

Elizabeth Creighton

I wanted to kiss her. She was not looking at me, but her eyes glittered with a kind of self-assurance and contentment. I think she knew I wanted to kiss her. She put the two pages together, folded them neatly and placed them in the same envelope with my apology.

"He'll take George out of the school," I said.

"He might." She was not smiling.

"I'm sorry."

She licked the envelope, sealed it, put two stamps on it and handed it to me. "You mail it."

I looked at it, feeling so grateful you'd have thought there was money in it.

"Here's what I want you to remember from this," she said. "You meet parents on Parent–Teacher night to shake hands and let them know what you're doing in the classroom. You answer questions. And that's it. You have nothing else whatever to do with any parent unless I request it."

I nodded.

"Any other problem will be taken care of privately and I'll do it."

"Okay."

"Let's hope Mr. Meeker cares about his business a little more than he does his son," she said.

I didn't know what effect Mrs. Creighton's letter might have on George's home life or even if he'd remain in the school. I couldn't change what George's parents were doing at home, but I could do something about what was happening to him in school, and as long as he was there I was not going to let the others torture him if I could help it. As the days went by, I realized he was not going anywhere.

What I finally did was not so subtle as my Nazi extravaganza, but I hoped (and believed) it might work out in some glorious way.

The idea for it came from a long conversation with Doreen about how to win back George's confidence. Since my conversation with his mother and the "bout" with his father, he had been reticent and totally uninterested in anything I had to say outside of the curriculum. He still did his homework, still took copious notes in class, and occasionally when I got discussion going a bit, he'd chime in with something. But when class was done, he'd get up and walk out without a glance back. He did not speak to me in the hallway unless I spoke to him. Polite and respectful whenever I addressed him, he greeted me with a look of utter disdain when I didn't.

So during a lunch break one day, shortly after the Thanksgiving holiday, I got to talking to Doreen about it and she said, "As long as he does his work, what do you care?"

I shrugged. I knew it was not in my job description, but something about George's predicament drew me to him. It was not a desire to be a better teacher. It had nothing to do with teaching. But it was, I think and still believe, a sincere desire to help another person. What causes that? Hasn't everybody experienced it to some degree? Everybody who is not a serial killer, or one of those awful, pea-brained people who claim to like and trust animals more than human beings? Isn't there a need for charity in every heart? Is all kindness insincere and born out of a desire to manipulate and control what happens to the people around us?

I'd asked Doreen these questions, but I realize now I should have addressed them to Annie. I even told Doreen what I thought Annie's answer would be.

"You have a Christ complex?" Doreen laughed. "Really." She was eating a tuna fish sandwich and sipping a Coke.

117

"What?"

"It's not news to anybody, believe me."

"Oh, what, now *you're* accusing me?"

"All men have a Christ complex," she said.

"Very funny."

We were sitting in my classroom, looking out on a dazzling array of green shadows and sun that filtered through the dead leaves on the oak trees. It was December, but you'd never know it from the weather. Sporadic breezes carried a slight hint of hard ice, but mostly the air was balmy and still. Just about everyone but Doreen and I had gone outside.

"Kindness is what you believe it is," Doreen said. "But true kindness, as far as I'm concerned—or at least sincere kindness—is done anonymously, for no credit or thanks."

"So if you get caught being kind, it's an attempt to get credit or manipulate?"

"What manipulate? Who said manipulate?"

"That's the nature of a Christ complex, isn't it?"

"You're his teacher. Why don't you pay attention to that?"

"But don't you see?" I said. "It isn't about teaching him, it's caring for him. Don't you care what happens to him?"

"Of course I do."

"Well?"

"I don't care if he has affection for me," Doreen said. I could tell she really thought she'd hit the nail on the head with that one.

"I don't either, but if he doesn't like me, even a little bit, how can I keep track of what is happening to him? How can I help him?"

"It isn't your job to do more than what you're doing right now. Anyway, he hasn't been beaten lately."

"Maybe the old man has found a way to disguise his brutality better."

"You've done what you were called to for the job. There's nothing more."

"I'm not talking about my job."

"Well," she said. "He'll come around. Just keep being kind to him."

And then she got to talking about a friend of hers who had won her over by throwing her a surprise party, and I got the idea. I didn't tell her about it then. I went into the office after school that day and looked up George's enrollment form. His birthday was, as you might expect if you believe the world is governed by a sadistic bastard, December 24th, the absolute second-worst birthday date ever.

Any birthday in December is pretty rough, but the degree to which it becomes sadistic is directly proportional to how close it is on either end of the twenty-fifth. The twenty-fifth is the big enchilada: the worst birthday date of all. You get up in the morning, and it's downstairs to "Merry Christmas in this corner, and that small group of presents over on the other side of the room there, that's Happy Birthday!!!"

Can you imagine it?

It's so ridiculously perverse I can't think of a single analogy to compare it to. What would it be like? It isn't painful or soul-destroying; it doesn't cause suffering, or disease, or any lasting or important human malady. I mean it's not an important hardship. It's just a circumstance that simply and effectively eliminates birthdays for anyone unlucky enough to have parents who got randy and acted on it anytime between March 21st and 29th; any time in March or April, to tell the truth, since birthdays diminish in importance the closer to Christmas, before or after, you get.

Gradually, though, I came to realize that my surprise party would be doubly rewarding for George, because it would once again make his birthday special.

I figured that was worth doing.

14

A Gathering and Sweetness

THE PARTY WAS on Thursday the 5th of December. All through that previous week, when everybody seemed giddy over the coming holiday—and when hearts were a little more charitable than usual—I worked on getting it set up. I got Mrs. Creighton's help, Doreen, Professor Bible, and the rest of the teachers did what they could. But the important work involved getting George's tormenters and classmates to kick in. That took some doing.

I scheduled individual conferences with each student in all my classes—ostensibly to go over grades and progress for the year, which took a lot of work by itself—and at the end of each conference, I broached the subject. I explained what I wanted to do in stark, truthful terms. Most of them knew at least a little of George's suffering; that the bruises on his neck meant something more than an accidental confrontation with a hanging branch, or a low-slung clothesline.

In truth, I was amazed at how uninterested and dispassionate the response was. Some said they wanted to help, but most simply looked at me as though I was crazy. I thought I had bitten off more than I could chew, but then I got help, miraculous help, from an unexpected quarter: Leslie Warren.

She strolled into my classroom one day shortly after the last class and flounced in a chair in the front row. "I hear you need help with something important." She was smiling. Her hair was pulled back into a single ponytail and she wore very small stones as blue as her eyes in each ear.

"Do you know George Meeker?"

"The little creepy kid who's always asking the girls to go out with him?"

I said, "He's not really such a creep."

"Maybe not, but he's definitely creepy."

I told her the story. She listened with real interest and when I was done she said, "God."

"So you see, he doesn't mean to be creepy."

She wanted to know what I wanted her to do.

"If you could get some of the kids to quit calling him *Gay-Org* and picking on him all the time . . ."

"I'll do what I can."

"It would mean a lot."

"To who?"

This question disarmed me for a second and I could see that she noticed it. I said, "To George. And to me too. It would mean a lot to me."

She rose from her chair, again with a confident smile. "You got it." Then she turned and walked toward the door. Just as she got to the opening, she stopped and turned around. "I think it's a kind thing you're trying to do."

"Thank you."

She leaned on the doorframe. I can't adequately describe the vision she made in the shadows and angles of light by the door. "Kind of like when you helped me the other day."

"Just courtesy," I said. "That's all."

"How old are you?"

"I'll be twenty-six in August. Why?"

"I was just wondering. Some of the girls were trying to guess."

"They all think I'm pretty old?"

She straightened. "No." Her eyes almost gave off their own light.

"Well now you can let them know."

She looked down at the floor, seemed about to say something else, then thought better of it and left the room.

The next day I had students coming to me—students I'd already talked to and asked for help, volunteering to chip in. Even those who had laughed at him and called him "Gay-Org" fell into line. Mark Talbot said, "If you want a few of us to rough up his old man, just let me know." I loved him when he said that, and for a brief moment, while he sat there watching my face, I actually considered it. "What I'd really appreciate," I said, "is a little bit of kindness for George. A little less ribbing and teasing."

"That's what Leslie said."

We were sitting in the classroom, shortly after I'd let everybody go for break. "Can I ask you something about Leslie?"

Kids are always on guard, ready for the unfair accusations of teachers, it seems; so this got his attention. His face turned serious and he removed his wire-framed glasses. "What about her?"

"I got the impression she gets in a lot of trouble."

"Who told you that?"

"It's just the impression I got."

"She gets teachers in trouble. Last year she went after Mrs. Gallant."

"Went after? What's that mean?"

"You didn't know? She got fired."

"For what?"

"Something to do with Leslie, man. I don't know. I heard Leslie claimed Mrs. Gallant tried to get her to have sex."

I had nothing to say to that. I think Mark noticed the shock on my face. He shrugged his shoulders and said, "That's what I heard, man."

"Well I never heard anything like that. What I was told was that Mrs. Gallant's husband was in the military and he got transferred."

"Maybe it's a big secret, what really happened."

"If what you say really happened, I think I would know about it," I said. I didn't believe it but I couldn't wait to talk to Professor Bible and Doreen. I figured if it was true then they had a whole lot of explaining to do. And even if it wasn't, I thought I deserved to be let in on the rumors and the dangers.

"Hey man," Mark said. "Leslie likes you. You got nothing to worry about."

"Did she ever go after anybody else?"

"I heard she accused Professor Bible but I don't know if that's true or not."

He got up to leave. "Should we bring presents?"

"Oh, no," I said. "Just being nice to him and having some of the cake will be fine."

"We're not going to have to sing that fucking song are we?"

"Would it be so terribly bad?"

"It would be totally embarrassing."

"Okay. We won't sing it then. Or at least I won't suggest it. Mrs. Creighton may want us to sing it."

"Then I guess we'll all have to sing it."

"If she insists, I guess." I watched him leave and it really did seem as though he strode a bit taller toward the door. I think he was feeling very good.

I saw a lot of other kids during the days leading up to the party. And Leslie came by regularly. She designed a big birthday card that I could get everybody to sign and brought it to me a few days before the party. Again she came by right at the end of my last class of the day.

This time she wore her hair down, and the shadows it made on the side of her face and around her eyes made her look oddly older—and tired. She showed me the card, which had a pretty good drawing of the school building on it, and lots of room for signatures. I told her it was very well-done. "Did you draw that picture?"

"Yes. It's not so good is it?"

"On the contrary. I think it's very good."

We talked about where we might hide it, and how we'd get it to everybody so that George wouldn't see it. Finally we agreed we'd keep it in Mrs. Creighton's office and send folks to her during the day to sign it. As I was getting ready to leave I said, "Thank you, Leslie. This is really thoughtful."

She said nothing, but nodded her head. Then, wanting to give her something—wanting to praise her and say something she might be glad for, I said, "You know, you could be a model if you wanted to. Or an actress."

She smiled in a way that told me she'd heard that a million times already. "Thanks." One single sweet note of music, but there was something in it that registered as sadness, or even distaste. Instantly I had the feeling I should apologize to her. She looked very sternly into my eyes, then turned and strode out. As I watched her go, I wondered how I would be able to stay on her good side. I couldn't tell if what I'd said was a good thing or not. At some level I actually felt threatened. I admit I also felt really stupid.

Mrs. Creighton didn't bake the cake, but she was kind enough to buy a very large chocolate sheet cake from the grocery store on the way to the school. She bought a box of candles and put sixteen of them on the cake. We decided to bring it into the English room, get all the candles lit and set everything up while George was in math class. We used a wide table in the back and then gathered all the other students in the other classes, except for George's class of course. Mrs. Creighton had announced over the intercom that morning an "assembly" in the "English Hall," and that attendance was mandatory.

When the math class was almost finished, Doreen lined them up to go to the assembly. She made George stand at the back of the line.

My room was the largest single space in Glenn Acres School, but it was not really big enough for an assembly. It had forty-one chairs in it and none of my classes were that big, so the room always looked huge. With everybody in the school crowded in, standing in front of the picture window—which darkened things considerably—and all along the front blackboard and my desk, it got pretty warm and really crowded in there once the final group filed in. Some stood in the rows between chairs. Mrs. Creighton stood at the back of the room, by the door.

George stood by the entrance from the Math room, his hands clasped in front of him. In his perfectly pressed gray suit and black-striped tie, he looked like an usher in church, except he was so short and thin and the collar of his light blue shirt was about a quarter of an inch too big, so his thin neck—that so often-bruised little space of skin—looked a bit like a white stem.

When everyone was sure he was in the room, I walked over to the table in the back and everyone stepped aside to make room for me. The cake already had the candles lit, and just as George saw it, everyone in the room hollered, "Happy Birthday, George!" I heard one snickering little shit mouth say "Gay-Org," but I'm certain George didn't hear it. The look on his face would have inspired a new religion; at first he seemed kind of puzzled, but then it registered, what we were saying to him, and what this was, and when he knew that, his face took on the beatific look of saintly gratitude and grace. Anyone watching would have accepted the idea that he had just then risen from the dead.

Of course everyone cheered, urging him to approach the cake. Mrs. Creighton had ordered it decorated, and an inscription across the middle said, "Happy Birthday George. We all love you." And at that moment, I think I did love him. Or at least I felt a capable urge

125

to embrace him and make his troubles go away. Maybe that's the higher side of pity—I did feel sorry for him, too.

As he moved across the room with everybody cheering, I noticed a thin, red-haired girl standing next to Doreen. *Standing* is too strong a word. It was more like stooping, because her head was down, her face exactly perpendicular to the floor, as if she'd lost a contact lens or something and needed to study the space at her feet lest she step on it.

I realized I had seen her before—my first day. I didn't much remark on it, except that I realized she was a stranger, and I hadn't seen her in any of my classes. I watched her while George blew out the candles and cut the cake. She did not look up. Doreen rested her hand on the girl's back for a second, as if to gently rub the fabric of her sweater, but maybe I imagined that. I would not remember this second encounter— if that's the word I want—except that I began to wonder if she would ever straighten up. I did not yet know her name, and I couldn't wait to ask Doreen about her.

When the cake had been served, a few of the students brought out presents for George. It was not a requirement—in fact, Mrs. Creighton insisted that people not bring presents—but some kids did anyway and nobody minded very much. Professor Bible stood in the hallway directly in front of his room, smiling, watching George, and then he looked up and saw me. He signaled that I should join him, so I made my way through the throng of cake-eating, laughing students, toward the back of the room. As I passed in front of Mrs. Creighton's office, I noticed Mr. Creighton in there getting his guitar ready. He had an amplifier, and a black cord he was unwinding. I leaned in and said, "You playing for this crowd?"

"Why not?"

"I can't wait to hear it," I said.

"Oh, you'll hear it."

When I got to him Bible said, "You got a cigarette?"

"In my desk, I'll go and . . ."

"No, no. Don't bother." He took hold of my arm to stop me. "You don't want to fight your way through that crowd again."

I turned and watched as Doreen and Mrs. Creighton passed out second slices of cake. Leslie Warren collected the used paper plates. Every movement she made was classic—her arms and hands, her wrists, the way she bent her legs and leaned over to reach for a plate; she carried herself with such pure artistry. It was like watching a very subtle ballet.

"I have to tell you," Bible said. "This is a very fine thing you've arranged."

"Thank you."

"I never would have thought of it."

"Well," I said. "I didn't see why he should have to suffer here."

"And that's a good point."

"Did you see the look on Mrs. Creighton's face?"

"No. Why?"

"I didn't either. I bet she was pleased."

"Oh, she loved the idea. She said that to me this morning."

I was unreasonably happy at that moment; it's possible that it was the purest happy moment I ever had at Glenn Acres School.

15

The Beginning of the
End of Something

THE NEXT MORNING I went outside with Professor Bible to have a cigarette. It was during the break between my first- and second-period classes. I was still basking in yesterday's unreasoning happiness with the earth and just about everything in it. A slight breeze reminded us of the time of year, but it wasn't very cold. The weak sun warmed us when the air was still. We stood just outside the back door, both of us staring at the sloping driveway that led out to the main road.

"How was George this morning?" Bible asked.

"He was not the same kid."

"Really."

"He came running to the bus this morning. He sat up very straight in class, too."

"Maybe it will be enough for a while that he doesn't suffer here."

"I think he must believe that everybody doesn't hate him at least," I said.

He drew on his cigarette a bit. Then he said, "He may be lucky that he came to this school."

"Did I tell you what Mrs. Creighton said in her letter to George's father?"

"You did."

"God it was sweet."

"It might've worked," he said. "At least they didn't take George out of the school."

"And George will never know how she saved him."

"How *you* saved him."

"I guess we all had something to do with it."

"It was your idea for the party," he said.

"I wasn't sure it was possible, but you never know with kids this age. I couldn't have done it though without Leslie Warren's help."

"You watch out for her," he said.

"Is it true she got Mrs. Gallant fired?"

"Who told you that?"

"Mark Talbot."

"Well it's not true. Cindy's husband got transferred."

"That's not what the students think."

"There are always rumors when a teacher leaves. She had her problems with Leslie. We all have."

"What kind of problems?"

"Leslie simply will not be told what to do."

"Has she ever gone after you?"

"Gone after me?"

"Caused you trouble. Mark Talbot told me she claimed Mrs. Gallant tried to have sex with her."

Bible gave a short laugh. "She complained about Cindy but that wasn't what it was. Cindy would not allow her to simply get up and go outside for a smoke. So she went to Mrs. Creighton and her parents and said that Cindy had slapped her."

"Did she?"

"Probably. There was no one in the room but Cindy and Leslie. But that was all there was. Nobody got fired."

"What about you and Leslie?"

"She's never made any formal complaint against me that I know of. She's very intelligent. I find ways to insult her that require education."

"Like what?" I asked.

"Allusions, my man. Allusions. I'll tell her she reminds me of somebody in history. Like Ilse Koch. Sometimes she catches on, sometimes she doesn't. When she does, there's not much she can do about it."

"Who the hell is Ilse Koch?"

He smiled indulgently.

"Okay," I said. "I'm not that educated either."

"The Beast of Buchenwald. You've got your holocaust project and you never heard of her?"

"I know all about her. I just didn't know her real name."

"Most people don't. Anyway, that's how I get after Leslie when she becomes a pain."

"She's been nothing but a sweetheart to me."

"And that's fine. Just don't cross her."

"Really. She's that bad."

"She's beautiful, and she knows it. She's also smart and spoiled. That's a bad combination."

A burst of laughter came from inside the school. I waited for a bit then I said, "A lot of the girls want to adopt George now."

Bible smiled. But I could see there was something else on his mind. His face wouldn't capture the smile; his whole visage seemed to struggle against some interior strife. We stood there silently for a long time, listening to clatter begin to die down inside the building. Then I said, "Is there something you're not telling me about Leslie?"

"Of course not."

I let my cigarette drop to the ground and stepped on it. "Well we should be getting back in."

"Young man," he said. "Did you know this was my last year?"

"You're quitting?"

"I'm retiring at the end of the year."

"No, I didn't know that."

He looked at the ground, then shook his head. "I'm finished here."

"Finished?"

"I'm going to try to make it through the year, but I may not."

What he wasn't saying caused something cold to leak into my heart. "What?" I said. "Tell me."

"Don't say anything about this, to anyone—especially not Doreen or Mrs. Creighton or any of the students."

"I won't. What's happened?"

"I have an infection in my foot. I wouldn't even have noticed it, but the whole nail turned black and it started to bleed in my sock. I was afraid it was melanoma." I'm sure the shock on my face registered, but he almost smiled at me. Then he said, "It wasn't. It wasn't melanoma, but it was—well, I'm diabetic."

"They have treatment for that," I said. "You just . . ."

"I know. I've been on insulin since I was seven years old."

"Oh."

"They wanted to remove my big toe over the Thanksgiving break."

"Jesus Christ."

"I told them no. I'd have to be in the hospital for weeks. I can't afford that."

"I thought you just had to take the insulin, and . . ." I had not noticed him limping or favoring his foot in any way. Except for his emblazoned, almost crimson cheeks, he looked completely normal to me. "So what are you going to do? Just let it kill you?"

"Antibiotics might help, but with diabetes, you never know. So I just have to treat the infection the best I can. Keep taking my insulin, of course."

"And what if that doesn't work?"

"Well, that's what I'm worried about. The doctor said I could get sepsis—blood poisoning, and that it would either cause me to lose my leg or even kill me."

"Jesus Christ," I said. "Let them have the toe."

"I can't."

"Why?"

His eyes were unwavering and steady. "This will probably be my last year of teaching. I don't want to ruin it with something like this. The doctor said it could take weeks."

"But if the alternative is . . ." I didn't say it.

"The doctor was willing to let me try this—he said it was a bit risky, but if I wanted to try it for a few weeks, I could have until after Christmas to think about it. As long as I keep soaking the toe in antiseptic wash and taking my meds."

"Are you doing that?"

"Of course. He told me he's already scheduled the surgery for the first week in January."

"So he doesn't think it will work."

"A precaution," he smiled ruefully.

Then we were both quiet. With no cigarette to puff on, and all the quiet of classes seated and waiting, it was kind of awkward standing out there in what was becoming a fairly damp and cold morning. Finally I said, "I'm sorry about this."

"Well," he said. "What can one do?" He seemed relieved to have told me, and now he smiled again and I could see it was a superb attempt to make light of his predicament.

"I'm really sorry," I said.

"I got into this business—this profession—because it allowed me to talk about the most important things to young people, but you know, I can't talk to them about this."

"No, I guess not."

"It's—can you believe it? It's embarrassing."

I was so shocked and sad, I couldn't think of anything to say. I wish I had told him that it shouldn't be embarrassing. It hadn't really sunk in yet that this man I believed would be the first real mentor in my life was about to leave it. I didn't even get a full year with him. Those thoughts—all about me, I realize—didn't come until later.

"Under my goddamned big toe." He shook his head, and then tears came to his eyes. "I'm going to miss this place."

"It will miss you," I said.

"I hope and pray I can make it until graduation day."

I thought of the next thing I said while I was saying it. "Why are you telling me all this?"

He shuffled a bit, started back toward the door.

"Professor?" I said.

"There isn't anybody else," he said. "Would you believe it? I don't have anybody else I can tell."

I realized then how alone he was, and I knew at the same time that I might have to be there for him and take care of him in ways for which I was not even remotely prepared. I liked him, and he seemed the wisest man on earth to me, but I barely knew him. He became important to me because of his age, the way he dressed, and the way he carried himself as if he was a sage. I have to admit, he got me with the chalk trick. I was his disciple when I saw that. But it wasn't just that. He had just the right attitude where George was concerned, and he had rescued me from George's father. He rescued me in a way that was not particularly heroic, but rather crafty and smart—he wasn't Achilles, he was Odysseus. I believed he knew everything I wanted to know and more; that his mind would somehow connect in a very substantial way with mine and what I would learn would make me—well, there's no other way to say this—like him. I didn't want to end up like him, but I wanted to *be* like him. Does that make any sense at all?

He meandered on back toward the building and now I did notice a slight limp. At the door he turned back to me and said, "Remember. Don't tell anybody."

"I won't. You have my word."

"Especially don't tell Doreen, or Mrs. Creighton."

"I won't tell anybody," I said. "I promise."

He nodded, gave me another weak smile. "Yes," he whispered. "You're a good man."

"If there's anything I can do," I said, feeling kind of bleak and soulless. Suddenly the air felt like ice and smelled of dead tree bark. The breezes kicked up and started bullying the leaves and small branches. Professor Bible went in and let the door close, and I stood there, wondering what the hell was so good about the world.

16

Credence

Now I carried a secret around with me that gnawed its way toward the surface of my brain and tongue like a dark, flesh-eating worm. How could I keep from telling Annie, at least? Christmas break was going to be excruciating. The thing was she always knew when I was bothered by something. I'm not very good at dissembling, or pretending everything is the berries, when I'm worried. I couldn't get the idea out of my mind. (I checked all of my toes every time I took off my socks.) I was also worried about Professor Bible, and what it would be like watching him march toward what could be the end of the world.

I have always been absolutely frightened at the idea of leaving this earth—but especially of having one of those diseases where I can live on for a while, watching my own decline, not able to do a thing about it. Talk about fear cramping your heart—there aren't enough drugs in the world to numb me enough so that I wouldn't be a study in terror. Annie would have to take me around in a pillowcase.

Doesn't it bother everyone? Doesn't it bother you?

And every time I start thinking about that—every time I find myself worried that I'll get one of those diseases and I'll have days and days to think about my own end, it hits me that I'm living that way now. All of us are.

Sometimes I see all of life as a kind of ongoing, chattering, trinket-ridden, stupid process: lives going on all over the surface of the earth, driven by a small twisted double helix, or some kind of curling mitochondria, always changing, always losing ground against the dark, always casting out toward a pinched and deadly future; every blasted one of us collecting things—memories, photographs, movies, books, tapes and televisions, houses, hotels, cars and laws—and as we pass beyond all of it into oblivion, that is what we leave behind. Our legacy is mostly junk, pure and simple.

I made it through one day before I whispered Bible's secret to Doreen. I couldn't help it. She wheedled it out of me. She started by simply asking what Professor Bible and I had been talking about when we were having our cigarette the day before. "You guys were hatching something. What were you so serious about?"

I told her it was nothing.

"I saw him through the window. I thought he was going to start crying."

"It's nothing."

"There's something wrong. You haven't said one thing since you got here."

"I'm very busy."

"What's going on?"

I leaned back in my chair. I'd just picked up my gang and they were all outside smoking in the chilly, damp air. It was the last day before Christmas break, and I knew I would not be doing any work on this day. I was not at all busy and she could see I wasn't.

"I won't tell anyone," she said.

"There's nothing to tell."

"Come on, Ben." She sat down in the first student chair in front of my desk. "You don't trust me."

"No, I trust you."

"Then tell me. I know something's going on."

I looked around, realized we were completely alone. I could tell her if I wanted. But I had promised Bible I wouldn't tell anybody. "I've promised not to say."

This only got her more interested. I could see, too, that she was hurt by it. She said she'd known Bible longer than I had, and he wouldn't trust me with something and not her.

"Well, I'm sorry," I said.

"He wouldn't keep anything important from me."

"Well, see? It's not important."

She didn't start crying or anything, but her eyes glistened a bit and she started fidgeting with her hands, entwining her fingers and staring at them.

"Oh for Christ's sake," I said. So I told her. I couldn't keep a thing like that bottled up anyway.

Right away she gave in to her tears.

"Don't do that, now," I said.

It took her awhile but she got control of herself. "He's been such a good influence on me," she said.

"Me too."

"Like a father."

I nodded, but I didn't see him as a kind of father. He was better than that. He didn't judge me unworthy, and snicker at me all the time. I loved my father, but sometimes he thought I was overeducated and lacked common sense.

"Are you crying because he's retiring?" I asked. I handed her a tissue from a box on my desk. "He assumed I knew about it, so you must . . ."

"No, I didn't know."

"Aren't you worried about the infection?"

"If he doesn't get it treated, yes." She frowned.

"You think he could die?"

"I didn't say that."

"How worried are you about the infection?"

"What's the matter with you?"

"Nothing."

She wiped her nose with the tissue.

"I just wanted to see if you were crying about his illness, or what?"

"Why?"

"I guess I was wondering how much I should be worried about it."

"What do you mean?"

"If you're really worried then maybe there's something to worry about. But if you're not, then . . ."

"Then you don't worry?"

I didn't answer her.

"You are really strange." She sniffed. "Really, really strange."

I didn't know then, or now, what was so bloody strange. Maybe it's not the same for you but I can remain pretty damned calm as long as everybody else does too. I frequently gauge how frightening a situation is by the looks on the faces of people. When I get scared on a plane, all I do is look around me. If everybody I see is completely calm and continues reading, or chatting, or staring blankly into space, I feel pretty safe. Don't you?

17

Like Wildfire

ON THE FIRST day of our Christmas break I told Annie. We had been having a conversation about assholes and stupid people. We'd just spent a lovely Saturday afternoon lying in bed, watching Jack Nicholson in *Five Easy Pieces* for the third time. After the movie, we decided to go for Chinese, and while we were eating our appetizers we heard one of the other patrons of the restaurant ask the Chinese waitress if she had a "main squeeze."

The waitress said, "Pardon?" Her voice was lilting and soft and very polite.

"Your main squeeze," the guy said, a little irritated to have to repeat himself.

"Men squiz?" the waitress said.

"Yeah."

"I don't know what is men squiz."

"For Christ's sake," the man laughed. "Boy friend. Boy friend."

"Oh no," she said. "No boyfriend."

"Would you like one?" the guy said, really loud. He thought he was so funny, he laughed way too long.

"What an asshole," I said low, to Annie.

Annie said, "No, he's just stupid."

"I think he's an asshole."

She sipped her tea and said nothing.

"I wonder," I said, "If there are more assholes or stupid people in the world."

"What's the difference?"

"Everybody can be an asshole once in a while, right?"

"Sure."

"And everybody can occasionally find themselves doing a stupid thing."

Annie nodded.

"So, the chances of running into either an asshole or a stupid person at least once or twice a day are greatly increased by that fact."

She said nothing.

"Some people are born stupid, though. You have to *become* an asshole."

Again, she only looked at me, a slight smirk on her face.

"Doesn't that bother you?"

"Of course not."

"But think of it. You can't ever get away from either one."

"I guess not."

"Given a choice, which kind would you rather run into? A stupid person or an asshole."

She frowned impatiently. "What's the difference?"

I thought about it a minute. Then I said, "Remember that scene in the restaurant in *Five Easy Pieces* when Nicholson angrily clears everything off the table with one sweep of his arm? Well, he's being an asshole in that scene. And the waitress is a stupid person, right?"

"I guess."

"So . . ."

"Why isn't the waitress an asshole?"

"No, she's just stupidly following the rules in that restaurant. Some asshole may have written the rules, but she's just following them."

"I see."

"She's just being stupid. And he's an asshole because he throws that little temper tantrum and makes a mess in the restaurant."

"Okay." She smiled, which encouraged me. I always loved to make Annie smile, and I could see she was agreeing with me.

"Well," I said. "Which would you rather run into? An asshole or a stupid person?"

"A stupid person."

This surprised me. "Really."

"Yes." She picked up a spring roll and took a small bite out of it.

"But in that scene, Jack Nicholson is the one everybody identifies with. He's the one everybody laughs at."

"So?"

"I don't get it."

"You asked which I'd rather run into, not who I liked or didn't like."

"You liked the Jack Nicholson character?"

"Yes. I wouldn't want to be around him though."

"Why not?"

"Because there were three other people at that table and they had to put up with his tantrum, that's why."

I didn't know how to respond to that. She was right, of course. Annie always had the most capable understanding; she always seemed to know what was right, where the balance was. I should have listened to her more often.

Anyway, she told me she didn't think I was either stupid or an asshole. Then she told me I had done a fine thing by having that party for George. I started wondering what she would say about Bible's problem.

She finished her spring roll and picked up another one. The wait-ress brought our dishes, and a large bowl of rice. I ordered another beer. We ate for a while, then Annie said, "What's the matter?"

"Nothing."

"You got quiet all of a sudden."

"I'm eating." I'd been thinking about diabetes and infections, and the end of life. I'm not very talkative in those circumstances.

"Did I hurt your feelings somehow?" Annie wanted to know.

"No, of course not."

"Is there something you're not telling me?"

"Well," I said. I knew she would eventually get it out of me, and I didn't want to take up the whole dinner with the struggle not to say what I knew I'd say before it was over, so I told her about Professor Bible.

She didn't think I should worry about it. "Didn't he say he was working with a doctor?"

"Yes."

"Well what are you so worried about?"

"He's taking a pretty significant risk, not getting the surgery . . ."

"But his doctor said it was okay to wait, right?"

"I think that's what he said."

"So what the hell are you worried about?"

"I'm not really worried about him. I'll miss him."

She sighed slightly and shook her head.

"What?"

"Nothing."

"It's supposed to be a big secret, so don't say anything to anyone."

"Who could I possibly tell?" she said. "I don't know anyone there."

"You'll eventually meet folks. Just remember to keep it to yourself."

"How many people have you told?"

"Just keep it to yourself." In the space of two days, I had revealed Bible's secret to two people. At that rate, after a year, only 363 more people would know about it.

I'll leave it to you to decide if I was being stupid, or just an asshole.

I spent the Christmas break trying to forget how unfaithful I'd been to Professor Bible. Maybe "unfaithful" is not the word. I should have kept my word to him. I betrayed a confidence, and I don't really know if that ranks as unfaithful or disloyal or if it is in any way an actual betrayal. I just know I felt bad, and wished I'd kept my mouth shut. I would have enjoyed the time off much more if all I had on my mind was the satisfaction I derived from the party I had arranged for George; although, even that might have been cloyed by the knowledge that Annie's approval of it was very short-lived. We were lying in bed, watching a cold December moon sink beneath broad, violet clouds, when I mentioned getting back to school after the break and taking advantage of the good feeling of the party, and she said, "So I suppose you think the birthday celebration solved something?"

"I do indeed. He won't suffer so much at school. I did that."

"You think so?"

"Yes, I do. I can't stop what goes on at home, but I can sure help him at school. The kids will be better to him now; kinder."

"You really believe that?"

"Yes. You weren't there. You didn't see it."

She was not convinced. I pulled the covers up to my neck and gasped my relief at the end of the day. "I thought you said what I did was a good thing."

"I did."

"Now you've changed your mind?"

"No, it was a good thing. I never said I thought it solved the problem."

"What makes it good then?"

"It was nice. You did a nice thing."

I had no response. I was feeling kind of sad.

She said, "They will get back to him."

"What do you mean?" I turned over on my side and looked at her in the vanishing moonlight.

"They're nice to him now, but he's getting special treatment, isn't he?"

"No."

"Yes he is. Maybe not from you—at least not from you now, but he was getting it. And you just said the kids are treating him better. That's special treatment."

"So what?"

"Once they turn on him again—and it will only take one—it will be worse. Much worse, because he's had this period of being special. They will really give it to him because of that."

"You have such faith in young people."

"I know about kids," she said. She was not looking at me. I watched the side of her face, tried to decide if I should kiss her next to the corner of her eyes, or touch the hair by her ears. I wanted to do something to feel better; I wanted to rid myself of this capable impulse to shove her out of the bed. Not that I actually would, but goddamn it. I felt as though she had given me something valuable and then taken it back.

"I think you're wrong," I whispered.

She turned herself away from me, pulled the covers up around her shoulder and said, "You'll see."

18

Power and Pity

I DON'T WANT to give the impression that I had no other problems that first year, or that George or Professor Bible were my only concern. I am writing a long time after it all, and I don't want to infuse it with how I feel now, so that how I felt then is somehow skewed or lost. I want to be truthful, but it is also important that I be accurate. No doubt you can understand that in trying to remember how all this got started I must be a bit selective in what I recall.

That first year was a busy, hectic year. I spent a lot of weekends just sitting at my desk at home, grading papers, while Annie watched football or basketball and did the wash. In spite of George's problems, I would not have focused on them in the telling of this story but for what happened later. I had such a powerful sense of accomplishment after George; I think that might have led me to get so deeply involved with Leslie Warren. Or at least it led me to a sturdy belief in the idea of making a difference.

Most of the rest of that year George fared pretty well. He was no longer the butt of jokes and when he spoke up in class, people didn't laugh at him. Annie may have been right about the nature of young kids, and what might have happened if they turned on him again, but she didn't count on the renewed interest in his welfare every time he came to school with even the smallest bruise. If he came to class with a fresh bruise—one smaller and located on his cheek or his arm, one he could just as easily have gotten on the playground or riding his bike—the girls just fawned over him. It was almost embarrassing to witness. If you saw the look on his face as the girls gathered around to console him, to pat his head and hold his hand, you'd have to fight the notion that he might actually be grateful for his father's brutality. And he never did have marks around his neck again. His journal didn't mention many more "punishments" either. There were a few entries about getting slapped or punched, and one about being knocked down and kicked in the "rump" (I swear that's the word he used), but nothing at all about the bungee cord and the phone book. In fact, once or twice he talked about how his dad was "rewarding" him with fishing gear and trips to the movies. Believe me, we scrutinized George very closely, and I think I can safely say the abuse had been significantly curtailed.

A few weeks after Christmas, Doreen came into my classroom during lunch break with a letter in her hand. She sat across from me, looked around to be sure we were alone, and then said, "This is a letter from my sister."

I opened my lunch bag and unwrapped my peanut butter and jelly sandwich. When I looked up at her she was waiting for me, still holding the letter. I said, "I didn't know you had a sister."

"She knows somebody who had diabetes. Look at this." She unfolded it and handed it to me. In very clear scrawl her sister wrote this alarming story of a neighbor who ignored the effects of a diabetes infection in her foot and who lost first the foot, then her right leg, then her left leg, and then she died.

"Damn," I said, handing the letter back to her.

"We have to do something."

"What?"

"We've got to get him to let them remove his toe."

"Why? According to your sister it won't do any good whatsoever."

"It won't do any good if he waits too long. Didn't you read what my sister said?"

"How do we know how long that is?"

"He could die," she said.

"He's under a doctor's care. He said the doctor let him wait until after Christmas."

"Well it's after Christmas. Is he doing anything?"

"I don't know." I took a small bite of my sandwich. I did not want to be chewing during this conversation, but I was hungry and it was lunchtime.

"Talk to him about it."

"I guess I could do that, but I don't want to. It's his business."

"You have to."

"He knows all that, Doreen." I pointed to the letter. "The doctor told him. So maybe we should just leave him alone about it."

"What if he waits too long?"

"I doubt we could talk him into anything," I said.

Doreen touched the hair over her ears, a gentle sort of gesture that let me know she would not let herself get frustrated by my resistance, but she was fighting it. "I can't say anything to him because I'm not supposed to know."

"You better not say anything to him."

I could see the composure seep out of her face. "I wish he'd told me about it," she said.

"I wish he had too."

"I think you're being too . . ." she stopped.

147

"Too what?"

She considered for a moment. "You think you're . . ."

"I think I'm what?"

"Nothing." She got up and started refolding the letter.

"Were you going to say God?"

She scrunched her nose. "Of course not."

"Well, what then?"

"I don't know. I just wish you weren't . . ." she hesitated. "It's like you're in control of everything."

"I'm the one who thinks we should just leave it up to him. How is that controlling?"

"You're new here. I've known Professor Bible so much longer. Why didn't he . . ."

"He told me not to tell you."

She put the letter back in the envelope. Then she said, "I wouldn't let him know that you told me about it. But I have to say something to him."

"You better not. He didn't want me to tell anyone, but he said especially not you."

Her face changed. Something in her eyes softened and at the same time I saw her mouth—the only smoothly constructed, well-proportioned part of her pocked face—open slightly, as if she needed to slowly but surely take in air. At that moment, in that light from the big picture window, she was beautiful. "He said that?"

"He said, 'Especially don't tell Doreen.'"

She cast her eyes down, her head slightly tilted toward me, and I thought she looked as purely sad as any Madonna I'd ever seen staring down at the body of Christ. At times, in spite of her lean, mannish figure—her short hair, long thin nose, and pockmarked face—there was something youthful and oddly attractive about her. She carried herself with such confidence, such independent and assured awareness of herself, her body, her gleaming eyes, it was almost as if she had learned how to make people forget the acne and the scars; had found a way to make those little imperfections merely a feature of her own special charm.

"I'll talk to him," I said. "I promise."

She smiled in a virginal sort of approving way, then walked out the door. I finished my lunch, chewing my sandwich while I stared at the bulletin board on the back wall. Somebody, in the years before my arrival, had tacked individual letters across the top of the board that said, "Adventures in Literature." Underneath that was just orange paper stapled to the board, covering it like a tablecloth. No other adornments filled this space, so it was easy to stare at it and think nothing. I knew I'd have to get up eventually and walk across the hall to see Professor Bible. It would be a statement—a fairly loud statement—if I avoided him. Still I was always afraid he could tell by looking at me that I had divulged his secret. And what do you say to somebody after they tell you a thing like that? Every time I saw him I felt stupid for saying, "How's it going?" Could I walk in there and say, "How's your foot today?" He was seeing his last January as a teacher. What could I say?

I cleaned up my waxed paper and sandwich bag, and threw it all in a trashcan in the hall on the way to Bible's room.

"George is doing very well, now," I said.

He only nodded vaguely. He sat at his desk, as he always did, his head bent slightly toward the papers in front of him, a pure white forelock of his hair dangling across his forehead and just above his dark eyes. His face was ruddy and seemed more relaxed, as if he'd just finished a very successful chess match and was now ready for conversation. I think he might have been slightly embarrassed about what I knew.

"Did you get caught up on all your work over the Christmas break?" he asked. He didn't seem to want to face me.

I sat down in the chair next to his desk and said, "Pretty much. But it's piling up again."

He was quiet, reading a student paper in front of him.

"How are you?" I asked. I swallowed a little when I spoke and I think he misunderstood the tremor in my voice as suppressed emotion.

He looked at me. "Don't let's get maudlin here, okay? I'm fine. I'm getting used to the idea of the end of my career. Even the end of the world. You ever thought about the end of the world?"

"No." I was lying, of course. Most days, I can't get the end of the world out of my mind. Especially the end of *my* world.

"You know," Professor Bible said, sitting back in his chair. "Somebody once said, 'Even when you know you're going to die and the sentence will be carried out very soon, it's still extremely rude to sit in a corner and wail about it.'"

"You're not necessarily dying," I said. "You don't have to let this kill you."

"I've been doing a lot of thinking," he said. "A lot of thinking. I live alone, I have no family to speak of. Oh, I got a brother in Indiana that I talk to sometimes, but nobody else." He met my gaze, and seemed to understand something about what was going through my mind. "No," he muttered. "I haven't told him. He's pretty old—twelve years older than me. I don't think the old guy would . . ." he stopped. I waited for him to continue, but he just started lifting the corner of one of the papers on his desk. He studied the tips of his fingers, the edge of the paper, as if he was looking for something very small and likely to move.

"Don't you think your brother would want to know?"

"He'd forget about it the next day."

"Oh."

"We don't talk that often. When I call him, I have to tell him who I am."

"I'm sorry."

It was quiet for a while. He wasn't looking at me, and I was sort of watching his fingers and the edges of the paper. Then he said, "You know, I think I've done some good." He was still studying the corner

150

of the paper. "I've been thinking about my life. About all those years teaching. I can't remember when I wasn't a teacher. I was just working, doing my job, enjoying myself. Oh, I always enjoyed myself. But you know, I think I might have done some good." Now he looked at me again. His face was less flushed, but his eyes gleamed in the afternoon light that flooded through the windows, and he was smiling, just slightly. It wasn't the kind of smile that you associate with happiness, or joy, or good humor. It was almost not a smile. He looked deeply pleased. "I think I did some good in the world, Benjamin. What do you think of that?"

"Of course you did." I can't believe how sad I felt, then. Everything I said to him felt like a lie. As I said, I don't want to let what finally happened color my memory of this time. I was living it; I didn't know any of the later events in my short teaching career. At that moment I was deeply sorry for him because I believed his life had been so pathetic. I couldn't imagine a life more sadly devoid of meaning. To end up alone, in a classroom, with chalk on my hands, in an old linen suit, my tie dangling from my throat, my hair white and falling across my mottled brow—for his brow was mottled, and speckled with those marks old men get on their faces and hands and arms—to end up like that, and to have only the forlorn belief that I might have done some good in the world to console me against the end of my life was the most overwhelmingly sad and pitiable thing. I know it's possible that any life—no matter how fully lived—would seem pitiable and gloomy at the end of things; that's probably what made me so sad. I felt as though I was watching a man who was about to be hanged, and he strove to find something admirable about the rope.

"You *have* done some good," I said.

"You know, Benjamin, I used to say 'in the fall they come back.'" His voice broke and he averted his eyes. It was quiet for a moment, then he looked at me again, his eyes not quite swimming but there were tears there. "They always come back." Now he smiled, shaking his head. "I never thought very much about what it would feel like to know that one fall *I* wouldn't come back."

I got up. "I hope one day I can be a great teacher."

Again, it felt as if I was lying, and it's possible he didn't completely believe it, but he smiled more fully, gestured with his hand toward me as though he were letting me through a door. "Welcome, my boy. It is a job I recommend," he paused, looking now directly into my eyes, "Highly, very highly."

I admired him. I wanted to be like him in so many ways. But I did not want to end up like him. I said, "I hope to be a great teacher like you. I really do." I like to think that perhaps he could not really see what a bad liar I was. Maybe he believed me.

That's what I like to think.

19

Rumors

HERE'S THE THING about kids between fourteen and twenty-five or so: they think about death in the same way they think about their own birth. It's something far distant in time, and they've pretty much forgotten about it. (I never had that luxury because of what Annie calls an unfortunate fissure in my brain. I think about death every day, and I have two basic conditions: healthy, and dying. There's no in between. The first symptom, of anything, is always the onset of what will kill me. All my life—even during my childhood—I've been that way; but Annie tells me most people my age don't think about death at all, unless it sneaks up and bites them in the ass.)

Of course, kids *know* about death. They just don't believe it. That's why people under the age of twenty-five make such good soldiers—because it takes at least a quarter of a century of living to develop a sense of life; to become aware of what is to be treasured and even hoarded if you can do it. You can be persuaded to take a lot of risks you wouldn't ordinarily take when you've forgotten or don't admit the possibility of dying. What most kids are afraid of is humiliation. That above all else. So there is no balance in the sense of danger you find in young teens. They will shrink from an irate, angry looking fat lady in a McDonald's—make their escape as though they were fleeing the scene of a blood-soaked clash—and yet think nothing of getting into a car and roaring it up to speeds that would turn their bones to powder if they hit anything. Many of my students could get into their own cars and race me down the road once I dropped them off, but most were forced to ride with me every morning and every afternoon. If they were going to kill themselves, it wasn't going to be during school hours. Only a half a dozen or so students drove their own cars—Leslie was one of them.

I didn't mind driving the bus after a while. I could sometimes discern what the kids were talking about, and occasionally I could sort things out enough to learn almost as much about what was going on in their lives as I did from reading the folded pages of their journals. What I was listening for was, of course, anything having to do with drugs, but also how George was getting along. I got pretty good at hearing things while whistling to myself and watching the road.

The week or so after Doreen handed me that letter from her sister, I heard somebody say something about "poor Professor Bible." It shook me, so I really concentrated on that one voice in the din behind me. It was a conversation between two of the girls. I glanced into the wide rearview mirror above my head, but I couldn't tell which one of the open mouths I saw uttered the words I was hearing. I heard, "diabetic," and "dying." I also heard "love," and "it will kill Mrs. Creighton."

I had told Annie and Doreen. I'd kept my mouth shut after that. Annie had never been to the school and hadn't yet met anybody there, so the only way these kids could have known about Bible was if he told them, or Doreen did.

When I got to school that morning, I headed right for Doreen's room, but Mrs. Creighton stopped me in the hallway. "I need to see you a moment."

She was smiling so I didn't think I was in trouble. "I'll be right there," I said.

"This won't take a minute."

"Well I wanted to see Doreen about . . ." I didn't finish the sentence. Mrs. Creighton was not slow to pick up on things. She could see I was in a bit of a hurry and that something was troubling me.

"See Doreen about what?" she said.

"Nothing."

"Is something going on between you two?"

"Of course not."

"Well, what then?"

"I just wanted to—it's nothing. Really."

She waited.

"I was going to ask her how George Meeker is doing in her class, that's all."

"Still concerned about him?"

"Well, I'm keeping an eye out."

"Haven't noticed any new bruises, have you?"

"Not so far."

"Come in here a minute," she said, beckoning with her narrow bejeweled fingers.

I went in and sat down. She closed the door, walked around behind me, and sat at her desk. In front of her was a blue folder—the kind of folder I later learned she used for what she called "special" students. I'm not talking about learning disabilities, or discipline problems—although those could be among her "specials" as she called them. To Mrs. Creighton a student became "special" when she took a personal interest in that student's welfare. It didn't have to be any real condition or educational problem that got you nominated to the "specials" category. George was in there. So was Mark Talbot, both as bright as anybody and both willing to actually read a book, cover to cover, and talk about it. These were kids with sharp minds who did not want to waste their hours and days sitting in front of a television or walking around with a radio pinned to their ears. But when she sat me down that day and pulled out the folder, I didn't know what it was.

"I've been working quite some time with a student here," she said. "She's much damaged."

"Damaged?"

"I'm thinking of putting her in your class late this spring or maybe in the fall."

"Okay."

"I hope she'll be ready before the fall, but if not then definitely in the fall."

I nodded. She sat there, staring at me, and I realized she was expecting me to be a bit more inquisitive about it. "Who is it we're talking about?"

"Suzanne Rule. You might have seen her. She has bright red hair. She won't look at you."

"Is she the one who walks around looking at the floor?"

"Yes."

"I think I saw her at George's party."

"She was there."

"What's wrong with her?"

"There's nothing physically wrong. She seems quite intelligent. Her mother says all she does is read and study."

"It will be nice to have somebody who reads."

"She is painfully shy."

"Is that the damage you mentioned?"

"No."

I waited, she looked at me—considering, I think—whether or not she should tell me. Finally she said, "She was terribly abused as a child."

I shook my head, but I had nothing to say to that. Mrs. Creighton knew how I felt about parents who abuse a child.

"She was not beaten, if that's what you're thinking," she said. "She was sexually abused, repeatedly, by a member of her own family. It may have been the girl's father."

"My god," I said.

"But that's not the damage either. That's what caused the damage." She glanced down at the desk, as if she needed to find the damage on a list of some kind, but then she met my gaze again. "The damage is, she either cannot, or she will not speak. And she won't look anybody in the eye either. She just stares at the ground wherever she goes."

"The poor thing."

"I'm trying to get her so that she will trust me enough to let me sit with her in your class. Eventually, I want to be able to leave her in there and go do other things, but in the beginning, I will have to sit with her. If I can get her to go with me. That's what I'm trying to do right now. Get her to the point where she will go into your class with me."

"That would be fine," I lied. I didn't want Mrs. Creighton in there at all if I could help it.

"You're doing such a fine job with George. I think you can safely say that you rescued him, even from the troublemakers here. I think it was a grand strategy, even though I would never have talked to his mother the way you did." There was a slight smile verging on her lips and in her eyes and I felt unreasoning pride for what she was saying to me. "But your idea for George was perfect. It couldn't possibly work for every child going through that sort of thing—but it worked perfectly here because of that. Because nobody has ever done it in quite that way, it worked."

I felt as if I grew taller as she spoke. "Tell that to Annie," I said.

"Annie?"

"My g—my wife." I didn't want her to know that Annie and I weren't married. I don't know why except to say that I thought it might offend her.

"When are we going to meet your Annie?" Now she was smiling.

"I'll bring her around soon."

"Please do." She rose from her chair, put her glasses on and looked at her watch.

"Got to get to class," I said, and went out.

Doreen denied that she'd told anybody.

"Well how do they know, then?"

"I don't know. I guess Professor Bible told somebody other than you."

"Maybe he did."

We were standing outside my room, during break, each of us smoking a cigarette. Doreen looked annoyed when I first saw her that morning, and she still did. Sometimes she would get this fixed, cross look on her face, and the skin between her eyes would bunch up and two very distinct lines would form there—so that she looked as though she was staring into direct sunlight. Her mouth would turn down at the edges and she'd wear that look all day; a scowl that said: "Keep out. This means YOU."

"What's the matter?" I asked. "You don't have to be pissed at me. I didn't tell anybody else, but the kids on my bus were talking about it. What was I to think?"

"Oh, I don't care what you think. I'm not pissed at you. I just wish they didn't know."

"Who told them if you didn't?"

Doreen turned her scowl my way. "You think I'd announce it to my classes? I didn't tell anyone. Got it?"

"It's only a matter of time before Mrs. Creighton knows. You think we should tell her?"

"I don't want to be the one to do it."

"I'll do it. But you think we should? The students think he's dying."

"He may be."

"There's no reason to be alarmist about it," I said. "He *is* under a doctor's care."

"I don't think I'm being alarmist."

"If we wait, one of the students will tell her," I said. "And if she finds out we knew and didn't tell her?"

"How can she find that out?"

"Can't she?"

"I don't see how."

"Well, we'll have to pretend we are shocked if she tells us," I said. "Maybe our acting won't be very convincing."

She gave a little laugh in the back of her throat, and her face eased back away from the scowl momentarily. "You can carry it off."

"What if Professor Bible tells her we knew?"

"He doesn't know you told me. Remember?"

"This is all just fucked up as hell," I said.

She finished her cigarette and flipped it into the cement ashtray. I offered her another one, but she waved it away with her hand. I stood there, finishing mine, both of us watching the kids beginning to wander back up the walk to the building. Then Doreen said, "God. I hate the world sometimes."

"Yeah," I said. "Me too."

20

Close to the Bone

IN MY CLASSES that day, since Bible's situation had gotten me thinking about it, I had my students write about death. I couldn't very well have them write about diabetes, and I didn't think infections would spark much interest. (To tell the truth, I didn't want to read what they might write about infections.) So I told them we are all going to die and there's not a thing we can do about it. I asked them to think about dying, about the end of the world for each of them. I told them to leave out religion ("For God's sake, leave out religion," is how I put it) and then gave them an hour to write in their journals.

It was a mistake. Not one of them mentioned anything they'd heard about Bible.

Some of them had already had a taste of death—one girl lost her baby brother to leukemia. Her journal (I read only the unfolded pages) was full of prayers and lamentations of the loss. Of course she told her mother what the day was like, what she'd been asked to write about, and her mother called Mrs. Creighton.

The next day I was back in her office.

"I just wanted to get their attention," I told her.

"Well, you got that."

"So many of them aren't interested in anything, I thought I might . . ."

"Why can't you just stick to the writing topics in the text? First you get involved with this Hitler thing, the camps and the holocaust, now this."

"I'm sorry," I said.

"I like you, young man, and I wonder if you know your circumstances here." She didn't wait for me to answer. "You're here to earn your place in this school." She let her gaze fall to the desk in front of her, and with her left hand she reached across the surface and traced with a red fingernail the outline of the blotter. It unsettled me that she would not look directly at me. "After the business with George's parents, the complaints I received about your 'holocaust' lesson, and now this . . ."

I interrupted her. "You had more than one complaint about the holocaust lesson?"

She kept talking, only registering what I said with a slight frown. "This preoccupation with death; why death? In heaven's name, why death? Why don't you have them write about life?"

"That's where I thought the assignment might lead."

"Really." She was not convinced.

"You've had more than one complaint about the holocaust thing?"

"Mr. Jameson," she said, looking at me now, her patience clearly diminishing. "Just stick to the English curriculum, would you please?"

"I thought I was free to do whatever I wanted to teach them what they need. A certain spontaneity. I can't . . ."

"The English curriculum," she repeated. "You are a wonderful teacher. I believe that. But you just need to focus on the subject you are supposed to be teaching. English. That's why you were hired, and that's why I'm paying you."

"Well, but . . ."

She let her shoulders fall a little and she tilted her head. It was clear she did not want to hear any more about it.

"Of course I'll teach the curriculum," I said. "I just wanted to say that I thought the holocaust essays were wonderfully written. Those kids cared about what they were doing when they wrote about that. I think some of them were made more aware of . . ."

"I'm not saying it was a bad assignment," she interrupted. "For a college classroom it's probably fine. But some of these kids are just too young yet, too unready for such ugly truth."

"I guess," I said.

"You can still do things like that with the seniors, or even the juniors, if you want—though I still think you should tone it down. But the younger ones . . ."

"Certainly," I said. "I see what you mean."

She sat back a little and smiled. I had the feeling that she wanted to say something else to me; that she was considering it. But then she only waved her hand toward the door and said, "Have your best day of teaching today."

Doreen came to my classroom just as lunch was beginning. "I saw you in with Mrs. Creighton," she whispered. "Does she know anything?"

"Not yet. I'm going to see Bible right now. I don't know what I'm going to say to him."

"I wish I could go with you."

"I wish you could too."

To tell the truth, I didn't know how I was going to broach the business of his operation with him again. When I got to his room, Leslie was there, leaning back slightly in her chair, talking to him. Bible was seated at the desk, his arms folded across his chest the way he did when he was just listening, his white hair hanging over his forehead like the bill of a cap. His head was tilted slightly, his eyes on Leslie, and a bent but genuine smile on his face.

"I think it's a mistake," Leslie was saying. "I don't have anything against black people, but why should we be treating them like children now?"

"Why do you say that?" Bible asked. It was clear he was truly interested.

"Say what?"

"Like children. Why do you think affirmative action programs treat blacks like children?"

"Don't they?"

"Explain," Bible said, and there it was: The one word that cornered you instantly and rendered you helpless in the face of his expectant, amazingly critical intellect. Bible had extraordinary skill at getting answers from students, or even from colleagues. He'd said, "Explain," to me a few times already. He really was good at that. He'd utter that one word, a deeply curious look on his face, his eyes totally focused on you, and the silence was almost frightening. You just could not leave that space unfilled even if you went on to make a complete ass of yourself. But to his credit, most of the time he wouldn't let you know you made an ass of yourself. This was his gift. He could make the dumbest comment seem only strangely invalid or slightly misdirected. He would treat what you said with respect. That was it. But it all started with his fixed stare into your eyes, his head slightly angled away from you as he waited for you to: *Explain.*

"Well," Leslie said, but then she noticed me standing in the door.

"I'm sorry," I said.

Bible leaned a bit toward her and said, "Would you mind if he had a seat here with us?"

"No, not at all." She graced me with that smile. I sat down next to her and nodded her way. Bible leaned back again, his arms still across his chest and that look still on his face. "We're talking about why affirmative action programs are wrongheaded. Go on," he said.

"Well," Leslie said, her voice slightly quavering, but she was sure of herself. "My mother did not get a promotion where she works because of affirmative action. They gave it to a black woman who had only half the experience my mother had, who wasn't as qualified as my mother was. When you give somebody an advantage that isn't based on anything except wanting to provide that advantage—isn't that treating blacks as inferiors again really—like we have to haul them up to our level by giving them an unfair advantage? That's treating them like children. They can't do it on their own, so we have to help them."

As I listened I realized I agreed with her. What she was saying made perfect sense to me.

Bible said, "Go on."

"Well. That's it."

"Why is that parental, instead of, say, a socially desirable remedy at law?"

"What do you mean by that?" Leslie really wanted to know and so did I.

"You have a condition," Bible said. "A seemingly permanent circumstance based on the location of people. Whole cities have been segmented and divided along racial lines because of racism. In those separate segments you have housing, jobs, and schools. White housing in the white segments, black housing in the black segments. White schools in the white segments, black schools in the black segments." He talked deliberately, calmly, slowly, in a normal tone of voice—but the sense of it, the way he was putting things, became almost rhetorical, as if he were making a fervent radio address or quiet public speech to people who can't stand noise. He went on, "White businesses and jobs in the white segment, and . . ." he paused, still not looking away from Leslie's astonishing eyes. "Finish that sentence."

"What?"

"Finish that sentence."

"What was it again?"

164

"You weren't listening."

"Yes I was."

"Okay, finish this sentence: white businesses and jobs in the white segment, and in the black segment . . ."

Leslie said, "Black businesses and jobs."

"No," Bible said. "You don't have black businesses and jobs in the black segments, you have white businesses and jobs."

"And that's because of racism," I said, wanting to be part of this teaching effort.

But Bible said, "No, not directly. It's because the schools in the black segments are underfunded, and therefore scarcely capable of providing the kind of education the white schools provide. Since for decades the 'separate' education was not sufficient, the level of education among the populace in the black segments was always inadequate. In consequence, you have poverty in the black segments of most cities, and the businesses and jobs are mostly white. Blacks can't get jobs that provide economic wealth as well as self-respect and dignity, so the poverty only gets worse. Because of the poverty, and lack of education, people naturally judge black men and women to be inferior. This feeds the racism. You have the poverty because blacks can't get good jobs, and they can't get good jobs because of job discrimination, and we have job discrimination because blacks in the black segments are undereducated and therefore are judged inferior. It goes in a circle like that, on and on. This feeds a kind of racism most of the white population would deny now, but still you have job discrimination because black men and women are judged to be ill prepared and badly educated. So the condition persists. Year after year and decade after decade. It feeds on itself and festers. You want to change that, right?"

"Sure I do," Leslie said, and it was clear she intended to say something else, but she stopped. Nothing Bible did or said made her stop. I think her own bright mind caught up with her and she could see where Professor Bible was going. There was a long silence.

"How?" Bible said finally, and then he waited, the question out there like something musical and full of longing. Then he said, "You can't move whole segments of cities. You can't take houses and apartment buildings in the black part of town, pick them up and move them to the white side of town and vice versa. You can't move black schools and white schools around. They are where they are. So you have to move people. You open up housing opportunities to blacks. That's first: equal housing. While you're waiting for the two races to begin to equalize in location, which takes a lot of years, you bus black students to white schools and white students to black schools—you mix them. You open up the colleges and universities to black students—which has taken the army and U.S. Marshals in some places—but eventually, with time and with programs to get black students admitted to good schools—also an 'affirmative action' program—you begin to equalize education. And all of this will be completely useless, unless you do something to equalize the situation with jobs."

Leslie nodded her head slowly. I could see she was definitely listening and I couldn't help myself. I blurted out, "I sure hope you do get into my class next year, Leslie."

She turned to me and smiled.

"So," Bible said. "You see my point?"

She was still looking at me.

Bible went on, "You begin to chip away at the job discrimination by providing affirmative action; by insisting that folks look for qualified blacks." It seemed as though Leslie had stopped listening, that she was only paying attention to me, and I suddenly felt anxious and sorry for Bible so I faced him, hoping helplessly that Leslie would do the same. "That's all affirmative action is," he was saying. "That's all it was meant to be. It is, simply, a remedy at law, used to cure a very bad, socially undesirable situation." Now Bible unfolded his arms and laid them on the desk in front of him, leaned forward so that his face was not more than a foot from Leslie's face. "See?" he said, gently.

She turned back to him. "Yes, sir," she said.

Bible smiled, then looked at me. I could see he was once again happy in it—feeling the joy of his work, and I felt again a terrible stab of sadness at what was waiting for him at the end of the year. He looked so satisfied and happy, smiling sweetly at his young student.

Knowing that some errant part of me wanted to be like Professor Bible, I was suddenly frightened; sick with fear that I'd end up in the same place. He thought he'd made a difference to Leslie, and maybe he did. It occurs to me now that I can't say for sure he didn't. He changed my mind about the whole affirmative action thing. But you don't normally change a person's mind with oratory, or questions, nor with leaning over a desk and saying, "See?" And even if you could change one mind that way, what difference would it make, really? What if Bible actually changed Leslie Warren's mind about affirmative action? That difference was no more remarkable or valuable than the difference you make when you stand on a beach and pour a shot glass of whiskey in the water. It's still the ocean, and your whiskey disappears in it. When a student Leslie's age—even a good smart student, as she clearly was—expressed an opinion about politics or morality, she was only spouting what Mom and Dad believed. And as soon as Leslie got home and told her mother and father what Bible had "taught" her, they'd go to work on her. They'd get in there and stir it all up again about blacks being treated like children. And what would Leslie do then? She'd eventually reject what her parents believed about it, but that was bound to happen anyway. What was Bible's affect on her? Really, what was it? And to live your whole life for that? To go around saying you were doing some good? I didn't see the difference between that and saying you were engaged in changing the ocean to whiskey with a shot glass.

When Leslie had gone, I asked Professor Bible about how the treatment of his foot was going. I did not say anything about the letter Doreen got from her sister, of course, but I told him I thought it was very dangerous for him to wait too long to have the procedure that might save his life. He surveyed the room and the hall outside as if I had just revealed something secret to him, but he said nothing. The expression on his face was inscrutable. I could not tell what he might be thinking or feeling. His deep blue eyes, looking almost gray in the afternoon light that leaked through the venetian blinds, seemed to freeze on me.

"I thought I should say something to you again," I told him.

"It was kind of you," he said quietly. It was almost a whisper. "But . . ." He didn't finish. Again he was silent and I sat there looking into those eyes, wondering what the hell I was supposed to say.

"If there's any chance," I said, weakly. "I mean if it gets worse or . . ."

"It's not any better. I'm to see the doctor this afternoon," he said, and then he folded his hands again across his breast. "Is there anything else?"

"I'm sorry." I wanted to tell him that I had told Doreen and Annie, but I didn't.

"I don't suppose you brought some cigarettes with you?"

"No."

"I feel the need for a cigarette right now."

"I hope they can do something so you don't lose anything more than the toe."

This made him impatient. He seemed to be looking for someplace to let his eyes fall, then he got up out of the chair. "Go get me a cigarette," he said. "Would you just do that?"

"Yes, sir," I said.

I went and got him a cigarette. He sat down at his desk and lit it. He was almost in a hurry to get it going.

Days went by. I didn't know what else I could do. I couldn't keep bringing it up to him. Still, Doreen wouldn't let me alone about it. What was he doing? Had he seen his doctor? Was the treatment working? My answer was always, "I don't know Doreen, he won't talk about it."

"Well it's silly," she said, one day. "Everybody knows about it now."

"Mrs. Creighton knows?"

"Well doesn't she?"

"I don't think she does."

"I've heard my students whispering about it."

"I have too, and they weren't whispering."

We were standing in the parking lot, getting ready to hop on our respective buses and drive students home. Doreen was smoking a cigarette, one foot up on the steps leading into her bus. I stood next to her, my keys in my hand. Her passengers were all loaded and jabbering and so were mine. It was an unseasonably warm, late February afternoon, and I wasn't in much of a hurry. Annie was going to be working late, again, and I really had nothing to do.

We watched Bible emerge from the building and limp to his car.

"I think I'm going to say something to him," Doreen whispered.

"No you are not."

"He must know the secret is out now. He must."

"You've got to wait until he comes to you."

"I wish you didn't feel like you have to always tell me what to do," she said, in a normal voice, now—and not too warmly either.

"I wasn't aware that was happening."

She looked me in the eye, told me I was a control freak, and then climbed up into her bus. She flipped her cigarette at my feet and I stepped on it for her. I leaned down to pick it up, and caught her looking at me, with this odd, crooked smile on her face. It was a look of frustration, I guess, but I think I saw scorn too.

"See you," I said.

She shook her head, smiling now, and drove off.

I made up my mind not to worry about Professor Bible. I had a pile of journals to go through, and I didn't want to waste time thinking about something I could do nothing about. I hated feeling so helpless.

(George) folded

2-16-86

Mark Talbot told me that Bible is dying I don't know what he's supposed to have but he's going to die. You could never tell. Yesterday Bible told us a story about when he was a young teacher and I thought he was going to cry at the end of it. Must be sad to be at the end of yourself like that. Dad hasn't hit me in a long time. He still yells sometimes but not so much anymore. I'm better than I was and feel more like I do now than I did before.

2-18-86

This wierd chick in biology. Suzanne Rule walks like she's looking for a four-leaf clover head bent down. She's skinny and stick like. Looks like one of those things the shepherds carried around in Bethlehem. She's got bright red hair and ugly freckles. The big red kind all splotchy like she spilled beet juice all over herself. She doesn't talk and yesterday before Miss Nagle's math class Mark Talbot and Happy tried to get her to straighten up. They were bending down trying to look up in her eyes, get her to look at us, and Happy got down on the floor on his back and scooted under her bent over head just like she was a car and he was a mechanic and he was going to have a look under her. She was wearing a dress and she didn't understand what he was doing. They were laughing and all, just trying to get her to be more comfortable, but then Happy got up real fast and said shit she's crying. I saw water I guess it was tears, dripping on the floor. She was definitely crying. I felt sorry for her. I think I should tell somebody what happened.

(Happy) folded

2-16-86

Suzanne Rule is really fucked up.

(Mark Talbot) folded

2-16-86

Here's a secret for you. If you're unfolding these pages and reading them, and I think you are—I think you are, because I would and everybody I know would—Professor Bible has Millenium's disease, or something like that. And at the end of the year he's going to die. Whatever kind of weird disease he's got you can't tell he's got it. He looks the same, but at the end of the year, when folks will be graduating from this place, Professor Bible's going to be graduating from life. I guess he's old enough to move on. Must suck to be him though. I wonder how old Bible is. He said something in class today about the meaning of history, and then he sort of let out this croaking sound like a frog or something and tears in his eyes.

2-18-06

I think when birds die they must fly too high and let the sky take them. You almost never see one lying on the ground. I wonder how old they get. Bible told us about listening to the heart of the world and everybody laughed at him. Jaime Nichols actually asked him what the world's heart sounds like. Everybody really laughed at her and so I told them all to shut up. Bible made me sit in the back of the room. Jaime watched me the whole time, and then after school I took her down to the railroad trestle, near where she lives and we made out for a while. I gave her some dope and got her good and high and then she says, let's fuck, and I said sure. So we got up on top of the bench near the back of the trestle and I took her clothes off and then I took mine off and then she proceeds to say come in from behind and I went ahead and did it. She is really nasty when she gets excited. I hope she doesn't get pregnant. She's a slut is what she is and dumb as a bag of grass seed but I think I might get her to go back down there with me sometime.

I spent most of the night after going over the journals trying to figure out what to do about Suzanne Rule. I was not bothered by the revelations of sex and dope. There was nothing I could do about that and

171

I knew it—they would have their excesses in spite of what any of us might dream up to stop them, but I didn't see how I could overlook the small, stupid harassment of Suzanne Rule. From the point of view of the boys, it was just a mistake. I believed the journal entry. I didn't think they meant her any harm, but I couldn't decide if what happened was worth revealing. I would have to let it be known that I was reading the folded entries. I wondered if I should talk to Mrs. Creighton or to Mark Talbot and Happy about what had happened. Could a stupid prank cause lasting trouble? What kind of damage did Mark and Happy do? The poor girl was crying and no matter what they intended, they were looking up her skirt. I realized there was nothing I could do but keep my eye on all of them.

21

Certain Things Come to Light

A WEEK OR so later, Professor Bible stopped at my door just before the eight o'clock bell and asked me if I could come to his classroom at lunchtime for a talk. His expression was serious, almost baleful—and I think I might have thought he was angry. I know I did not look forward to whatever our talk would be about, but when the time came, I took a pack of cigarettes out of my desk and went to his classroom. He was not sitting at his desk. He stood at a small bank of double windows that looked out on the field and the highway that ran by the school. He had his hands hitched in the back of his pants at the belt, the tail of his jacket hiked up sort of on his elbows, and he stared out the window as if he were judging everything in his view, taking it all in with his graying eyes. I know he must have been thinking of his retirement; of the end of all this; but there was no expression on his face, and when he turned back into the room, he took in what he saw with the same slow, concentrated apprehension. He seemed to be looking for something as he approached me, and then he said, "Time,

Ben. I'm thinking about time." He said this as if time was something he might just buy if the price was right; as if he was appraising the view from the window to determine if it would be worthwhile to buy another decade.

I had not done anything about those journal entries about Suzanne Rule. In fact I had not asked anyone about them. Not even Annie. But I was feeling tremendously affectionate toward Professor Bible at that moment and I knew there was no one I could trust more completely to guide me in the right direction, so I thought this might be the best time to broach the subject. I showed him the cigarettes.

"Well," he said. "I think I will." He opened the window, then sat down in one of the student desks next to it, and signaled me to hand him one. I did and he lit it right there.

"You sure Mrs. Creighton doesn't mind you smoking in here?" I said.

He didn't seem to hear me. He reached over and unlatched the dusty screen then propped it up with a ball point pen. It was a gray, icy day, with occasional salvos of sleet and freezing rain. I stood there watching him smoke, and felt the cold air filtering into the room. Outside, cars hissed up the wet streets in steady surges, almost like the sound of waves on a beach.

"I've discovered a sort of problem," I said. "In the journal entries of . . ."

"Ben," Bible said. "I'm afraid you've let me down."

I had nothing to say to that. He was not looking at me, and suddenly I wanted to get out of there because I was pretty sure I knew what was coming. He waited for me to respond, but I just sat down in the student desk nearest him and remained silent. Without looking at me, he got up, crossed the room, retrieved a piece of paper and handed it to me. He sat back down and I said nothing.

"Read that," he instructed.

It was a letter, apparently from the parent of one of his students. In it, she asked him if he would please consider withdrawing from the classroom, so the young students in his classes would not be "exposed to the terrible thing that is happening to you."

"What," I said. "Is she afraid it's catching?"

"She doesn't want me to keep teaching while I'm dying."

My heart stuttered. "Who said you were dying?"

"She thinks it's insensitive of me to go on, letting the children watch my 'decline.' That's what she says, Ben. Go ahead, finish reading."

I didn't want to but I did. It said:

This is the time in the lives of our young when they should feel that the world is a good place and they can have what they want if they only try hard enough. I am so sorry for your condition, and when my son told me of it I prayed for you and I still pray for you. But won't you please consider what it might do to the young students in your class to be exposed to your suffering? Please don't take this in the wrong way. I will pray for you until the end of the earth; my husband will pray for you. But we both feel the young people are better served by a younger teacher—one who has the time and energy and youth, to devote to learning the important things. Our students should not be so worried about their teachers. My son actually broke down crying last night when he told me of this. So I know they love you. Won't you consider them now, too? I hope you can take this suggestion in the spirit it is offered.

Sincerely,
Tess Hayward

When I was finished I handed it back. "She's stupid," I said, lamely. "It's clear she hasn't a brain in her head and she's about as sensitive as a corncob."

"Is she?" Bible said.

"I'm sorry she—I'm sorry for this."

"For what."

"For everything," I said.

"I asked you not to tell anybody."

"I didn't," I lied. "I told no one but Annie, but it wasn't long after you told me that I started hearing my students whispering about it. Some of them wrote about it in their journals. A lot of them think you're dying."

He shook his head.

"Listen here," I said. "I'm no saint, and I'm just as bad as the next guy, I suppose, but a whole lot of people came to know about this, so I'm finding it hard to believe I'm the only person you told about it."

"Now you accuse me?" he asked. "It's my fault, now?"

"Well who else did you tell?"

"I told you. That's all."

So it must have been Doreen. I didn't know what to say to him. I think I mumbled something about Mrs. Creighton not knowing about it yet or something like that.

"It doesn't matter," he whispered. He turned back to the window and drew a long pull on his cigarette. I watched the thick smoke billow out into the cold air. "She'll come to know it soon enough, now."

"I'm sorry," I said. "The only people I told were Annie and . . ." I paused. I knew I had to tell him about Doreen, even though he had told me expressly not to tell her. "Doreen," I added, my voice trembling on it. "Doreen. I told Doreen. I know you told me not to, but she noticed something wrong with you—she saw that you were not—that you were not the same, and she asked me what was wrong. She said she would find out, and I didn't want her bothering you. So I told her."

He nodded, took another pull on the cigarette. His eyes were absolutely inscrutable.

"I really am sorry," I added.

Now he turned back to me. "What did Doreen say?"

"She was very concerned."

He glanced downward, toward the floor.

"In fact," I went on, "she was the one who insisted I keep after you about getting it treated." I told him how she had been hounding me ever since to see if he had done anything to pursue the treatment. "She won't leave me alone about it."

He had no response.

"Well have you?" I asked.

"Have I what?"

"Have you decided to let the doctor treat this?"

"What treatment?"

"Didn't you say he wanted to cut off your toe?" I said, not a little exasperated. "That he'd already scheduled the surgery?"

"Oh," he shook his head, and continued to shake it, slowly as he spoke. "I showed it to him and he said it looked a little better, but it wasn't completely healed either. So we're going to keep treating it with the antiseptic baths and I'm to keep taking my antibiotics and insulin."

"I can't believe it."

"So now they all know about it," he said.

"Well not all of them," I muttered, but I didn't believe it. Death has a way of occupying center stage in any scene and people tend to tune into it even when only a slight acquaintance falls under the sweep of its blade. And the rumor, unfortunately, had included the sad, but untrue fact, that Professor Bible was dying from "millennium's disease."

Professor Bible flipped the rest of his cigarette out into the drizzling rain and closed the window.

"Most of them think you're dying," I said.

He turned to me and the sadness in his eyes did something to my soul; it left me no hope, that's what it did. His eyes murdered hope—not just for him, but for myself, for Annie and the world. I felt so desolate, and responsible too. There was that. As if I had caused not only this pain but his disease and its rumored prognosis. I didn't know what to say, so like a fool I stammered, "I will pray for you, sir."

I am horrified to this day that he heard me say that.

"You'll pray for me?"

I didn't know what to look at. I couldn't stand his eyes, his drooping, sad eyes. "I'm not a praying man, but yes . . . I mean . . ."

"Mrs. Creighton will have to let me go when she hears of this," he said. "She will insist that I get it treated and all, but her main fear will be the health insurance. My disease can be very costly."

"She wouldn't fire you."

"She'll insist that I retire now," he said. "I had hoped . . ." but he didn't finish the sentence. He went to his desk and sat down. From my place at the window, he looked like the perfect image of a teacher; like one of those photographs the colleges and universities put on their brochures to entice students to their campuses. He leaned over the desk, his white hair drooping over his brow, his white jacket bunched at the shoulders, the desk covered with papers, and behind him, a chalkboard with diagrams of the state legislature and other houses of government.

I walked over and stood in front of him. "Professor Bible, I am so sorry."

He waved his hand. "I know you are. I know it." He wouldn't look at me. I stood there another minute, thinking to offer him another cigarette, but then I just turned and walked out, slowly. I didn't want him to get the feeling that I was running away from him, but that was exactly what I was doing.

I guess I've given the impression that if I explain what happened with Professor Bible it will shed some light on everything else that happened. In a way, it will, although I could not have known that back then. Annie argued that I should just forget about it—that it was Bible's life, and none of my business. She also scolded me for telling Doreen about it. In the end, I promised her I would never try to influence events around me again. I really did intend to work on letting things be; on staying out of everyone's business but my own. I know I said that to her, but I can't say even now if I really meant it. Being a teacher sort of involves you in the lives of other people whether you want it to or not.

I have to say I agreed with Annie about Doreen. I should have kept my mouth shut. I didn't think I would ever trust her again, and knowing that, it became increasingly hard to talk to her. I couldn't very well avoid her, but I tried. I'd leave my class during breaks and go into Mrs. Creighton's office, or I'd march outside and walk down to the basketball courts and smoke with some of the students down there. She could tell I was avoiding her, though.

One day sometime around the middle of March it snowed in the afternoon and we had to pile in the buses right away and get everybody home before the roads got too covered. She stood in the door of my bus and waited for me.

When I came around the front fender and saw her I gave a start of surprise. She put her hands on her hips and frowned.

"What?" I said.

She asked me what I was trying to prove.

"I'm not trying to prove anything."

"Why are you making yourself so scarce, then?"

"I've just been kind of busy," I said.

"Really." She didn't believe it, and the scowl on her face sort of embarrassed me. She had no emotional hold on me whatsoever—I did not care about her even in any superficial collegial way—and she was berating me as if we were old friends; as if we were on the brink of love and our deeply satisfying and charming alliance would get us through it. There was something affectionate in her scowl and in the tone of her voice, and that made her simply pathetic. "I've noticed you scurrying off to smoke with your students and hiding in the office," she went on. "Don't you think I didn't, Mr. Ben Jameson."

179

I tried to go past her but she blocked the door.

"Go on," she said. "Explain yourself."

"Please," I said, not too firmly, but I let her know I meant it. "I'm not going to talk about this now."

Her expression faltered. "Is something wrong?"

"Yes, and I'm not going to get into it here."

She only briefly met my gaze, but then it seemed to humiliate her, and she looked away. She moved her head down slightly and walked past me. I saw the white, smooth skin on the nape of her neck—the only smooth skin anywhere above her shoulders—exposed to the cold air. She moved off, awkwardly, her brown hair bouncing on her shoulders and neck in a way that was almost comical, and suddenly I felt really sorry for her.

Sometimes I feel sorry for all women.

Once, on the way to what I thought would be an important job interview—it was at a finance company for a part-time position in the loan office—I passed a car beside the road with a woman sitting in the driver's seat, looking pretty alone and frightened. We were miles from a gas station or a phone. There was a traffic light up the road a ways, and I had to slow for the traffic. As I passed by her car, I saw that she was very definitely in some kind of trouble. She was probably in her fifties. I was dressed up for the interview but I had plenty of time. I'd left myself at least two hours to get lost or have my own flat tire and still be on time for the interview. I wanted to see if she needed any help, so I pulled my car over in front of hers, backed up a bit so I could get close to her car, and got out to ask her. I wore a blue blazer, a pinstriped shirt, a navy blue tie, white slacks, and tan shoes. I don't think I looked particularly menacing, but I didn't want to scare her further. As I neared her she frantically locked her door—which is what I would have done—but I knocked gently on the glass, smiled and asked if she was in any kind of trouble. I saw her decide to trust me. She let the window down a crack and with tears in her eyes, said she had a flat tire. I didn't see it as I approached the car, but when

I walked around behind it I saw that in fact the right rear tire was flat. I called out and asked her to open the trunk of her car. I told her she could stay in the car if she was worried about me, but if she had a jack in there, I'd change the tire for her. The trunk popped open, and I removed the jack and the spare. This was sometime right after I graduated from high school, before I ever dreamed of going to college. It must have been July or early August. I took off my jacket, loosened my tie and got to work. The whole time I was changing her tire, she stayed in the car. I got my hands dirty as hell, moving the bad tire off and replacing it, working the jack and tightening the lug nuts. When I was done and let the car down, I cursed myself for wearing white slacks that day. I just knew I'd get my dirty hands all over those pants and I'd instantly look like a street bum. And what would that do for my job interview? She got out of the car to thank me (she called me "honey" which made me feel sort of odd), but then she noticed my hands. "Wait a minute," she said. Instantly she was as concerned for me and my welfare as I had been for hers. "Never mind," I said, not wanting her to feel bad. "It's just a little washable grease and road dirt. I'll stop in a gas station up ahead."

"You'll get yourself all dirty." She went to the backseat of her car, and retrieved—are you ready for this?—a box, a huge box, of Mini-Wipes—you know, those little packets they hand out in restaurants that serve barbecued chicken and ribs. Apparently she worked for a restaurant distributor and she had a supply of those things. So there she was, breaking open each miniature packet as quickly as she could, working like a hurried servant beside that road, in the winds of passing traffic, unwrapping little Mini-Wipes for me, while I essentially scrubbed my hands.

She took care of me, you see, even in those circumstances. I felt mothered—pampered, to tell the truth. When I was done, and I couldn't find a speck of dirt on my hands, I had to prove it to her—she threatened to open another packet or two—but I really was clean. She inspected my hands the exact same way my mother used to when

I was a little boy on my way to school. So, when I went to get in my car, I ended up thanking her for rescuing me.

And that little episode has always been emblematic to me of what women are and what they mean to me. And I'm not talking about cleaning me up like a servant either. I'm talking about the rescue; about how she so naturally thought of me and tried to help me in those circumstances. It's not that most women are incapable of self-interest; it's that it almost never occupies center stage, and it is far—sometimes very, very far—down the list of their apparent faults. It hardly ever occurs to them—even when it ought to. This is not because they are calculating some recompense in later lives, or credit from some other worldly auditor of good deeds—it's because self-interest truly doesn't occur to them. They are always so much better at thinking *of* people rather than *about* them. That woman, I'm certain, has probably sung my praises to the heavens, told hundreds of folks about the way I rescued her, and has yet to mention her role in saving me. I could almost guarantee it. And yet—here's the rub—if I had told her something secret, that I could not afford to have her tell anybody else, ever, at pain of my own soul, and she knew other people who knew me, all of them would know it before I got to my job interview.

You tell me what that is. I have no idea. Maybe I haven't lived long enough to know yet. But it's vitally important in the world, for it makes loving a woman as essential as anything on earth. How else can one learn generosity of spirit? But it also creates a real need for reticence, even perhaps certain caginess, whenever you are within five feet of a woman.

22

The Will of the People

THE NEXT DAY I was going to go to Doreen and finally tell her how I was feeling, but then Bible wasn't there and I thought when she noticed that she would come to see me. I had just finished my second period class, and sure enough she walked in and sat down in the front row. I told her I was going out to have a cigarette, so she followed me—not too happily either—and when we were outside I stayed by the door near my classroom so we could talk. I lit her cigarette for her, then my own.

I asked her what was up, thinking I'd just wheedle my way around to the subject at hand.

"Professor Bible resigned yesterday," she said.

I think I staggered back into the door. I could not think of a thing to say. Doreen fought back tears, puffing madly on her cigarette. I had that terrible feeling of desolation again. I didn't want to be there. I didn't want to be anywhere. Everything I looked at made me sick. It was quiet for a very long time. Finally I said, "He never said a word to me."

"He told Mrs. Creighton all about it. She knew it anyway."

"Did you tell her?"

"I didn't tell anybody."

I decided to ignore this obvious lie. "Well," I said. "Now he's gone."

She said nothing.

After a long silence, I said, "I wonder who will teach his classes the rest of the year."

"Mrs. Creighton's got some retired friend of hers who used to teach here to come back until she can hire somebody else."

"I'm sure going to miss him," I said.

Doreen searched my eyes, tears running down her face. "He taught me everything I know about teaching," she said.

"I know. Me too."

"He always said, 'It's a balancing act. A high-wire walk without a net.' And he meant it."

I agreed, I guess. I don't remember. I think I was wondering what she meant by that, or rather, what Bible meant by it. I mean it sounds nice to say and all, and maybe he believed it—but I didn't get the metaphor, unless teaching is somehow dangerous; unless one has to conquer fear in order to do it. I wasn't ever afraid of my students. In the short time I was a teacher, I always knew what I wanted to do with them, and how to go about it. Most of the time, to tell the truth, all I worried about was how to use up the time, and keep them busy; and I confess I also worried about finding ways for my students to do some kind of work I wouldn't have to read too closely. It was just too hard to grade so many papers, if you can find a way not to.

"It's going to be a pretty boring place without Bible around here," I said, lamely. In truth, I didn't know what to say to Doreen. In some ways, I believed she caused the whole thing. Her sadness didn't count for much in the light of that simple fact, so it felt disingenuous to me. I finished my cigarette and left her there with her tears.

At my first break, I went right to the office to see if I could find out what was going on. Mrs. Creighton was sitting at her desk, leaning back a little in the chair and staring out the window, when I knocked on the doorframe and asked her if I could come in.

She didn't even nod slightly, but she turned her gaze toward me and waited, a slight, welcoming smile on her face. I moved to the chair in front of her desk and sat down. She said nothing, though, so finally I told her what I had heard.

She nodded, and the smile left her face.

"He's not coming back?" I asked.

"He's retired."

"I'm sorry to hear it."

"You know what is wrong with him?"

"Yes," I said. I would have lied but I was afraid she knew the truth.

"He's getting treatment. He thinks it won't do him much good, but he's going to get it anyway. He's afraid of losing his leg."

"His leg? He was barely starting to limp."

"He said the infection is being stubborn."

"What are they going to do about it?"

"Who knows what they're doing. It's another language. I know he's having some kind of treatment or surgery on his foot."

I nodded.

Then Mrs. Creighton said, "I want you to teach his classes until I can get somebody to take over."

"Me. I can't teach . . ." I stopped myself. "We have classes at the same time."

"It's only for a few days. Get them working on something. I'll take over your classes. I'm an old English teacher myself."

This had the unwanted effect of causing my heart to quiver like a bag of kittens. I was not using lesson plans; I had no true curriculum that I was following. What would I tell her I was doing in there? I had been spending the past few days having them write in their journals so I could investigate the folded-page entries. (I really did feel as though I should be vigilant there after what happened to Suzanne Rule. I know, from a certain point of view one might think I was also looking forward to a little voyeuristic pleasure, but that never crossed my mind. When my students wrote about their sex lives it embarrassed me.) I'd also given them Dickens's *Great Expectations* to read, and I'd been spending a portion of each class talking about their own dreams of the future; you know, that stuff that gets them talking about themselves and each other and has the terrific benefit of getting them to think out loud.

I had no plan.

It's possible I was too nervous for it to occur to me then—but I may have remembered what Doreen had just said to me about Bible's balancing act, and the knowledge of that flitted across my mind. At any rate, I now see, what I was doing in the classroom back then was a kind of freewheeling venture, every day, and if that's not a balancing act or a walk on a high wire, I don't know what is.

Mrs. Creighton said, "Just leave me some notes for each class about where you are in the lessons and I'll pick it up."

"Well," I said. "That's not going to be as easy as it sounds."

"I beg your pardon."

"I mean—I don't—I can't just sit down and sketch it all out, I'll need some time." I think it raced through my heart that I could always make something up.

"I wanted you to start with them today—the afternoon class."

"Oh I will."

"Just leave notes for fifth period today. And tomorrow we'll make the complete switch."

"Sure," I said.

"There's one other thing."

I had started to leave my seat, so when she said that, I sat back down and waited. She took a long time to say anything directly though. It was so quiet I could hear the clock ticking in the hall outside. Finally she said she assumed Professor Bible and I were friends. Good friends. I nodded at that. She asked me how well I knew him. I told her not so well as I'd like to. She smiled, as if she were offering the unwilling acknowledgement that I had amused her, but then she pressed on. "I assume you've been to his apartment, you know how to . . ."

"No."

"No what?"

"I've never been to his apartment."

"Well, he lives just up the street a few blocks. At the Bridge-water Apartments. I assume you've gone out to eat dinner with him and . . ."

"No."

"I see."

"We eat lunch together almost every day," I said, and she smiled. "Or we used to anyway."

"You know he has no friends to speak of outside of this place. A few people from his apartment building, the old woman he sublets his apartment from. He has no family to speak of and he's going to be— alone. A lot of the time." She paused, and I had the feeling she was looking for just the right words, so I tried to supply them. I told her the treatment was going to involve surgery and that he would probably be fairly disabled afterward. In fact, I think I used the word "helpless."

"That's right," she said. "He's going to need a lot of people to help support him while he goes through this, until he's, until he's . . . back to normal."

This didn't seem to call for a response so I said nothing. Some people find it easy to promise they'll do a thing in the vague future while counting on some ingenuity or other creative method to get out of it once the future gets more specific, but I didn't want to be that way. I knew I could offer nothing, so I said nothing. There was another long silence.

"I hope you'll be willing to visit him once in a while."

"I'm going to do the best job I can in his classes," I said.

"Well yes. That, too."

"I'm sure Doreen will want to look out after him."

"What do you mean?"

"I'm not real good with this kind of thing," I said, weakly, and feeling pretty weak too. "Illness—I don't bear it well."

She shook her head slowly, her eyes still fixed on me.

"It's just the truth," I said.

"Well you know he's asked me if I would explicitly talk to you about this. He said he was counting on you." Her tone was not sad. It was judgmental, in a way, and also kind of incredulous—not at what I had said, but at the irony of it. "He said you were his friend."

"I guess I am," I said. But I didn't think of myself as his "friend." I knew him, I worked with him, but he was a mentor—superior in ways that precluded friendship it seemed to me. I admired him, but my affections were bound up in sorrow for him; even pity. How can that be friendship? I said, "He's been very good to me."

"Will you do this for him?"

"He said to ask me?"

She wrote his address on a piece of paper and handed it to me. "He said he knew you'd probably stop by occasionally—that he wouldn't be lonely."

"Really?" I stared at the address.

"Why does that surprise you?"

"It's just that I never thought of him as a friend. He was—" I realized I spoke of him in the past tense. "He's my mentor." I shrugged.

"Apparently you give the wrong impression to people."

"Maybe I do."

"You fooled me." She was having a hard time looking at me again, and then I remembered how I had betrayed Bible's secret to Doreen, and I figured I owed it to him. So I told her I'd be glad to do whatever was expected. I told her I wouldn't want to disappoint Professor Bible.

"Or me. You shouldn't disappoint me, either," she said.

23

Substitution

Mrs. Creighton figured out that something was wrong with my "curriculum" after only one day of teaching my classes. She called me into her office and wanted to know exactly what my students were supposed to be doing. I had to go over my "plans" with each class, making it up as I went along. I had to make up things that my students wouldn't immediately reveal as totally new to them—things that would not cause suspicion. I knew she would not approve of classes that were not planned right down to the last second. I could not think fast enough to convince her.

"You don't really have a plan for these students, do you?" she said. I couldn't tell if her voice registered scorn or sadness or a little of both.

"Well," I said. "I like to wing it a bit in my classes."

"Wing it?"

"I think you have to get in there and talk with them, see where they are in their lives and then . . ."

"You don't have a lesson plan."

"I have plans, but not each lesson. Not daily, no."

"So, how can I show the State—when it comes to licensing and accreditation . . ."

"The State?"

"I have to have approved curriculum. Virginia requires that certain subjects be taught."

"I'm teaching writing," I said. "You've seen some of their essays."

"But what kind of writing?"

"Just writing."

"They're supposed to be working on summary, on definition, description, comparison contrast; on analysis and on proper grammar, proper uses of . . ."

"They are." I got a little loud. Then more quietly I said, "Mrs. Creighton, I'm teaching them the best way I know how."

"I want you to have a curriculum—goals and . . ."

"I do."

"I want it to be clearly stated, both for me, the State, and our students."

I had no response to that. I knew it meant a lot of work, and a lot more careful thinking about adjectives and adverbs and other ridiculous terms about which I had no clue. I mean, I could say "predicate nominative" but I had no freaking idea what it was.

"Do you understand me?" Mrs. Creighton said. It wasn't a pejorative question, she really wanted to know. "If you can't do that, I still have copies of Cindy Gallant's lesson plans. You can use those, if you have to."

"I understand."

"I realize you started immediately after you were hired—that you didn't have a summer to prepare these things, but I want you to have them for me as soon as possible."

I nodded, but I was already thinking my glory days as a teacher were over. Sheepishly, I said, "Can I see Mrs. Gallant's plans?" I saw her eyes sink—something happened to the expression on her face that told me she was disappointed so I hastened to add, "I mean, you offered them and all. I can use them while I'm drawing up my own curriculum. Just for reference."

"And only for reference," she said.

Mrs. Creighton's replacement for Bible was an elderly gentleman named Steven Granby. He had worked at Glenn Acres more than ten years before and was an old friend of the Creighton family because of the years he had put in at the school. He was tall, thin—with a black-checkered vest that was so loosely fitted it might have blown off him in a stiff wind. He also wore a baggy, thinly woven short-sleeved white shirt—you could see his flesh beneath it, which is probably why he insisted on the vest—and black, tightly fitted jeans that made his whole frame look as if it was supported by stovepipes. Every now and then he wore a different pair of pants, and the shirt might change, but he always wore the vest. He had a long, deeply lined face, and very white skin.

That first time I saw him he was sitting in his chair as if someone had strapped him to it and they were going to pull the switch at any minute and electrocute him. His arms rested on the arms of the chair, his back rigid and totally upright—an exact ninety-degree angle from the hips—his legs bent perfectly at the knee and his feet in the proper place at the base of the chair. He spoke slowly and deliberately. His hair was gray and so sparse he scarcely combed it. It just sort of clung to the top of his head and moved about where the breezes took it over a smooth, oddly curved, almost pointed dome. His ears ran almost the length of the side of his head, but they didn't stick out much.

"This is Mr. Granby, History and Government," Mrs. Creighton said.

He did not get up. I reached out and shook his hand. Mrs. Creighton introduced me and I smiled. Still holding onto my hand he said, "Steven Granby."

I told him I was glad to meet him, and then I withdrew my hand.

"And you teach?" he looked at Mrs. Creighton for his answer and she gave it to him. When she told me he was going to be replacing Professor Bible, Granby said he was aware that he had his work cut out for him. "I know what kind of teacher Professor Bible was."

"He's still a great teacher," I said.

Mrs. Creighton said, "Professor Bible was a lot more organized in his lesson plans than Mr. Jameson here." This might have wounded me, but we'd been all around and over that problem.

Granby turned out to be a little crazy. Doreen hated him. She said he was always stealing her lunch out of the refrigerator—Mrs. Creighton had put a small refrigerator and a water dispenser in the combination break room/counseling office. (Glenn Acres had no counselors, but Mr. Creighton frequently closed the deal on new enrollments in that room. It was in the far corner of the building, a long way from North and South and the daily morning deposits.) Granby's main fault as far as I could see was that he loathed all of our students. It was hard to listen to him for five minutes. He thought all of them were criminal, uncivilized, and barely human. In his best moods he saw his job as a kind of informed stewardship of juvenile delinquents; in his worst, he believed we were no more than cultured guards watching over an unlawful population that might at any minute rise up and kill us all. He had nothing but contempt for anyone who had not read all of Shakespeare's plays and sonnets, or who had no knowledge of the Hundred Years War. This meant of course that he hated everyone, but you had to infer that from things he said, not from any actual stipulation he might make to you. In other words, he was perfectly civil in conversation.

He also smoked cigarettes, but he bought his own. Aside from his age, his smoking habit, and I suppose a fairly thorough knowledge of history and government, he had absolutely nothing whatsoever in common with Professor Bible.

I missed having Professor Bible around at the school, but I ended up visiting him fairly often during his recovery. I went to his apartment shortly after his surgery and sometimes I helped him bathe his surgically wounded foot.

You heard right. "Bathe" and "foot." I had to be in on that. But it wasn't really so bad. I'd get him clean towels, or a cup of tea, so he didn't have to get up. It's just that on some of my visits I had to be there, in the same room, with that foot, you know? And have you ever seen a foot, with a lengthy cut along the outside of the big toe, after it has soaked in warm salt water for several hours? From certain angles, it looks like a newborn infant before it opens its eyes and takes its first breath. It will make you shudder to look at it, even for a little bit.

My memory of the rest of that first year is a blur. Nothing much went on that would shed any light on what eventually happened. I remember very clearly the work with George—I still kept close watch on his neck, to be literal—and this new student Mrs. Creighton kept telling me I should watch out for: Suzanne Rule. She never got to the point where Mrs. Creighton felt comfortable putting her in my class, but I kept running into her—in the hall, or sitting in Mrs. Creighton's office (She sat the same way she stood, bent over at the neck. She looked, when sitting down, as if she were looking for something very small in her lap.) I said hello to her a couple of times, but she said nothing. She was just this strange creature with red hair. I'd never seen her eyes. I'm not sure anybody had, except those boys who had scooted under her and looked up to see the tears beginning to fall.

I also remember learning to accept Steven Granby, in spite of Doreen's constant barrage of bad news about him. Once you got used to his unvarying bitter news about our students I didn't mind him so much. Sometimes, he was pretty accurate in his criticisms, and he could be mildly amusing if you didn't take him too seriously. I can only remember one time when he got to me.

We were smoking cigarettes outside my classroom during a break and Doreen had just finished hers and gone back inside. He watched her go, then turned to me and said, "She's got a real problem with men." I said, "No, she likes men," and he said, "I didn't mean that. I meant men don't like her."

"I like her and I'm a man," I said.

"You may be the only one."

"Why?"

He seemed to consider for a long time, then very thoughtfully he said, "Well, she is strong-willed, intelligent, and fairly forceful, isn't she."

I agreed.

"She says what she thinks, and is not afraid to disagree with you."

"Yes."

"In short, she's a bit of a cunt."

I didn't like the way his lips curled when he pronounced the word *cunt*. I said nothing at first, but I stopped puffing on my cigarette. I held it in my hands, just looking at it, and he chuckled to himself. "A rummy bitch like that would shatter a good man's balls," he said.

He was old enough to be my father, and as far as I can remember, I'd never spoken disrespectfully to anyone more than one or two years older than me, but I couldn't help it. I felt my face starting to burn.

"Just now . . ." I said through my teeth, "I think you'd better finish your cigarette, old man."

He made this sound in the back of his throat and his face changed. He looked exactly like he'd just seen something suspicious dripping from my mouth. I checked to see if anybody could hear us. Then I said, "You know she doesn't like you very much either."

"She can go to the devil."

"Why don't you shut the fuck up about her," I said. "How about that?"

"I had no idea you were . . ." he didn't finish. His visage softened a little and then he said, "I really am sorry. I didn't know you cared about her in that way."

"I don't. Not even slightly. But I do care about her. I mean we've worked together all year." I don't know why his sneering talk about her made me so angry. I really didn't have what you could call sincere affection for Doreen, at least not then. The only thing I can say is Granby pissed me off. I was angry at him for saying things like that about her when she was not there to defend herself. I knew Bible would never characterize her in that way, and maybe my anger over all that had happened up to that time just boiled over.

At any rate he stood there, looking silly, and I said nothing except to repeat that I was not romantically involved with Doreen. "She's not somebody I have any interest in that way," I said.

"Well, all right then."

I threw the cigarette down at his feet. "Shit," I said, and left him there.

What he said wasn't that bad, but it made me furious anyway. Perhaps I reacted so angrily for another reason. I believed Granby was partially right when he said men didn't like Doreen. She was too strong for them, too capable and sharp. It didn't bother me, but I could see how it might bother others. Especially the usual lot of young power brokers and former athletic types, who drank light beer, slapped their prosperous stomachs, watched ESPN vigilantly, and who only liked lesbians if they could watch them having sex once in a while. But Granby should have been better than that. Maybe I was angry for that reason too. He should have been better.

24

A Kind of Rescue in the Snow

IN LATE MARCH a terrific snowstorm crept up swiftly from southern Virginia and began to cover the ground almost instantly. Mrs. Creighton decided to let school out early. Because of the bad weather we would not drive the buses, so parents had to pick up their children and take them home. Some students had their own cars and left immediately. The others had to wait. Mrs. Creighton let me borrow her big silver Oldsmobile to go home. "You go ahead, honey," she said. "Mr. Creighton will come pick me up in his car."

I was happy to get out of there. A snow day is like a gift from heaven—as if the gods themselves have said, "take the day off."

On the way home I got caught in traffic. Only a mile or so from Glenn Acres, everything came to a stop. I sat there in Mrs. Creighton's car while snow piled up all around us. I heard sirens behind me. There was nowhere to go. A fire truck came alongside the road, in the gravel of the shoulder, its siren blaring, the red lights whirling. It made its way up the highway. Whatever it was, we would not be moving for a long time. I had no cigarettes, no water in the car. The radio didn't work.

Snow kept falling; it began to collect on the windshield wipers. But it fell straight down, so I could see out the side windows. On the windshield, only the path the blades made was free of snow. I was in the right lane. I looked at the car next to me, a Ford Escort, and realized it was Leslie Warren. She seemed to be crying. I watched her awhile, to see what might be the trouble. She did not notice me. Still the traffic did not budge.

I didn't know whether I should keep looking at her. She was not happy about something. I wanted to ask her if she had a cigarette, but she wouldn't look my way. She concentrated on the road in front of her, squirming a bit in the seat. I rolled my window down and tried to catch her eye. When she finally saw me, she leaned over and rolled down her window.

"Do you know what it is?" she said.

"No. I think it must be a bad accident."

She shook her head. "Do you have a radio?"

"It's not working."

"I can't get a traffic report."

She had tears in her eyes, but she only sounded frustrated. I nodded toward the traffic in front of us and said, "It can't last much longer."

Then she looked at me with such pure sadness. "I have to pee." It cost her everything to say that to me. She rolled her window back up and sat back behind the wheel. She looked like she was suffering terribly. She would not look over at me again, but her eyes told me she was fighting with every ounce of strength not to give in. Her jaw was set tightly. Every now and then she would shift angrily in her seat, then recapture whatever it was that let her sit still and bear it.

We were going to be stopped a long time. Most of the drivers up ahead had turned off their cars. Snow fell steadily and with what seemed like purpose—as if the sky was falling in great bursts of little white flakes. It was absolutely silent, except for the few motors still murmuring around us. I heard Leslie scream, "Fuck," as loud as I've ever heard any one scream it.

I was wearing a long, tan overcoat and I realized it might be useful to her. So I got out of my car and stepped in thick snow around the back of hers. People in other cars watched me. I got to her window and knocked gently on it. She had seen me get out and knew I was coming around to talk to her.

I smiled. "I can help."

She cracked the window.

"Look," I said. "I got this big coat. You can open your door so nobody in front can see you. I'll turn my back and hold my coat out so nobody behind us can see. You can pee and then get back in the car."

She said nothing. She was stirring in the seat, trying not to be dancing in place fighting it. I noticed a pack of Marlboros on the console in her car.

"Seriously," I said. "I won't look. I'll keep my back turned and you can make sure you're all done and seated in the car again before I turn around. Then all you have to do is give me a cigarette, and that will be that."

I watched her consider it. Then she put the car in park, opened the door and scooted from under the steering wheel. She did not look at me and she was in a big hurry. She picked two tissues from a small box in her console, and then she took off her jacket and threw it in the backseat. I turned around, unbuttoned my coat and held it out on both sides with my arms stretched as wide as I could, like a cape, and she squatted down and peed there in the little triangle we made between her car, the door, and my coat. It took her a long time. In the silent snow and the muttering cars, I heard her sigh with the letting go of it. Snow collected in my hair and eyebrows. I felt it collecting in the collar of my coat, beginning to leak down my neck.

I don't know why, but I started laughing. And then she was laughing. We both absolutely howled, without changing position or looking at each other.

When she was done, she got herself back together, jumped behind the wheel, and said, "Thank you, Ben. Thank you thank you thank you." She was still crying but now it was from the laughter. And I loved it that she called me Ben.

I buttoned my coat and turned only slightly toward her. I didn't want to embarrass her by seeing the stream she had made. She handed me four cigarettes from her pack. "Let me know if you smoke all of these," she said. "You are a savior."

I took the cigarettes and made my way back to my car. We sat there for another hour, until it started to get dark. But here's the thing: the snow continued, the cars remained exactly as they were, and Leslie never once glanced my way. She studied the traffic in front of us, looked down at her console or something on the radio dial, and back up to the traffic. But she absolutely refused to look at me. I didn't feel bad about it. I think I understood it.

Still, doesn't the whole episode reveal something about the precarious nature of help and gratitude? I remembered the middle-aged woman whose tire I'd changed all those years ago—how she ended up rescuing me. I wondered if Leslie knew how her four cigarettes made it possible for me to endure the boredom of sitting in traffic with no radio and nothing to read.

And why not feel like a savior once in a while? It's a great feeling. Still, if it weren't for my helplessly rewarding tendency for rescue, maybe things would have turned out differently.

25

Prom Night

ONE MEMORABLE EVENT near the end of that first year was the prom. We all had to attend in formal attire. I think that was the first time everybody met Annie, who wore a long white sleeveless gown and spiked heels that made her look a lot taller. She wore a white pearl necklace that only made the bones in her neck and upper chest look even more silky and elegant and structurally beautiful. I really couldn't take my eyes off her.

Doreen wore a tuxedo that looked a lot like the one I had rented, and when Annie first got a glimpse of it she looked at me and winked.

"What?" I said.

She whispered, "Didn't you tell me Doreen was gay?"

"I said I thought she might be. I don't *know*."

"Well I guess we do now."

"It's just a style. She just dresses stylishly."

"Yeah," Annie said. "Right."

Mr. Creighton played the guitar for part of the evening, and I think even the kids enjoyed it. He really could make a sweet, rippling sound come from that guitar, his fingers dancing over the strings, his gold rings glittering in the spotlight. He was a bit overweight, and looked like he ought to be playing "Begin the Beguine" or some other Harry James song, but there he was, under the lights, playing James Taylor, Eric Clapton, and Neil Young. He did a rendition of "Southern Cross"—just the music mind you, no singing—that had everybody in the room trying to sing it themselves. It really was kind of amazing and sad at the same time. He worked so hard under those lights, sweat running down, and Mrs. Creighton talked to the kids and paid no attention at all. The kids wouldn't dance until Mr. Creighton sat down and let the DJ Mrs. Creighton had hired play some of "their" music. (That's what they called it. "Their" music, as if they had made the songs themselves.)

I think Annie had fun. Everybody mentioned how beautiful she looked, and we danced a bit in spite of the obvious attention it produced from the kids. (They never expect a teacher to actually have a life outside the classroom.) I really was feeling kind of special, too—since many of my students came over to talk to us and they didn't seem as if they wanted to avoid our company. Also, I think I looked pretty well distinguished in that tuxedo.

It was a hot night—one of those early summer nights when even the crickets seem to complain—and the dance was in a rented hall, about two blocks from the school. With the doors open to let in air, the sound of music probably got a lot of attention in the neighborhood. It's just possible one of the kids invited trouble by telling friends from other schools what was going on that night, but who knows? At any rate, just when the evening was about to wind down—I'd already said "hello" to a couple of parents who had arrived to round up their kids— Doreen came running across the dance floor with a look of real panic on her face.

Annie said, "What's the matter?"

"There's trouble," she said.

I sat up a bit. "What sort of trouble?"

"Mr. Creighton is trying to kick some kids out who don't belong here, and one of them is refusing to leave."

Annie looked hard at me and I said, "What?"

"You don't have to go over there."

"Of course I do."

"He's a big kid," Doreen said. "I mean really big."

"Why doesn't somebody call the police and . . ." Annie didn't finish. Doreen broke in with, "Mr. Creighton is an old man. He's been sweating up there playing guitar all night, he'll really get hurt if he gets into anything with this guy. Normally I'd go to Professor Bible, but he's not here."

"You're sure the fellow isn't one of ours?" I asked. "A cousin maybe? Or a big brother?"

"No. He's a friend of somebody here. I know that. He knows somebody here."

"Well," I said. "Can't you find out who that is, and have them take care of it?"

"It's happening now," Doreen said.

"I've never been very good in a crisis," I said. "I tend to think the worst and either panic or fly off the edge and start looking for a weapon."

Doreen was very worried. I saw her decide not to rely on me, and so of course that propelled me to my feet. "Oh, all right, I'll go over there."

"Stay here!" Annie said. "What do you think you can do?" But I was already moving away. I walked through the mingling kids to the entrance. There in the doorway stood Mr. Creighton, his fists curled tightly next to his pants legs, staring up at a huge kid in a Coca-Cola delivery uniform. The kid leaned toward him, a deeply resentful and threatening scowl on his face. As I approached, I heard Mr. Creighton saying, over and over, "Are you going to leave? Are you going to leave? Are you going to leave?" and the kid stood there, his fists also coiled. The muscles in his jaw rippled and his chest heaved, but he said nothing. I really believe I got there in the last five seconds before one of them would throw the first punch. It was that tense, and that close. I realized Doreen was right behind me, and perhaps it was the arrival of reinforcements that caused what followed, but it was astonishing, even to me. The big kid looked at me when I stepped into their range, and when I was close enough for him to hear me, I said, "Hey, what do you say you and I go out front here and smoke a cigarette before the police get here and cause all kinds of trouble."

I don't know what made me say it—except that it seemed a really appealing idea to me then; after all, it would get me out of harm's way. If the kid refused to go, that's what I was going to do: get out of there and smoke a cigarette. But it worked. The kid looked down at me, at the pack of cigarettes I'd produced, and said, "Okay," real softly, and both of us strode out to the front of the building and lit up. He stood there, smoking his cigarette, getting his dignity back, and I chatted with him about how fine a cigarette is after any kind of exertion or trouble.

Annie told me later that Mr. Creighton came back to the table where we had been sitting, singing my praises. "Never saw anything like that in my life," he said. "Your husband just stepped up to this big bully, whispered something to him, and just like that the guy turned around and walked out with him. It was a fair miracle." She didn't bother to tell him that I wasn't her husband. (And when she told me that, I was unreasonably glad. Something about her willingness to have people think we were married made me proud.)

Doreen said to me the next day, "And you said you're no good in a crisis."

"I'm not," I said. "That wasn't a crisis."

"Yes it was."

"No, it was about to become one. When either one of those guys throws the first punch, you got the crisis. And that's when you'd find it really hard to find my ass."

She laughed, but I don't think I convinced her.

26

Visits with Bible

THE REMAINDER OF that first year and most of the summer that
followed was completely taken up with Professor Bible. His condition
worsened for a time—I thought he'd have to spend the rest of his life
in the hospital—but eventually he came out and went home, and
that's when I started my regular visits. It was not too difficult to stop
by and see him because, as it turned out, his apartment complex was
only a few blocks up the street from the school. I could stop by after
classes on the way home. The building he lived in was an old, red
brick, square, flat-roofed structure just off the highway that ran in
front of the school. It looked like a sort of guardhouse compared to
the more modern buildings that crowded the slopes behind it.

I continued to learn from him. I was his only student, and he
couldn't stand not teaching, so eventually, I ended up reading the books
and articles he suggested, and bringing him books to discuss that he
thought I might learn from. (I would never have read Alexis de
Tocqueville or Adam Smith or John Kenneth Galbraith if not for

Professor Bible.) I also brought him cigarettes occasionally and we'd sit in his den smoking and sipping brandy while he soaked his foot. He did not lose his toe; only a small portion of it, and what was left slowly began to heal. Our conversations ran on and on sometimes, and most of it cannot be recaptured—even if I wanted to. It was like any class: a haze of lectures, conversations, and debates over a period of time that slips away so quickly you can't believe it is comprised of anything so long as a semester. The truth is I really was in a sort of class, Bible's class, all by myself until the end of my first teaching year, and nearly all of that summer.

Bible was in love with America. The idea of it moved him. "It's the most exquisite idea human beings ever dreamed up," he said to me once. "Liberty. A government founded on the notion that you—you, yourself—have an unalienable right to be happy; to seek your own happiness. Think of it."

"It's amazing," I said.

"Is it any wonder that every single country on earth is represented here?"

"Represented?"

"America has attracted people from every culture, every country on earth."

"Maybe some were captured and forced to come."

"Did you know that American English contains more words than any other single language? You know why? Because every language on earth is represented in English. Every culture on earth has sent its poor and its disadvantaged and they have brought their language with them and given us words and words and words."

I played devil's advocate, just to get him excited; to get him talking about anything but the future. "Wasn't all that immigration just cheap labor?" I asked. "All those slaves in the beginning, and then the poor immigrants who came later, they went into the factories and worked on the railroads and died in sweat and squalor so the earlier English, German, and Dutch settlers could prosper, right?"

"You are way too cynical for a man so young," he said. He was smiling, and I had the impertinence to think he rather enjoyed my gentle resistance to his idealistic notions. Still, he really believed everything he said to me, and the sad truth is frequently I didn't believe much of anything that I said to him. A lot of the time I just took the opposite tack because it challenged him, got him going, and also—to tell the truth—it made him more eloquent and interesting to listen to.

Here's the only detail that I remember vividly—besides the foot and the bath, the details of which I have already failed to spare you. Anyway, I don't know if this is important or not but as you will see there's a good reason that it sticks in my memory. This happened near the end of the school year. I was overcome with papers to grade and with the new lesson plans I was creating to show to Mrs. Creighton. I was in a hurry, so when I got to Bible's place all I wanted to do was give him a few cigarettes, chat for a bit about the weather, and then be on my way. We had been talking about de Tocqueville at our last visit, his essay on America, and Bible brought it up again. In fact, he held the book in his lap. I don't remember what he said; something about "the dream," and then suddenly he got misty-eyed and turned away from me.

I sat in a hard chair across from him. He was in a large cushiony recliner, and in front of him was a round blue basin full of salt water in which he bathed his foot. One pant leg was rolled up to his knee. I looked up when I noticed that he had fallen silent, and then I saw the light reflected off the tears welling in his eyes.

"You okay?" I said.

He nodded, but I could see he wasn't. It's possible he wanted me to ask him again if he was okay.

Then he said, "This was such a great idea."

"What?" I thought he might have been referring to the idea that I visit him once or twice a week, but I wasn't sure.

He pointed to the book. "America. The whole notion that peasants and rubes could govern themselves."

"Is that what we're doing?" I said. "Our President is a former actor . . ."

He picked up the book, flipped through the pages with his gray fingers, and when he came to a place he had marked by folding the top edge down, he said, "Listen to this." He cleared his throat, got better control of his emotions. "This was written in the 1830s. De Tocqueville's talking about his realization that in fact—though he doubted it at first—democracy in America works. He says 'the middle class can govern a state.' Then he says, 'Despite their small passions, their incomplete education, their vulgar habits, they can obviously provide a practical sort of intelligence and that turns out to be enough.'"

This time I had nothing to say. I was in a hurry. But I did wonder silently, what could possibly be construed as a middle class in mid-nineteenth-century America? If I'd wanted to argue with him, I would have said something about an entire population of people—several populations of people—left out of the whole thing: Indians, Chinese, and Blacks, probably most of the immigrants who came to this country before the civil war, and most who came after.

"You see what I mean?" Bible wanted to know.

"I do," I lied.

"Until this country came on the scene, the world was ruled by simple inheritance and force; by nothing but accidents of birth, or brute strength and mostly passion—since reason requires thought and less action, and action is the main component of power and force. But Americans are all about action, Ben. Do you see how important and ironic this idea of self-governance based on reason is?"

I didn't know what he wanted me to do. Sometimes I think he liked it when I argued with him. But I was in a hurry, so this time I only said, "I see."

It got quiet for what seemed like a long time, and then I tried to change the subject. "You should see George these days. He's started working out with weights. I think he's more confident."

"Really." He lifted his foot carefully out of the bath and wrapped it in a clean towel. He let it rest on the floor next to the basin of water. I carried the basin to the sink, emptied it and refilled it with warm water and salt. While I was doing this, I kept talking over my shoulder about George. "He's started a sort of growth spurt, I think. He may be a little taller than he was the last time you saw him. I bet his bones are killing him."

"His bones?"

"All that fast growth. Annie says that's got to hurt."

I came back to where Bible was sitting and put the basin of water in front of him. Then he unwrapped his foot, lifted his leg a bit and lowered the foot down into the water. "Not too hot is it?" I asked.

Alexis de Tocqueville was still in Bible's hands; it was still open to the page he had been reading to me. I looked at it, and realized in some ways I was watching the book the way a man watches a sleeping baby, for fear it will wake up and start crying. I wanted Bible to put the book down.

"Listen to this," he said.

"Do we have to?"

This seemed to take him back. He cleared his throat. "I'm sorry," he almost whispered. "I thought you were interested in this."

"I am. But I can't take the time today. I mean I don't—I have to get going and I don't want to get into an involved discussion of . . ." I didn't finish the sentence. He got misty-eyed again. "I'm sorry," I said.

"It's not you," he said. "It's just that—you see it's just that I am always very moved by human folly and all attempts to thwart and avert it."

"Really."

"It is the story of the rise of goodness in the world."

I made a last attempt to change the subject. "Well, you talk about rising in the world, George is doing very well. Someday he will be taller than his old man and if he keeps working out he'll fill out nicely. I hope he keeps it up with the weights."

"Do you know what?" Bible said.

I looked up at him.

"I've been thinking about my time in this world. The time left to me . . ."

There was, of course, no adequate response to that. Often in these visits he would begin to talk about the end of his life, and I would listen simply because I didn't know how to get him off of it. In truth, he was not very wise about his own life—or about life in general. For all his knowledge of history and the world, he could get pretty dreamy and romantic when he talked about the meaning of existence. Not that I know anything about it one way or the other, but I do know it doesn't have a lot to do with any person. He would go on about the world as if it was this momentous and enlightening place; as if it was truly the miraculous garden of each man's providence, the place where life teaches its eternal lessons. "We are temporary witnesses to God's grandeur," he'd say, "and in the end we will have to say what we have seen, and how we have added to it or changed it."

I think of the world as this temporary patch of blue and green in a frozen, empty, almost lightless universe. In my soul I believe I have not got a soul, and neither does anybody else. I am a conscious creature, driven by mitochondria to go on eating and surviving so the mitochondria will survive, not so I will. I don't matter. Nobody else matters.

You know where morality comes from? Not from God, or Allah, or Buddha or Marduk, or any other imagined deity. It comes from the simple human ability to imagine and perceive the future. That skill led to the compulsion to choose; to a little thing called human will. If we were driven by instinct alone, we would not have developed this idea of "good" and "evil." Animals don't have it. You don't see animals writing legal opinions or arguing with each other about goodness or beauty, or right or wrong. If animals could talk, they wouldn't have anything to say except "gimme gimme" and "stop that." Every now and then, one might say, "Goddamn that itches." Or, "Get away from me." But they would have nothing whatever to say about goodness or evil, unless you gave them consciousness of the future and the capacity to choose their own behavior. Once we got those things—a great gift and a great curse, if you ask me—we were able to "choose" a thing and then decide if it was "good" or not. We crawled into our morality; slowly but surely we stood up and worked toward what we believed would keep us standing. From that, and from that alone, came this notion of good and evil, right and wrong. The world has no idea what we're doing here, anymore than a large dog has any idea what the fleas are up to in its fur.

And in the beginning of our discussions, I would say these things to Bible in the secret—maybe not so secret—hope that he would talk me into his view of things; that he might induce me to believe that life really did have meaning. I always wanted it to have meaning. And he was always trying to convince me, but he never did, and I soon tired of his oddly provincial ideas about God and Man and the universe. He was too educated for those beliefs, frankly. That's what I believed. How could an educated man, a man who knew as much as he knew, still believe in the ancient fairy tales about God and heaven? How could he believe he would survive his own death and then get to mourn his own loss? When you're gone, you're gone.

At any rate, that day when he said again that he had been thinking about "his time in the world" I knew where he was headed. I said, "You're not going to die from this." I had told him that many times in the past.

"I know," he said. "But you will admit that I'm near the end of things."

"No, I won't admit it." I stood up and looked at my watch.

211

He was sitting back in his chair, and his white shin and calf seemed to reflect the dim light that came through the windows. His foot looked stony and immense in the gray water. When he saw me look at my watch, he got this hurt look on his face. "You got another cigarette?" he said.

I gave him one and he lit it. I stood there, my arms folded across my chest.

"You're so young," he said, picking at his lips as if a bit of tobacco had gotten stuck there.

"I really do have to get going," I said.

"So young." He was sort of wistful now.

I said, "You ever been married?"

"Once, long ago."

I waited but he didn't go on so I said, "What happened?"

He shrugged. "Divorce."

"I'm sorry to hear it."

"We did nothing but argue." There was no affection or melancholy in his voice. He may as well have been talking about a Buick he had sold years ago.

"How long ago were you married?"

"You mean when did I do it, or when did it end?"

"Both."

"I got married right out of law school, and divorced six years later, when I started teaching."

"You never wanted children?"

"Oh, I had so many every year teaching. In the fall they come back, Ben. Remember? I always had children."

It was quiet for a long time, then I said, "You went to law school?"

"Yes I did."

"Were you a lawyer?"

"I was."

"That's what I want to do."

"Really." He shook his head slowly, the ruddiness in his face seeming to increase a bit. I was certain he was getting ready to say something else, but he didn't. He looked out the window and sighed. Then he turned back to me and said, "The law wasn't a lot of fun, you know? Not for me. It was hard work and I hated it." He said nothing to advise me one way or the other about it—which was definitely not his attitude toward teaching, or my life in it.

"You don't think I should be a lawyer?"

"I believe you should do what makes you happy. You should especially do that. Then, when you're on the threshold—when you're getting ready to leave this life and go on to the next . . ."

"You're not getting ready to leave this life."

He shook his head, but he was smiling.

"Sometimes I wonder how you can think what you think," I said.

"About what?"

"God and all that nonsense about an afterlife, and . . . you know." Feeling superior to somebody so much older than I was felt really creepy, as though I was confronting God and letting him know exactly how I felt about cancer and cobras. "I'm sorry."

"I shouldn't be afraid to die," he said quietly, almost as if he was talking to himself. "I've been dead before. We've all been dead before. It wasn't so bad."

"I thought you were going to heaven."

"I hope I am. I pray for it every day. I was trying to console you."

"I'm fine."

"I know you think that," he said. "But it's not the afterlife that I'm worried about with you."

"What are you worried about with me?" I asked, and immediately regretted it.

"This won't take a lot of time," he said, smiling.

I really did have to get going, and I realized my interest had faded with the smile. I was afraid this was going to be an evangelical conversation, and I hated having to listen to one of those for five minutes so I said, "Can it wait until Friday?"

"You know," he said. "Life is a misleading tramp of a girl, and she seduces you for all the wrong things."

"Friday, then?" I said, getting up. "I really should . . ."

"Listen here," he said. "We are always tricked by life—I want you to understand what I mean by this."

I stood there in front of him, waiting.

"You've got to understand it. I'm not talking about the afterlife. That's one thing. I'm talking about life. Right now."

"Okay," I said. "But I'm kind of in a hurry."

He looked hurt—as if I had ridiculed something he was proud of—so I sat down again and settled myself.

He said, "Human beings carry the future, Ben. They have it in themselves as they go into it. They cast out and go on through the days with something in mind up there in the future."

"I know," I said. "It's what I've been saying to you . . ."

"It's where we're going; what we want; a place, maybe, or a condition; a way of being, even—a desire for knowledge or position, or simply more comfort; more time to play. Always something in the future, something up there in front—striving for, or lazily heading toward—it's there, for everyone. And then we get to a certain age—it happened to me with this infection, in my midsixties—but perhaps others go on a little longer before it happens to them. You get there, Ben. You arrive."

I struggled mightily against a yawn beginning to stretch and awaken in the back of my throat. He looked right at me, and waited for me to say something. I watched him reach over and snuff the cigarette out in an ashtray. He had barely puffed on it. Finally, I said, "You've arrived then?"

He made a slight chop through the air with his hand, for emphasis. "Yes," he said. "I have. And do you know what?"

I shook my head.

"It's, nowhere, Ben. I've arrived finally—I'm in my future and it's nowhere. I realize now, only now when it is too late, what I should have been doing all those years of getting here: I should have been paying attention to all those days that I let pass, one right after the other, on my way here. All those days I paid almost no attention to, because they were not exactly right, or because it wasn't ready to be summer, or fall, or a perfect day; all those non-perfect days that I rode down to the last hour, not ready to enjoy them because I was on my way here." He was almost laughing, but I could see again the slight mist in his eyes. "It's nowhere. Bloody nowhere. When your future runs out, and it shrinks to a small fraction of all the time you've lived, it hits you then—by God, it hits you then—well here I am, and I've got no place to go. And really, no place I want to go. This is it. And it's nowhere."

I was as silent as I could be. I think I might have been holding my breath.

"Doesn't that make you sad?"

"Yes it does." I believed he was done too, but I hated that he was thinking like that. It would do him no good; it meant a loss of the one thing he needed to keep taking his shots and working to get better: hope. And anyway, no one really knows if they are done in life, right? He might find other uses for his talents; he was smart and charming and highly educated. He would not end up a crossing guard or tele-marketer. Still, a person has to eat so the goddamn mitochondria can go on.

It was quiet for too long, then like an idiot I said, "Well," letting breath out with it, as though we'd been chatting about football and it was time to go. I tried to recover from it. "You've done wonderful things with your students, though. You didn't waste your time." My voice shook. "You didn't waste your time."

He nodded, half-smiling at me. Then he said, "Remember this, Ben. Remember it. Life's not about getting anywhere; it's about being somewhere, all the time. Figure out where you are and be there, Ben.

Be there." He clasped his hands across his stomach and turned to stare out the window. "Thanks for coming to see me today," he said. "If you can find it in your heart to come back I would be grateful. Every day, I thank God for you. I hope you know that."

"I do," I said. Then I told him I'd see him in a few days and turned to leave. I looked back his way when I got to the front door but he was still gazing out the window.

I tried to open and close the door as silently as I could. You'd have thought I'd just put Professor Bible down for a nap.

27

The Whips and Scorns of Time

AFTER THAT DAY, thinking about what Bible said to me, it was pretty goddamn awful for a while being anywhere. The school year was over by then, and what kept going through my mind was this stifling, churning passage of time. Bible at the end of things, Mr. and Mrs. Creighton approaching it, the faculty, including me, in the middle, and our students—all these young faces—embarking on their own passages—toward what? Professor Bible did what he wanted in life. And still there he was at the end of it with nothing. Nothing. I couldn't get his sad visage out of my mind. He was always there, sitting in that beveled shaft of sunlight, staring out his window, saying, "I'm there, Ben, and it's nowhere."

The mind is a damned nuisance and cruel jokester sometimes. As I'm sure I said earlier, I admired Professor Bible. I think he was a truly good human being—a person I cherished and looked up to, and for good reason. I admired his vast knowledge, his skill with people and his work with students. As I told Annie many times, I wanted to be the kind of teacher he was. But I was absolutely terrified I would "end up" like him. I thought about that, and almost nothing else, and then one day it hit me like an express train what I was really afraid of: I was terrified that I would live. I would get to be Bible's age and be conscious of the end of whatever life I had led; of whatever work I chose. How do you deal with that kind of fear? When I told Annie about it, and how my mind would suddenly give me the grand finale of my life, she told me, again, that I was sick.

"What, you've never had your mind give you something like that against your will?" I asked.

"I just did, when you said it."

"Well?"

"But my mind didn't conjure it. Jesus."

We were walking on a beautiful spring morning, down to the end of our street to get coffee. There was a small, fragrant bakery there, on the corner that we discovered the second day it opened. We'd leave our apartment before anybody was ready for work—the sun just beginning to bleed over the horizon, in perfect red weather on clear days—and only the joggers and newspaper delivery boys were out and about. It was our time together, before she went her way and I went mine, and it was usually wonderful and pleasant sipping coffee with her and talking about what we were going to be up to in the coming day. We got to the corner on this particular morning when she called me sick and then we had to stand there, waiting for the traffic to thin out so we could cross. My feelings were hurt but I didn't want to let on.

"I don't conjure it on purpose," I said. "My mind gives me those things."

"It's sick."

"Stop calling me sick."

"Well it is."

"You never have thoughts that come to you unbidden."

"Unbidden?"

"You know what I mean."

She saw an opening and began crossing the street and I followed. Inside the bakery, after we got our coffee and a piece of vanilla pound cake, and we had seated ourselves, she said, "I've never imagined myself old and used up, I can tell you that."

"Why not? How do you keep from thinking about it? Do you just forget that you're temporary?"

"Really." She looked away.

"Have you ever imagined dying?"

"No."

"Sometimes, when I sleep very deeply, without dreaming, it's like getting a little taste of death, and I wake up and say to myself, 'That wasn't so bad.'"

"Good lord."

"You've never considered what it would be like to die?"

"No."

"Have you ever had a close call? Certainly you've had a close . . ."

"Yes, and what I did after was laugh. Really hard."

"Everybody laughs. Nervously maybe, but they laugh. But what about after. You ever thought about it after?"

She sipped her coffee, staring at me now. Then she said, "Are you serious?"

"I'd just like to know."

"Let's talk about something else."

I said nothing. We didn't talk for a while, then she said, low and under her breath, "You're so morbid."

"I prefer to think of myself as a realist."

"An obsessed realist."

It wasn't an obsession. I mean I didn't very often picture myself lying in a casket, or strapped to a gurney with plastic running out of every opening in my face, but still—everything I did was now somehow tinged with the knowledge of the dark; what Bible did to me, really, was warn me not to be trying to get anywhere. "Just be where you are," he said.

I guess I didn't know how to do that. I wanted hope for the future back, that's what I wanted. I tried to explain that to Annie but she didn't want to hear anymore about it.

"Why don't you shut up about that," she said finally.

She could tell it hurt me, but when she reached for my hand, I withdrew it. I had nothing more to say to her and I wanted her to know it. The last thing I said to her that morning was: "You just don't understand."

I stopped going over to Bible's so regularly sometime near the end of that summer. One Thursday in August, I went down the street and had coffee with Annie, and then she and I played a little tennis. I came back to the apartment, took a cool shower to wash the sweat off, and then instead of driving down to Bible's place, I decided to take a nap. I think I was planning on stopping by later that day, but I slept way too late, and then it was dinner time so I just didn't go. I thought about calling him, but I was afraid he wasn't close to the phone and he'd have to get up and limp to where he could answer it. That's what went through my mind anyway. His foot was getting much better, though. He'd made good progress during the time of my regular visits.

He didn't call me, and naturally I thought that meant he didn't need me. So Monday came around and then Wednesday and then another Thursday. I didn't show up for two weeks and still he didn't call me. When I finally went back there he acted just as though I hadn't missed a visit. He was always glad to see me.

I thought I was free of the responsibility of my visits. Maybe even, in a way, free of him. I realized, of course, that I didn't really wish to be free of him—and even if I did, it wasn't an important wish. I mean, I did miss him in the spaces when I didn't go by there. He was nice to know. If it wasn't for the talk of endings and all, I might have enjoyed visiting him a lot more often than I did. Our conversations were, as I said, enthralling and mostly entertaining. I learned more than I can say, to tell the truth.

Sometimes he called me "Lad." I guess I liked that, too.

28

In the Fall They Come Back

THE SUMMER ENDED, and oddly enough I was not too unhappy about it. I had another year of teaching in front of me and I felt a bit more confident about it. I knew I wouldn't be getting any kind of raise, and I knew I might someday decide to try something else—maybe even further graduate study. I didn't want to feel settled into anything. I'd find a profession—there was no doubt about that in my mind at all. I just wasn't ready for more graduate work and I couldn't think of anything that I'd rather do than teaching. Anyway, I came to see higher education as a kind of prison of the mind and the teachers were the guards. I realized I'd rather remain a guard for another year before once again becoming an inmate. I know that sounds dramatic and a little prosaic, but that's how I felt.

The second year was when Leslie Warren came to me. She was a senior, *for the last time* according to Mrs. Creighton, and she would be in my English class. We were at the first faculty meeting that

September, the week before Labor Day, and when she announced that Leslie Warren was coming back everybody groaned. Even Doreen looked at me and rolled her eyes.

But I kept my mouth shut. I listened to the other items on the agenda, the announcements of new students and important dates, and when the meeting was over I went to Doreen's room and asked her about it.

"You'll see," she said.

"Did you have trouble with her last year?"

"Not so much."

"I know her a little bit," I said. "I don't think she is so bad."

"Well then. You'll see."

"I'll see what?"

With mock exasperation she said, "Oh not now, Benjamin."

The best thing about the second year was I didn't have to drive a bus anymore. Mr. Creighton finally decided to sell all four of them, which would compensate for the small loss of enrollment in the first year. He was certain folks would find a way to get their children to the school and he just didn't want to do the maintenance any longer. I had an extra hour and half of sleep in the mornings, and I got home an hour earlier in the afternoon.

The seniors were gone, but I still had George to deal with—a slightly bigger and more capable George—and Mark Talbot, Happy Bell, and Jaime and a few others. Mrs. Creighton came to believe that Suzanne Rule was ready to actually sit in a class, so she put her in my senior English class. I wouldn't have minded very much except Suzanne required that a guardian angel accompany her, and that angel was, of course, Mrs. Creighton. For every one of those classes—at least in the beginning of that year—Suzanne crouched in next to Mrs. Creighton, bent so low she looked like one of the dogs. She and Mrs. Creighton were always early, and Suzanne would sit in a desk in the corner that faced the center of the room, so that her side was to me, and Mrs. Creighton would sit in front of her, the chair facing me, which made it easier for her to write notes on Suzanne's pad. (She also whispered to Suzanne a lot, which really irritated me.)

She tried to write down everything I said, and of course I had to numbingly and trippingly stick to the fake lesson plan that I'd drawn up for the class over the summer. It was the most excruciating experience trying to follow my "plan." We had classes on prepositions, and commas, and subjects and predicates, and verbs, adverbs and adjectives, and even gerunds. (Gerunds!!! Most of those terms sound like some sort of weird anomaly in one's reproductive organs. "I'm sorry Mr. and Mrs. Kettlewell, but your gerunds are totally adverbial and you're suffering from a dangling participle. It doesn't look like you will be able to conjugate children.") And I hated having Mrs. Creighton there to observe everything I tried to do. I'm pretty sure the kids hated it too. One day, in an early class, Mark Talbot actually raised his hand and asked what Mrs. Creighton was doing there.

"She's just visiting."

"Are you in some kind of trouble?" he asked.

"No, of course not."

"Pay attention to your studies young man," Mrs. Creighton said. Suzanne Rule did not budge. She sat staring at the surface of her desk and the yellow pad Mrs. Creighton made notes on. With her head down and her scraggly red hair dangling, I could not even make out the slightest feature of her face, and like I said, I don't think anyone—except a few of the boys last year—had ever seen her eyes.

Around the second or third week of school Doreen and I stepped outside my classroom for a cigarette. Just as we got outside, Leslie drove her car into the driveway and behind the building. We were standing in the smoking area where the early students normally gathered, but on this morning each student seemed to make the awkward decision not to join the two of us. They began to gather a little way down the embankment toward the basketball court. It was a self-imposed aristocracy, teachers high on the hill looking down on the students, who also watched Leslie cross the parking lot. She stopped under the big tree on the other side of the building, just on the edge of my sight. I wanted to move to the outer corner so I could see her better, but I resisted it. Doreen lit my cigarette for me. We stood there, in the shade, watching Leslie Warren.

Then Doreen said, "Any trouble from the bitch yet?"

"No," I said. "Now you're ready to talk about her?"

"Oh yeah. I'll talk about her." We had some time before the beginning of classes for the day. Doreen wore her penny loafers, white jeans, a blue, puffy blouse and a thin black belt. Her hair was damp and the splotches of red acne along her jaw looked almost like a birthmark. "She thinks she's so beautiful."

"She is," I said. "She really is a beautiful young girl." No one could help but notice her beauty—and I'm sure if you saw her it wouldn't be long before you remarked on it either. It gave me a kind of exquisite pleasure just to look at her. I swear to you this was not sexual; there was no desire in it. As I've said before, this was pure aesthetics. It simply provided a kind of intellectual delight to look upon something so perfectly rendered, so beautifully designed. She had perfect light brown skin, a lovely, bright smile, and sparkling eyes that froze in your mind like the memory of certitude and permanence. "So why should I watch out for her?"

"She's a pain in the ass," Doreen said. "And real dangerous. You'll see."

"Dangerous?"

"She can ruin a career."

I laughed.

"I'm not kidding. She knows how she looks, and she knows men, too."

"I'll be on my guard."

Doreen looked up at me gravely. "You can make light of it. But you just watch yourself with her."

"It's hard to think of this place as . . ."

"As what?"

"A career."

"Well, aren't we proud."

"To tell you the truth, lately it's hard to think of anything in my future, much less a career."

"What do you mean by that?"

"Nothing," I said. "I'm just feeling fully mortal today."

"Maybe you should quit smoking."

"Isn't it possible Miss Warren will behave this year? It's her last chance, right?"

"Oh, she'll get another chance. People who look like that always do."

A cool breeze brushed the smoke away from my face. "Tell me about her."

"She is a troublemaker in and out of class."

"Well," I said, "she hasn't done anything wrong yet. We're in the third week and she's been quiet and listened carefully."

"You've got Mrs. Creighton in there with you. Wait until she's gone."

"Maybe it's too early to vouch for Leslie in my class, but I've seen her out of class, and she's been just fine. She was a big help to me with George and the party and all. Was she that bad in your class?"

"I couldn't complete a sentence. She's got a dirty mouth, too."

We were quiet for a while, then I said, "It surprises me to hear you, of all people, talking so badly of her."

"Why 'me of all people?' "

"Well, you're a bit of a rebel yourself, right?" I hoped this didn't offend her, since we'd never talked about it and I was reading her manner of dress, her demeanor, and her general carriage—but I could see she was pleased. I think it's safe to say that most people like to be called a rebel. At least those of us who are young do.

"She's not just a rebel. She's a criminal."

"A criminal. What crime has she committed?"

"I know she's into drugs."

"How do you know it?"

"I hear the kids talking."

"How do they know it?"

She said nothing.

"I want Leslie to talk in my class."

"Really."

"I want to encourage discussion."

"Believe me," she said, "it won't be discussion."

"They *can* have ideas," I said. "They just don't seem to know anything. Do you have Jaime Nichols in your class?"

"The little one? Dark hair, kind of a deep voice?"

"That's her. When I first met her, she didn't know who Adolf Hitler was. Now she knows. I'm proud of that."

"Yes, we've all heard of your Adolf Hitler project."

"That's not what I called it."

She leaned back, frowning as though she was disgusted by something on my face. But then she said, "I have to say, Jaime's a very good student now." We were quiet for a minute. I wanted her to credit me with the blossoming of Jaime Nichols. I wanted credit without asking for it, but if it came down to it, I wasn't above pointing it out again. Then she said, "You don't really believe she didn't know who Hitler was, do you?"

"Of course."

She smirked. "Really."

"What?"

"Nothing."

"No. What?"

"She was just playing you and you fell for it."

"She doesn't strike me as the sort to play games like that."

"Why not?"

"She's so—well, she's so small and mousy."

Doreen laughed. "How could she exist for one hour in this culture—does she watch TV? Listen to the radio? Has she been living in some forest, in a bubble—how could she live in this culture without . . ."

"I was amazed, too."

"She already knew who Hitler was. She was just giving you the business. She's just as much a wiseass as any of these kids."

I smoked quietly for a while, watching the group of students down the hill increase. I was certain that Jaime was sincere in her ignorance, but I realized that saying that to Doreen could be taken as a sort of indictment of her teaching, not to mention Professor Bible's. Suddenly I was thinking of Bible again. I hadn't seen him for nearly a month, and I wondered how he was doing. I looked at Doreen and when her eyes met mine I almost said something to her about how he had made me feel; about the loss of any longing for the future. But she looked away and said nothing.

I was always planning on stopping in to see Bible again. He was never far from my mind, but like I said, I had wandered away from the regular routine and it was hard to get back.

"Here comes the mute," Doreen said, and she flipped her cigarette into the grass.

A blue Chevrolet Nova came up the drive very slowly. Sitting in the front passenger seat, her shadow bent over and frozen, was Suzanne Rule. A large, heavyset woman, wearing a purple shirt with large yellow flowers, baggy yellow pants, and white boat shoes, got out of the car and came around to Suzanne's side and opened the door. When Suzanne leaned over to get out of the car, she stayed that way. She did not say anything to the woman in the baggy pants, but she let her hand touch the side of her leg as she passed. The woman closed the door, got back in the car and waited until Suzanne had gone into the building—which did not take long, because Suzanne almost ran to the door, still bent over and curled like a question mark.

"You know her story?" I asked.

"I've heard it, but who really knows?" Doreen shook her head. "She always runs in like that. When she rode my bus she'd jump down and scoot like she'd stolen something; like she's got to go to the bathroom really bad."

"How does she learn anything?"

Doreen laughed. "You know what? She gets straight As. She could probably recite the Constitution."

"She ever have to do that?"

"What do you mean?"

"Did Bible ever ask them to memorize anything?"

"No. Of course not. What could they learn from that?"

"Mrs. Creighton wants me to have my students memorize poems."

"But that's a good thing, isn't it?"

"You know Bible always said the same thing, but I think it's crazy."

She looked at me. I'd known her for a full year, and she knew that Bible had taught me everything I ever learned about teaching, so it was an awkward moment—I felt as though I'd spoken rudely about one of her parents. I said, "I just mean you guys must know something I don't know. I don't see the value of rote memory for much of anything except the multiplication tables, valences, and the law of cosines."

We breathed in the perfect September air for a while, saying nothing. Finally Doreen said, "You really must want to teach these kids something."

"I think they have to want to learn, too." I threw my cigarette into a rubbish can filled with sand next to the door.

"Really," she said. "They wear some folks down over time, but if you really believe in school . . ."

Whenever she talked like this, I realized school was a belief for her, as it was for Bible and probably Mr. and Mrs. Creighton; a belief like Christianity or Buddhism. She was only a hypocrite about smoking. Everything else was entirely moral and, in its own way, beautiful. "What we do," she went on, "we are called to do by this profession. Nobody gets into this business for the money."

"Tell me about it," I said.

"I spent my first two years in the public school system. Bloody drug-recruiting centers for Christ's sake."

"Some of these kids are into the same things."

"I'm just trying to warn you," she said. "If something happens to your idealism because of Leslie Warren, I don't know if . . ."

"I'm not an idealist," I said. "I'm not even really a teacher. Sometimes I think this is all just temporary."

"So you've said." This was a statement. Her face seemed on the verge of a kind of knowing smile.

"I do like some things about it."

We were quiet again for a moment. Then she said, "Hell, who would ever want to do this for the little bit of money we make?"

"You got me."

"So what are you doing here?"

"I don't really know," I told her. "I felt very lucky to get this job. Most times I try to remember that."

"You know, it's probably a good thing we don't make a lot of money. I wouldn't want to work with anybody who got into this business for the money."

"Nor would I."

"You're so young," she said.

"I'm not that young."

"Wait until you turn thirty, then talk about ambition and what's temporary."

"You're thirty years old?"

"Thirty-five." She seemed proud of it.

"I had no idea you were that old."

She only stared at me, shaking her head. Leslie Warren had moved out of sight on the other side of the building. I really wasn't worried about her. I figured we already had a pretty good relationship.

29

Adventures in Literature

DAYS, THEN WEEKS went by. As I expected, Leslie Warren was perfectly fine. She sat at her desk, quietly; she worked when I asked everybody to work. She wrote entries in her journal about clothes and actresses and movies and the places she had traveled. She was always impeccably dressed—every day she looked like a fashion model. I said a few things in class that made her laugh, and when I did I counted it as a major triumph.

Eventually, Mrs. Creighton felt comfortable leaving Suzanne alone in the room with me. She took her own notes, but kept her chair turned to the side, so all I saw of her was the red hair hanging down by her face.

One day, about a week after Mrs. Creighton stopped attending, Leslie got up in the middle of class and started for the door.

"Leslie, where are you going?" I asked.

"I'm going out to have a cigarette."

"Wait until break time."

"I want one now." She had a reasonable tone. She was explaining to me.

"I'd like one myself," I said. "But let's wait until class is over. It's only another twenty minutes."

She frowned. I thought she was going to stamp her foot, but she only bent at the knee a bit, and then stood flat-footed again. "But I want one now," she whined.

"But class is not over. I've not finished."

There was a long silence. She extended her lower lip until she looked like a five-year-old, pouting. Her head tilted slightly downward, her eyes gazing at me under those dark, ill-tempered brows, she said, "Can't I just go have one now?"

Everyone was watching her.

"Leslie," I said. "I wish you wouldn't."

She stood there for a moment, considering, then she took her seat. No further argument, and very limited petulance, or attitude. I wished Doreen had been there to see it.

Things were going well enough in all of my classes each day, and I had plenty of time to finalize and present my lesson plans to Mrs. Creighton. She frowned when she saw I was bent on repeating my holocaust project with the juniors and seniors, but she said nothing. I showed different films this time, since most of my students had been with me the year before. I still wanted films that showed the bodies, the bulldozers, the long lines of naked men, women, and children, but I also gave them a good drama or two about the struggle to conquer such evil in the world. They saw *Days of Glory* with Gregory Peck, and *Battle Cry* with Van Heflin and Aldo Ray.

I typed up the numbers for each class. In bold type I wrote: *Of the millions of Jews deported from occupied countries, almost no one over fifty or under twelve was allowed to live.* I showed them pictures of the bodies, the survivors, the ovens, the roving gas trucks, the SS firing squads, and the killing ditches. "This," I said, "was Hitler." It didn't take long, but they all knew. After each film or handout, I had them write in their journals. I didn't read the journals too closely, right away—I scanned rather cursorily, just to get the flavor of them. I planned on a lot of rewriting for everybody.

I had the seniors fourth period, and every day Leslie Warren was first to arrive. She always came in slowly, watching me; then she'd sit in a chair to my left, her back to the books that lined the sidewall. I had arranged the desks into a U-shaped pattern, down one wall, across the back, and up the other. Behind the back chairs was Suzanne's desk. Most of the seniors would take the time between classes to go outside and smoke cigarettes, but Suzanne Rule always came in next, head down as usual. She'd take her seat. Leslie always smiled over at her and said politely, "Hello." And Suzanne would nod her head a bit; start to raise her hand a little. Some mornings she'd almost look up, but then something would fail in what appeared to be a mechanism in her neck and her head would sort of slump back into position. Leslie did not ever say anything else to her, and it never seemed to bother her that she barely got a response from Suzanne. Then George Meeker would wander in, not paying much attention to anyone. He always sat in a chair in front of the large picture window. He'd nod my way, take his seat and stare out the window.

Except for this awkward beginning to what was my second-to-last class of the day, Leslie Warren was a model of behavior, and Suzanne Rule was—well, you can't really worry overmuch about the behavior of a statue—Suzanne Rule was a model of behavior as well. I could only assume she was hearing what we talked about in class.

I probably should have left things as they were, but one day in late fall, I just had to try to break into the awkward silence that always ensued after Leslie, Suzanne, and George were seated and comfortable.

"Isn't it a lovely morning," I said, very loud. I wanted to be cheerful. The day before I had just returned a huge stack of their papers. Suzanne Rule earned an A with a paper entitled "Monkey

Paw." She described a method of trapping monkeys by putting part of a banana inside a gourd attached to a sturdy rope. The monkey puts his open hand inside the hole to get the banana, but when he forms a fist, he can't get his hand out of the gourd. He's trapped. "It never occurs to him to let go of the banana and open his hand," she wrote. She likened the monkey trap to "the human condition." We are "given life (the banana) and we hold onto it, even when the world turns out to be a small hole." It was pretty good, though a little frightening. The tone of it was humorous, though, so I didn't worry overmuch.

George wrote a paper about how much he enjoyed weightlifting; he said he'd "finally gotten into something [his] dad was proud of." I really believed the beatings had pretty much stopped.

Leslie got a C on her paper. I thought I was being fair. I didn't want to give her a C but it was not much of a paper; in fact it was a little below average—something she clearly dashed off the morning she turned it in. It was one page, and told the story of an Embassy dinner she attended with her father—a "top executive at Exxon" who "traveled the world for the biggest oil company in the world." At the dinner, Ronald Reagan made an appearance and she shook hands with him. When she saw the grade, she sat up straight and glared at me. I thought she was a little shocked that she'd passed the assignment.

At any rate, that morning I felt sort of invincible, and as I said, I wanted to break into the uncomfortable silence. Also, I thought it was time to get beyond the Nazis. But when I said, "Good morning," I got no response. Leslie paged through her loose-leaf notebook, and Suzanne simply stared at her desk. George smiled.

After a long silence, I sat down and waited. I cleared my throat, and when I caught Leslie looking at me, I said, "How are you this fine morning?"

"Do you like being so tall?" she asked.

"Ah." I felt my face begin to take on color. "Well, I'm not really all that tall."

"I heard what you did at Prom last year."

I really did not know what she was talking about at first, so I just stared at her.

"Miss Corrigan raved about you in class. She said you just—oh, what was the word she used. It was just perfect. I've got to think of it . . ."

I didn't want her to go on about it, but I have to say a part of me was glad Doreen had been talking about me, and Leslie thought I was a hero. Wouldn't that please you? "I think I know what you're referring to," I said. "Believe me it was nothing."

"No. Miss Corrigan said you—the guy was a big, mean-looking dude and looked like he was going to kill Mr. Creighton, but you fixed it."

"We just went and had a cigarette."

"Defused! That's it. She said you *defused* the situation."

"Yeah, well."

"Is that what you did?"

"I suppose."

"Why did I get a C on my paper?"

This took me back a bit. She sat there, staring at me, her face expressionless.

"You got a C because it was a C paper. I wrote on it about what you should have done to get a better result. Did you read my notes?"

Nothing could have prepared me for what Leslie said next. Her eyes sort of half-closed and she leaned toward me a bit and in a breathy, lilting voice said, "I bet you fuck real good, don't you."

"Pardon?" I heard her, but I didn't know what else to say.

"I bet you're real good in bed." She let her voice linger on the word *real*.

What would you say in a circumstance like that? I didn't say anything. I mean, Suzanne Rule was sitting right there, listening with her little red ears. George pretended to be reading in his journal, but his eyes moved my way a little then went back to the page he was reading. I looked at the book on my desk—*Adventures in Literature*—and tried to get my mind to recognize other words again. I'd like to say that I was thinking about how sad it is that to sell the greatest ideas and thoughts that ever shimmered through the human brain, educators believe they have to present literature as though it's an amusement park ride. I struggled to keep my eyes from wandering over to Leslie Warren's knees. I could not think of even one word. I didn't remember any ideas; not love, or charity, or mercy, or anything. Seconds crawled by, then Leslie said, "I bet you do it so slow, don't you?" She was smiling on every syllable but I did not face her. I wanted somebody else to come into the room. I was acutely aware of her eyes, staring at me, her legs slightly splayed. She shifted a bit, moving her feet further apart and leaning back in the desk chair. "I bet you and me could really fuck sweetly," she whispered. Suzanne Rule had not moved. She remained bent over her desk, staring at the blonde wood.

You know what I said, finally? I coughed, on purpose, stalling for time, then I said, "That will be enough of *that* kind of talk, Leslie."

I saw Suzanne Rule's hands move a little bit toward the edge of her desk. I did not want to swallow or make any sudden movements with my face or my hands. I felt my heart increasing and my whole head felt like it was burning. I looked at my hands.

A student named Harvey Mailler came in, smelling of smoke. I was never so glad to see anybody in my life. He wore cowboy boots, and a long draping coat that was too warm for that time of year. "Hey Leslie," he said.

"Hey." She sat forward a bit.

A few others filtered in and sat down.

"Harvey," I said, gulping. "I'm glad you're here." He glared at me suspiciously. I said, "Could you open the door and tell the others it's time to come in?"

"Sure, Teach."

Leslie ran her fingers through her hair, stroking it, still staring at me. Her lips were darker today, and so were the shadows over her eyes. Suzanne Rule moved slightly in her seat, a small adjustment for comfort, turning her head a little more toward the wall, but I could definitely see that she was upset.

I didn't know what was happening on my face, but I still felt heat in my jaw and behind my eyes. I might have said something more, if I could find any thoughts in my soft, buttery brain, but nothing was happening there.

Then suddenly the words *so this is what everybody is talking about* raced through my brain and I realized I was angry. I felt betrayed; I had been nothing but kind to her and didn't deserve this treatment. I might not have gotten so involved with Leslie if I had not done what I did next: I walked over to her and lifted her out of the chair. She came up easily enough and we walked to the door where I gently placed her outside in the hall. I didn't push her, I merely kept her moving, and I insured she would be outside the room when she stopped moving. I know, I did lay a hand on her, but it was only to get her out of the room. "Go to Ms. Creighton, right now," I said.

"For what?" She was peering up at me, her lips slightly parted, an expression of limitless sorrow and innocence on her face.

"Just go there. I will talk to you with Mrs. Creighton, after class." I closed the door and went back to the front of the room.

She opened the door and started to come back in.

"Go to the office," I said, and I was pretty loud. She did not seem to know much about what was happening to her expression. In spite of her apparent intelligence and power over others, her mouth was open almost as loosely as one of the hounds.

"Did you hear me?" I said.

"I'm going to report you, for saying that to me," she said.

"Report me."

Harvey came back in, and most of the others trailed in behind him.

"Thanks, Harvey," I said.

"Sure, dude."

The crush of students entering and taking seats seemed to silence Leslie. She stood there with her hands in front of her and the lovely hair draped over one side of her face, covering one eye. She stared at me as if she believed her gaze would eventually wear away flesh and cause wounds. "I'm going to report you," she said again.

"For what?"

"For saying that to me."

"Saying what to you?"

"You know what you said."

I looked at the top of Suzanne's head. "I didn't say anything but to go to the office."

"You said more than that."

"Go on," I said, more loudly now and really angry. Then I yelled at her. "Get out! Now!" The whole class jumped.

She glared at me a second longer, then she turned to Suzanne Rule, whispered, "Bye," and closed the door. Suzanne Rule reached up and pushed a few strands of hair back over the top of her ears, then went back to the same position.

"Suzanne," I said. "You heard what happened."

She did not move.

"George?" I said.

He looked at me with a pleading expression; begged me with his eyes. He did not want this trouble.

I stood there until everyone was seated and settled, then I said, "Before we start today, I want to give you all a writing assignment."

They groaned, opened backpacks and got out notebooks and pens. Still shaking a bit inside, I walked around and sat on the front of my desk. When the confusion subsided and they were ready I said, "I want you to answer some questions for me but I want you to put your answers in the form of an essay."

Some of them looked around, exchanged knowing glances.

"How long does it have to be?" Harvey said.

"I want you to write it until you're finished, and when you're finished I want you to stop." A few of them laughed. I wrote the word "civility" on the blackboard. "I want you to write about this word. Write about what it means to you."

"You mean a definition?" Jaime Nichols asked.

"Well, if that's all you can say about it. I want to know how you define it. How would you like to be treated? What do you see as civil behavior?"

Mrs. Creighton came in and took a seat in front of Suzanne Rule. She did not look directly at me, but her face was not expressionless. She looked very concerned.

When the class was over, I collected the essays. The place emptied as quickly as it always did, and only Suzanne Rule and Mrs. Creighton remained in the room. I stacked the papers in front of me and waited. Mrs. Creighton was writing on a pad in front of Suzanne, whispering to her. Suzanne stood up finally, as far as she ever stood up, picked up her notebook with the pad of paper in it, and slouched out the door.

"Well," I said.

Mrs. Creighton took her glasses off and let them drop on the chain around her neck. She was not facing me, but I could see she was thinking about what to say.

"I'm sorry I had to send Leslie out like that. But—"

"I'm sorry too."

"She was being very disrespectful."

"I know she can be that way."

"I wouldn't have—I'm sorry it came to that," I said. "But I just couldn't let her remain in the class."

She turned to me. "Did you say anything to her?"

"I told her I would not allow her to speak like that in this class."

"What did she say?"

Somehow, I managed to tell her. I don't know if the words even registered. Her face did not change. "You said nothing else to her?"

"I told her to go to the office."

"You made no comment about her—about her sex?"

"What, you mean gender?"

"No. I mean her sex. Did you comment on her—did you say anything at all about having desire for her?"

"What did she say I said to her?"

She glanced above my head, briefly, as if she were considering, then she met my gaze again. "I don't want to repeat those words."

I wanted to say, "You didn't mind making me repeat them," but I said nothing.

"You didn't tell her you wanted to have sex with her?"

"Of course not."

"She says you did."

"You know I didn't."

"Was anyone else here?"

"Suzanne was here. So was George Meeker."

She shook her head. "Are you absolutely certain that you said nothing she could have misunderstood?"

"I'm certain."

She shook her head, then went to the door. "I believe you," she said, standing in the entrance. North came lumbering down the hall and she reached down and began to scratch him behind one of his floppy ears. "I hate this kind of trouble," she said quietly. "I hoped to avoid this kind of thing."

"It's happened before?"

"It's bad for the school—even though it is clearly a fabrication."

"I'm sorry," I said.

"If you hadn't embarrassed her by sending her to the office."

"What was I supposed to do?"

She looked at me. Her eyes were kind and sad. "You probably had no choice," she said. "That kind of language is—"

"She knew what she was doing," I said.

"Yes, I'm sure she did. But there's her father, and the fact that she absolutely needs to graduate this year."

I said nothing.

"There's no telling the lengths to which she might go."

"Well, I do have two witnesses."

She shook her head very slowly. "I wonder if Suzanne can take this sort of thing. I mean, it might get very public; she's—well, she's so—so fragile. And George? He's not ready for this sort of thing either."

"It's not like you have to have training for it."

"That's not what I meant. He's been the center of enough trouble here. Things can pile up on a person."

"They both heard everything, though . . ."

"Leslie has made a complaint and now she has to do something about it and so do I. I can and will make sure the truth comes out, but . . ."

"I really am sorry," I said.

"Sometimes children don't know the harm they do," she said.

"I guess not."

"I'm afraid Leslie does know. That's the one thing I'm most afraid of."

"Leslie's no child," I said.

"Yes she is. She may be more of a child than any of us can possibly know."

30

The Center Cannot Hold

THE MORNING AFTER Leslie lodged her complaint against me Granby and I were the first to reach the smoking area outside my classroom. I realized he knew Mrs. Creighton as well as anybody and I wondered if he had any experience with the sort of complaint Leslie had lodged against me. I guess you could say I was worried and needed to know what Mrs. Creighton might do. So, while we were smoking, I decided to tell him about all of it.

Granby smiled. "Really? She actually said you and she could fuck sweetly?"

I nodded.

"Did you tell her you fuck like the ambassador of love?"

"Very funny."

He laughed. "She's a lot of trouble. I figured that the first time I saw her."

"You ever had a student say anything like that to you?"

"Can't say I have."

"It really shook me up," I said.

"Really." His face got very serious. "And you said nothing—you didn't say anything of a sexual nature, right?"

"I just said it was a beautiful morning."

"Has she ever complained about anyone else to Mrs. Creighton?"

"I don't know."

"Mrs. Creighton never told you of any other complaint? It would be a good thing if she'd made the complaint before. The more the better."

"Why?"

"You don't want yours to be the *only* one. People tend to give credence to single incidents. If she's made other complaints about other people, they can just chalk it up."

"I'm not going to worry about it," I said, but I was terrified. "Doreen warned me."

"If folks are warning you about her, then she has some sort of reputation. I wouldn't worry about it."

"Mrs. Creighton told me her father is some sort of a big shot oilman," I said. "Represents Exxon all over the world. People like that can pretty much do whatever they want."

"Don't her parents care about her behavior?"

"You would think."

"It's a hell of a thing," Granby said, staring out beyond the entrance to the driveway. "Speak of the devil," he said.

I turned and there was Leslie, coming up from the front drive, strolling again in the morning sun, her gold hair flying by her face. She wore a light blue skirt, a white blouse, and black pumps with white socks—she looked like a little girl, but she walked more purposefully now, and I believe she was consciously not looking my way. Suddenly I felt sorry for her. And terribly estranged—as if she had once meant a lot to me, and now I felt nothing for her. It was among the most extraordinary sensations I ever discovered simmering in my heart and I didn't know what to do with it. It is very possible, I now see, that what I felt was nothing more than the earliest intimations of hatred, although I really can't say, even now, whether or not I actually ever came to fear her enough that I could hate her. She walked regally around to the other side of the building, and as she passed out of view a white cloud gulped the sun, and the world seemed to close down a little—as if she took the sun into the building with her.

"I wonder if Bible would have sent her to Mrs. Creighton," I said.

"Mrs. Creighton doesn't miss much," Granby said. "I don't think you need to worry."

"Is Leslie in any of your classes?"

"Social Studies. I already despise her."

"What'd she do to you?"

"Nothing, yet. But I hate anybody that looks like she does and knows it." He leaned down and put his cigarette out on the heel of his shoe, then threw it in the trashcan. "I'm going to make sure she never goes to Mrs. Creighton about me, though."

Doreen came around the corner, carrying a large cup of coffee, her books, and a heavy purse. She wore a navy blue jacket and dark jeans. "Give me a break," she said, balancing everything in her hands.

Granby understood what she meant and scurried immediately to the door of the English room and opened it for her. She whisked by and disappeared inside.

"She looks good today," he said.

I said nothing.

We waited awhile, to see if Doreen would come out. When she didn't, I said, "What should I expect from Leslie now that she's 'reported' me to Mrs. Creighton?"

"If she comes to your class, I'd ignore her."

"I can't act like I don't know about it."

"Yes you can." He moved a little closer to me. I realized he wanted to help, sincerely, and for a brief span of time I felt bad for disliking him so much. It was not his fault that he wasn't Professor Bible. "Look," he said. "What she reported about you was clearly a lie. So we know she can't be trusted to tell the truth about anything. And she's used to being believed. Can you think of a worse combination?"

"I can if you give me some time. You think she's dangerous?"

"To a career? To your reputation and character? You bet your ass. But you can count on Mrs. Creighton. She won't let this get out of hand."

"Well, she made it clear to me yesterday that she knows the truth of it." I said this with some apprehension, because I did not, on the whole, believe it.

"This school is a business," Granby said. "Leslie Warren is a customer. Do you know whose side Mr. Creighton will be on? He's the one you got to worry about."

"Mrs. Creighton said she believes me."

"Do you have any witnesses?"

"Suzanne Rule and George Meeker."

"There's a procedure," Granby said. "So things will have to be said and reported on. And your only witnesses are a mute and a timid little freak like George."

"Well, Suzanne can talk, can't she?"

"You got me. She's never spoken a word in my class." The slight hair on top of his head looked like silver wire in the sunlight. He smoothed it back with a bony hand. "You'll probably have to meet with Leslie's parents."

I didn't want to think about that. Icy fear numbed my mind. I felt as if I might be fired before the day was over. But then I remembered Mrs. Creighton telling me she did not believe Leslie. "Mrs. Creighton will back me up," I said. "She believes me."

"I'm sure she does."

"I'm afraid of facing Leslie's father. It'll be soon, if the bastard's in the country."

"You should hope you don't have to have lawyers in this."

"My girlfriend said I should get a lawyer."

"Like you can afford it."

"I know. I'm shit out of luck if it gets to that stage of things."

"Just make sure you leave the little bitch alone."

"And pass her no matter what she does."

He shook his head. "Doreen says most of the teachers at this school have flunked her without giving it a second thought. I think even Bible flunked her."

I said. "And I'll fail her. If she does no work, I won't have a choice."

"Well she knows it's her last chance. Maybe she thinks she's found a way around the work."

"Why would anyone want to graduate that badly?"

"She begged to get into French class. There's only one boy in there, and that's George Meeker. So, what do you think?"

Later that same day I got hold of myself. I decided to take action. First I gave my god assignment to the seniors. I did it solely to make an effort to get something from Leslie Warren. I realized I did have some power; if she wanted to graduate, she was going to have to go through me and my class.

Before the period began I went to Mrs. Creighton and told her I was going to have everybody writing in their journals. "You don't have to be there for Suzanne if you've got other things going on," I said. The truth was I worried she might think to come back to the class to steady things with Suzanne and perhaps observe Leslie's behavior. I didn't want Mrs. Creighton in the room.

"You think Suzanne will be okay without me?" she asked. She was on the phone when I came in, and put her hand over the receiver.

"She'll be fine. Everybody's just going to be writing."

She nodded. "I do have a lot to handle today."

In spite of the fact that Mrs. Creighton had pretty much told me it was a mistake to send Leslie to the office that first time, I decided I was going to do it again if it was necessary. When she came in—this time with all the others—and flounced down in her chair, looking bored and insulted for having to be there, I went over to her and whispered, "What are you doing here?"

She looked up at me, puzzled.

"What are you doing here?" I spoke out loud now. The other students fell silent and watched us.

"I'm here because this is fourth period English."

"Senior English," I corrected.

"And it's fourth period."

"And what are you doing here?"

She shook her head, still staring up at me. "What?"

"I was under the impression that you did not want to be in this class."

This seemed not to register. Her expression of puzzlement did not change but it was clear something was brewing in her.

"Please," I said, indicating the back door. "So I can begin my class."

She started packing her books in front of her, slapping them down on the desk and forcing them into her backpack.

"Why are you so upset?" I asked. I stood over her, but now she did not look up. I stared at the crown of her head as she packed her books.

"I'm not upset," she said, quietly.

"That's not how it looks. When you slam books around like that . . ."

"Fuck you," she muttered.

I wanted to be sure the rest of the class heard her so I said, "What did you say?"

She repeated it, louder, and the rest of the class let out a unified gasp. I folded my arms and continued speaking quietly to her as she zipped up her backpack and slung it down on the floor next to her desk. "I'm sorry about this, Leslie," I said, in the most tender voice I could muster. "I really do want to work with you."

She got out of her chair, pulling the backpack up and throwing it over her back. She started for the back door, toward the office.

"You didn't want to stay, did you?" I asked.

She stopped and looked at me. "What?"

"I asked if you wanted to stay."

"Whatever," she said.

"If you want to pass Senior English, you better sit down and do some writing in your journal, don't you think?"

She stood there, glaring at me.

"Perhaps you can write about being trapped in the snow, in traffic. Remember that?"

"I don't need this now," she said, fighting tears. She turned and went out. The rest of the class stared at me.

"Today," I said, "We're going to do some free writing," and I went into the assignment.

31

Witchcraft

LESLIE CAME BACK while the class was writing about my contention that God did not exist. It was quiet, so she politely made no noise going to her desk and taking her seat. She opened her backpack and took out a composition notebook, opened it, and began to write. She did not look at me.

I walked over to her and knelt on the floor next to her desk. She did not face me, but I leaned in and whispered, "Do you know what to write about?"

She looked at me. In the shadow of her hair, with her head bent slightly forward, her eyes were as deeply dazzling as anything I had ever seen. "I know what I want to write about," she whispered.

"Good. I'm glad. Write about anything you want," I said as I struggled awkwardly to my feet. "That's all I ask."

She went on writing and I made my way to the front of the room. I thought I had definitely made some progress. I didn't know what happened when she went to the office, but the fact that she came back and prepared herself to work was a good sign.

I was still thinking fatalistically, fearing the meeting with her father, worried about how strong Mrs. Creighton would be if he, or worse, Mr. Creighton, demanded that she fire me, but I had to admit there was a glimmer of hope that I might actually have saved something between Leslie and me; perhaps reminding her of what we had already shared, and my tender suggestion that I wanted to work with her registered as a kind of charm.

Later that afternoon I picked through the journals to find what she wrote. She had put her name at the top, in the middle, as though it were a title. She put a little heart over the *i* in *Leslie*.

(Leslie Warren) not folded

9–22–86

The funny thing is, I'm eighteen years old. I should have graduated already. I can do anything I want, even vote. I can even drink now, at home. I'm eighteen. And still in school. My father won't let me just go and get a GED and he makes me take classes here because I can't go to the public schools. I hate this place. It's not even really a school. Everybody gets to do just what they want. The teachers don't care. All Mrs. Creighton wants is the money for tuition. She talks to me like I'm so special, but she doesn't really do anything for me. My father said this was my last chance to get a diploma. If I don't get out of school with a diploma now, he won't give me another penny and I'll have to pay my own way to Europe this summer. He wants to talk to you. I wish I had something to eat right now.

I like rocky road ice cream a lot. And the beach I like going swimming on a hot day at the beach. Randy promised we'd go to the beach this summer. He's just a boy though. And he says he's going to be going to join the army and go to Europe himself. Once he's in the army I guess it won't be long before he's gone. Why would anybody want to join the stupid army.

Every Friday night i go to a bar in Fairfax called Jolito's. Randy works in the kitchen there. Buddy Harper, a bartender there gives me licqor. He puts whiskey in my coke and he's always good to me. I been in there when he isn't there tho and I don't much like it then. Lots of guys hitting on me. I hate it when they think they're being attractive to me. They're such boys most of them—even the older ones who are married. They think I'm impressed if they can drink alot and if they have a good body and all. Like I should be interested and want to be with them. Like they're powerful and strong and can protect me and show me a good time. I hate the way they call me babe. Or the stupid ways they have to tell me i'm beautiful. I hate the following words: gorgeous, babe, dollface, movie star, beauty. I hate the way their eyes shift down to look at my breasts. I can always notice it, no matter what I'm wearing. If I'm showing a little it's really kind of sad and definitely pathetic. How can they be so obvious and still think we don't notice that's what they're doing.

Well this is several pages and I think that's probably all I want to write now. Now I'm going to write something private and fold the page over so you don't read it.

The page was not folded over. She just left a few spaces, then she wrote:

Last night I had sex with Randy in the back of his station wagon he was very excited and when he took my panties off I said, fuck me now and then I kissed him and pushed him away and got on all fours and he put it in. His legs were cold against my back side, but it was hot when he put his cock in me. It felt so good. He kept moving it in and out and I felt it everywhere. It only seems like a long time if your stoned. I was to high to remember much of anything that happened, but when he put it in me it felt kind of like I was being filled up by something hot and soft and silky.

I like hot soft silky things. I love fucking so much.

She signed it *Leslie Warren*, again with a little heart over the *i*.

252

That part about having sex with Randy got me going a little bit. I felt suddenly as though I was being watched. I looked around the room, studied the silence, and the early afternoon light that crossed the empty chairs in parallel beams through the shades over the picture window. I hadn't realized that she was eighteen. I knew she wrote all that about Randy to get to me, and I resolved not to pay much attention to it. I didn't show it to anybody either. I had an image of her smirking face, and realized she had manipulated me without even being there; she must have known what effect this writing would have on me, and it struck me suddenly that her power over me had been complete. I laughed out loud. "This is witchcraft," I muttered to myself. "Damnable, beautiful, uncanny witchcraft." I couldn't wait to show it to Annie.

I wrote in the margin of the section about Jolito's, *I've been there, it's pretty good food and I think it's funny and pretty accurate what you say about men.*

At the end of her entry, where she said she would fold the paper, I wrote, *Nothing really got you going yet—but you write well enough, and maybe this is a good start. Focus on one thing—what you say about men, about your friend joining the army, or even public school—any one of those things is the beginning of a good idea so try again.* Then I went into Mrs. Creighton's office and made a copy of the last page for my defense if I should need it. I placed it in a folder I labeled *Leslie's Complaint*, and placed it in the center drawer of my desk. Then I folded the paper for her. If she really did forget to fold it, I didn't want her to know that.

I was interested in everything Suzanne Rule wrote as well. She had no folded pages either.

(Suzanne Rule)

9–22–86

If there is a God, would that being know of earth? The world is a tiny place—a spec of dust in a giant ocean of sand. Would a God who owned all that sand know what was happening on one tiny spec of dust lodged on one small grain of the sand in the desert? Would he know what was happening in the microbial heart of one tiny being among eight billion beings scurrying around on that spec of dust?

Why does it seem more probable that we are without help?

I am young and new to everything in the world, and I have been taught religion and I still can't believe any child believes in these myths about a "lord" and "kings of kings" and all that royalty when we threw all that baggage off 200 years ago. Why would anyone devoted to democracy want to go to a heaven ruled by a king? Ruled by a king of kings. One who created cancer, and tornados, and men. Men and all the horrors of earth?

It's just as you say. It's all a myth. We created God, not the other way around.

I wrote on the last page only. I said,

Excellent beginning draft. Now you must develop some of these ideas more fully, though. It isn't complete yet, but I like what you have so far. Why do you condemn men particularly? I mean, it seems like you are adding men in the specific gender sense here, rather than the generic sense. It violates the tone of what you've written.

I felt oddly successful, responding to Suzanne's ideas. As if I had somehow broken through and gotten an ape to talk. Maybe she would never say a word out loud, but what she had written was a kind of talking and she was talking to me. I was certain of it. I was actually hoping for a future where I could get to know Suzanne Rule through these essays. Maybe she could learn from me, and I might communicate with her in spite of her handicap. Writing is a miracle. Before I packed up my things, put the rest of the essays into my briefcase and got ready to leave the room, I had already envisioned what I would say to my classes tomorrow about how writing transcends distance, time and place, and even death.

Just as I was about to leave, Mrs. Creighton came in. She approached the front of the room with a serious look on her face. She sat down in the front and let out a loud sigh, and I turned to the things I was putting in my briefcase.

"What a day," she said, softly.

I looked at her again. I thought, *This is it, I'm fired.*

"I'm trying to get Leslie to withdraw her complaint."

I said, "Thank you."

"Her father wants to talk to you, and he's not happy. But he wants her to graduate, and she wants to do well, so . . ."

I shook my head. I was glad to have her on my side—or at least still claiming to be. "I hope you don't have to go through a whole lot over this."

"I hope we don't have to." She rose from her chair, smiling. Again I realized that at one time not too far back, she had been a beautiful woman. She stood there, thinking, and then she said, "I won't tolerate crude behavior in anyone."

"Do you think she'll withdraw the complaint?" I asked.

"I told her if she went through with it that I would dismiss her from this school and she would never be allowed to return. I said that to her father, too." She smiled. "We'll see what that does." I was so proud of her, and rightly so. I almost told her what Granby had said about how she would come through for me, but I didn't. What I said was, "Thank you for believing me."

She said, "How did Suzanne make out without me today?"

"She was fine." It was quiet for a beat, then I said, "I'm sorry about today."

"What about today?"

"I know I shouldn't have sent Leslie to the office again, but I thought it might . . ."

"You sent her to the office again?"

I nodded.

"I never saw her."

"It was right at the beginning of class. She wasn't gone long."

"She never came in. I saw her coming out of the restroom just around then. She must have been afraid to see me."

I shrugged. "Maybe that's a good sign."

"How so?"

"Well, she came back in and actually did some work for me." I was suddenly afraid Mrs. Creighton would want to know what I was having them all write about. I wasn't quite sure what she believed about God, but I knew it was a dangerous subject in any case. "Leslie worked the whole period," I said. "She wrote almost as much as Suzanne." We were standing about five feet apart. I realized she was waiting for me to say something else and she had this skeptical look on her face—as if she expected that now the real truth would emerge. I remained silent. Finally she said, "How long was she gone?"

"It couldn't have been more than five minutes."

She shook her head, and I pushed open the door and lifted my briefcase a bit to wave good-bye. "I got to get going or I'll be late getting home."

"Being late would be nothing new in your case," she said. I smiled, but I didn't think she meant to be charming about it. I had the feeling as I walked to my car that perhaps Mrs. Creighton did not believe me after all. I wished I hadn't said, "Thank you for believing me." That sounded like I thought she was doing me a favor, and it was just the thing a liar might say. Have you ever felt like a liar while you were telling the truth? It is pretty goddamned eerie, I can tell you.

32

False Accusations

ON THE WAY home that day all I thought about was Leslie Warren. Was there a way to break through to her, and get her to pay attention to her own future a little bit, instead of working so hard to ruin the future of others? The poor thing had probably never gotten the truth from anyone about her talents. She would only have elicited praise for how she looked; people would naturally try to please her, and give her whatever she wanted. People—even professional people—find it very difficult to treat somebody who looks that good like they would treat anybody else. From the start, beautiful people are lied to. Just like rich people, they can never know if people have befriended them sincerely, or out of a secret wish to get their hands on some of that wealth, (or beauty, as the case may be). But maybe I could teach her how to turn her beauty into an advantage; how to use it to get something better out of life other than rebellion, diffidence, and suspicion. Maybe I could teach her that if you don't always try to manipulate people, you get to behave as yourself once in a while. It was worth a try.

I did not know what I was going to do about Suzanne Rule. I knew I couldn't rely on her as a witness. Thinking about Suzanne only made me remember what she'd written in her journal. She was definitely a capable and intelligent writer, in spite of her odd thinking about men and the evils of the world. I was certain whatever reason she had for harboring those thoughts was probably as good as any; and one I'd rather not know about. At any rate, I saw no reason why she would want to help me since I was a man.

When I got home, Annie wasn't there. I waited awhile, and then I decided to make myself something to eat. I was sitting on the couch, eating a bacon sandwich with potato chips and a Coke when she came in. I'd made enough bacon for her, if she wanted it, but I was hoping she didn't, so I could finish it.

"Where you been?" I said.

"A few of us stopped for drinks after work." She threw her purse on the dining table and swept out of the room. I could hear her down the hall, changing her clothes. When I was finished with my sandwich, I got up and went to the kitchen, which was to the left of the thin hallway that went back to the bedroom.

"You want a bacon sandwich?" I hollered.

"No. We had chicken wings at the bar."

"Really." I picked up the four remaining slices of bacon and lay them across a piece of bread, then went to the refrigerator and got more lettuce, a slice of tomato, and the mayonnaise. "I wish you'd called me," I said.

"What?" She was way back in the bedroom now, maybe even in the closet searching for what she'd wear.

"I wish you'd called me," I said louder.

"It was happy hour." She came down the hall. "Free snack food."

She had changed into a pair of Levis and a blue sweater.

"You look nice," I said.

"How was your day?"

I told her about Mrs. Creighton trying to get Leslie to withdraw the complaint.

"Well that's a relief." She sat down on the couch and brushed the hair off her forehead. "You think she'll do it?"

"Believe it or not, Mrs. Creighton stood up to her and her father. He knows if she's going to get a high school diploma, it will be through me."

"Why's that such a big deal to her father?"

I didn't know. After a pause, I took another bite of my sandwich and said, "Mrs. Creighton told me he's a big oilman. Works with worldwide markets and diplomats. Maybe that's it."

She put her feet up and groaned. "People are so strange."

I wanted to tell her about what Suzanne Rule had written in her journal for the God assignment. I was so proud of myself for getting her to write so much. But when I told Annie about the assignment, I could see she was horrified. "Why do you get them to write about such controversial stuff?"

"It gets them interested."

"You think Mommy and Daddy won't object to what the evil English teacher is doing to their little Johnny?"

"You know. I'm trying to play the part."

She sighed. "Play the part."

"Teacher. I'm a teacher."

"And you want to change the world."

"How is that changing the world?"

"You can escape only so many times from these little traps you lay for yourself."

"What are you talking about?"

"Hitler, now God?"

"It's just something to get them motivated and pissed off enough to write. I used the same assignment last year."

"You taught Jaime or whatever her name was about Hitler, but it didn't change the fact that she got to be a junior in an American school without ever having heard of Adolf Hitler."

"I never said I wanted to change the world. I'm just looking for things they can get their teeth into. Things I can get them to write about with passion."

"You think."

"Well, I'm hoping for that."

She said nothing for long time. I finished my sandwich. I could see there was something on her mind.

"Who's *we*?" I said.

"What?"

"You said *we* stopped for a drink. Who's *we*?"

"Steve and me and a few other people." Steve was her officemate. Had been for almost a year. He was "just a good friend to have in a place like that," Annie had said. She often talked about him. And sometimes weeks would go by and she wouldn't mention him at all. Steve had dark hair, a long aquiline nose, and smart blue eyes. He was not much taller than Annie. They looked good together.

"Steve, huh."

She stopped and looked at me. "Yeah?" She had a puzzled look on her face.

"You see a lot of him at work, don't you? Then after, too?"

"You going to be a jealous husband before we're even married?"

"What jealousy?"

"That's what it sounds like."

I shook my head. "Maybe you want me to be jealous."

She sank back heavily on the couch and put her feet back down on the floor. "Puhlease," she said.

I sat down next to her. She pointed to my plate on the table, the empty glass. "You going to leave those there?"

"What if I'd cooked you dinner?"

"You didn't."

She looked tired, and her dark eyes seemed ready to draw down her eyelids. She'd been drinking and it showed. The pink skin around her pouting lips made me restive. I wanted to kiss her. "It just would have been nice," I said. "If you'd called me maybe I could have joined you."

"Next time I'll call."

We fell quiet for a while. I took the empty plate and glass into the kitchen, then poured myself a shot of whiskey. "Want a drink?" I said from the kitchen.

"No." Her voice was soft, far away.

I came back in with my drink and sat down again. "Want to watch TV?"

She was chewing on the tip of her forefinger closed against her thumb, twisting her hand a bit, her eyes straight ahead. I waited, but she did not answer. She was gazing off in space, lost in thought. "What?" I said.

She looked at me. "Nothing."

"What? You're thinking about something."

"God forbid I should think."

"What were you thinking about?"

"Nothing important."

"You've got something on your mind."

"I do?"

"Is this a game?"

She seemed to slump down a bit, and again her face had this pained expression. "I'm just tired, okay?"

I sat there for a while, sipping my whiskey, then I got up and turned the television on. "Want to watch the news?"

"If you want to."

"What do you want to do?"

"I'll watch the news."

"But do you want to?"

"Yes, I said I wanted to."

"No you said, 'I'll watch it,' like that. Like you were doing me a favor."

"Jesus Christ," she said.

I sat down again, leaving the television on, but with the volume turned down so far the sound was barely audible. "Jesus Christ what?"

"I want to watch the news, okay?"

It was quiet again for a while and we sat there looking at the TV, then she said, "Turn it up."

I said, "Do you want to fight with me tonight?"

"I never want to fight with you."

"Well what is this?"

"I'm just trying to watch the news. And you seem to be in a bitchy mood."

"I'm not in any kind of mood," I said. I didn't know what we were arguing about.

"And this wouldn't have anything to do with the fact that I went out with some friends after work today."

"No. Of course not." It really wasn't about that and her thinking it was truly angered me, but I contained it. "I can't believe you think I'd do that."

"Do what?"

"Take out my feelings like that."

"Sometimes we don't know what our motivations are."

"Maybe this is something *you* want."

"And you're not picking a fight."

"No."

"Well that's how it feels."

"I'd hate to think . . ."

"You know what I want?" she said.

"What?"

"I want a cigarette."

"I leave them at work. I don't have any. The way you smelled when you came in, I'd say you had quite a few in the bar."

"Do you know what else I want?"

"What."

"I'd like it if you'd just watch the fucking news and shut up." She got up slowly, almost regally, her head held high. "I'm going in to take a bath."

"Good night," I said.

Later that night, lying in bed, she snuggled up and apologized for not calling me. "I'm sorry about tonight, too," she said.

"You don't have to apologize."

"It was insensitive of me to leave you out like that."

I held her in my arms and we talked about how silly our argument had been. "At least we communicate," I said. "That's really important in a relationship." I did not really think we communicated at all, but I thought saying it might make it true somehow; perhaps it would make her conscious of the ways in which she refused to tell me what was on her mind.

I said, "I don't know how people who never say how they feel can live."

She nodded.

"I guess it bothers me more than I let on when you accuse me of being jealous."

"I'm sorry." She did not mean it this time. She was hiding an unshakable feeling of certitude about it, she didn't really care if it bothered me, and I could sense it. "You have to admit," she said. "You do get a little testy whenever I spend any time outside of work with Steven."

"No, I don't have to admit it. It's not true."

She smiled knowingly, and for a brief second I tasted a vestigial flicker of anger again, but I said nothing. It was quiet for a long time, then she said, "Tell me about the rest of your day."

I said, "Know that student who never talks at all, to anyone?"

"You're sure she's not retarded, or injured in some way?"

"She's definitely not retarded. She may be the brightest person in any of my classes."

"Smarter than you?"

"She's been enrolled there for three years. Mrs. Creighton says she'll graduate this year and that I'm to leave her alone."

"That's bizarre."

"I'm trying with her, though. I don't want to leave her alone."

"There's something going on with that little girl," Annie said. "Abuse, or something."

"I guess." I didn't see the need to tell her what I'd heard about Suzanne. Males were tricky subjects with her anyway. She often characterized me as a rare bird; she'd say things about "most men" that would make me cringe. I didn't want to tip the scales completely against me just because I've got the extra chromosome.

We were quiet for a while, and I listened to her breathing, wondering if she might be falling asleep. But then she said, "I feel sorry for Leslie Warren."

"Why?"

"She's probably quite intelligent, but she'll never discover it."

"Why not?"

Annie raised her head a bit and looked at me. "She's just too beautiful to ever understand imperfection."

"So?"

"Nobody will ever be good enough for her. She will expect perfection in everything and everyone and when she doesn't find it, she will begin to hate people."

"Maybe," I said.

"How about you? Can you be perfect for her?"

"Oh, I'm not going to try. I'm just going to tell her the truth and she'll hate me for that."

"Nobody could possibly hate you."

I smiled and said, "Sure."

"I'm serious."

"Nobody's told Leslie no, ever. I can tell."

She let her head fall again on my chest. "How can you tell a thing like that?"

"She's spoiled rotten. She's always gotten just what she wants."

"I always got what I wanted," Annie said.

"And you're spoiled rotten, too."

"I am not," she laughed.

"And you're also beautiful."

She breathed deeply, but she said nothing. I listened to the clock ticking on the nightstand, thinking of Leslie's fine golden hair, the brown curve of her knees. Maybe I should feel sorry for her. Then I said, "I was thinking, I bet nobody ever told Leslie the truth."

"Why not?"

"Beautiful people never get the truth from folks."

"You never told me the truth?"

"Well, of course . . ." She laughed and I held onto her. I wished that I knew her better, or that she knew me. Sometimes she seemed like such a stranger. I went to sleep looking forward to the promising fall weather. It was the beginning of October, and the air took on a bright finish with the waning sun, a bracing quality, and mornings remained crisp and speckled with leaves and gusts of cool wind.

In spite of all that was going on, I really was kind of happy.

33

Purpose in Small Things

IN A WAY I admired Leslie's determination. As the days and then weeks went by she maintained a defeated, less than subtle resistance to everything I tried to do in class. She was not disruptive, not even disrespectful, but she would position herself—let her face drop, or move her head down, or sit lower in her seat and look at me with scorn—and I knew she was not interested or amused by anything I said, or anything anybody else said in the class. She was not a discipline problem and she did her work—not much more than the minimum, to be sure—but just enough to get by. Every day I was hurt by the way she looked at me. And each day I waited to hear from Mrs. Creighton about my talk with Leslie's father, or the progress of the complaint. I never had the nerve to ask her. I just waited, thinking no news was good news.

Leslie's journal entries—all unfolded, she wanted me to read them— were always lurid: full of the details of her sexual encounters with Randy and an older gentleman named Raphael, who knew her father and was "so sophisticated." He told Leslie that he "knew how to touch a woman's breasts." Then she went on to describe the way he did it, how her nipples got erect, and how smooth his cock was when she put it in her mouth. They always had their "meetings" in the best hotels.

I made a copy of each entry and put it in the *Leslie's Complaint* folder in my desk. I had so much ammunition against her I wasn't worried overmuch about her complaint. And I was beginning to think she was pretty stupid for saying those things directly to me in writing. But I realized it wasn't so much stupidity as it was simple arrogance. She had always had her way, and for the first time in her life she was confronted with something she could not control: Glenn Acres Prep School, and me. It made her furious and careless. When she was angry, she did not consider consequences.

I don't know why it was so important for me to win her over, but I was always trying to do that with or without her false accusations. I was not worried anymore about my job. If I was worried about anything, it was Leslie's promiscuity. The more she wrote about it the more I fretted over the danger. Sex was lethal again—very lethal—and I wrote in the margin of her journal things like, "You could get very bad diseases if you're not careful," and "For heaven's sake take precautions." I did pay more attention to her most of that year, but that was because I had to. It bothered me to feel disliked, and the truth is I just could not stand the fact that Leslie had no regard for me and she did not like my class. That's not an easy admission for any teacher to make, but I'm human. Isn't every teacher a little worried about that? In spite of a certain awareness of this vainglorious need of approval and affection, I still believe that what I must have wanted all along was to save Leslie from herself. I don't think I should be proud of myself for any of it.

On the last Sunday in October Mr. and Mrs. Creighton threw a little party at the school for the faculty. The weather turned as cold as a

New Year's Day, and just as windy. Mr. Creighton cooked out on a huge rented barbecue grill, and all of us sat in the English room eating hot dogs, hamburgers, baked beans, and potato chips. Mr. Creighton filled the cooler with a few six-packs of beer, and in spite of what turned out to be an absolutely clear, sunny, and bone chillingly cold day, he insisted on standing outside in front of the grill, cooking the dogs and the burgers, with an ice cold beer in his hand. From my desk in the English room, I could see him through the plate glass window standing with his shoulders hunched, breathing out puffs of steam, sipping his beer. Mrs. Creighton sat in the back of the room, smiling, munching on cut strips of carrot dipped in blue cheese dressing. Doreen looked like a young man in Levis, loafers, white socks, and a flannel shirt. Fat Mrs. Brown wore the usual kimono, but it was made of wool and didn't drape very neatly off her broad shoulders and hips. She looked so uncomfortable. The hair on the French teacher, Mrs. Nagler, looked like something damp had flattened it. She insisted on speaking nothing but French, so only Mrs. Creighton was willing to speak to her.

Granby wore his vest, and chatted with Mrs. Creighton about the Washington Redskins, and tennis and traffic in the Washington area. I knew he was going to ask her for a raise, and I listened for it—hoping to hear how he might engineer it. I thought maybe Mrs. Creighton or her husband might say something about Leslie's complaint but they had been just as silent as ever about it. I watched Mrs. Creighton awhile to see if perhaps she wanted to get my attention. When she spoke French, her cheeks would tremble a bit and her face got red.

After a while, I turned back to Mr. Creighton again; the cold air had brought tears to his eyes. Smoke from the grill blew away so fast, I knew he was standing in a frozen gale of wind, and yet when he saw me through the glass, he raised his beer toward me and took a sip out of it.

I realized he was doing all he could do. He always felt out of place talking to the teachers because, he said, "You people know about so much, and I don't know nothing. I'm just a salesman." He hunched over that grill, trying to get some kind of warmth from the hot coals, and I actually felt sorry for him; I wasn't feeling superior to him. I looked up to him. Any man who could play the guitar like he did was a gifted artist. But I thought I might teach him that he shouldn't say things like "I'm just a salesman." In my life, I'd never met a salesman I didn't like or one that wasn't as quick of mind and witty as any teacher. Can you believe it? I wanted to make him feel better about himself because I thought he was feeling disliked.

When he came in with the burgers, his face red and cheery, breathing through his mouth as if he'd run a marathon, he said, "Come and get it. Dogs and Burgers." He'd stacked them on a plate. He set them down on my desk, which was covered with a white sheet. "Damn," he said. "It's cold out there for this time of year."

Then while we were eating, he wanted to drink a toast to all of us. "To knowledge," he said.

I drank to that.

I thought I had knowledge.

I know. The mark of a truly stupid man is that he cannot comprehend the enormity of his own ignorance.

Near the end of the party it began to rain. Mr. Creighton closed up shop and everybody headed for home.

As we were leaving, I shook his hand and said, "Great party. Great party."

"Well thank you." The smile on his face was genuine and I could see he was happy, even perhaps grateful.

"Have you ever thought of teaching the guitar?" I asked.

"Nooo." He still held to my hand. "I'm no teacher."

"You're a bloody genius on the guitar," I said.

The smile on his face got a little brighter and he squeezed my hand a bit harder. "You're a good man for saying that."

"I mean it."

He nodded, looked up a little at the freezing rain, and then turned to leave. I watched him ducking in the wind and rain on the way to his car. When he got there he looked back and waved at me, still smiling. I don't know if it mattered to him really, but I thought it did and it made me feel better. In fact, I felt damned good.

On the way home I started thinking about every moment I'd spent with Leslie. I ran a little montage through my mind, of Leslie picking her things up after she fell on the wet pavement, smiling carelessly as she handed me the big birthday card; looking pensively at me as I talked to her about George and his problem; listening to Professor Bible and debating with him about affirmative action. I saw her glaring at me with a lustful, lilting pout on her face. I couldn't remember if I'd ever praised her for anything; ever written "Good work" on one of her papers, or admired her thinking in a class discussion. I realized I'd never told her anything wonderful about herself except the truly stupid remark that she could be a model or an actress if she wanted to.

Annie got home a few hours after I did that night. She called and said she would be late so I had dinner by myself. When she got home we spent the evening watching television. I don't remember anything we might have said to each other. When I went to bed, I was still thinking about Leslie. Not in any romantic way—I am not unmindful of how that sounds—but in the same way you think about any insoluble, complex, frustrating problem.

Annie thought I was just a little moody because she came home a little later than usual and we missed dinner together again.

34

A Little Voice

WHILE I WAS paying attention to Leslie's moods and measures, something new and very promising developed with Suzanne Rule.

Sometime early in those first few weeks, and for most of the rest of that second year, I began each class by reading a poem. I'd pick poems by the best contemporary poets—people like Henry Taylor, James Dickey, Jane Shore, Sharon Olds, Denise Levertov, Anne Sexton, George Garrett, Roland Flint, Alan Shapiro, Gregory Natt, Richard McCann, and Ted Kooser. I'd simply start reading the work out loud and the class would quickly fall silent, and when I was done with a particular poem, I'd put it away and begin teaching whatever I was going to teach. I'd make no comment, no effort to explain or help them understand. It wasn't studying poetry, it was hearing it. Just, hearing it. I wanted to give them a wondrous thing. Doesn't everybody want to do that? Isn't it normal? If you knew someone who'd never seen a movie, how long would it take you to drag them into a theater? Think of being able to give a person something so extraordinary and enthralling as watching good movies. It's the same thing with poetry. People just don't know how goddamned wonderful it is. To offer it to someone is a pretty nice thing to do. The problem is, it isn't ever really offered. Poetry is usually forced on people and they're told they "ought" to like it. I'm convinced that if teachers of literature in high schools and colleges were entrusted with teaching films almost no one would ever want to watch a movie.

At any rate, one morning late in November—I think it was not too long after I sent Leslie to the office the first time—I found a small piece of notepaper on my desk, folded neatly in half. No one was in the room yet, so I thought it must be a note from Mrs. Creighton. When I opened it this is what was written on the page, in pencil:

Jewels on a Woman's Throat

> *diamonds look blue as ice,*
> *but slip the light*
> *and red stones darken even bone*
> *rain falls down like diamonds and*
> *blood drops like rubies,*
> *green petals catch the rain*

It was unmistakably Suzanne's handwriting. As a poem, of course, it was nothing to write home about, but I liked the fact that it was so concrete, so full of exact detail. It was an attempt at a poem, and not a bad one at that. I folded the paper back up and decided to return the favor. I'm not a poet, but I figured I'd find one I could give her. I opened the *Adventures in Literature* text and began paging through it looking for a poem that might be appropriate. I spent the rest of that day—during breaks between classes, lunchtime—searching through that text. That night, I took it home with me, and finally found what I thought might be just right. In fact, it was absolutely perfect. I used a pencil and copied it onto a small piece of paper.

In the Fall They Come Back

Maid Quiet

Where has Maid Quiet gone to,
Nodding her russet hood?
The winds that awakened the stars
Are blowing through my blood.
O how could I be so calm
When she rose up to depart?
Now words that called up the lightning
Are hurtling through my heart.

—*William Butler Yeats*

It was probably the title, and then the reference to a "nodding russet hood" that drew me to the poem. I'm not stupid, I realize from a certain point of view the thing is a love poem. But I didn't intend it to be and I don't think she understood it that way. Certainly I wouldn't want to vouch for anyone else's interpretation. I already said I thought it was perfect.

I put it on her desk the next morning.

She had already been there, though, because I found another one on my desk. This one said,

Cold Spring

Birds object to the shivering of the trees
Wind slaps sails and foils the early bees
Beneath rocky clouds, buried sky
Every yellow jonquil stricken by
Icy air, sways a green neck, tattered leaves.

I wasn't worried, nor would I ever worry about the tone of these poems. The first one might get one to thinking—that reference to the way blood falls—and this last one which described what most people would say is the opposite of spring—or at least the opposite of poems about spring written by high school girls—might be a cause for concern. Perhaps the trained eye might have seen early warnings of depression and suicidal thinking, but I never thought about it, and that's the truth. I was just so happy that she was now sending me these little poems. I hoped she might leave one on my desk every day, but she didn't. It was mostly sporadic after that. A poem or two in one week, then nothing for two or three weeks, then maybe two or three poems in the space of a few days. Each time she left me a poem, I'd find one to give to her. Mostly I just looked for poems that I thought she'd like. Not that I knew her well enough to know that. I guess I went by what her poems seemed to be about. Maybe I was responding to the mood she created.

One day she left a poem about the tree outside our picture window. It said,

The Tree

It looks like a lung
Turns yellow in fall
Leaves scurry down
Arteries, veins and
Capillaries glistening and still
In rain, white as anguish in snow

I was sorely tempted to write something on this one—about the wildly inappropriate image of a tree as a lung. I wanted to say, "This one doesn't work," but I was afraid if I did that, she'd stop writing them for me. It was important to keep getting them. So I did nothing. I found another poem I thought she'd like, "Resuming Green," by Roland Flint. I gave her George Garrett's "The Dancing Class," and Gregory Natt's "Scrapbook."

Just before Christmas she wrote this poem:

Linen

Soft as rose petals
supple and compliant
stiff as cold air at first
touch, and smells of mother
before night falls

I wasn't sure what I could say to her. It hit me after the first dozen poems or so that none of them referred to her; or anyone, really. Was it a breakthrough that she mentioned her mother in this "linen" poem? Or was the word "mother" generic and not specific? Something was happening between us—a bond that might blossom into the whole world for her. Talk about success as a teacher. Think of it: you can bring a person back from the darkest place in their own soul in the light of words. I studied her poems over and over trying to discern an idea—something she might be trying to say to me.

Working so hard to do exactly the right thing with Suzanne's poems took my mind off of Leslie and her complaint. It gave me reassurance in classes where Leslie would refuse to even look my way. No matter what might happen with her, I believed I might be nearing a breakthrough with Suzanne. We tend to settle in the direction of success, and the more I found myself failing with Leslie, the more I gravitated toward Suzanne. I admit I was having fun working out our small communication.

And then I ran into Leslie at Jolito's.

35

Saving Grace

NOW I KNOW this is going to be hard to believe and I hate to be in the position of having to rely on something others have found quite impossible to accept as true, but I went to Jolito's for a drink by myself that night because it was close to my apartment, and I wanted to be out when Annie got home. I did not go there looking for Leslie. It wasn't even a Friday and you must remember, she said in her journal that she went there every Friday. You also must remember that Annie and I had had a bit of a spat over her happy hour meeting with Steve and the office gang. Being the fellow left out, sitting home—wondering where your soul might light if you let it free for a second—is not the most pleasant feeling in the world. Perhaps others have experienced it too; for me loneliness is a physical sensation, a simmering nameless thing very much like fear that saps your heart. So I was a little more upset over being left alone that night than perhaps I should have been. Anyway, Annie didn't come home right away and I sat there waiting for her. I waited a long time; I baked some chicken and potatoes, steamed some broccoli, all the while feeling more and more anxious. Then she called. I didn't answer the phone, I let our new-fangled answering machine kick on and there she was, a little embarrassed, and clearly a little pierced by a few glasses of wine. She apologized again and said she just stopped for a "drink with the guys." I could hear the guys in the background laughing and having a high old time. I heard her say to somebody, "I wonder why he didn't pick up," laughingly, as if I was always right there at the other end of the line. She was not worried either. So I just decided I was not going to sit at home waiting for her. I left the house determined to stay out later than she did—leaving no call, no message on the machine. I wanted her to get home and sit around wondering where the hell I was for a change.

So I went to Jolito's. It was pretty crowded for a Wednesday night. Places like that are all the same—a wide, wrap-around bar at the far end of the room, and tables surrounding a small dance floor and stage to the left. On the right was a big juke that could be played pretty loud when there was no band. Tonight, the dance floor and stage were empty. The people at the bar had their eyes fixed on the color TVs high at either end—some sort of news or sports talk show.

I didn't see her at first. The grids of soiled neon bulbs in the ceiling distributed the light only weakly, and in the shadows it was hard to discern anyone's face. The room smelled of wet teak-wood, fried shrimp, cigarette smoke, and beer.

I sat down near the end of the bar and when I looked up, eyes acclimated, there she was, Leslie Warren. She was sitting to my right, just where the bar swung around for the other side of the room. Her silky light brown hair framed the side of her face, and in the falling light she looked almost saintly. She seemed not to have noticed me, and at first I considered slinking away from the light, getting the hell out of there. But then I noticed the look on her face.

I would not say it was fright or anything like that. But she was clearly not comfortable. She was smoking a cigarette, looking furtively at two men playing darts on the other side of the bar, directly across from where I was sitting. One of them kept raising his hand and waving at her, but each time he did, she'd look away. He was well-built, if on the short side, his hair closely cropped. Whenever he waved at her he let out a strange sort of howl—barely human—as if he were calling to her across some Paleolithic swamp.

It clearly irritated her. Finally, he strode over and installed himself on her right. He leaned close and stared at the side of her face. I got myself out of the light and moved by slow degrees over to where she was sitting.

"See that shot, babe?"

She nodded, leaning back away from him. She still hadn't noticed me.

"Come on," he said. "Come over to the table so you can see better. Helluva game."

Leslie wouldn't look at him. "No thanks," she said, her voice small, rising up from what could only be fear. I couldn't believe it. This was the young woman who had the entire faculty cowed and on edge?—in thrall to this barely literate bar jockey, this dumb little, loud mouthed, dart-throwing *ape*?

"Least tell me your name," he demanded. " 'Kay, babe? Least gimme *that* much."

She stared at the ashtray in front of her.

"I *know* you got a name. Right? Mean, nothing this beautiful should go without a name." He leaned in real close and started whispering in her ear again.

I don't know what got into me, but I couldn't stand watching him sully her space like that. So I moved over, sat down next to her. "You ever get in touch with the babysitter, hon?" I said, leaning over the bar just next to her, busy fielding the bartender's attention.

She looked at me, the shock of recognition barely even registering. "No," she said, ever the quick study. "I thought *you* were going to call her."

I wish you could have seen the look on the dart jockey's face. He stepped back, and as I put my hands up on the bar, Leslie leaned into me, holding onto my arm. "Fuck, man," he whined. "I'm, like, sorry." No threat or anything—fucker could have torn me in half—but, as if he'd accidentally insulted my mother, or bashed my religion: Very, very sorry.

When he was gone, Leslie let go my arm, took a strangely calm drag on her cigarette.

"Sometimes I feel as though I should apologize for all the men in the world," I said.

She smiled without looking at me. "That was pretty clever," she said. "What you did there."

"*You* sure picked up on it right away."

She laughed. I liked the sound of it—the small notes of it, like rippling water or a piano in the mid to higher registers, but soft . . . really soft. She was relaxed now, sitting there next to her English teacher, the English teacher she'd lodged a complaint against.

The bartender came over to me and I ordered a beer. Leslie didn't want anything. I waited for my beer while she finished her cigarette. I asked her what she was doing there.

"I'm meeting my boyfriend, Randy."

"Really."

"He works in the back."

"Sure you're allowed to sit at the bar like this?"

"They don't mind," she said. "Long as I don't, you know, order anything."

She still wasn't looking at me, but I could see the light refracting through the incredible blue cornea of her eyes, sparkling like some sort of precious stone. "I can't even drink a Coke at the bar, you know? Or a 7 Up," she said. "Might have *liquor* in it."

The bartender brought my beer, and I took a swig. "Want to move to a table, then? So you can have a Coke?"

"Okay," she said, rising before I could. "Which table?"

"How about over there." I pointed to a table in the corner next to the front door. We walked over and sat down. I lit the candle in the middle of the table. "Well," I said. Then I signaled a waiter who was about to pass by, ordered Leslie a Coke.

"Will your boyfriend—what's his name? Randy? Will he be able to see you over here?" I asked.

"Oh, sure."

"What's he do in the back, anyway?"

"He's a cook."

We sat there silently awhile. I wondered if I should bring up the complaint. Now that I had pretty well rescued her a second time, maybe she'd be willing to forget the whole thing. Not that I really wanted to bring it up. I was less than ten years older than this girl. We might have been a couple, I half thought to myself—and just like that, something happened to my resolve. I wasn't so much interested in the complaint, you see, as I was in Leslie; I wanted to know her better. Not for romantic reasons or anything . . .

I suppose that tension is always there between men and women, and I can't say I was unaware of it. Still, I was determined not to do anything that might be construed by anyone—her above all—as, you know, pursuit.

"What are you doing here?" she said.

"Oh, I just came in to get a burrito and a beer. It's right around the corner from where I live. I was surprised to see *you*, actually."

"I come here a lot."

"Really." I took a thoughtful pull of my beer. "Maybe you could write about this. You know, your experience with the dart-throwing crowd."

"*Write* about it?"

"In your journal."

"Oh," she sighed. "That."

"It's okay. We don't have to talk about school."

She smirked. "Yeah, let's not."

"Why'd you come back this year? You're eighteen, right?"

"I had to." She looked directly at me now. "My father."

"You know what eighteen means?" I said. "You don't have to do what your father says anymore." We sat there, staring at each other. Was it easier for her to look at me here, dim as it was?

"I don't want to hurt him any more than I already have," she said, simply.

I hadn't expected that. For all her usual rebellion, her spikiness, the general wise-guy attitude, Leslie seemed right now governed solely by the mallet of her father's love.

"That's so sweet," I said, stupidly, and the stare she fixed me with could have frozen the torrents playing over Niagara Falls. "Well," I said, clearing my throat. "I hope you get what you want."

"I will."

"Though it won't be with . . ." I stopped. *You won't get anywhere with this grievance against me,* I'd nearly said, before thinking better of it. I didn't want to sully my rescue with any notion of recompense or reward.

"Won't be with *what?*" she said.

The waiter brought her Coke and I paid him, then finished my beer and settled back to look at Leslie. She sat slightly away from the round table, legs crossed. She wore a blue skirt, and a bright white blouse. Her hair was held back a bit on one side with a barrette that had a very small red ribbon on it. She studied my face, waiting.

"You know what," I said. "We don't have to talk about it."

"It won't be with what?" she repeated, the whine in her voice by now almost friendly in its teasing relentlessness.

"You're going to have to graduate by doing the *work*," I said. "I'm not going to graduate you for any other reason."

She nodded, the recognition of what I was saying evident in her eyes. "I'll do the work," she said.

"Good."

"Good," she agreed.

"I'm glad," I said.

"I bet you are."

"Leslie, you won't get lies from me. Ever."

She looked puzzled.

When I think of her behavior now, I wonder if she might have been waiting for me to say something about it—to beg her maybe; or perhaps she just wanted me to acknowledge that we might make a new start if only she were to drop the damn complaint. It is also possible she was afraid of what I might be up to, possible she was preparing herself to fend off yet another slobbering attempt at seduction. At any rate, she seemed to be waiting for something.

"I think I know what it's like to look like you," I said, finally. The awkwardness was immediate.

"What's *that* supposed to mean?"

I'd thought maybe if I could get her to think about the ways she'd been lied to, she might weaken in her resolve, might regret her lie about me. Because it was clear enough: this girl was just too attractive to have heard the truth from anybody. See, people will say anything to remain in the company of that kind of beauty. Everywhere she went she would have been greeted with only bits of the truth, packs of lies clustering around her as people sought primarily to please.

She didn't like it that I'd brought up her looks. Her face seemed to shrink a little—as if the air had leaked from behind her eyes. "*You* know," I started to stammer. "To—to be so—so . . ." What other way was there to say it? She was waiting there, braced for it, and I had no idea what to do about the red flush that must have been blossoming across my face. "So beautiful," I said, finally.

She shook her head.

"Don't get me wrong," I hastened to say. "I'm not coming *on to* you."

"Right."

"I'm not. It's just . . . you obviously understand you're not . . . ordinary, you know? I mean, you must know how breathtakingly attractive you are."

"I don't . . ." But she didn't finish.

I took a sip from the already empty glass in front of me, stalling for time. But we were into it by this point, and I wanted her at least to understand. "Look," I said. "Can we forget for a minute that I'm a man? Or that you're . . . a woman?"

She was suspicious, but waited.

"You are strikingly beautiful, okay? And make no mistake, when people say *striking*, they really mean that—that your beauty almost *strikes* them. Stops them. Like, it *hurts*."

Still silent, she had relaxed enough to take a drink from her Coke, her eyes never leaving mine. I couldn't tell if she was merely humoring me. Could anything I was saying be sinking in?

"People who are extraordinary in that way—you know—who are so damn attractive it's all anyone ever notices about them—well, it's a burden, I expect, to carry around with you."

"Tell me about it," she said, sarcastically. I could see I'd hit a nerve.

"You can't go anywhere that men aren't . . . *throwing* themselves at you, right?"

She nodded.

"And they're not very good at it, I know—believe me; most men are *awful* at it. And the ones who *are* any good at it, they probably got that way by coming on to way too many women. I mean, they're probably the ones you should avoid most of all . . ."

Suddenly she broke into a smile. I can't express the joy I felt in the light of that smile. I was getting somewhere, I could sense it. "So you have this constant battle," I said. "Right?"

"Exactly."

"You get stared at, wherever you go."

She nodded.

It was like I was hitting jackpots in a guessing game. "I understand," I went on. "You know? I really do. And who can blame you for not trusting anyone? I wouldn't either."

She lifted her Coke, watching me over the edge of it, the smile gone, her face inscrutable, impassive. She put her lips on the straw and began to drink.

"But you can trust *me*, Leslie. That much I promise."

We were quiet for a long time after I said that. I took my empty glass and bottle over to the bar, then walked back to the table and sat down. "Looks like your dart-playing friend finally cleared out."

She looked across the room at the clock on the wall. "Yeah . . . Randy gets off in, like, half an hour."

"You won't need me anymore, then."

She said nothing. I sat there a moment longer before getting to my feet. She leaned forward, put her arms out in front of her on the table, and looked up at me. Her face was sad, and for the first time, she seemed to me . . . vulnerable. I wanted to caress her shoulders, wanted to tell her everything would be all right. I'd forgotten her complaint, to be honest. It was just two people, coming to a kind of understanding. "See you tomorrow?" I said.

She didn't say anything, but smiled again. Only this time it wasn't so enigmatic. It was a smile of recognition, of affection even—the kind of gift bestowed by a grown woman who understands the world, who knows what it means to trust a person.

36

Many Happy Returns

THINGS WERE DIFFERENT with Leslie after that. She worked harder. She was suddenly a part of the class, still speaking out of turn, but now without wanting to shock or disarm, but because she was interested. The next time I collected journals, I read every page of hers. She did not mention Randy, and there were no folded pages, just descriptions of daily activities, and events in her life. In truth, she wrote like almost any normal teenaged girl, except that the events in her life revolved around embassy parties and cordial dinners at her family's house with oil executives and foreign dignitaries and other "Washington snobs," as she put it. Every now and then she would address me directly. She'd say things like, "Don't you hate it when people act like snobs, Mr. Jameson?" Or, "I know you can understand how I felt." That kind of thing. It always thrilled me.

The dreaded meeting with her father never materialized. What he did was send a brief note to me that said:

Dear Sir:

*As I am sure you have been made aware, Leslie needs to graduate this year.
She has promised to work very hard. I am conscious of her impetuous
nature, and I know she is also prone to exaggeration when it suits her
needs. If in this last scenario you were in any way as crass or obscene as
Leslie initially claimed, I would have taken the appropriate action you can
be sure. But Mrs. Creighton and her husband have come to your defense,
and Leslie has since changed somewhat her initial response to your remarks.
For the rest of this year I expect you to comport yourself in such a way, that
if Leslie cooperates her goals will be achieved. In your own way, you can
therefore take part in her success and provide for her a lasting rescue from her
own recklessness and folly.*

He signed it, *Robert Wilson Warren.*

The relief I felt upon reading this letter was almost orgasmic.

The year was going well, but I don't think I was feeling self-satisfied.
I started thinking again about George Meeker. Talking with Leslie
was possible because my experience with George had empowered me
in a way. I realized how important it can be to simply talk to a person
one on one. I didn't think my little meeting with George's father had
solved anything, but it set wheels in motion. Mrs. Creighton's letter
threatening his business probably did the trick.

At any rate I decided to sit down with George one on one and see
how he was doing. Before I could get it arranged I had a fight with
Annie about it. We were sitting in our living room, sipping on wine
and getting ready to watch a movie, and I mentioned what I was planning. She said, "Why can't you just do your job, grade their papers,
teach them the rules of composition and so on, and then let them go
home?"

"That's not all a teacher does."

"It's all my teachers did."

"Well they weren't very good teachers."

"Maybe they were. Maybe they were doing what they were supposed to do and nothing more."

"Forget it," I said. "I don't want to talk about it."

"It's because of your . . ." she stopped. I waited for her to continue but she didn't.

"Because of my what?"

"Nothing."

"No, because of my what?"

"You know what."

"No. Say it."

"Your need to control things," she said. "You're a control freak. At least you should admit it." I have to say I was beginning to see expressions on her face that I didn't like very much—I mean, maybe I was getting used to her, but she would sometimes let her mouth get twisted in a funny way, or crinkle her nose up toward her brow, and in truth, she was pretty awful to look at. Don't get me wrong—she was very attractive, in a clean, plain-looking kind of way. Her pale skin was flawless. But just sometimes when she crimped her face, I thought she looked almost ugly.

"I am unable to distinguish between your definition of a 'control freak' and caring about people," I said, and moved away from her on the couch.

"I know," she said. "That's your problem."

"Yeah, well."

"Really, you just can't see it, can you?"

"I said I didn't want to talk about it."

Now she scooted over and poked me, smiling. "I don't want to fight. I'm just talking here."

"Well I don't like what you're saying."

"What if I tell you a little story?" She wrapped her arms round my arm and snuggled up against me. "Want to hear a little story?"

"Don't," I said.

But she continued. "Once upon a time there was this parrot lying in the desert, on its back, its little feet in the air."

"I said I don't want to hear a story."

"Just listen, will you?" She scrunched her nose up again. I know it is entirely possible my reaction to her facial expressions was a product of the words she was saying to me—the judgments she made of me all the time. She could pass sentence on me with a small flicker of her eyebrow. "So anyway," she went on. "This parrot is lying on its back and a traveling nomad comes by riding on a camel. He says to the parrot, 'What do you think you're doing?' And the parrot says, 'I'm holding up the sky with my feet.' And the nomad says, 'How can a little bird like you, with those tiny, spindly legs, and little twig-like feet, hold up the sky?' and do you know what the parrot says?"

I remained silent.

In a very high, squeaky voice she said, "'One does what one can,'" and then she started laughing.

I laughed with her, but I was wondering what she was trying to say to me. She continued to laugh and after a while I said, "It's not that funny."

"It struck me funny," she said.

"So what's it mean?"

"You don't get it?"

"I get it. It's just not that funny."

"You're the parrot," she said, laughing. "Don't you see? You're the parrot. You're always holding up the sky, or trying to."

I came so close to saying, "Fuck you," I don't even want to think about it.

I sat down with George the day before Christmas break. I wished him a happy birthday, and he smiled a little weakly and thanked me. We were in my classroom, both of us sitting in student desks. I had put them together so that we would be facing each other. Before he sat down, he pulled his desk back a little, but he left it facing me.

"George," I said. "How are things at home?"

He said nothing, but he nodded his head a bit.

"I think you know I wouldn't ask you that question lightly."

"What do you want me to say?"

"I want you to tell me the truth."

He shook his head, slowly. "There's nothing to tell. Things have been great since—since—well, you know."

"I haven't noticed anything in your journal about it. You've stopped writing very much at all about—fishing, or your father, or . . ."

"My dad and I get along now."

"I'm glad to hear it."

"I'm still a fuck-up. But I'll be leaving soon," he said.

"Where are you going?"

"I'm a senior. When I graduate, I'm going to join the army." He asked me for a letter of recommendation and I told him he wouldn't need one. The army would be glad to have him. I complimented him on his growing physique—I told him the weightlifting was definitely beginning to show.

"It's my dad," he said.

"What?"

"My dad makes me do it. To punish me."

My heart sank.

"I keep fucking up."

"You know I want to help you?" I said.

"I know it." He looked away from me.

"Tell me about it."

"What?"

"George, I can't help you if you won't tell me what's happening."

"I keep fucking up. I'm no good for anything."

"That's just not true."

He looked at me. His eyes were gray, dead looking.

"I'm telling you it isn't true. I've seen enough of you, worked with you enough to see that you have talent, you . . ."

"I have talent?"

"You're smart. You can write."

"I'm trying to get an A."

"You'll get an A. But you got to work with me here."

"What do you want?"

I realized I really didn't know. What could he do? Could I ask him to swear out a complaint against his father? I wasn't even sure this was abuse anymore—but it was definitely cruelty. I was suddenly absolutely stumped. "George," I said. "I wish I could save you from . . ." I didn't finish the sentence.

He made a sound in the back of this throat and I could see he was fighting tears. But then he smiled and his eyes seemed to brighten. "I'm a screwup, though. I know that. But look at me. You can tell I work out. I'm building muscle."

"Yes, you are."

"So it's a benefit. My dad and I work out almost every day. We spend a lot of time together."

"All as punishment?"

"No. But the workouts get more intense when I mess up. And I'm such a screwup . . ."

"You're not a screwup," I interrupted him. "Everybody makes mistakes. You don't have to be perfect." I went on about the idiocy and stupidity of expecting perfection, but gradually I came to see that he wasn't really listening anymore. He nodded his head, but what I said didn't even slightly register. He was impatient to get out of there. I hoped he would ask me something—anything—to keep the conversation going; perhaps he would provide me with an opening. But he said nothing. Finally I patted him on the shoulder and told him if he ever needed to talk, I'd be there for him. When he got up, he paused for a second, still looking at the floor, and then he said, "I'm really okay, Mr. Jameson." He spoke barely above a whisper, but I think he meant it. He glanced back at me briefly, a nascent smile on his face, and then left the room.

I collected journals a day or so later.

(Leslie Warren) unfolded

12-16-86

Did I ever thank you for saving me from that DNA case at Jolito's? I am beginning to think that Miss Corrigan is right about you. She said you are a natural kind of hero because you are a gentleman. I think she's in love with you. Mrs. Creighton thinks you have great potential. She said that to me when she begged me to drop my complaint.

Did she tell you about it?

I dropped it because I want to graduate and I'm so tired of being in trouble. I know I'm smart, so I thought I'd do the smart thing for once.

Do you need me to help you out with Suzanne? She looks kind of lonely now that Mrs. C isn't sitting with her anymore. I'd be glad to sit next to her if you want me to. And yesterday George Meeker asked me on a date. I think he's asked every girl in the school. I was very gentle with him. I told him I already had a boyfriend but if I didn't, I would sure like to go out with him. He smiled so wide I thought he was going to burst out laughing.

I'd like to try to help Suzanne.

I wrote in the margin next to this:

Be very careful with her. She is very delicate and should be treated as gently as possible. But if you want to sit next to her and befriend her, you're welcome to try. She has not spoken to anyone as far as I know, so don't try to force it on her.

I also wrote that I'd heard from her dad and I knew the complaint had been dropped. I thanked her for it. I tried not to think about why Mrs. Creighton had not told me about it. Then I realized she probably liked it that I was feeling so tentative and threatened. She would expect my best behavior under those circumstances.

(Suzanne Rule) unfolded

12–86

I read all day sometimes. It is a way of listening that almost makes my soul feel warm and safe. I like books that make me think. I've always read every kind of book and now I want to read more poetry. I am surprised to find that I like poetry as an art form, because it allows one to speak from the heart. I see it now as a way of expression; of images and intimations that come from somewhere deep in the heart, or even memory and desire. I wouldn't want poetry to teach me anything. You can't write a poem that would teach about geometry, or trigonometry, or history, or French. I wouldn't want to learn French with poetry but I think I would like to read a poem in French. I never read poetry before this year. In school before this year, poetry was always thrust upon me like some sort of test of my intelligence; teachers insisted on their own interpretations of meaning and if I didn't see it their way, they made me feel inadequate and not up to the work mentally. I never got the feeling poetry was alive anymore, I thought it was dead like Latin, or classical music. Now I like how free I feel from reading it.

I wrote in the margin:

I am so glad you like poetry now, Suzanne. I think it is among the most beautiful developments from language of the human race. By the way, classical music isn't dead. People still play the great composers of the past— Mozart, Beethoven, Brahms, and so on. And people alive now are making their own classical music. People like Bernstein and Copland. Did you know it?

In her next entry, she wrote:

I think music is too mechanical for some people who play it. I had piano lessons when I was five and all I remember is counting and memorizing scales and counting some more. It's a hateful thing. I like listening to the piano when my mother plays it. I love it when she caresses it and makes her fingers move so fast the piano sounds like a stream of falling water, smashing against rocks and clattering too fast over tree branches and stones. I like it because it soothes me.

Suzanne was now talking to me directly, about herself; telling me about her likes and dislikes. I really did believe I was on the verge of something wonderful with her. I can't put into words how it feels to get to a point like that with a student who is so completely withdrawn and damaged. The way my second year was going, I didn't even remember law school. I was doing the most meaningful work there is. That's the only way I can express it. It was meaningful and worthwhile and important work and I was beginning to make a difference.

It didn't occur to me then, but just now I see what I had. Why do anything else with your only life?

37

Visit, and a Fall to Earth

AFTER CHRISTMAS I went to see Professor Bible. It wasn't easy to get up the nerve to do that, but I felt a growing need just to talk with him. I hadn't seen him since the summer so I guess you could say I abandoned him. Somehow it seemed like a major breach in relationship logic to just show up at his door. Annie suggested I send him a letter, but that felt cowardly to me. So, one cold and bracing Saturday morning, after a long jog across the park, I realized I was near the school and I could walk up the street to his apartment. Even though I had been walking for a good mile before I knocked, my breathing still sent wisps of steam his way when he opened the door. He was standing with no cane. Although he was in his robe, he was wearing a pair of white, puffy-looking tennis shoes. His hair, as always, was piled high on his head and as white as the tennis shoes, but now he had a short, very thick and wiry beard. It was also white, so white that it made his mustache look steely gray, and darkened his face a little. He looked quite distinguished.

"Well young man," he said, smiling. Under the darker mustache his teeth shone white and healthy.

I said hello, or something innocuous like that, and he opened the door wider, as if to present his whole self to me, but he said, "Look at you."

"I haven't seen you in awhile," I said.

"Come in out of the cold." He stood back and waved me in. The warm air shocked me. "Wow, you've got the heat turned up in here."

"I don't like the cold." He shut the door, then walked back into his kitchen. I followed him. He had a fire going under a simmering pot of vegetables and what looked like chunks of beef.

"Making a stew?"

He said nothing. He went to one of the cabinets and got down some cups and poured us each a cup of coffee. While he was doing this, he asked me questions about the school, and Mr. and Mrs. Creighton, and George Meeker. He didn't wait for answers; he just let the questions fly, and sort of answered them himself, like this: "Everything okay at the school? But of course it is. How are Mr. and Mrs. Creighton? I hope they're doing well. They always do manage, don't they? And George Meeker? I bet he's beginning to grow a bit, eh? He'll be close to seventeen now, am I right?"

When he had settled himself at the kitchen table, he pointed to the chair across from him. "Sit."

"How's the foot?" I asked as I pulled up my chair.

"Fine. Never better."

"I'm glad to hear it." There was one dull bulb in the ceiling fan above us, but most of the light came from two windows over the sink. It was early enough in the morning that the sun was parked in one of the upper panes and it leveled a wide, sharp beam of light at chest level across the room. When we sat down, we sat under the beam, which left beautiful shadows on the table and seemed to add a gentle kind of warmth to the steamy air. "I spend my mornings in here," he said.

"It's a lovely room."

We sipped our coffee for a while in silence. Finally he said, "So. What seems to be the trouble?"

"Trouble?"

"Something's bothering you."

"How can you tell?"

"I'm an experienced man. I've worked with young people all my adult life. I grew old doing it. How do you suppose I could tell?"

I shrugged. I guess I wanted him to be right, but I was not really troubled by anything except the unalterable fact that I had neglected him since August. It's possible that he assumed I was in trouble because of my sudden, unannounced visit. At any rate it was clear to me that he wanted to help, so I realized I needed to give him something to help with.

I took a tentative sip of my coffee, trying to think of what to say to him. What could I tell him that would make this visit seem less like charity and more like a natural result of my need for help?

He said, "So are you going to tell me?"

I was on the spot. I simply couldn't pretend I was there for an easy chat in the natural course of events between friends. I hadn't seen him in almost three months. So I just started talking. I told him everything that had happened so far that year in school. I told him about getting trapped in the snow with Leslie, my night at the bar with her, and my failed attempt to break through with George. I even told him about the poems I was getting from Suzanne Rule. I did not tell him that I was feeling utterly triumphant, or that I was on the verge of real success with Suzanne. I didn't tell him about Leslie's complaint, but I did say she had become one of my best students. He listened, patiently, sipping his coffee and without much comment. When I was done, I said, "So I guess I just wanted to see what you thought about things."

"What things?"

"Well," I said, and as I spoke, I realized I really was troubled about something—deeply troubled. "Annie says I should just mind my own business, teach my classes and go home. She keeps telling me I have a Christ complex or that I'm a control freak. But I think I'm doing the best job I can."

He looked at me over the cup. His dark brows and gray mustache made him look almost evil in that light. Like a deranged Hemingway.

I added, "She makes me feel like I'm doing things I shouldn't be doing."

He smiled sort of ruefully. "That comes with the territory."

"What does?"

"You've always got that conflict to figure out."

"The conflict between people who teach and those who don't know . . ."

"The conflict between what you know is your job and how to do it without going beyond what it calls you to."

"Well what did you do?"

"I was more traditional."

I put both hands on my cup and leaned forward. "You mean more traditional than me?"

"I would not have gone to Jolito's to meet Leslie Warren."

"I didn't go there to meet her."

"I would have avoided even the possibility that someone would think I did that."

"It worked, though."

"I know Leslie Warren. She is poison. Plain and simple."

I shook my head. "She's not. Not anymore."

He sipped his coffee again, looking at me over the steamy brim.

I said, "She's much better in class since I talked to her. I've won her over."

He lowered the cup and studied the table now, thinking. Then he said, "You may have. It's possible. She is human and human beings can change. I believed that all my teaching life. One has to believe it. But I'm telling you only what limits I would set in that situation and that's one of them. I would not have approached her. I would not have spent an evening sipping a beer with her sitting across from me. Nor would I have confronted George."

"But you did confront him. You told me . . ."

"It was a mistake. I lost him by doing that. You may now lose him too."

"He wasn't angry."

"He didn't show any anger with me, either. But I lost him."

"The abuse has stopped, pretty much," I said. "Now his father forces him to work out with him—that's not very nice, but it isn't abuse. And it's good for him."

It got quiet for a while. I finished my coffee and tried not to let him know it was gone. I kept sipping at an empty cup, feeling as though I'd been forced to defend myself. I could see that he pretty much agreed with Annie, and I was beginning to realize that coming here was a big mistake. But then I remembered what kind of teacher he was; I remembered why I admired him so much. I said, "But you never just came to work, taught your classes and went home, did you?"

He smiled.

"I can't believe you ever did that. How'd you lose George if you weren't getting in there and trying to help outside of the class?"

"There's that too. One must find a balance. It is very very hard."

"Seems easy to me. If you care about it. If you care about a student—about really teaching something that . . ."

"But you see, son. It's a service job. It's work we value ourselves, yes. But to everybody else, it's a service job. No different than that of a cook, or waiter, or dishwasher, or butler."

"I get it. I understand that. But isn't it also a kind of profession like being a lawyer, or . . ."

"No," he said, and then he leaned forward and spoke loudly, angrily. "You don't get it. We are not like lawyers, or judges, or even accountants or business managers. We don't count as much as a telephone repairman, or a plumber. A teacher is part of the service industry: short order cooks, waiters, butlers, maids, and so on. It's always been that way. Aristotle was a servant in Prince Phillip's household. All through the ages teachers were always among the servants in the great households; paid little, and given the responsibility of educating the upper classes. All the great kings and queens of England, France, and Spain, were educated by mere servants, people who lived and died without mention anywhere, in any book. What they passed on, what they prepared their students for, was the whole world—the whole bloody world—and not one of them was any more important than a common scullery maid!" His voice quavered a little at the end there, and it may have surprised him. He was deeply sad, but he didn't want me to see it. The tone of his voice at the end almost broke my heart. He got up and took his cup to the sink. It was as if he had announced to me, at the very moment he himself discovered it, that he had wasted his life.

"I'm sorry," I said.

He rinsed his cup and set it in the sink; then he stood there, looking out the bright window toward the climbing sun.

"I'm sorry," I said again.

He turned back to me a puzzled look on his face. "Sorry?" he said. "What in heaven's name are you sorry for?"

"I guess I'm sorry I brought it up about . . . I mean . . ."

He waved his hand, almost laughed. "Ah, forget it. You got nothing to be sorry for. I'm sorry I went at you like that."

I didn't know what to say.

"You're a good teacher, Benjamin," he said. "A fine teacher."

I said nothing.

"Just don't ever take it too seriously."

"I won't."

"And remember that each person you have to deal with is a separate entity—a completely separate and whole entity."

"What do you mean?"

He pointed to his head. "A universe, young man. A universe. Every student you see will be different from every other student you see every day of your teaching life. If you remember that—if you never forget to see people and not types of people—you will be fine."

"I will remember," I said, but I would have said anything. I was so ashamed for bringing this tender and benevolent man to such an extremity—to the realization of what his life finally meant—and to be honest I was already thinking about how to make an exit from his kitchen as soon as possible. My sense of triumph was in flames. In a way, I was glad of our conversation though, because it made me see, with absolute clarity, that maybe I should only teach a few more years, and then get on to law school. It seemed to me that I should eventually get very tired of being among the servants.

38

The Second Coming

Suzanne's next poem opened with this:

Here comes to the earth a
being—incredibly powerful

Then it went on:

Not Superman nor savior,
though he benefits from good press
The papers say He is all loving, all powerful, all good.
He waves a finger and miracles happen
sunsets, dawns, millions of blossoms
white blooming clouds in columns of light
cathedrals of light
cells divide, multiply, life

mushrooms from the dark miracles of life and
miracles of death (life, birth, immortal cancer
cells that cannot die).
But children can. By the thousands.
Countless others burn in fire
under walls of hunger or in floods or landslides
earthquakes and fires and fires and fires
The babies die, we all die
But oh the miracle of those sunsets in fall
those black towers of green leaves and white
roofed mountains shimmering in ice blue lakes
and oh that love, thrashing in human hearts

He maims in traffic of blood and cells
in genes, in mitochondria
in skyscrapers and machines and rooms and
cellars everywhere
He ordains, He wills, He waves that finger
every day He does these things
every second He does these things
and will not stop

He will only keep choosing, electing
Here will be orange sunrise, white swirls of cloud
in blue and here will be death and disease and horror
and here will be love and here will be hate
here will be motherhood, and here will be murder
no one gets out

Yet does He love us. He loves us so
Yet is He the one the true the only
and here He comes to the earth this being

There He is! Look, He is right there rising over the earth
like the sun in morning
like a spirit growing from the ground
He moves toward us
He loves us
He might do anything! He might do anything!

Fear not.

The poem was called "The Stampede."

Now, what would you do with that? It was clearly some sort of development of the ideas I had put in her head with my God assignment. It was not a good poem—it wasn't even close to her earlier work. I didn't know what I should do about it though. It wasn't school work; this was not a creative writing class and I was not a creative writing teacher, so I didn't think it would be a good idea to give it back to her with comments and suggestions for revision. What would I say to her about it anyway? That the idea of the poem isn't new? Who expects new ideas from a high school student? Could I tell her the poem wasn't really all that poetic? That her imagery—except for the bit about the trees and the mountains—was prosaic and a little confusing? That poets rely on connotation and nuance, the true souls of words, and using the word *miracle* while describing suffering children was perhaps a bit of a violation of some basic poetic principle of which I was completely unaware? I had to admit, I couldn't really tell her what was wrong with the damn thing. I just knew it was bad.

But how could I criticize it? I didn't think she wrote poems and left them on my desk for that reason anyway. I could have responded to the *idea* of the poem, I guess, but I was working with the fear that if I did anything differently she might stop writing them; might stop leaving them on my desk. I liked finding her poems in the morning because she was communicating with me, having another sort of conversation with me, even if I had never looked her in the face and didn't even know the color of her eyes.

I wanted only to encourage her, but I guess I thought it might also be a bad idea not to respond to her ideas. I didn't want her to think I was simply ignoring her sincerity, her sensibility. I'm not stupid. I could see she was attempting to touch a nerve with me; that she was writing that poem to me directly. I considered asking Leslie to read it but then thought better of it. She had taken to sitting next to Suzanne, and speaking to her gently at the beginning of every class, but nothing developed from that. (Leslie wrote in one of her journal entries that she thought Suzanne was very sad, and I replied that it was probably best to leave her alone.)

I read the "Stampede" poem over and over. But I didn't talk to Annie or anybody at the school about it. Frankly, I'd grown tired of Annie and her attitude toward my students and their problems. But I did have somebody I could go to.

When I was in graduate school I knew a guy named Wally Drummond who claimed to be a poet. Everybody called him Drum. He and I worked for a while on the school literary magazine, and in my last year of graduate school, we used to have a cup of coffee each morning before a class we both hated, called "Myth and Symbol in the Literature of Ireland." He always joked that the class should have been called, "No Thing Simple in the Literature of Ireland." (Reading too much James Joyce could do that to a person.) At any rate, I always thought Drum wasn't such a bad guy, and I figured he might be willing to read the poems and talk about them. (I know. It should have been clear to me then what sort of movement I was making away from Annie; if I couldn't talk to her about Suzanne then what could I talk to her about?)

I hadn't seen Drum in quite a while, but when I told him what I wanted he agreed to see me. He was working at the public library just up the road from Glenn Acres, so we arranged to have a quick lunch one cold, wintry Wednesday near the end of January. I took all of the poems Suzanne had written. I hoped he might know what I could say to her that would be useful—especially about the last poem.

The first thing Drum did was read all of them. He sat across from me in a bagel bakery and read each poem as if he were trying to decipher one of the Dead Sea scrolls. When I asked him if he wanted some cream cheese for his bagel he held up his hand and shushed me, frowning in concentration. I slathered my bagel and sipped my coffee and watched him. He was a tall, thin, sharp-pointed kind of man—his face filled with corners and crags. He wore a thin mustache, and let the beard on his chin grow just enough to show. His brow hung over his eyes, making them look sinister and threatening, like something hiding in the shadows, under the lee of two curved stones. In spite of his dark countenance, he was almost meek and it always stunned him when anyone took him seriously.

I was nearly finished with my bagel when he finally put her poems down and picked up his own bagel. "You say she's a high school student? I gotta talk to her."

"You can't do that." I told him all about her while he prepared his bagel and sipped his coffee. "She's as shy as a wild animal, for reasons we can scarcely guess at," I said once I'd finished.

"So she reads a lot."

"She sure does."

"It shows."

I took a sip of coffee and waited for him to continue, but he added more cream cheese to his bagel, stared at it for a bit, and then started eating again. He looked down at the poems.

"What can I say to her about that last one?" I said.

"Why do you have to say anything?"

"Well, I feel as though I've put those ideas in her head."

"So?"

"I don't know if I want that responsibility."

"Really."

305

"Not for that," I said. "Not for a vision of the world so bleak that she might . . ."

"Oh," he said, understanding me before I did. I realized as I was telling him about it that I was more concerned about Suzanne than her poem.

"Her life has been miserable up to this point," I said. "I think I can believe that absolutely. What if my suggesting these things to her leads her to try something awful?"

He nodded, chewing his food. Then he pointed to the poems and said, "Can I have these?"

"No. They're mine."

"How about copies?"

"What do you want them for?"

"I'm still poetry editor of *Hounds-Tooth*."

"You're kidding."

"Maybe we'll publish one or two of them."

"Really."

"That would be my response to her. Do her a big favor. Get a few of them published, then hand her the book and see what she says. I bet that would be a terrific way of motivating her—if that's what she needs."

"You're a poet. You think her poems are good?"

"Nobody really knows what a good poem is. Some poets can recognize a bad one when they see it. But poems are like wines. People take what they like. Most people in this country think a good poem is anything that rhymes."

"Most people like bad poetry."

"That's because good poetry makes demands on them."

"Yeah, well."

"Poetry has always had a very small, very select, very special audience."

"James Dickey said a poet in America is ludicrous."

"That was a criticism of America, not poets."

"I know that."

"Anyway, I think some of these show promise."

"What about that last one, about God the brute?"

"Didn't you ever read W. B. Yeats? 'The Second Coming'?"

I shrugged.

"How's it go? Something like, 'What rough beast with lion body and the head of a man, its hour come round at last, slouches toward Bethlehem to be born?'"

"I remember it," I said. "Maybe I can get her to change her title to 'The Second Coming Revisited.' That is better, don't you think?"

"Her poem isn't just about God, it's about us. Why don't we run from such a God, eh?"

I shook my head, more in amazement than anything else, but he took it to mean that I disagreed with him.

"See?" he said. "You don't like it. I do. It's not perfect, but nobody ever wrote a faultless piece. It's the best poem I've ever seen by a high school senior I can tell you."

"But what do I do now?" I said. "What about how I respond now?"

"I'll publish these, or most of them, in *Hounds-Tooth*."

"You can do that."

"I'm the poetry editor."

I shook my head. "Don't you think I should get her permission?"

"The magazine is copyrighted. Her name will be on the poems. What could she object to?"

"I don't know. It feels wrong."

"Shit, Anne Bradstreet's uncle or some sort of family friend took a bunch of her poems to London and published them in a book without telling her."

"Really."

"It might help you break through the shyness if you could show her a magazine with her poems in it."

I thought about what that would be like. Placing a new copy of *Hound's-Tooth* on Suzanne's desk one morning, watching her pick it up and begin to leaf through it. "When does the magazine come out?" I asked.

"The first week in April."

"Okay," I said. "Take them. Go ahead and do it. But I want them back when you're done."

"Sure."

"What do I do in the meantime? Shouldn't I have some sort of response to this last poem?"

He smiled, and with those dark eyes he looked almost evil. "Give her Blake's poem about the tiger."

I realized he was exactly right. That poem would be perfect. So here is what I put on her desk the next morning:

The Tyger

Tyger, Tyger, burning bright,
In the forests of the night;
What immortal hand or eye,
Could frame thy fearful symmetry?

In what distant deeps or skies.
Burnt the fire of thine eyes?
On what wings dare he aspire?
What the hand, dare seize the fire?
And what shoulder, & what art,
Could twist the sinews of thy heart?
And when thy heart began to beat,
What dread hand? & what dread feet?

What the hammer? what the chain,
In what furnace was thy brain?
What the anvil? what dread grasp,
Dare its deadly terrors clasp!

When the stars threw down their spears
And water'd heaven with their tears:
Did he smile his work to see?
Did he who made the Lamb make thee?

Tyger, Tyger burning bright,
In the forests of the night:
What immortal hand or eye,
Dare frame thy fearful symmetry?

Suzanne came in as she always did, before anyone else. I watched her from outside. I was in the smoking area with Doreen, who stood with her back to the door so I could see over her shoulder through the top window on the door. We were both freezing, but she agreed to stand there with me until Suzanne got there. The cold air made Doreen's eyes glitter and she let me know she didn't want to stand there too long. Suzanne went right to her desk; she did not have a new poem for me. When she sat down and put her books under her chair, she picked up the piece of paper and began reading.

I couldn't see her face. I never had seen her face, but she did something that got me worrying a little bit: when she was finished reading, she held the paper against her breast and started rocking a little, back and forth, like in prayer or something. I looked away, but Doreen noticed something was bothering me.

"What?" she said.

"Nothing."

She started to turn around, but I stopped her. "She'll see you and know we're talking about her."

"We're not talking about her, are we?"

"Don't women hold things against their chests when they are thinking romantically about it?"

"What?" The look on Doreen's face was so puzzled and contorted you would have thought I'd asked her to explain quantum mechanics.

"When you treasure something—a piece of paper, or cloth, or maybe a small doll or . . ."

"What the hell are you talking about?"

I could see now that Suzanne was reading the poem again. Her red hair, draped as it was next to her face, concealed all of her features, but I saw her wipe her eyes with the sleeve of her left hand. Then she took the paper and folded it carefully, reached back under her desk and retrieved her notebook, and placed it reverentially inside.

I must have made a sound in the back of my throat, because Doreen said, "What's wrong with you?"

"I think I've made a mistake giving Suzanne Rule those poems."

"Why?"

"I'm afraid I might be sending her the wrong message."

"Are you writing them?"

I looked at her, trying to remember what she said.

"The poems, the poems. Are you writing any of them?"

"No."

"And the ones she writes for you, do they express deep devotion and love?"

"No. Nothing even close to that."

"Then you got nothing to worry about."

"You didn't see what she did with that poem I just left for her."

"She's a high school senior. Believe me, if she's thinking what you're afraid she's thinking, you would know it."

"I would."

"She say anything in her journal?"

"No."

"And you still read them, all of them."

"I read hers."

"So, don't worry."

But I did worry a little bit. I was not completely unaware of what might happen if Suzanne got the wrong idea about me.

We got through January (no snow days) and well into February, and I was so busy with classes and grading papers and journals that I didn't have much time for anything else. I graded papers all weekend, every weekend, and most of each night during the week. The only day I refused to work at home was Friday. Annie was busy with some project of her own at work, so I didn't see much of her either.

As I said, Leslie had been behaving wonderfully since our meeting at Jolito's. She'd done her homework and spoke up in class and generally behaved herself. Even Mrs. Creighton could not believe it, and although I never told her about meeting Leslie outside of school, she attributed much of Leslie's improvement to me. She finally told me that Leslie had dropped her complaint.

"I know," I said. "The letter from her father mentioned it."

"I think you handled it just fine," she said. I thanked her. "You are good with them, I have to admit that," she added, more to convince herself than me.

"Well, she'll graduate this year. That's what matters to her. It's not me, it's her."

"Don't be so humble."

I was happy to remain silent and bask in the credit, I admit it. I don't wish to be immodest, but it really was because of me. No matter how anybody looked at it, Leslie had to be viewed as one of my clear successes.

And it felt wonderful to stand in front of the class with her eyes on me, actually listening and taking part. I know I keep saying it, but to make progress with a difficult student is so invigorating and even satisfying it sort of intoxicates you. With Leslie it was like winning the love of a beautiful and distant impossibility. You know what I mean—like a peasant winning the love of a princess. That really is what it felt like. And in the same class, Suzanne Rule was writing poems and leaving them on my desk in the mornings before I got there. I was feeling pretty powerful, I guess, and better than I should have been feeling. As has since been pointed out to me, I wasn't really all that aware of what anybody was learning, and my attention to the various personal details of a few students might have robbed me of a certain efficiency that high school teachers cultivate and develop. I didn't pay much attention to curriculum, mine or anyone else's. I made up things to do each day with Leslie and Suzanne in mind. I had already started reading poems to begin each of the senior classes, and before it was over, I was reading poems before every class. I'd pick really good poems—from the greatest modern poets. I knew poets like George Garrett, Sharon Olds, Roland Flint, Jane Shore, Gregory Natt, Henry Taylor, and Ann Darr were good because so many other poets admired their work. So I kept at it, on and on.

Then I'd have "discussions" of what the poems brought to mind. Not interpretation, but what did the poems cause my students to think? What came into their minds?

We talked about everything from AA meetings to wicker furniture. I didn't care.

Then I'd get them to write what was on their minds. I'd make them take class time to write in their journals, and sometimes I'd have them write essays that I insisted could only be two pages or less, no more than 500 words.

One day I read one of Whitman's civil war poems. We ended up talking about the civil war. Happy decided he would write his paper on the confederate cavalry officer Jeb Stuart. I had told the class their essays had to be at least 500 words, so Happy wanted to know if I was going to stick to that.

I said, "It has to be at least 500 words."

"What if it's four hundred ninety-seven words."

I said, "Add the sentence, 'And that's true.'"

He smirked a little and went out.

Here's what he wrote: *Stuart's men rode over the rise and saw the blue-coated Yankees.* That was twelve words. After that he wrote *Bang.*

312

Bang. Bang. Bang. Bang. Bang. He wrote it 485 times. At the end he wrote, *And that's true.* It was exactly 500 words.

I gave him an A.

That's how it was going.

Then something happened that changed everything, forever. And as I said at the very beginning, I want to understand it. I don't think it was my fault. I hope it wasn't my fault.

39

The Rough Beast

ONE DAY SHORTLY after I went to see Drummond, Leslie came to class late and I could see she had been crying. I wondered what might be wrong, and if there was anything I could do. I didn't want to embarrass her in front of everybody, so while I had the class writing in their journals, I ripped a small piece of paper out of my notebook, wrote, *Are you okay?* and left it on the edge of her desk. She looked at me, her eyes so darkly sad I almost picked her up out of the desk right then to hold her in my arms. Nothing can compare to the look of a woman's eyes when she is sad. Nothing. She only stared at me for a moment, considering. Then she looked back at the journal in front of her on the desk. She had not been writing in it at first, but now she started writing furiously. The effort seemed to both calm her down and revive her spirits.

I watched her for a moment, then went back to the front of the room. I don't know how much time went by. In my short time as a teacher one of the things I discovered is that when a group of students is working silently on something it's never really very silent. Some-body is always sniffing, or coughing, or sneezing. It's really quite extraordinary and even, in its own way, kind of charming. I know some teachers have been disgusted by those noises. Professor Bible once told me that on average a class period of fifty minutes contains between thirty-five and forty sniffs, five sneezes, two coughs, and "at least one or two other expulsions we should not think about."

Outside it was blustery and cold. Every now and then it would turn dark and great blasts of wind only slightly wet with rain brushed through the trees and herded leaves, drenched and heavy, across the field and the basketball court. I watched out the window for a while, amazed at the quick change of bright sun, dark wind and rain, then sun again.

Sometime near the end of the period, I noticed Suzanne Rule fold over several pages in her journal, then go on writing. In all her other journal entries she had never folded a single page; she had never said anything even remotely personal either. In fact, her writing was only interesting for how much she could say about everything under the trampled moon without revealing much at all about herself. I didn't have time to think about what I might learn from her confidential entry because I realized that Leslie had looked up just as Suzanne had folded her pages, and as though it had reminded her that she could do the same thing, Leslie folded her pages as well. Then she looked at me. I felt caught by her eyes—caught staring at her; admiring her, really. I froze, too. I couldn't look away from those unbelievable eyes.

Then she raised her hand. "Mr. Jameson?"

"Yes."

"When we fold the pages in our journal that means you won't read them, right?"

"That's right." She knew that.

"I just wanted to be sure." She looked small, sad. But then she forced a smile and unfolded most of the pages purposely, so I could see her do it. I smiled as gently as I could, but to be truthful, the way

I was feeling right at that moment, to say that I lit up would not be entirely inaccurate.

I couldn't wait to read at least two of the journals that afternoon, so when the period was over, I collected them. Everybody groaned, but Leslie actually worked up to a smile, before her face once again took on the crestfallen look of a new widow. She walked out of the room without looking back. Suzanne handed her journal forward, then slumped out of the room.

It was a hard choice to make, but I decided to read Suzanne's journal first. She had folded the pages for the first time and I couldn't wait to see what she had to say.

(Suzanne) folded

The poem about the tiger will always be one of the favorites among the poems I got from you because it presents notions about creation and God that imply a blacksmith made the earth. I am so used to reading history and biography, I can't believe poems like this one have eluded me all this time. I Don't think you should see this entry. It's stupid. I wish some day I could talk about poetry the way you do. I had a teacher in Baltimore who said poetry is a funny little twit's version of art with a lot of whining and raving about things nobody wants to talk about. I think it may be about what nobody can talk about. And maybe people who don't read poetry are twits. Like people who don't listen to music, or go to the movies or read books. Really interesting sorts, right? They can't talk about anything except what's happening right now on the TV or in the news or on the radio or in the sports world. Or they talk about the price of everything. They all laugh at the right time and say, "Oh that's funny." And they chatter happily about nothing that matters and disappear into thin air, into their graves without ever understanding or feeling anything deeply. Is that a judgment? Should one be judged on what slice of the arts she is interested in? Can't a person who only takes apart race cars and talks about gears and tools be interesting to anyone else? I know some people who think being an artist is a waste of time. My mother says I should remember what bores some artist

types can be. I'm not saying you are a bore. I don't know what I'm saying.
Sometimes I really wish I was dead. I cannot bear to think about any days
except the one I'm living right now. The thought of other days, tomorrow
and the day after and after that, and after and after—it just terrifies me.
Death is like going home. It's not an escape it's a retreat to home and peace.
When I sleep, I welcome the departure from the world. I'm not going to let
you read this entry.

I was kind of sorry that I'd seen what she wrote. I wished I hadn't
seen that reference to death. I folded over the page and set her journal
aside. I was tempted to tell her about what Drummond was going to
do with her poems, but I decided it might be a better surprise to
simply hand her the magazine with her poems in it. That was what
Drummond suggested and it seemed the thing to do. I admit I was
probably a little afraid that she might tell me to get them back—
might hate the idea of being published. After all she was so painfully
shy, and publication of one's poetry is about as broad a breach of
privacy as I can imagine. I worried about that a lot, to tell the truth.
What if her "debut" only served to drive her further into her own
skin? What if it further depressed her or worse drove her to something drastic and final. She might try to kill herself. On the other
hand, what if seeing her poems in print operated as a sort of coming
out for her; what if it made her less susceptible to panic and better
prepared to look other human beings in the face? I didn't know.

Next, I looked at Leslie's journal.

(Leslie)
You ask if I'm okay. I don't know if I can tell you what has happened to
me if you will understand, or just be like my parents and all the other adults
in the world. I am seeing somebody he is a lot older than I am (older than
you too. He's thirty.) He's not really from this country. He is the son of one
of the men my father works with in the foreign service, but not from the us

but from columbia south america. I don't know if I will be able to say what has been going on with him. Randy hates him and knows a little about him but not all of it and I've been with Randy too. I've been with Randy and with this other guy who I should not name here or anywhere. If my father knew or anyone else knew it would be just the most tragic thing because this guy from columbia is married last year when I was in England he came there to work with my father as his assistant or something translator or whatever and the embassy had a dance and he danced with me. My father said we were cute. We don't get along most of the time but he made me feel good when he was proud of me for dancing with his assistant. You may as well know—I've already talked about him in this thing. It's Raphael. That's all I can say. Anyway all last year Randy was my boyfriend and when Raphael came to our house with his wife to visit I would see him but nothing really happened with him until one night I took a cab to washington to go to a club where I was going to meet Randy and I saw Raphael at the front of a restrant near where the club was. He said hello and wanted to know where I was going. I was wearing this long chiffon gown and black stilleto heels and my hair curled down both sides of my face and I felt very beautiful but he didn't say anything about my beauty at all. He just smiled and seemed really glad to see me there and then he asked me if I wanted a drink. So I went with him. I didn't even think about Randy. He was very mad but I didn't tell him where I went. I made up some lie about my parents and he said he forgave me and then he forgot about it. But I kept seeing Raphael. Some weeks I would see both of them. I liked the danger of it. I liked how exciting it was to be with Randy right after school and then go see Raphael in the evening, dressed in a white gown and with perfect hair. Randy treats me like a girl and likes me to be a girl, but Raphael treated me like a woman. Like you did, that night in Jolito's. I felt like a woman that night when you rescued me, and it was fun getting to know you a little bit; sitting with you in the bar and drinking my coke and feeling like we were a couple. I liked the way you rescued me, too. It was so smart, in a way. Not too clever or anything, just natural and smart. And I didn't deserve it. So many men fall all over themselves to tell me I'm beautiful, I wanted to use my beauty to hurt you. I wrote about sex in my journal just to get back at you. I wanted to tempt you and all because you gave me a C on my paper, and it was the first paper in a long time I tried to do well on. I really did work on it. Then in Jolito's you told me about the truth. About people not telling me the truth and it hit home. It all hit home. I understood what you tried to do for me.

I'm stalling because I hate trying to say what is wrong with me. You taught me that I should look for the truth, and that's what I thought I got from Raphael. I fell in love with him. I am deeply, passionately in love with him. If you see smears on this page its where I wiped off tears. I know that sounds just so immature and stupid. I am no different than any other high school girl in trouble. I'm pregnant. And I don't know if its Raphael's or Randy's. I don't know who to tell or what to do. I can't tell Randy if its Raphael's and I can't tell Raphael for the same reason. I can't make the wrong man take care of this; or the right man take care of it. I can't take care of it myself. I don't know what to do. I love my father and mother I really do. But I am terrified of my father. He is very religious and he expects so much from me. He trusts me thats what he keeps telling me that he trusts me and he takes me overseas with him sometimes and asks me to take notes or listen to conversations in french or even spanish and I have to tell him what I've learned. I try so hard and I don't fail him when he needs me over there. The only place I've failed him is in school. I've tried and tried, but when you've been in the great cities of Europe with royalty, when you've been in embassys and palaces talking to the highest kind of people, it's hard to sit in a small wood chair and listen to somebody with a piece of chalk in his hand. No offense. I like listening to you, I really do. I mean I like it now. Once I started listening. You are so much more mature than everybody I know. My father said I should like you because you are different and you don't go with the mold. that's how he put it. I wish he wasn't so religious. When his religion comes into it he can be meanly cruel. When I was a little girl he made me kneel on uncooked rice in the kitchen for two hours. I couldn't stop crying and he wouldn't let me get up unless I did stop. Finally he took me out into the car and put me in the back seat and said I was going to stay there until I stopped crying. It was winter. I was cold. I started screaming. He wouldn't come to get me. Finally my mother came out and brought me inside. I went through all of that because I said "Jesus Christ." He taught me spanish and french and even some farsi. He spent all his hours with me when he wasn't traveling. I know he loves me. I know it would kill him if he knew I am pregnant. Or he would hate me. I am so important to him. Yesterday, I went to the bathroom and tried shaking up a bottle of coke and letting it shoot into me. Nothing happened. I just cried and cried. Every morning I feel dizzy and nausius and I can't eat. I think I know exactly where the little thing inside me is growing and dividing and becoming. I think I can put my finger on the place where it is making me sick and where it will soon make a crib of my body. I hate it and want it out of me so bad. At night I dream that it is climbing up my ribs. But I can't make it go away without telling my mother or my father. I am afraid to go to a clinic. I don't know what they will do. I don't know if they tell your parents or if they have to have the father's permission or what happens to your records or how long you have to be in the hospital if you get an abortion. I don't think I want to know, but I can't think about tomorrow. I hate the idea of tomorrow and whenever I think about just the next day, just the next few hours, I get sick to my stomach, as sick as I am in the morning when I get out of bed. I hate tomorrow. So when night falls and I have to come to a standstill someplace or I have to sit somehere or eat dinner or whatever I get sick thinking about what is coming now what is happening is the night is falling and then it will get dark and cold and still outside and I will have to sleep and when I do the sun will come up and it will be morning and I can't stand the idea of morning. Sickness again and another day, another day in front of me where this is true and its not going to go away, and then I have to eat again and I watch the sky loose its light and I know its going to be the time soon when I have to stop this somehow. I have to do something about it somehow. Because night is falling again and its going to fall again tomorrow and I hate tomorrow because this is true, this thing is true inside me and its growing and becoming itself and I am so afraid of it.

320

When I was finished I had tears in my eyes. At the bottom of the last page, I wrote,

Can you come to see me after class so we can talk? I want to help. If you can't come after class, what about Jolito's. Can you meet me there? I really do think I can help.

I knew damn well I could help.

40

First Lessons

I DIDN'T EVEN think about asking Annie about it. I went right to Doreen because I trusted her and I knew she would not judge me. At the end of that day I cornered her in the parking lot. The wind had calmed down a bit, but now the cold rain seemed to fall more steadily, though it was still closer to a mist than a downpour. She was standing by her car, trying to close her umbrella when I approached her and said, "Can we talk?"

"What?" she said impatiently.

"If you're busy . . ."

She finally got the umbrella closed and opened the car door. "I don't have any cigarettes," she said, throwing the umbrella on the floor in the back of her car.

"I don't want a cigarette. I need to tell you something and ask your advice."

"Well get in the car." She walked around and got in on the driver side. I cleared some papers off the front seat and got in next to her.

"Well?" she said.

I told her I had a student who was pregnant. I didn't tell her who. I told her I wanted to help if I could, that the student was paralyzed with fear and self-loathing and that it would be the best thing if she got an abortion. But Doreen surprised me. The first thing she said was, "Well it's none of your business. It's a family matter. She has to work it out with her mother and father."

"She can't tell her family."

"Well she has to."

"Could *you?*"

"Why should *I* tell them?"

"No, I mean could you tell your own parents if you were pregnant?"

"If I had to. Who is it?"

"I can't tell you that. And I don't want you to ask me again."

She started her car and turned on the heater and the windshield wipers. "You can tell me," she said. "Your secret's safe with me."

"Right."

"What's that supposed to mean?"

"I didn't mean anything by it. I just can't tell you or anyone." There was no way I was going to broach the subject of Professor Bible's illness and her fortitude and resolve where that secret was concerned.

"You don't trust me," she said.

"If I didn't trust you, I wouldn't be sitting here asking for your help."

"Well what do you want?"

"Okay," I said. "What if she wanted to get an abortion? What would she have to do?"

"Why would I know that?"

"You go to a clinic. You see a woman's doctor, a gynecologist, right?"

"Yes."

"Does he do abortions?"

"Every other weekend."

"I'm serious."

"So am I. That's the truth. He performs them at the open clinic in Alexandria. Every other weekend."

"How do you know that?"

"He's got pamphlets about it all over his office."

"So, if I took her to him . . ." The windows were fogging up pretty badly.

"Whoever it is, I would definitely not take her anywhere."

"I mean, if I gave her his address and she went to him, he would do it?"

"Yes."

"Would he insist that her parents know about it?"

"How old is she?"

"Eighteen."

"It's Leslie. It's Leslie isn't it? Come on, you can tell me now. She's the only one who's already eighteen."

I didn't know what to say.

"It's Leslie isn't it," she said again.

"She's not the only eighteen-year-old in the school," I said.

"I think she is. I bet she is."

"Of course not."

"I know it's her already, you don't have to try to backpedal away from it."

"It doesn't matter. If I tell this student to go to your gynecologist he'll arrange the . . ."

Doreen interrupted me. "He won't arrange anything. She has to go to the free clinic in Alexandria on one of the Saturdays he's there."

I nodded. In the silence that followed I became aware of the windshield wipers sloshing back and forth in the rain, which had increased now, and was steady and forceful. Then I said, "How can I find out if he'll be there this Saturday?"

She picked up her purse and opened it. "Here," she said, and handed me a piece of notepaper and a pen. "It's the Alexandria Free Clinic and Family Planning Center. It's in Arlington Ridge Shopping Center. You can get the phone number from information."

I wrote down what she said, then handed back the pen.

"It's just too bad," Doreen said. "Leslie was doing so well, finally."

I said nothing.

"And here you are," she said. "Stepping up to be the hero once again." She smiled and her eyes seemed to sparkle with it.

"I'm not a hero," I said.

She leaned toward me. I didn't want to embarrass her by recoiling from her, but that is what I wanted to do. I looked into those hard, steel-glinted eyes—saw close up some of the scars on her cheeks, and before I could pull back, she put her arms around my neck and kissed me. It was a very soft kiss—and longer than a mere friendship smack on the lips. She missed the mark a little, and it wasn't open-mouthed, but it got to me anyway. It was sexual and with the steamy windows provoked a kind of license. I put my arms around her and kissed her back. Now we sort of found the right position and got centered for it and it blossomed into a full-blown kiss with all the accoutrements. I realized we were both suddenly breathing very fast. I pulled back first, I think. Or perhaps she did. It's possible that we both stopped at exactly the same time. I said, "What was that?"

She laughed. "It was a kiss you dodo."

"But, but . . ." I sputtered. "What *was* that?"

This made her laugh harder. "Don't worry," she said. "I'm not trying to seduce you."

"Doreen," I said.

"Don't be so shocked," she said. "I always wanted to kiss a hero."

"Really."

Now she smiled in a ruined sort of way. I know she wanted to be seductive, but it really only looked as though her shoes might be pinching a bit. "I didn't dream that my hero would kiss me back."

And goddamn it that is what I had done. I sat there, looking at the gray, steam-covered windows, the heat from under the dash beginning to cook the skin around my collar. I didn't know what to say.

Doreen still smiling said very quietly, "Well?"

"Jesus Christ," I said. "I'm engaged to be married."

"Don't be so paranoid," she said. "I'm not trying to break up your stupid wedding."

I looked at her.

"Or whatever it is," she said. "You're safe." Now she moved her purse from the seat between us to the floor in the back. I watched this, wondering what she was about to do. We were in the parking lot of Glenn Acres School. The windows were so fogged by now we could have taken all our clothes off and humped away and nobody would have seen us—although they might've noticed her Malibu wobbling a bit. I wondered who saw me get in with her, if we might get away with something. But then I remembered myself. I didn't want to do anything like that. I really didn't. I knew what kind of trouble that would cause in my life and Doreen's.

She moved over and pressed herself against me. She ran her hand down the side of my face and whispered, "Don't fret my heroic little coward. I was just interested in a nice little roll in the hay. Nothing more serious than that."

I swallowed something that felt the size of a tennis ball. It wouldn't go down.

She traced my jawline with her fingernail. I looked into her eyes and felt the most profound sadness. So I said, "You were right. It's Leslie."

She scarcely reacted to what I said, but I saw her eyebrows weaken a bit. Then something seemed to occur to her and she pulled back. "She's not pregnant because of you is she?"

"Of course not," I said way too loud. It took her back a bit. It also had the beneficial effect of destroying the ambience of the moment, or whatever it was that she was working on before I said it. She moved back behind the wheel.

"I'm sorry," I said lamely and immediately regretted it.

"Don't be." She put the defrost fan on high, turned the heat down to cold, stared at the windows as they started to clear.

"Look," I said. "I want to be faithful. That too is heroic, right?"

"Sure."

"That's all. I wanted to kiss you. And I guess I must have wanted . . ."

"Don't be so analytical about it."

"I'm sorry."

It was quiet for a while, then she said, "You have the name of the clinic?"

"Yes."

"Then why don't you get out?"

"Oh," I said. "Sure." I opened the door. She still gazed straight ahead, waiting for me to shut the door. The windshield wipers threw water at me. "Please don't tell anybody about this."

"I won't."

"I mean it. You can't tell anybody."

"Okay," she said impatiently.

"I'm sorry," I said again and shut the door. "I'm not really a coward." She put the car in gear and drove off. I don't think she heard that last part.

All the way home I was kicking myself for being so vulnerable to Doreen—or more accurately for letting her be so vulnerable to me. I swear it never even occurred to me that she might be interested in me that way. I thought she was gay, for Christ's sake. I was also fairly certain I would not tell Annie about it. In fact, I would never tell Annie about it.

By the time I had parked my car and walked to the front door of my apartment, I was thinking about how perfect it would be if Doreen looked like Leslie and only wanted a friendly "roll in the hay." I didn't want to have that thought, but by Christ that's what I was thinking. And I didn't believe I would be able to resist, either. I think I'm a fairly ordinary man—believe me, I know I'm no hero—and still there I was, fumbling for my key, thinking about what it might be like to have Leslie offer herself to me like that. How great it would be. I actually got to the part about wondering where we would go, and then of course it hit me—what a rotten, snout-like thing a man is when he's enthralled by a beautiful woman who suddenly appears to be possible. I wonder: Do women seek men the same way? Would a woman be so turned on by a gorgeous man? So deeply beguiled by something as meaningless and superficial as physique?

I opened the door, pondering this issue, and I almost decided I could find a way to ask Annie about it, without letting her know specifically why I was asking, but once again the apartment was empty. She wasn't home.

By the time she came clamoring in, apologizing for being so late and all (she'd stopped off with "the gang" to celebrate some terrific budgetary reconciliation, a "real breakthrough"), I didn't want to talk about desire and men and women anymore. I didn't want to talk about anything.

41

The Typical Offerings of
an Ordinary Adult

LESLIE AND SUZANNE were in my fifth period class, the last one of
the day. I spent most of my time that day trying to avoid seeing
Doreen, feeling quite certain that if I did the embarrassment would
kill both of us. Of course she must have been avoiding me as well
because I didn't see her that whole day, and there was no way we
could miss each other in a building so small. I only saw Mrs. Creighton
once, in the hallway between first and second period. I went out
there to get a drink and she was standing outside her office tacking
something on the bulletin board about the coming Spring Festival.
This was in early March, but she was already excited because she had
found jonquils in her backyard over the weekend. She announced this
to me as I was rushing to gulp all the cold water I could get before I
dashed back into my classroom to avoid Doreen. When I was finished,
I stood up and wiped my chin where plenty of water had dripped
down onto my neck and shirt collar.

Mrs. Creighton ran her hands down the outside of my arms and then took both my hands in hers. "Mr. Jameson," she said. "You have done a wonderful job with Suzanne Rule."

"Thank you," I muttered, trying ever so slightly to free my hands and back away.

"She is actually beginning to thrive."

"Really?"

"She's started writing me little notes."

"And you write back?"

"Oh yes." She smiled. "We have a correspondence. I'm actually getting to talk to her through those notes."

"Good." I pulled again slightly and she let go my hands.

"That was your idea, wasn't it?"

"What?"

"Communicating through notes?"

"No," I said. "It started with Suzanne. She started leaving those poems for me in the mornings before class."

"But you had them writing in their journals so much, and that's a way of communicating with their teacher, right?"

I agreed it was—but I felt kind of like a fraud. I had them writing in their journals so often because I hadn't prepared anything for class and I had a stack of their papers to grade.

"Well," Mrs. Creighton said, "I'm so glad it got started, no matter whose idea it was. Do you know that little girl tried to kill herself last year? And now, maybe . . ."

"She tried to kill herself?"

"Yes."

I thought about her last journal entry. "Has she written poems for any of the other teachers?"

"Just notes and such. But you know, since she's been here, mostly all she's ever done is listen. Do what we say. Now she asks questions in her notes. She's actually breaking out. Communicating, for the first time; you had something to do with that."

I nodded, and then I said I had to get back to my classroom to prepare for second period.

Once I knew Suzanne had tried to kill herself, I didn't care that she was writing to her other teachers and to Mrs. Creighton. I had no control over what any of them might say to her, but now I realized how important it was to respond exactly right to her poems. I was glad that I had been so careful up to that point, although I worried even more about letting Drummond publish some of them. I don't know if I can accurately describe how it felt to have that whole thing hanging over me so completely. I was sick with both anticipation and dread; I had set something in motion that might be dangerous or really good and I didn't have the wherewithal to stop it if I wanted to.

Leslie put a note on my desk when she walked into class the next day. It said, *Did you read my journal? Can we meet again at Jolito's?* I immediately turned the note over and wrote, *Have you told anyone else about this yet?* When I gave it to her, she read it, then looked up at me with a look of shock on her face and shook her head no. I nodded and said, "Good."

She crumpled the note up and put it in her pocket, then seemed to relax a bit, as though everything was settled. But I still didn't know what time we would meet at Jolito's. I had their journals piled on the corner of my desk, so I said, "You'll all be glad to know that I will return your journals today." Of course they groaned. Getting the journals back meant they'd have to do more writing in them. Before I passed them back, I pretended to be getting a last look at some of them. I even made some notes in one or two—you know, *Thank you for sharing,* and *good*—then when I got to Leslie's journal I found what I'd written at the end and I added, *Three today?* I handed it to her and saw her go to the back of it to read my comments. She looked up and nodded. There was such hope in that look; I don't think I will ever forget it.

．　．　．

After school that day I went right to Jolito's. The place was almost empty. It took a while for my eyes to get used to the darkness in there, so I went immediately to the bar and sat down.

When I turned around and faced the light of the entrance, I saw Leslie sitting in the same corner where we had sat before. I ordered two Cokes and carried them over to the table. "I assumed you'd want a Coke," I said, and sat down across from her.

She said nothing. Her face was so beautifully sad—as though she were waiting for the last breath of life; as if she knew in the next moment she would have to say farewell to everything and everyone she loved. She took the Coke when I handed it to her, then looked around the room, still holding the Coke in her hand. She did not take a sip. When her eyes met mine I felt the need to say something soothing but I couldn't think of anything. Perhaps I wanted to offer her the possibility of simply having the baby. Couldn't I convince her that she would come to see her child as a wondrous gift? My plan was to get her to tell her parents about it. I went over all the ways I could say that to her, but nothing presented itself. What I saw in her eyes told me for certain that she would not want me to say anything that sounded like the typical offerings of an ordinary adult. A long silence ensued while I tried to figure out what to say. She looked at me blankly, waiting there. Finally I said, "Looks like the dart crowd isn't here today."

She gave a little smirk, then resumed the look of sadness and fear.

"Trust me honey," I said. "Tell me what you want and I will help you if I can."

"I don't want to be pregnant anymore."

"We can do that if you want."

"Do what?"

"An abortion. It's perfectly legal."

She started crying softly and quietly. There was an unlit candle on the table, and an ashtray. I lit a cigarette, then the candle. She did not look at me, but I saw tears, glistening now in the candlelight, running down her face to her chin. Her nose was running. I handed her my napkin and she wiped under her eyes.

"I'm sorry," she said.

"Leslie, have you considered having this baby?"

"I can't." She started crying again.

"You've considered it."

"I don't want this to happen to me. Raphael would never have me if he knew."

"How do you know?"

"He's married," she said this with a little bit of a sob.

As gently as I could, I whispered, "Is he in love with you, honey?"

"I don't know. I don't know." She sounded so much like a little girl. It took all of my strength not to just take her in my arms and hold her. She cried so hard that saliva started collecting on her lips, tears streamed down her face. She kept wiping them away with the napkin. "This can't happen to me."

"Well it won't then. We can do everything without letting anyone know."

"We can?"

"Yes."

"No one will know?"

"I will and you will. The doctor and maybe a nurse or two. No one else."

"My parents?"

"Don't have to know. It's no one's business but your own. You're eighteen. An adult."

She wiped under her eyes again, started to get control of herself. "If I was an adult I wouldn't be so stupid as to let this happen to me."

"It happens to lots of women," I said. "Adult women."

She only looked at me with those shimmering eyes. Up to that point she had seemed so self-possessed and willful she emanated nothing but control and even a kind of supremacy over everything and everyone around her. It was possible to admire her and even to fear her a little bit. If only her critics at the school could see her now, they would not be so quick to judge her unworthy.

"When you are lost in passion," I said, "It's supposed to be bad form to be considering the future."

"What?"

"Nothing. It was a stupid thing to say." I reached into my pocket and got the name and address of the clinic in Alexandria. "Here's where you have to go. This Saturday."

"I can't go alone," she said.

"Why not?"

If you could have seen her eyes—the way she pleaded with me with just a helpless look. "I'll go with you," I said. "In fact, if you want I'll drive you there."

Now, in the midst of her tears, she smiled. It was absolutely perfect. In movies and on television, I've seen the most beautiful women on earth, made up as perfectly as the makeup artists can do it, under the most favorable lights, with the exact camera angles to produce the most unreachable allure, and all of them would sadly pale next to Leslie's tearful smile in that candlelight. I wanted to reach out and touch her face, just to confirm that it was real.

She cast her eyes down again briefly, then she said, "Why are you doing this for me?"

I didn't know the answer to that question and I didn't want to think about it. I am aware that some will say I was falling all over myself to help her because she was so beautiful; that if she was less attractive I would have ignored her problem, but I just don't think that is true. I wanted to help her because she so desperately needed help, and I knew I *could* help her. What would you do? It's not like I was in love with her or anything. I barely knew her.

42

An Impression of Fall

THAT SATURDAY, IT took a while to convince Annie that I was only going to the mall to see about getting a new pair of shoes. (There was no way I was going to tell her the truth about what I was up to.) I told her all that standing up and walking back and forth in my classes was killing my feet and I needed to pick up some shoes that would be soft and cushiony. She suggested a pair of black tennis shoes, or maybe some Bass loafers. "Do they still make Hush Puppies?" she asked. I said I'd look into it. She offered to go at first, but I told her I wanted to walk into the shoe store, get the pair I wanted and walk out again. She likes to wander around the mall for hours, so she told me to go on and get my shoes; she really didn't want to be impatiently herded in and out of the mall because of my insanity.

At the right time, I got in the car and drove to Glenn Acres where I met Leslie, then I drove her to Arlington Ridge Shopping Center—which was only about ten miles up the road from Glenn Acres—and the Alexandria Family Planning Center and Free Clinic.

We drove most of the way in silence. She fumbled with her car keys, then shoved them down into her jacket pocket. It was a windy day. Bright sun and a cloudless sky. The wind was relentless; it would not stop. Simply walking into it gave you the feeling that you were moving at thirty or forty miles an hour. Leaves swirled in the bright sun and gave an impression of fall, although that was long past.

I was surprised at the efficiency of the clinic. We barreled through the door, struggling to settle from the disarray of the wind—Leslie's hair was all over the place; I had leaves in the collar of my shirt—and even as we stood there in front of everybody putting ourselves in order, a black woman shaped like a cannonball came from behind the counter with a clipboard and a pen attached to it. She welcomed us, bade us have a seat.

"Please fill out the form completely, okay?" she said. "And then we will set you up with a doctor. Fill this little card out first and give it to me, so I know your name, honey, okay?" She smiled at both of us, clearly assuming we were there for some sort of "family counseling."

"Just a friend," I said, with a tight smile.

Leslie looked at me, and I shrugged. "Well, I *am*." Remember, I was all of nine or ten years older than she was.

She found an empty seat and began filling out the form. I remained standing by the door. The room was small, and close. Blue plastic chairs sat in rows from one side to the other, almost all of them occupied. I was the only man in the room. Some of the older women, I felt, eyed me suspiciously.

The procedure was complex and took more than two hours. Not the abortion, mind you—just what Leslie had to do before she went in for it. The black woman came back out and took her form. We waited for what seemed like a very long time—Leslie standing next to me now, watching the others in the room who one by one were led through the door into the back offices. Finally it was her turn. The receptionist came out and led her on back. I waited by myself, though more women came in, one with a fat man who sat right across from me, his belly bulging out of his sweat suit. Every so often he'd snap the pages of the *Wall Street Journal* he was reading, and between snaps he breathed so loudly through those tight little nostrils of his, it was as if I were sharing his every intake of air.

Finally, Leslie came back out. I could see she'd been crying. She came right up to me and put her head against my chest. I put my arms around her and held her a moment. It was as innocent as any hug on earth. I wished I was her father, to tell the truth, so I could forgive her, you know? So I could offer her . . . absolution.

She remained there a long time. "What's the matter?" I whispered.

"Nothing." She moved next to me and I kept my arm around her shoulder. I didn't even know if it was done yet.

"Is it . . . I mean, have they . . ."

"No," she said. "I had to talk to a counselor and then fill out a whole other form."

"Oh."

"I had to, you know, agree to the procedure and all." She sniffed, wiped her eyes. She was hardly more than a child. "And then I had to sign this new form that said I had seen and signed the *other* form."

"Jesus."

"Like, they want me to be sure of what I'm about to do."

"Case somebody wanders in here and thinks they're in for a fucking mud bath?"

She smiled, even managed to laugh a little through her tears. "You're so funny sometimes," she said.

I couldn't help feeling rather proud of myself. I don't want to go into the reasons. It just seemed unerringly right: getting her to laugh a little in that situation; nothing romantic about it, just the joy of a kind of release. Hoping to score another laugh, I said, "What do they think? Like, somebody might wander in here expecting a yoga lesson?"

But her mind must have returned to the procedure. She got this scared look on her face, tears brimming in her eyes again.

"Sure you want to do this?" I asked.

She nodded.

"Did those forms . . . upset you?"

She shook her head no, but tears were still running down her face.

"Leslie you don't have to do this if you don't want to."

"No. I *want* to," she said. "I have to."

"Okay."

"I just don't think it's right." Now she put her head on my shoulder and took hold of my arm. "I know it isn't right."

"Well then you shouldn't do it," I said.

"I have to."

"But you *don't* have to. You really don't."

She buried her head against my chest again, sniffling.

"Honey," I said. "Maybe you should trust your parents in this, okay? They might handle it better than you think." But then I remembered what she'd said about being six—a six-year-old girl—when her father made her kneel on uncooked rice, and realized I didn't believe a word of what I'd just said.

She looked up at me, her eyes searching my face, and I couldn't help myself. I leaned down and kissed her very softly on the mouth. It was the only kiss I've ever given out of . . . I don't know . . . a kind of innocence? It was pure, perfect. I loved her then with only love—nothing else. Understand? There was no sex in it at all in that moment.

It wasn't a long kiss, and when I pulled back from it and looked at her, she smiled as if she knew what it was; as if she understood it completely. Tears still filled her eyes and ran down her cheeks. As tenderly as I could, I brushed them away.

She didn't say anything. A few minutes later, a nurse came out and called her name, startling her. I held her a little tighter, to reassure her. She looked up at me, gave a half smile of what? Determination? And then she was gone.

I waited a long time. It didn't seem right to look at a magazine, so I just I stared out the window, watched the wind swirling the leaves.

When she finally came out again, she was silent. She looked as if she'd just awakened from a very long nap. Her eyes were puffy, and her hair seemed to have lost some of its luster. She walked carefully, as if it hurt the bottom of her feet.

"You all right?" I asked.

"Fine." Her voice was normal, slightly disinterested even.

I drove her back to Glen Acres. Again we rode in silence. I couldn't think of anything to say, and didn't want to keep asking her if she was all right. In the parking lot of the school, before she got out of the car, she leaned over and hugged me. "Thank you, Mr. Jameson," she said.

Like an idiot I said, "You're welcome."

I wanted to kiss her again. I think now, to be honest, I needed to kiss her again. But we only stared at each other for a brief moment. "Ben," she whispered. "You really are the very best teacher I ever had." And I knew at that moment, looking into those dazzling eyes, that I would never be anything more than that. She would go on with her half-charmed life, graduate in the spring. Whatever she might do about Randy and Raphael would be none of my business. I wished with all my heart that I could think of something memorable to say, because I also knew at that moment that I loved her in the only way I ever could.

She smiled fully now, understanding all of it. I kissed her on the forehead, and then she got out of the car and without looking back, trudged over to her little Ford Escort. I watched as she fumbled in her pocket for her keys, got in, and then a moment later pulled out of the lot.

I still had to go buy a pair of comfy shoes and I wasn't sure what I would tell Annie, since I'd been gone most of the day. It turned out that Hush Puppies were not all that hard to find.

In the end I didn't tell Annie anything. She was napping when I got home, and when she woke up, didn't seem interested in my day. I showed her the Hush Puppies I'd bought and all she did was smirk at them. "Who wears gray shoes?"

"They're gray?" I picked them out in a hurry and I wasn't sure of the color. I would have said they were light brown.

"You idiot. You don't know what color they are?"

"Didn't they all use to be gray?"

"God what a silly name for a shoe."

"Oh yeah, and *mules* isn't."

She laughed and that was that.

43

Aftermath

LESLIE CAME BACK a little after that day. I mean she was beginning to be interested again in classes. We did not communicate outside of class at all, and all she ever said to me directly was "Hi, Mr. Jameson" (I never could get her to call me Ben), and at the end of the day, "Bye," with a glamorous wave of her hand. But she took part in the class discussions, worked in her journal when I asked for it, and turned her papers in on time. (She wrote an A paper about the rock group Foreigner that was insightful, involved, and a pleasure to read. She said she was afraid the band was for older listeners and had been around too long. She compared them to Talking Heads.) I was beginning to wonder what she was thinking about my kiss, and then one day in early April, I stayed in my class during the last break of the day, and she came in very early, walked up to my desk and said, "Can I see you?"

"Sure. What can I do for you?"

"After school."

"Oh." The idea flustered me and I found myself wondering what to do with my hands. I said, "Sure. How about Jolito's?"

"Can you give me a ride? My mother has my car today."

"From here?" I was worried about how that would look, but I didn't say that to her. She didn't answer me. There was no one in the room yet, not even Suzanne.

"Okay," I said. "Wait for me out back."

She turned, went to her desk, and started unloading books and settling herself for class. Under a dark blue sweater, she wore a white dress with a small leafy pattern cut into the fabric around her neck.

Suddenly I was worried about what she might want. I still felt so protective of her, and I didn't want her to misunderstand anything between us. I didn't know what to think of it myself. I knew I felt a kind of tenderness for her, but it was not romantic as much as it was spiritual. In fact, it was almost religious. How could I tell her that?

That afternoon, I walked to my car and she was waiting there beside the front door, holding her books in front of her. She almost curtsied, as I opened the door, then she got in the car, sweeping her dress in with her legs. I closed the door and walked around the back of the car, trying not to look furtive; trying not to check the windows and other cars to see if anybody was watching us. Of course people were watching us. The place was crowded with folks scattering to jobs and home. I wondered if Mrs. Creighton saw me. Or Doreen.

I had kissed Doreen too. Or she had kissed me. She started it anyway, and it wasn't the same kind of kiss. I know I should have wondered what was wrong with me, but I really didn't. I believed I was in love with Annie; I believed I had been faithful. In the one case, Doreen had sort of ambushed me, and for a few minutes I gave into it. I'd never say this to her, but it's possible I responded because I felt a little sorry for her. And, it's also possible that some part of me was interested, because when she turned her head in a certain way, or when she laughed through something she was saying, she could look pretty sexy. Still, I had been shocked into it and we had been avoiding each other ever since.

When I kissed Leslie it was as if some elemental facet of my humanity wanted to touch her as sweetly and gently as possible. It was an offering. Nothing more.

But what if Leslie had seen it as romance? What would I do? I actually wished I could ask Doreen about it.

I felt so alone and I was in dangerous territory.

We drove to Jolito's without saying very much. She held her books in her lap and stared out the window, her face inscrutable. When we got there I found a place to park and turned off the car. "Are you all right?"

"I'm fine." She put her books down between us and got out.

I followed her into the restaurant. When we were seated at the same table as the other two times, she said, "I want a Coke."

I went to the bar and ordered two Cokes.

When I came back she was smiling, her eyes bright and gleaming in the candle on the table.

"Did you light that?" I said.

She nodded, still smiling.

"Well," I said, sitting down across from her. "What's up?"

She looked down at her hands, began playing with the tips of her fingernails. "I was just wondering what you were thinking."

"What I'm thinking?"

"About . . . stuff."

"What's the matter, Leslie?"

She shook her head, then looked at me. "What do you think of me?"

What could I say to her? She stared at me, anticipating some kind of response. She was eighteen and I was twenty-six. The only thing between us it seemed to me was that I was her teacher. At that moment, I did not even remember Annie. "You know what I think of you," I said.

"No I don't."

"I think you are beautiful, that you . . ." I saw her face change. You would have thought I had called her "babe." She did not look away. "What do you want me to say?"

She raised her brows slightly, letting her eyes fall.

"I'm sorry," I said. "I think we might . . . if I wasn't your teacher . . ."

"Do you think I'm a killer?"

"What?"

"A killer."

"What do you mean?"

"I killed my baby." With this, she started to gulp, to choke back tears. She took a quick sip of her Coke and then wiped her mouth with a napkin. "I'm sorry."

"Leslie, you did not kill your baby."

"Raphael doesn't want to see me anymore."

"You told him?"

She couldn't look at me now. She studied her hands, the slow toying of her forefinger with the edge of her thumb. "He's Catholic. He got angry when I told him what I'd done. He called me a murderer."

"It was not murder. Raphael is an idiot."

"I thought he loved me." Her voice broke. I waited for her to begin sobbing again. But she didn't. She took the straw out of her Coke and started bending and folding it. I could not take my eyes off her face.

"It will be all right, Leslie."

"My father talked about abortion last night. He had friends over for cards and I heard him say it. That it's murder."

"You told him about it?"

"No. That's what they were all talking about. My father and his friends and my mother."

"Well it's not murder."

"They all agreed."

"They're wrong."

She did not seem convinced.

"Look here," I said. "It's just name-calling. People say things like that because they have pea brains and they don't know any other way to argue."

"My father doesn't have a pea brain."

"Forgive me. But if he thinks like that, he's got a pea brain."

"He says it's murder."

"You know how many women are on the pill? Millions of them. And every last one of them is having spontaneous abortions almost every month, but you never hear anybody calling them murderers."

She looked puzzled but she was definitely interested. She didn't understand how the pill worked. She'd never been on the pill, so I had to explain it to her. "The pill convinces the body that it is already pregnant. So all fertilized eggs—all of the tiniest embryos—get sloughed off by the body. They can't attach to the uterus. But they're still embryos."

She took a slow sip of her Coke, meeting my gaze now with a kind of warmth. Her eyes still glittered, but she'd mastered it. She was not going to cry. We sat there for a long time without saying anything. Then she said, "Thank you, Mr. Jameson."

"For what?"

"Everything. For helping me."

I almost took her in my arms right then. I wish I had. I might be holding her right now, if I could have had the courage to reach across the table and just touch the side of her face. But I was a mere mortal, engaged to be married. I knew for certain that if I pulled back from the light of her eyes, I would remember that I was in love with Annie. Everything I loved about Leslie had to do with her allure, her unmatchable beauty, and I knew it. I cared for her, I wasn't in love with her. So I didn't say anything. We finished our Cokes and I drove her back to the school so she could call her mother to come and pick her up. When she got out of the car, she smiled at me again, reaching back in to get her books. "See you in class tomorrow," she said.

I went home feeling as though I had made a real difference in her life. And perhaps I'd made a difference in my own. I felt clean, to tell the truth. Ethical. It was not a bad feeling.

I cruised into April not thinking much about what the end of the year would mean. Leslie came to every class. She was quiet, and never happy, but she was getting through it, or seemed to be.

Annie talked a lot about law school and she kept telling me if I was going I needed to begin sending out applications. So finally one weekend I got everything together, wrote a few application letters, and sent them off. But I was going through the motions. I figured I could stall at least until the end of the decade. I applied at the University of Virginia, Georgetown University, and The American University. Of course we hoped for American or Georgetown, since both were close to home and all. But I was willing to move to Charlottesville.

At the end of April, I found another poem from Suzanne on my desk.

Under ground

In the dark
Seeds have secrets
Small chances
Where walls come down and
Membranes fuse in damp
Breathe in dark soil
Everything small
Big as the earth

I wanted so bad to write *membranes fuse? Yikes.* And hand it back to her. Get some sort of dialogue going about the work because I think she did have talent. But I was just too afraid of what might happen if I came at these little gifts critically.

346

I went to Mrs. Creighton's office and started searching among the English texts in there, trying to find a poem to return to her. I searched all through my break and was almost late for class, but I finally found another by Blake that at least seemed appropriate for the time of year. It was the last poem I gave her.

To Spring

O thou, with dewy locks, who lookest down
Thro' the clear windows of the morning; turn
Thine angel eyes upon our western isle,
Which in full choir hails thy approach, O Spring!

The hills tell each other, and the list'ning
Vallies hear; all our longing eyes are turned
Up to thy bright pavillions: issue forth,
And let thy holy feet visit our clime.

Come o'er the eastern hills, and let our winds
Kiss thy perfumed garments; let us taste
Thy morn and evening breath; scatter thy pearls
Upon our love-sick land that mourns for thee.

O deck her forth with thy fair fingers; pour
Thy soft kisses on her bosom; and put
Thy golden crown upon her languish'd head,
Whose modest tresses were bound up for thee!

I put it on her desk, but I didn't see what she did with it. I assumed she put it with the others she was saving.

As the weather warmed, we could take breaks outside again and smoke cigarettes. Doreen and I had gradually overcome our embarrassment over that kiss, so we could stand outside my room and talk about the weather, or about one of the students in our classes. We never ever talked about the kiss, but it was always there between us, like some sort of gauze we had to speak through. Every now and then she would smile knowingly at me, but I'd look away not wanting to be appraised. I told her about my application to law school, but not anything else. She never pressed me to find out what happened with Leslie and I didn't volunteer it.

I don't know if I could say I was hoping for anything. I was so busy with schoolwork—grading paper after paper, reading journals, or riffling through them pretending to, and just trying to keep my head above water. Five classes a day are hard to manage for an entire year.

Early in May, I noticed that Leslie was beginning to slip a little. Her demeanor was the same, pretty much, but now she brooded more in classes. Her journal entries were beginning to scare me. She wrote about killing, about how it feels to have ended a life for a man she was "completely in love with," and being thrown away "because of her desire to protect him." I wrote back of course and told her again that she had not actually done that. *A life begins*, I wrote, *when a baby is born or is viable outside the womb, not before. And Raphael simply did not have the courage to leave his wife.*

In another entry she wrote:

My baby is there in me or she is and I am the earth. I am the world and how could I take away all color and music and taste and softness and summer fragrance. It was my baby. My baby. I have killed my baby.

I wrote:

Leslie honey, you have not killed your baby. It might have been your baby if you had waited a very long time and perhaps suffered through a lot of illness and discomfort. But you did not kill a baby. Millions of women take the pill because they want to stop their pregnancy before a baby is

even possible. That's what you did. You chose for your body not to keep a
fertilized egg. You sloughed it off before a baby was possible. It was not a
baby. A human being is only a baby when it can live outside of you.
Don't you see?

But she seemed to pay no attention to that at all. In class she began
to stare out the window, and she stopped taking care of her hair. She
no longer looked like a fashion model, that's for sure. She didn't
have to wear much makeup to adorn that face; her eyebrows were
naturally curved perfectly over her light blue eyes, and her lips were
fairly puffy and dark to begin with. But I noticed she was not paying
the same attention to her appearance. She began to look sort of pale
and weak; as if it took all of her energy to remain upright.

Mrs. Creighton came to me one day and wanted to know if I'd
noticed anything different about Leslie. I told her I saw that she was
not so prissy anymore about her beauty. I think that is how I put it. I
was a little scared of what would happen if Mrs. Creighton found out
what I had helped Leslie to do, so I didn't want the old woman to
notice anything at all if I could help it. "She's just growing up," I said.

"I think something's wrong. Is she writing in her journal? The
folded pages?"

"She just wrote an A paper for me." I was standing in front of my
desk, in the first week of May, putting papers in my briefcase. I
wanted to get out of there.

"I'm worried about her."

"She's fine."

"I think she's losing weight."

I hadn't noticed that and said so. "I'll have her write in her journal
tomorrow and I'll let you know if she says anything."

"Okay. Thanks." She turned, made her way through the rows of
chairs to the back of the room, but before she went out, she stopped.
"I should tell you I'm a little worried about Suzanne, too."

"Why?"

"Has she said anything to you about death? Or dying?"

"In one of her poems she said something about it. She said she doesn't like to dream when she sleeps."

She waited there for me to say more, but I didn't know what else to say.

"She wrote in a note to me that she'd rather be dead," Mrs. Creighton whispered, almost to herself.

"I think she's just coming out to us," I said. "Just letting us in a little bit. It's probably a good thing."

She nodded, slightly, then waved her hand and went out.

In her journal, Leslie started talking about loving another man.

(Leslie) unfolded

4-08-87

I learned so much from my experience with Raphael. Now I think I really know what love is. Someone else taught me by everything he did for me. I think I understand now why people talk about how important it is what is inside a person. Who a person is. No one is what they look like and I am not beautiful until I learn what it means to care for and love another person without thinking about how they look or if they are cute or handsome or not. The only thing that matters is if they are too interested in their own selves rather than others. I broke up with Randy. I didn't want to hurt him but he is so imature he is not like a real man yet and I don't care anymore how good looking he is. I've fallen in love with a man who is so much better and so much more beautiful in every way.

She drew a little smiley face after the last word. She had one page folded over. On it, she wrote, *I love you, Mr. Jameson.*

I folded it back with tears in my eyes. My hands shook. Fear made my heart stutter and I couldn't think. I was alone in my living room and Annie would be home any minute and I paced around as if Leslie was there and I had to get her out of the house. I knew this was dangerous. But, to be accurate and truthful, it was also incredibly thrilling. I knew what it was, though. She was only grateful to me for helping her and she would eventually come to see that she was not really in love with me at all. I knew that. And I knew what the right thing was. I knew I could do the right thing.

Since I had promised not to read folded entries, I pretended I hadn't seen what she wrote. I commented at the end of the unfolded entry:

> *I am glad you have started to have feelings for another. Whoever this new man is, he is lucky to have you because now you are a fully grown young woman. You know, I'm getting married soon. Being in love is a wonderful thing, but it takes time to let it develop so don't be in a hurry. My fiancée and I have known each other for three years. Love is the sweetest thing, especially in the spring, but you should be patient and watchful of how it develops especially when you are coming from heartache. The writing is still developing beautifully. You have talent Leslie and I'm proud of you.*

When I returned the journals next day, she turned to the back and unfolded the page to see if I'd written anything there. When she saw nothing her face changed slightly—almost as if she had confirmed something for herself—then she read my comments. She closed the journal and placed it in her book bag. Her face did not change, but I saw her brush her hair back a little with a trembling hand and I felt as though I had purposely injured her.

I never saw anyone so completely transformed before; in spite of her former beauty and power, she was now vulnerable and sad and I had the temerity to feel sorry for her.

44

Small Triumphs

THE SECOND WEEK in May, Drummond called me with the news that he had magazines. I met him at the same restaurant where we'd gone before only now it was a beautiful spring day. Warm breezes caressed everything as I got out of the car and strolled into the bagel shop. "What a day, eh?" he said. "I love April and May in this area."

We decided to eat outside.

When he handed me *Hounds-Tooth* I was shocked at its quality. It had a glossy cover, with a picture of an old mining town, high in the green mountains of Tennessee or Virginia, the sun crouching behind one of the mountain crests, making shadows along the dusty streets. The picture was taken sometime in the thirties or maybe the late twenties. A boxy black car seemed to be making its way toward the camera, and people in high hats and dark tresses walked on the streets.

Inside, the pages were deeply white, with fine dark print and good pictures and artwork. The top of page thirty-eight read *Poetry by*, and at the top of thirty-nine it said, *Suzanne Rule*.

Under that banner, printed down the middle of each page (with a little artwork along the sides that looked like the drooping leaves of a weeping willow tree) were three of Suzanne's poems, including "Stampede."

It was really impressive and I said so.

"You think she'll like that?" Drum said.

"Absolutely."

"You sure I can't talk to her?"

"That would be impossible," I said, still gazing at the magazine.

"Why?"

"I told you. She's so completely impossible, Drum." I looked up at him. "I've been working with her all year and I still haven't seen her eyes."

He took a bite of his bagel then wiped a bit of cream cheese away from his lip. He seemed in a hurry to chew what he'd bitten off, so he could continue trying to persuade me, but I went on. "She's so utterly shy if you tried to talk to her it might do her harm."

"Harm?"

"I'm serious. She's not only shy, she's very fragile. She has not spoken to anyone since I've been there. Except for the few times I've heard her cough and once or twice when she sneezed, I've never heard her voice. As far as I know, no one at the school has."

"Well, shit," he said. "She sounds unbelievably interesting."

"Maybe to you."

"Come on," he said, irritated at my ignorance. "Emily Dickinson was just as banked and withdrawn."

"Well, she's no Emily Dickinson," I said.

"But she has talent. I'd like to work with her."

"I really can't allow it."

He looked at me.

"Thank you for this," I said, holding up the magazine. "It really is a wonderful favor."

"I didn't do it for you."

"I know."

"It was my idea, not yours."

"Well I wanted to show you the poems. I must have had a reason. Maybe I helped it along a little."

He smiled, then let out a very loud laugh. "Goddamn Jameson, you got into the wrong business. You ought to be selling insurance or Fords."

"Anyway," I said. "Thank you for having the idea and for getting this done. It will mean a lot to her."

I couldn't wait to show the magazine to Suzanne.

I got to school very early the next day. It was May 10th and the deep blue sky was filled with high white puffs of cloud that opened just enough to let the earliest rays of sun leak through. North or South or both had left his usual morning deposit—it had been so long since I'd gotten to the place that early, I almost forgot the odor that always preceded Mrs. Creighton and her Mr. Clean and chlorine bleach. I stood outside with the magazine, waiting for Granby and Doreen so I could show off Suzanne's work. But nobody was as early as I was. I waited awhile, then went back in my room and put the magazine in my desk drawer. All through the day, I tried to forget it was there. I didn't show it to Doreen or Granby after all. I could have held onto it for a day and then showed it to them maybe in the smoking area after school or tomorrow, but I was too anxious to put it in Suzanne's hands. In the end, I didn't even do that. Right before the beginning of my last class of the day, before she got there, I put the magazine on her desk with a note attached that said, simply,

Suzanne,
For you, and just the beginning, I hope.

Ben

The seniors filed in and I noticed Leslie take her seat, not looking at anyone. She only had her notebook with her. The others talked and joked as they got settled. Suzanne came in, head down as usual, and sat down. I saw her pick up the magazine, and stare at it. She ran her fingers over its surface, studying the cover. She took off my note and put it in her bag. Then she put the magazine down under her chair. She almost didn't look at it. I got everybody to be quiet, then I said, "Take some time and read in your texts for a while. Or whatever you want. We'll have a little quiet reading time."

I didn't look directly at her, but I saw her reach under her chair and retrieve the magazine. She opened it and began paging through it. I watched her now. The others had settled down and were reading quietly. I was standing at my desk, leaning back against it, and when Suzanne got to pages 38 and 39 she seemed to freeze. It was almost as if someone had shouted at her from the surface of her desk. She ran her long, white, fingers over the page as she read what was there, and then by god she raised her head up and looked at me. Her eyes were green, brimmed with tears, and beautiful. Her bright red hair draped on either side of her face made her look almost angelic. For a flawless moment, she stared at me, and I stared at her. I think I had this ridiculous grin on my face. I know I was very happy that she was actually sitting upright and looking at me with those eyes. And something else happened to me. I don't know how to explain this—I mean I can't say why it made me feel this way—but I wanted to understand it and still do. I was ecstatically happy. I had no reason for it, but that is what it was: Happiness, pure and simple.

Somebody sneezed and broke the trance. Suzanne looked down at her desk for a second, then she closed the magazine and holding it against her breast, got up, grabbed her book bag and ran out of the room.

I wasn't sure what to make of that. I think she was crying. I made sure everybody was working, then I ambled out into the hall. I didn't find her there, so I went into Mrs. Creighton's office. Mrs. Creighton was sitting at her desk with those glasses on, writing on a pad. When she noticed I was there, she looked up.

"Did Suzanne come in here?" I asked.

"No."

"Well—she just got up and left my class."

"Maybe she went to the bathroom."

"You think?"

"I can have Doreen check, if you want."

"No," I said. "I'll wait and see." Then I asked if she could talk for a bit and she nodded. I sat down and told her what I had done with Suzanne's poems.

"And they're published?"

I was still proud of it, so I was smiling when I said, "They sure are."

"What were you thinking?" Mrs. Creighton said, an expression of horror on her face.

"What?"

"That little girl is so private, so terribly afraid of . . ."

"No," I interrupted her. "Nothing in the poems is about her. I don't even think the personal pronoun *I* appears in them. They're all very abstract."

"They are." She was gazing at me, still with that look on her face.

"Yes. And what's more, she looked up when I gave her the magazine."

"What do you mean?"

"She sat straight up and looked me in the face."

"And you think that's some kind of breakthrough?"

It was a trick question. I could see she already thought she had the answer. She sat back and placed the tips of her fingers together so that her two hands made a sort of temple between her face and mine. It didn't matter how happy I was, she was not very pleased. I wondered if maybe she knew something about what had gone on with Leslie. I didn't know where to place my hands. Finally I said, "I don't think it's a breakthrough, but isn't it progress?"

"You think so." This was a statement.

"Has she ever looked at you that way?"

"No."

"Or anyone else?"

"She looks at her mother."

"Now she looks at me," I said. "Her eyes are green, by the way."

"I wonder if you know what kind of chance you took with her."

I shrugged. I guess I knew it was a chance, but Drummond convinced me it was a good thing. Who complains about being published? "I thought it would be a very good thing," I said. "The poems were good enough to publish, apparently."

She took a very deep breath that turned into an exasperated sigh. "You don't have any idea of taking precautions do you. You just act. Just go ahead and do things without considering consequences."

"No I don't. I mean I consider consequences."

"You don't. That's the one thing I've noticed about you."

"I hadn't noticed."

"At the prom last spring, did you think about what might happen when you challenged that big bully to go outside and have a cigarette with you?"

"I just suggested we go have a cigarette. I didn't challenge him." I couldn't believe that was her take on what I had done. I thought everybody agreed I had pretty much saved the day.

"It was a reckless thing to do."

"Mr. Creighton said . . ."

"I know he was impressed. I wasn't." She put her hands down in front of her and stared at me, still frowning. It looked as though she was trying to read something written very small on my forehead. "I want you to consider things a little better than you do. Understand?"

"I understand," I said.

"Now you should get back to your class. Let me know if Suzanne doesn't return."

I was pretty dejected, to tell the truth. I think she saw that.

As I was leaving she smiled. "Don't worry, I still believe you will be a wonderful teacher."

I said nothing. I waved slightly and went on back to my class.

45

Roses in Spring

SUZANNE DID NOT come back to class that day. Apparently she waited outside until the end of class then when her mother came to pick her up she simply took the *Hounds-Tooth* home with her and that was that. If I wanted to see the magazine ever again, I'd have to get it from Drummond. I never got any poems from her after that, either. It was so late in the year though, she might have been done writing poems by that time. They had thinned out near the end there anyway. But I was still a little worried about her, to tell the truth. You have to be vigilant with such a delicate and fragile person. Annie said I had again pulled a *bonehead* play. But Suzanne had actually looked at me. I saw her green eyes, bright with wonder. Suddenly she was alive for me in ways she never had been before. I realized that was what her look was: a sign of life. And that is probably at least part of the reason it made me so happy.

I didn't argue with Annie about Suzanne though. I thought I did the right thing, and still do. The only thing I argued with Annie about was the prom that year. I was really hurt that she refused to go with me. "I've been there," she said.

"Well, I have to go."

"You can pretend to be sick."

"No, I can't. It's expected of me. I don't want to go alone."

"Well I'm not going. I don't want to buy a new dress and I'm certainly not going to wear the same dress I wore last year."

"Why not?" I asked. "Everybody said you looked beautiful."

"You don't wear the same dress the next year, you just don't."

"I'm going to wear the same tuxedo."

"You don't have to. Rent something different."

I didn't want to argue. We'd been doing nothing but arguing that whole year it seemed. I was always disappointed and saddened when I got home in the late afternoon and she wasn't there—but on the other hand, sometimes, even in my sadness, I reveled in the solitude. It's hard to be under scrutiny all the time, and lately it seemed as if Annie was always looking for faults.

The prom that year was earlier in the spring—the third week in May—because it had been so hot the year before. I rented the same tuxedo, and Mrs. Creighton rented the same hall. Mr. Creighton again put on a show that stopped everyone; he played a version of The Allman Brothers' song, "Blue Sky," pounding on that guitar with such energy I couldn't sit still.

Doreen wore a dress this time. A pale blue sleeveless gown with some sort of cloth configuration in the middle under her breasts that looked like a white rose. It had a white ribbon that trailed down in front. Her hair was cut a little shorter but parted in the middle, and it shone under the spinning overhead lights in such a brilliant pattern, she really was kind of attractive. Her eyes were dark—especially in that light—and her dark thin eyebrows curved perfectly over them.

You couldn't see the scars on her jaw and chin or on the cheeks either side of her nose. That was a function of the light, but also probably some pretty heavy foundation. She sat by herself again, at a table not far removed from Mr. and Mrs. Creighton, Granby, and me.

Since Annie was not with me I was a little reluctant to be anywhere near Doreen, but I realized she couldn't be left to sit by herself like that. It might have been easier if there was some booze to help me out, but finally I decided I had to say something to her. I figured I would ask her to join us, but then a shadowy, tall, slightly portly figure crossed the dimly lit room and sat down next to her. She smiled and he kissed her hand and when he leaned into the light to do that I realized it was Professor Bible. Mr. Creighton finished his set, and I could see the disc jockey setting up behind him. The quiet couldn't last too much longer.

I walked over and said hello to Professor Bible and he said he was glad to see me. I motioned for him to remain seated, and then I too kissed Doreen's hand. "You look lovely," I said. "All the ladies do."

"Have you seen Leslie?" she asked. It was not ironic; she was enthusiastic about the way Leslie looked. "You've never seen such an angel."

I sat down next to Bible. "How've you been, sir?"

He smiled. "Lost a little weight. I'm taking it easy."

"It's good to see you."

He turned back to Doreen. I felt as if he were sort of leaving me out there with my tuxedo; almost as if he were excluding me. I sat there for a while as he talked to Doreen. His back was to me and I couldn't hear a word he was saying because the disc jockey had started playing his records. But as I started to go back to my table he grabbed my arm and yelled, "Where you going?"

I shrugged.

He pulled me back toward him. "Come on, sit with us."

I sat back down and he leaned away from the table and put his arms over the backs of my chair and Doreen's. When the music stopped momentarily he said, "It's good to see you guys again." I wondered what he would say if he knew what I had been up to.

Then I saw Leslie. She was standing next to an older gentleman who was very lean and tall. He had slightly graying hair over his ears and a broad forehead under dark hair combed straight back. I realized, just as Doreen announced it, that it was Leslie's father.

"Wow," I said.

"Imposing fellow," Bible said.

Leslie caught my eye and gave a slight wave of her hand. She did not smile. She wore a white dress that was open in the back, but that covered the front of her completely. It had some sort of filigree, or lacy pattern above her chest, dark patches of skin and shadows showing through. She wore pure white pearl earrings and a pearl necklace that wrapped around her throat above the dress in three rows. It was an absolutely stunning effect. The dress was floor-length and seemed to have layers of lace and delicate silky white cloth. Wrapped around her waist was a series of bows and ribbons, all whiter than the dress if that was possible. The dress made her skin look dark and smooth. She had two bright red roses in her hair, on one side, just above her ear, which seemed to keep her gold hair back on that side. Her father wore a black tuxedo, and he was a full head and shoulders taller than she was. He took her elbow and sort of moved her into the darkness on the other side of the room. I wondered what kind of asshole would insist on accompanying his daughter to her senior prom.

Then I saw George. He was attending his first prom. He wore a purple tux with black lapels and a black cummerbund. Something about the way he carried himself made me proud. I know I had nothing to do with it, but he showed more confidence now—he'd grown of course from last year and all that weightlifting was paying off. I noticed some of the girls looking at him when he came in. As a date he'd brought a cousin—later I learned his mother had forced this on him—but his cousin was dark and pretty and he didn't seem to mind.

I watched others file in: Jaime Nichols, looking a little frightened and tentative; Harvey Mailler with his gangly walk, wearing a white tux with some sort of fluffy shirt underneath. He looked a little like a pirate. Mark Talbot in a black tux with tails and a white tie; Happy Bell in a white tux with black socks, an outfit I'm sure he designed himself; Pam Green in a dress that seemed to puff her shoulders and the fat around her shoulder blades. All of them walked in as though they were prancing before a camera, as though the evening news would be reporting their arrival.

Suzanne Rule, of course, never came to prom.

The music kept the room shaking enough that I didn't have to explain Annie's absence to anyone. In fact, I didn't have to say very much to anybody if I didn't want to. After a while, Bible turned to me and patted my arm. His lips moved but I couldn't hear his voice. I leaned closer and signaled to him that I couldn't hear.

He hollered, "You decided what you're going to do next year?"

"I don't know," I screamed.

Doreen looked at me. Then she took a little piece of paper out of her purse, borrowed a pen from Bible and wrote, *You better be back here next year, you bastard.*

I thought it was really sweet. She took the tone of one of the boys with me. She had long ago let me off the hook for our kiss, and this note was further confirmation that we would be okay. I smiled.

To tell the truth, I hadn't really thought much about the next year. It was too early. I had sent out some applications, as I said, but it was really just to see. I guess you could say I was letting my applications decide for me.

It was good to see Professor Bible that night. He looked healthy, and maybe happy. Mr. Creighton came over and shook his hand and they made a joke about the Washington Redskins. Mrs. Creighton nodded his way, and smiled at me every time I looked over there.

Sometime in the middle of the evening, Professor Bible, Doreen, and I went outside. It was a bright, cool night. The moon made shadows everywhere. Bible took a flask out of his jacket and the three of us sipped a little bourbon.

"Good stuff," Doreen said through her teeth. It definitely made her squint.

"That's a really nice dress," I said.

"Thank you."

"I liked the tux, last year."

Bible said, "Tux?"

"I wore a tuxedo last year."

"Really."

"In protest because you didn't attend."

Bible laughed.

The three of us stood there. Bible said he wanted a cigarette. Breezes picked up and moved swiftly through the leaves around us. I had this secret burning its way through my mind. What would he say if he knew about Leslie? But I was determined not to tell him.

Doreen brought it up. "So, if I go inside and bum three cigarettes, will you tell me what happened with Leslie?"

Bible looked at me.

"Nothing happened," I said.

"Tell her," Bible said. "I want a cigarette."

I shook my head.

Doreen said to Bible, "Leslie is pregnant. And this guy wanted to know about abortion clinics."

Bible's expression did not change, but he let his eyes fall slightly— as though the news reminded him of something painful.

"Go ahead and get the cigarettes," I said.

Doreen went back inside and Bible and I were alone. Across the lawn and down by the road, cars lined up at a traffic light. Each time the light changed we could hear the small, distant, muffled increase of motors. I thought of all the corners in the world—all of them, in every single hamlet—just like this one: filthy cars and trucks, buses and motorcycles, crowding together always, for all time engines burning inside, each one blowing invisible poison out of its pipes. It didn't seem possible that the earth could possibly survive.

It was quiet a long time, then finally Bible said, "Is there something you want to tell me?"

"I thought we'd wait for Doreen."

"What happened?"

I looked at him. "To Leslie?"

"You can start there."

"Well, she did get pregnant." I couldn't look at him. Inside, the music stopped and everybody began cheering. Then somebody said something into the microphone and the music started up again.

"Go on," Bible said.

Doreen came back with a pack of Marlboro Lights.

"Where'd you get those?" I asked.

"Bummed them from Leslie's father."

"Really. That's ironic as hell."

She smiled broadly and passed out the cigarettes. "Go on," she said. "What did you tell Leslie?"

"I gave her the address."

"And what happened?"

"She's not pregnant anymore."

Doreen's mouth dropped open. "No."

Bible lit his cigarette and handed me the matches. I lit mine and Doreen's. Then I told them the whole story. I was pretty plain about it. I didn't mention the kiss, Leslie's tears, or how I had brushed them away from her eyes after I kissed her.

"I can't believe you went there with her," Doreen said when I was finished.

"I didn't think she could do it alone. And she did ask me to."

"She asked you to?"

"Yeah. She said she couldn't do it unless I went with her."

Throughout this exchange, Bible still had not said anything. I wanted to know what he thought, so I looked at him. I was standing next to him, so I could only see the side of his face; I couldn't read an expression there. It was quiet for more than a minute, and then I said, "So, what do you think?"

"You sure you only went with her because she asked?"

"What do you mean?"

He paused for a beat, then he looked directly at me. "Was the baby yours?"

"Of course not."

I think the vehemence of my response took him back a little. Doreen said, "Good lord, you better hope not."

"It wasn't mine. I don't have that kind of relationship with her."

Bible said, "Still, I would not have gone with her."

"She was so afraid," I said. "I didn't want another George Meeker on my hands."

Bible looked at me now. "Her father was abusive?"

"I don't know. She said he would be rough on her. That he would die if he knew."

I told him about the uncooked rice and Leslie's devotion to him.

"I wonder if you realize the risk you took, young man?" Bible said.

"I know."

"Perhaps you don't know. It could ruin your career."

"She won't tell anybody." I looked at Doreen. "And you won't either, right?"

She seemed hurt. "Of course not."

"I'm not just talking about your career," Bible said. "Young girls like that. She could have formed an attachment."

"Yeah, well," I said.

"It is every bit as much a danger to her as it is to you," he said.

We smoked for a while in silence. I had the feeling Professor Bible disapproved of me now, and it made me want to defend myself. "She really was desperate," I said. "I couldn't just sit by and watch her founder like that."

"What if it was little fat Pamela Green?" Bible said. It was the most crude sentence I'd ever heard come out of his mouth.

"What do you mean?"

"I wonder why you chose to get involved in this one case."

"I've been involved with all of my students," I said. Now I felt as though I was arguing with Annie and I didn't like it. "If you had heard her talk . . . if you had read her journal, you would have tried to help her."

He nodded a bit, but I could see he didn't believe it.

I finished my cigarette and flipped it into the bushes. Bible did the same. Doreen tried to get a last puff or two out of hers and then she said, "I think light cigarettes burn faster."

Bible let out one small huff of a laugh. I made a move to go back in, but he stopped me. "Listen young fellow," he said. "You are important to me. This thing—this involvement with a woman to the extent . . . to where she might have been harmed, or her parents might have had deeply religious objections—you understand that you risked a whole lot more than a simple reputation, don't you?"

"Yes," I said.

"You put her at risk too."

"I think I saved her," I said.

"It's not your job to save anyone. Not your job to even determine if someone needs saving. Not in a classroom, anyway."

I had no response to that.

"You move in traffic of ideas and notions. You teach them to unlock this," he pointed to his head. "How to think about thinking."

"I know."

"You don't intervene so completely into their private lives."

"Sometimes, you're drawn in. Isn't that what happens in every life?"

"All of us get involved to some degree," Doreen said, defending me. A few students came out to smoke. The three of us watched the traffic at the bottom of the hill for a while, then Doreen said, "Anyone want another cigarette?"

"We should get back in," I said.

We moved back into the room. The disc jockey was playing "Smoke Gets in Your Eyes" and in the middle of the dance floor, Leslie Warren danced with her father. He would turn slowly, guiding her. I saw her thin arms, her long, slender fingers spread wide on the back of his black coat. I couldn't see her face. Then his face would come round, and the back of Leslie's head, her hair brilliantly lit, reflecting like something woven from gold. They were a striking couple. When the song was over, he stood back and clapped, and I saw her eyes glistening as she looked up at him. He watched the disk jockey as he clapped, but she watched him. I think it is sometimes possible to see love in a woman's eyes, and that is what I saw in Leslie's eyes that night. She clearly idolized her father. So much so that I was beginning to think maybe I was wrong about him being an asshole. Perhaps she insisted on bringing him to the prom instead of one of her many suitors. I was proud of her that night and I couldn't wait to tell her father that she was going to graduate.

I was also glad I had been spared from an individual conference with him over the earlier troubles with Leslie. He was such a tall and imposing figure. He might have talked me into passing his little girl whether she did any work or not. I really mean that.

Later that night she introduced me to him. He had a firm, eager sort of handshake, and he smiled a lot. Leslie told him I was now one of her favorite teachers. "That's quite an accomplishment," he said.

I thanked him, and smiled at Leslie. She glanced over at Doreen and said, "Hi." She waved sort of automatically at Professor Bible.

"Your daughter will graduate this year," I said to Leslie's father.

"Well, thank you," he said.

"It's Leslie's doing," I said. "She's the one who has buckled down and done all the work. She's been . . ." I smiled at her. "A fine student this year."

He put his arm around her, and she looked up at him. "She's my little girl," he said. Then he talked about his travels, how he was always on the road and always thinking of his family. He said he didn't like being so far away, that he used to call Leslie at all hours of the night, but she never minded it at all.

"I didn't," Leslie said.

"Did you know she speaks three languages besides English," he said proudly.

"Well yes, I guess I did know that."

"I always tried to include her in things I was up to—especially downtown here. Sometimes, I'd take her with me to Europe. I like to have someone with me I trust." He squeezed her and the smile left her face.

"I agree," I said a little too loud.

"You do," he said. I had the feeling he knew more than he was letting on; that he might know all that had happened with his daughter, and it made me tense and uneasy. Suddenly I wanted to be away from him.

Leslie looked at me, a slightly puzzled frown on her brow, then she smiled. Something intimate passed between us. That's exactly what it felt like: she and I shared a kind of intimacy and it made me feel rather extraordinary: nervous, and excited, and even a little triumphant. And frightened too. For her. I was conscious of her looking at me during the rest of our conversation with her father, and I felt admired, as though winning Leslie's trust and admiration was an achievement. But I really didn't want her to be in love with me. I wanted to believe she was mature enough to realize that a lot of girls fall in love with their teachers. Her father whirled her back away from us when the music started again and I watched them dance. She seemed completely okay just then.

Back at our table, Doreen said, "I think Leslie's father is hot."

I said nothing.

After a while, Professor Bible wanted to know how Suzanne Rule was doing. I was still staring at Leslie and her father. I heard Doreen say, "I wonder what happened to her."

"Tonight?" said Bible.

"No. I mean before she came to the school."

Bible said, "You really don't know?"

I turned to him. Doreen too was paying attention now. "You know what happened to her, too?" I said.

"I heard something from Mrs. Creighton about rape," Doreen said. "Or some kind of ongoing abuse by her father, but I don't know if it's true or not."

"Mrs. Creighton said her father was involved," I said.

"Her father had sex with her for most of her life. He even let his friends in on it."

"Jesus," I said.

Doreen shook her head, still staring at Bible. "His friends?"

"It was his way of getting back at his wife. His hatred trumped any other emotion with him. I'm surprised you didn't know about it. I thought everybody did."

"I don't think Mrs. Creighton knows," I said. "She said she didn't . . ."

"She knows. She just probably made up her mind not to tell anybody. It's private."

"Of course," I said.

"And anyway, it doesn't matter what kind of abuse," Bible said. "That's not what matters now." We fell quiet for a beat, then he said, "What you should be worrying about is how to reach her. How to get her to learn."

I knew who he was addressing but I had nothing more to say on the subject. I might have bragged a bit about getting Suzanne published, and about her poems to me and all, but I figured after everything we'd talked about that night, I wouldn't mention it. Besides, I think I knew what he might say. I admired him enough that I was afraid of his judgment.

And I realized nothing could save Suzanne Rule.

46

A Formal Feeling Comes

AFTER THE PROM I tried not to worry about Leslie too much. She still came to school looking worn out and sad. Her hair was frequently unwashed and hung down limply by her ears. But she smiled a little more and I knew she would eventually get over everything and come back to herself. I counted it a triumph when I made her laugh a little bit in class. It seemed to me that we had this bond of affection between us because of what we'd been through. (I really did think of it as something we had both endured.) I did not want to encourage her feelings toward me, but more and more I found myself wondering at the possibilities; at all the things that might develop once Leslie graduated. I didn't want to have thoughts like that; it felt like a kind of plot in the back of my mind, ready to hatch at any further sign of Leslie's readiness.

I would never consciously pursue her as long as she was my student. It's just that suddenly she was possible and that knowledge changed something in my heart. We talked to each other almost as equals when we were not in class and, to be completely honest, at some level I must have wanted to charm her; to win her over again, not in any romantic way, but to bring her back from guilt and rejection. If she ever actually fell in love with me it would have to be in completely different circumstances. I don't really think that is what I wanted though. If it was, I did nothing to bring it about. I was afraid of that, to tell the truth. I didn't want to do anything that might threaten my relationship with Annie. I loved Annie. Or at least I thought I did and the idea of breaking up with her made me sick at heart. But to come close to falling in love with Leslie—to have her think for a while that she was in love with me—was so intoxicating I would be lying if I said it was not on my mind. I really was balancing on a kind of high wire, trying to be everything my job as a teacher called me to without taking advantage of either my knowledge or my influence, so that I might win her trust again—not in me but in her own capacity for love; in the human potential for healing and restoration. Why should that desire be any less ennobling than the wish to teach her the world?

Then near the end of May, during a long period of unusually hot weather, Leslie came to school one day looking the way she always used to: her hair perfectly quaffed and her makeup just right—understated but with a hint of glamour, so that her features just seemed to glow with loveliness. She wore a white skirt, a light blue blouse, with a red scarf tied loosely around her throat.

"Well, look at you," I said, for she was early and there was no one else in the room with us. "You are the picture of spring this morning."

"Thank you," she said, with cheer in her voice.

I watched her take her seat. She looked at me, then averted her eyes, but she was smiling. We were simply glad to be in each other's company. That's all it was. Then Suzanne came in, hunched over as usual. She sat down in her chair and stared at the surface of her desk. I said good morning to her, and she nodded slightly. Eventually the whole class filed in and we got down to work. Leslie really had regained something of her old, spirited self. Everything awakened in her bold blue eyes—she was animated and alluring. I was teaching the difference between inductive and deductive reasoning and when I started talking about syllogisms she raised her hand excitedly and announced to the class that she knew what they were, that she'd been working with them at "the London School," in her freshman year when she and her family had been in England. I enlisted her help in explaining how the syllogism works and she showed that she knew more about them than I did. I knew the basic form—premise A plus premise B equals conclusion C. The most famous syllogism is, of course the old saw about Socrates.

All men are mortal
Socrates is a man
Therefore Socrates is mortal.

But I didn't teach it like that. I wanted to get their attention so I wrote it like this:

Some day all human beings will be rotting humus
We're all human beings, therefore
some day we will all be rotting humus.

Then I showed them what fun you can have with syllogisms. I wrote the old joke on the board:

God is love
Love is blind
Therefore, Ray Charles is God

Everybody laughed, including Suzanne Rule I think, but then Leslie started talking about the "undistributed middle term" and other things that I'd never heard of. I was so proud of her.

At the end of the class I went over to her and patted her on the shoulder. "Very good, Leslie. Even I learned something." She smiled and thanked me. Her voice was strong and sweetly girlish. I was elated that she had gotten beyond her guilt. I wished Annie and Bible could see her now; I wished they could have witnessed her gradual return to happiness. As she picked up her books and started out of the room, she turned and bestowed a glorious smile, waving one lovely hand. Once again I had the most profound sense of well-being; I felt exactly as I had when Suzanne Rule sat up and looked at me with those amazing green eyes: buoyant, and lucky. Like you feel on the finest day when you are young and free; free to enjoy every second of it. It was a feeling that had the purity of youth and all the great possibility of a long future bound up in it. I think people get to a certain age and they forget how that feels. And isn't that the very beginning of old age—when you can no longer actually feel the exquisite permanence of youth? I knew I would go home, find Annie smiling a greeting, and I would forget my anxiety about Leslie. All that was going to happen between us had already happened. I was absolutely convinced of it. I almost skipped to the parking lot and my car. Maybe, I thought, this is truly what I was meant to do.

And on that warm, windless day, while I drove home from school, marinating in my joy, Leslie Warren went home and put a bullet through her head.

47

The Sky, It Seems,
Would Pour Down

THERE'S SOMETHING KIND of disingenuous about teenage expressions of grief. Don't get me wrong. They're sincere enough, I guess. But you have to admit, when the newspapers report that a young teen's funeral has been attended by at least a "thousand of her closest friends," it gets a little hard to swallow. I attended Leslie's funeral. So did Doreen, Mrs. Creighton, and most of the people from the school. Even Suzanne Rule made a stooped appearance, her hair hanging scruffily by her face, her white ears sticking out like potato chips through a red curtain. I watched Leslie's parents. I don't think I've ever seen people more stricken, pale, and distraught in my life. They looked as if they were continually witnessing Leslie's death; watching her fall.

What happened the day she killed herself was pretty clear. According to her mother, Leslie came home, bounced into the family room, threw her arms around her neck and said, "I love you." Mrs. Warren said she hugged her daughter and told her she was a "wonderful young woman, now." Then Leslie said she had to do some homework. She did not call her father, as some newspapers reported. He was in Ireland. She went into her father's den, took out one of his pistols—a .22-caliber revolver he'd taught her how to shoot, the *Washington Post* reported ruefully—went into her room, put the gun against her head, just above the left ear, and pulled the trigger.

There were early reports of a possible homicide. "Young women don't kill themselves this way," the Fairfax County chief of police said. But apparently she had been planning it for a long time because a few days after the event her parents got a letter from her. She had composed a suicide note the day before and posted it to her mother at the home address.

That whole week was just a blur. I know the sun came up; the days were warm and slightly breezy with just enough clouds to make the sky a wreath of white in blue sorrow. The song of birds in the morning sounded vaguely insulting; as if sweetness had not withdrawn from everything. When the leaves on the trees hissed in the warm, swift breeze, it sounded like something that rose out of hatred; as if the whole world scoffed at anything lovely. I hated anyone who made the argument that a tiny bundle of cellular tissue is a human being.

At first I was angry. I mean really enraged at the insipid stupidity of it. How could she have done that? She was so happy and normal the last time I saw her. How could anyone with such promise destroy all the bloody future? I couldn't get my mind to grasp it. But eventually everything I looked at came to me in light of her place in it—the rooms of the school, the parking lot, the chair she sat in—as if every single angle of repose was empty of her shadow and lacking something essential, something that made life real and sweet and apprehensible.

I know now that I loved her more than I could possibly know.

I think on some level all of us loved her—even when she was being the most difficult and mean-spirited little brat. There was something so discordantly lovely about her.

But I still don't think I loved her in a sexual or romantic way. I loved her because she was my student, and a human being. I didn't want her because she was beautiful; I didn't want her at all. But I loved her because she was smart, and she had something to offer the world, if only somebody could find a way to help her see whatever it was the world would need from her, or what she might have to offer. That's what I thought I was doing. Was it my fault? I ask you. Was anything that happened truly my fault? I'm not looking for absolution here. I really want to know.

I never saw Leslie's note and I can't say, even now, what it said. I know what was in it, though. Shortly after the funeral Mrs. Creighton called me into her office. This was in the last week of classes.

I sat down glumly, still feeling the shock of what had happened. Mrs. Creighton looked at me with withering eyes and I knew instantly something was up. She told me about the note.

"I think the papers said something about it," I said. "Didn't she mail it?"

"Do you want to tell me anything?" she said.

"Pardon?"

"I want to know what was going on between you and Leslie Warren."

"Nothing was going on."

She frowned, glanced down at the papers on her desk. Then she softened a bit, seemed to remember something pleasant. "I told you once that I thought you were a wonderful teacher."

"I know it."

"You know what?"

"That you said that."

"But I told you not to go too far. Do you remember that?"

I nodded.

"You are always in danger as a young teacher," she said.

I nodded again.

"Things happen between people. We're all human beings."

Still, I didn't see the point in saying anything.

"And where else is love more likely to take place than in a class-room? It's natural. You can have a true meeting of minds—the most vital and deeply rewarding contact between people."

"I don't understand," I said.

"You are a very young man. Only a few years older than Leslie was, right?"

"I'm eight years . . . I'm twenty-six," I said.

"Leslie's mother says the note mentions you, it talks about being passionately in love, a pregnancy. The loss of that love. You know nothing about that?"

I didn't know what to say. I looked at my hands fumbling together in my lap as though they were looking for a place to hide. "She wasn't in love with me," I whispered.

"Do you want to tell me what was going on?"

"Nothing," I said. "Not what you think."

"You were sleeping with her weren't you."

"I was not."

"It's not a punishable charge," she said, wryly. "Mrs. Warren already looked into it. Leslie is—Leslie was eighteen, and so . . ."

"I wasn't sleeping with her," I said. "Jesus Christ."

I saw the corners of her mouth start to droop a little and realized she was fighting tears. "If you have anything to tell me," she said, struggling with herself, keeping everything back. "I want to help you if I can. But you must tell me the truth."

"It is the truth."

"Do you have anything else to say?"

"I'm sorry."

"I want to know what was going on," she was a bit stronger, now. Not loud, but in control of her sadness.

Mr. Creighton came in, pulled a chair up next to the desk and sat down. I was facing the two of them.

"Mrs. Creighton," I said, "I think you've got the wrong idea, here." I tried to keep my voice steady. I was still in shock over what had happened; still had not talked about it to anybody. Even Annie. I said nothing to any human soul. I walked around like somebody who's been placed under some sort of robotic spell; unconscious, mechanical, deliberate. I wasn't really human; I was a doleful contrivance, with circuits and gears. But now I had to talk about it.

I said, "I . . . I . . . wasn't . . ." I couldn't control my voice.

Mr. Creighton said, "You better have something to say for yourself young man, because you've put this entire school in jeopardy."

"I have?"

"They are suing us," Mrs. Creighton said. "The Warren family is suing this school and you."

"Me?"

She picked up a piece of paper on the desk and handed it to me. It was a legal summons. My name was at the top of it.

"Good god," I said.

"You're going to need God," Mr. Creighton said. "You're going to need a good attorney too."

"I don't have that kind of money."

"Tell me what was going on," he said. "You have to tell all of it."

"Nothing was going on. She got pregnant, I tried to help her."

"Did you meet her at Jolito's after school?" he asked.

My heart turned to ice. They knew about Jolito's. I said, "I met her there once or twice. It was during her trouble over the, over her . . ."

"You didn't get her pregnant."

"No. Of course not."

Mrs. Creighton said, "The Warrens think you had an affair with their daughter and that you got her pregnant. And when she told you about it, you abandoned her. Threw her away."

"Did her note say that?"

"No."

"Well how'd they get the idea then?"

"They were suspicious about who she was—about how she was spending her time." She fiddled with a document on her desk.

I waited.

"So Mr. Warren hired a private detective who followed Leslie. Your name was in his report. He says you met with her at Jolito's, twice, and that you drove her to the clinic in Alexandria where she apparently got the abortion."

"I met her at Jolito's three times. I accidentally ran into her there the first time. And yes, I drove her to the clinic. She was desperate. I wanted to help her."

"And you helped her get an abortion?" Mrs. Creighton said.

"That's what she wanted. She said she had to."

"She did."

"I didn't get her pregnant." I almost said, *Leslie didn't know who got her pregnant*, but then I thought of her—of her fright and desperation—and I wanted so bad to protect her in some way, rescue her from this judgment, I said nothing more.

Mr. Creighton said, "Did she say who did?"

"No sir, she didn't." I had my *Leslie's Complaint* folder in my desk. I also had her journal. I could take everything out and show them all her entries about Randy and Raphael. It would save me from all of it, but I couldn't make myself say anything else. I remembered Leslie's eyes, her note to me on the folded page of her journal, the last smile she cast my way, and I stopped talking.

"You don't know who she was sleeping with?"

"No."

"But you could find out. She's written it somewhere."

"I don't have anything more to say. I've told you all I know."

"Tell me what she told you," Mr. Creighton said.

I explained Leslie's desperation, her guilt afterward. They listened patiently, and I thought again that I might save myself without talking about her journal entries. I wanted to find some safe ground. But when it came to what I knew, I just couldn't make myself betray her that way. It was just too important and private to share it with anyone. I went on a bit about her unreasoning guilt. Then I said, "I think she may have misunderstood my help. She got to think, briefly, that she was in love with me."

"And you threw her away," Mrs. Creighton said.

"No. I never let on that I knew."

"What do you mean?"

"She wrote it on a note she didn't want me to see. She didn't know I saw it."

"You're sure of that."

"I told her she would find love again, but I don't think I—I guess, for sure I didn't convince her." I felt my voice break.

"Her mother thinks she wasn't just despondent over the abortion," Mrs. Creighton said. "She believes you used Leslie then cast her aside when she got pregnant."

"It's not what happened."

"How else would Mrs. Warren get that idea?"

"I don't know. It wasn't me."

It was quiet for what seemed like a long time. I think I could hear Mr. Creighton's watch ticking. Then finally he said, "Well?" and looked at Mrs. Creighton.

In a trembling, barely audible voice she said, "I'm afraid we're going to have to let you go, Benjamin."

"Really?"

"I'm afraid so." Now she did have tears in her eyes. She looked out the window, struggled to catch it, suppress it. She took a deep breath and went on. "I want you to finish out the year. It's only the rest of the week. But then—well, you were planning on something else anyway, right?"

"I was going to go to law school."

"Well, perhaps that's for the best."

I said nothing.

"If there is some way you can prove that you weren't involved with Leslie. If you could . . ."

"You'll have to take my word for it."

"I wish I could." She shook her head. "I wish you had not helped her get that abortion."

I got up to leave.

"One thing," Mrs. Creighton said. I stood over her desk and watched her searching for words. Mr. Creighton got up and walked out through the back of her office. He had nothing more to say to me. Mrs. Creighton said, "I would prefer if you didn't make any announcements about your—that you're leaving."

"Okay."

"And don't tell anyone—especially any of the students—about this business with Leslie and her pregnancy and everything."

"I won't," I said. "You can count on that."

She was obviously finished with me. Still I couldn't leave yet. I knew I should say something else, but I couldn't think of it. So I just stood there looking at her.

"What?" she said, when she noticed I hadn't gone.

"I can't think," I said.

"What?"

"I wanted to say something, but I'm caught by surprise." My voice broke again.

"Go ahead."

"I can't think of it."

"Well I'll be here when you do."

"What about the lawsuit?" I asked.

She looked at me.

"I'm named in the suit. What should I do about that?"

"Nothing will go forward until they've talked to all the parties," she said. I thought again of the copied pages and Leslie's journal and felt a sudden, terrific sorrow that erased, for a brief span of time, everything else I could remember, and I knew for certain that I would take the folder and her journal out and burn them the first chance I got. What her parents would come to know about Leslie would be what they remembered about her. Nothing more. Mrs. Creighton looked at me and said, "You aren't out of this just because I'm firing you."

I didn't feel fired until she used that word. My heart sank even further, if that's possible.

"I'll try to keep you out of it," she said. "Once I explain the situation. You're lucky that her mother is not against abortion; she would have made sure they helped her if she had gone to them."

"I told her she should do that."

"Well. I'll explain that you were just being a friend to her . . ."

"That's what it was," I interrupted.

". . . and that you have some very strange ideas about how to be a teacher."

I said nothing. I stood there watching her for the longest time, then it hit me what I had wanted to say earlier. I had a hard time saying it, because tears welled up in my eyes. "I'm sorry I let you down."

As she went back to the work on her desk she said, "Don't forget to keep quiet about all this."

"I will," I said. An easy promise to make. I didn't feel like talking about Leslie and what happened ever again in my life. For sure I wasn't going to say anything to Annie about it. She thought Leslie was troubled and just turned out to be one of those "teen suicides." But you see, she wasn't just another "teen." She was an extraordinary and distinct human being, with a mind and intelligence and a powerful spirit; something in her eyes told you she was worth paying attention to, and I'm not talking about her glamour, either. I'm talking about who she was. How could someone with such promise turn away from the earth? It was all such a terrible waste.

No, I would not tell Annie one bit of it. I didn't think I would ever tell anyone about it.

48

Final Exam

MY LAST WEEK went a little too fast. There was nothing in it to
savor, but I still found myself carrying on as though I was going to
lose something grand. I don't know how to explain it. I walked around
looking at the shelves of books, the desks, the notes on the board as
though I was going to leave not just the school but this life; as though
my leaving would be from all the earth.

I said at the beginning that I wanted to tell the truth as accurately as
I can. I would not want to sully Leslie's memory or the tragedy of her
family by being prosaic now, and I am perfectly willing to accept my
responsibility for all that has happened. But so many factors played a
role, and I am trying to understand so much more than culpability.
Even if the whole thing was my fault I wonder what I might have done
differently. How could I be other than I am? What is a teacher's job,
anyway? I had to watch George Meeker get brutalized by his father—
I knew it was happening. I saw the marks on his neck, the bruises on his
cheekbone and the side of his head, and I was helpless against it. I had

to teach him about prepositions and pronouns, sentence fragments and parallel constructions, so whenever he finally discovered enough hate in his heart to report his old man, he could describe his own suffering accurately and with style. Is that all a teacher is responsible for?

I still don't know if I should have refused to help Leslie. She was so desperate and sad. How could anyone have said no to her?

Mrs. Creighton stayed away from me most of that last week. My classes, as I said, went way too fast. I was finished with grading, mostly. I had the freshmen and sophomores write one final essay about their plans for the summer, but most of them wanted to write about Leslie and how much she had meant to them. I got to read a hundred essays about the shock of her death and the terrible sadness of it. They all wished they had said some final thing to her about how much they loved her. Jaime Nichols wrote: *I just know Leslie died so God could teach me to treasure those I love.* I wrote: *What kind of God do you believe in exactly? What if somebody else wanted to teach you an important lesson by killing a person?* I admit I wasn't very gentle or lucid. That kind of thinking has always angered me. I can't think of anything more profoundly selfish or self-centered than a "Christian" with a "personal" relationship with God. Leslie died so Jaime could learn something important in her *own* life. Jesus Christ!

Another student wrote: *Leslie's death is God's way of teaching us the meaning of beauty because her beauty couldn't save her.*

I didn't bother to respond to that.

Suzanne Rule wrote nothing in her journal about Leslie or anything else.

The seniors, of course, continued to grieve right through graduation. They made speeches at the ceremony about what they would remember most about her. All of them believed that Leslie was as dear a friend as any of them would ever have. And all of them had fond memories of their time with her.

I did not see any reason to point out that our memory of the newly dead is always slightly marred by our own apprehensions; or that counterfeit grief is really simply a kind of offering, in the hope that death will be satisfied with our suffering and leave us alone for a long time to come. I guess it is also a result of the romantic notion that if we can give meaning to the life of someone we barely knew, we can lend a little importance to our own lives.

On the last day, Mrs. Creighton stopped me on the way to my first period class and whispered, "Good luck, young man."

"Thank you."

"I don't think you need worry over the lawsuit. Leslie had a boyfriend her parents knew nothing about. And there was another fellow—it's a huge mess."

I wasn't glad to hear that. I felt so sorry for Leslie and her parents. I wonder why it is such a terrible thing to discover that somebody you have loved and cherished is simply human. It would be a long time, I realized, before I thought anything in the universe was good. I nodded at Mrs. Creighton and started to turn away, not wanting any emotional displays, and she stopped me. "One more thing. Her parents wanted me to let you know how much Leslie respected and admired you."

I had nothing to say to that.

"I wish . . ." she paused. Then she touched my sleeve, seemed to watch as her fingers ran down the side of my arm. "I wish . . ." Now she looked at me. "I wish things had gone differently."

"Me too."

"If you hadn't helped her get that abortion, I think Mr. Creighton would not object to you coming back. He really liked . . . he likes and admires you."

"I know," I said.

"Well . . ." she smiled, tears welling in her eyes.

"Yes," I said. "Good-bye."

"You know," she said, still fighting tears. "You are invited to graduation."

"I know."

"We do hope you come." She went on back into her office and I walked in to my classroom to start my last day as a teacher.

At the end of the last period, after everyone had filtered out, I sat at my desk and stared at Leslie's chair. I would have had to say good-bye to her on this day anyway. She was a senior and she would have graduated. She had earned an A in my class.

The room was brightly lit. Outside the air was balmy and sweet with the smell of wisteria and honeysuckle. Through the picture window of my classroom I saw the new leaves stirred slightly by mild, summer breezes. Broad white clouds blossomed and grew silently in the blue cathedral above the dark green trees. It was a beautiful day. A memorable day. I made up my mind I would not feel badly about anything but what happened to Leslie. I sat there a long time as the building emptied. I watched those clouds reforming themselves, changing from great churning puffs to thin, wispy hints of what they once were, and I knew I would go home, and prepare myself for law school and Annie. I was going to work on my relationship with her. I was bent on repairing it. She said on that last morning that we should "take the summer to reconsider things," so that is what I planned on doing. I was just too numb to apprehend what she really meant by that.

Finally, when I was fairly certain the building was empty, I got up and started putting papers in folders and arranging things in my brief-case. I cleaned out my desk, and put one piece of chalk—my only souvenir—in one of the inside pockets.

As I was closing the strap on the briefcase and buckling it, concentrating on it, I realized someone else was in the room. I looked up, and there—fully erect and sort of heaving with it, her red hair draped on both sides of her face—stood Suzanne Rule. She wore a blue sweat-suit kind of jacket, and blue sweat pants with white tennis shoes. When she knew I saw her, she took a deep breath, and then as if it was her first attempt at it, she walked slowly across the space in the middle of the room. She did not look down. It was as though she were walking a tightrope, but I will never forget her bright, green eyes, the small red freckles across her nose and cheeks, the look of pride and determination on her face as she approached me.

When she got to my desk, she paused. I wanted to say something—anything—to congratulate her for walking upright that long, for letting me see her face. I looked at her hands, expecting her to pass me a note of some kind, but her hands were empty. They grasped the sides of her sweatpants. When I looked up again I realized she was fighting tears. Her eyes did not meet mine; they seemed to study something on the wall just above and behind me as she said, "Thank you, Mr. Jameson. Thank you . . . for all this year." Her voice was delicate and sweet, like birdsong. I had tears in my own eyes. Before I could say anything, she nodded, and now she did look in my eyes. "Thank you," she said again, in a slight whisper. Then she turned around and walked out of the room.

I would not want to surrender how I felt at that moment for all the money on earth.

49

Commencement

GRADUATION TOOK PLACE in the bright, sunlit yard above the basketball court. It should have been a small celebration—we only had twenty-nine graduates, each of them dressed in a light blue cap and gown—but with family members and friends, it turned out to be a fairly crowded afternoon. Mrs. Creighton gave the graduating address. In her high, trembling voice, she talked of the future. She did not mention Leslie Warren, although when some of the seniors got up to speak that's all they talked about. It saddened me to realize that Leslie was an inspiration to all of them.

George graduated with honors. I watched him at the ceremony. In the cap and gown he looked taller and carried himself with a kind of strength, in a way that showed he was distinguished, proud, and ready. He would take what he wanted from the world. I saw him hugging his father and mother and a host of relatives and admirers. His father actually came up to me and shook my hand. He had tears in his eyes. "I sure am proud of that boy," he said.

"Well, he's a young man," I said. "Not a boy at all."

He looked at me without the slightest sign of recognition or awareness that I might remember what a prick he was. All I could do was let go of his hand and turn away from him.

I had one very proud moment.

Mrs. Creighton stood at the top of the small rise in the ground and called out the names of the graduates and asked each to come to the front and receive a diploma. When she called out Suzanne Rule's name, she stood straight up and walked across the open space between the graduates and Mrs. Creighton, who handed her the diploma with tears in her eyes. Suzanne looked out at the small crowd. It was so quiet suddenly, it seemed that the whole world noticed her posture and waited to see what she would do. Mrs. Creighton whispered to her, and then Suzanne gave a small, unpracticed smile and started to walk back down the hill.

The crowd let go a soft, scattered bit of laughter, which stopped her. She was in the middle of the open space of ground, holding her diploma in her small white hands, still standing upright. Mrs. Creighton had tears streaming down her face. Then people began clapping tentatively and Mrs. Creighton walked down and put her arms around Suzanne and held her for a quiet moment. Then everybody started clapping loudly and cheering. It was a small, beautiful thing to see.

Once all the names had been called and the graduates had thrown their caps in the air, I found my way to the parking lot and got in my car. I didn't want to stick around for the party. I already felt as though I had inadvertently stumbled into somebody else's revelry and I didn't want to suffer a lot of farewells. As I was pulling out of the place, though, I saw Doreen standing at the edge of the basketball court by herself. I stopped, rolled down my window, and waved to her. She came over to me, smiling.

"Where's Annie?"

"I'm going to get her now. We're going out to dinner."

She nodded. It was quiet for a long time. Then she said, "Don't be a stranger."

"I won't."

"I'm awful sorry," she said.

"Don't," I said. "Really. It's just how things turned out."

She touched my arm. "Weren't you proud of our Suzanne?"

"Yes I was."

"You should be proud of yourself, too."

"Yeah, well."

"You should be."

I patted her hand, then put the car in gear. "See you," I said.

She waved and I drove away from Glenn Acres for the last time.

I have not seen Suzanne Rule since that last day at Glenn Acres. I'll probably never know what happened to her. Shortly after I left the school I heard from Doreen that Suzanne and her mother moved to Florida. I don't know if she ever learned to face the world or speak to people the way I hoped she would. I would have loved to have given her that, too. But I am pretty sure I gave her poetry, and poetry is a terrific gift to give a person.

And maybe that is what a really good teacher is, finally: a man or woman with only the best intentions, bearing gifts. Imagine how you'd feel if you could hand somebody music, or movies, or books, or art, or history, or anything in the world worth knowing; if you could give somebody that kind of treasure in a few moments of time, every day, for just a little while. I still think of Suzanne Rule every time I read a poem. Every time I open a poetry journal I look for her name.

And I think of Leslie. I remember her smile, the tempting way she would turn my way when she thought she was going to destroy me, and how much that look seemed to mirror the other one—the look she gave me when I knew she was helpless and grateful, and how much it seemed to ask for a simple embrace. When I took Leslie in my arms I loved something totally other than glamour, or attractiveness, or sex. I loved her for herself, with no calculation whatsoever about my rights in the matter. As the poet said, I had no rights, since I was neither father nor lover.

A few weeks after I left Glenn Acres, Annie and I broke up. It turned out that what she wanted to work out over the summer was how to do that. She and Steven realized they were made for each other, which was not really a big surprise. I think Annie and I discovered over those two years I was a teacher that we were *not* made for each other. Anyway, I was so brokenhearted over Leslie I didn't really seem to notice what was happening around me until Annie was gone. I have to admit, I missed her for a long time.

50

A Long Time Ago

IT'S BEEN MORE than twenty years. Twenty-four new summers have come and gone, and now it's fall again, and I am working still for the U.S. government in the Antitrust Division. I have spent my life examining business contracts and corporation agreements; studying mergers and acquisitions; policing hedge funds and banking practices in the federal financial system. It is interesting work sometimes, but not at all what I believed I'd end up doing with my life. Sometimes I think of ways to change, to get away from it all and go back to teaching somewhere. I spend most of my time reading documents that were not written to be understood; I have to truly study every phrase to make sure very clever people are obeying the law, which is to say I am in the law library more than I am anywhere else.

I will probably think of my days at Glenn Acres for the rest of my life. Even after all this time, it is all so fresh in my memory, I don't know if I'll ever get to a point that it doesn't occupy my mind whenever I have a chance to think about things.

I often wonder what might have happened if I had refused to help Leslie, or if I had insisted that she take care of the problem herself. I think it's possible she might have ended up doing the same thing. On my worst days, I wonder what would have happened if she had gone to her parents and discovered love in their response. I also wonder how long I might have stayed at Glenn Acres if Leslie had been alive to attend graduation. Lately I've been trying to get up the nerve to take a weekend away from my work and drive out to see if the school is still there; I know Mrs. Creighton died not too long ago—I think it was 1999. I never saw Bible again but I'm sure he must have gone to feed the roses not long after I left Glenn Acres. For a long time after I left there, I kept in touch with Doreen. We saw each other occasionally over the years. She and I'd go have a drink and laugh over our brief time together. I was never really attracted to her the way I was attracted to Annie, and of course she didn't move me at all the way Leslie did, but I liked Doreen. In spite of our age difference, I trusted her then more than I ever dreamed possible. This truly surprised both of us since she knew that deep down she was so completely untrustworthy. I still have coffee with her every now and then. She told me about Mrs. Creighton's passing. Something about Doreen always made me feel as though I could say almost anything and I always felt comfortable around her. And now she's become the principal of a new school in Fairfax and she has asked me to consider coming back to teach for her.

I don't know if I ever truly missed teaching. I spent a lot of time in the classroom as a student when I was in law school, and I noticed things other teachers did. I watched the classroom manner of teachers who simply read from their notes and stood behind the lectern as though it was some kind of protection from a firing squad. While they read, the students tried desperately to write it all down, and the only one in the room who used his mind was the guy who fell asleep and had a dream. Why didn't "teachers" like that simply hand over their notes and be done with it? Why not save everybody a whole hell of a lot of time?

I'm not saying I knew any better. Or I shouldn't be saying that. I was such a failure at it myself. But I wonder about what my life would have been like if I had remained a teacher. I always thought I might get another chance at it someday, but I never really pursued it. After all that happened I didn't think it was actually possible. Could I leave something like Glenn Acres off a résumé? And how could I include, in any record of my professional life, what happened with Suzanne Rule? At times I believe that my one real success with her is the only memory from my short life as a teacher that cannot wane or darken with time. I think of it as something I possess that no one can take away.

I've gone on with my life, of course, and I am the best lawyer I can be. I've married twice, and failed at it both times, but I am not unhappy. Sometimes I think about those two years at Glenn Acres as though it were something in the recent past. I'll be sitting in the library, reading some case history in a law book, and suddenly I'll look up and stare at the yellow sunlight filtering into the high windows above me, or I'll hear a siren outside, or maybe I'll notice a cold rain dripping down the drains and trickling in the gray, watery light of those same windows—and I'll think of seasons gathering and passing and then I can't concentrate on much of anything. I remember all those faces, a few bright days, and Leslie's radiant smile the last time I saw her. It will always make me sad. But I also remember the look on Suzanne Rule's face when she first saw her poems in that magazine and she lifted her head and looked at me with those green, dazzling, secret eyes. I remember the harmonics in her trembling voice when she said, "Thank you, Mr. Jameson. Thank you for all this year," and before long I'm daydreaming about working with young kids again, about bearing gifts. At times like that I actually believe it might be possible that perhaps I will become a teacher once more.

Who knows?
Maybe I could do some good.

Robert Bausch
Stafford, Virginia
April 2014

A Note on the Author

Robert Bausch is the author of many works of fiction, most recently the novels *Far as the Eye Can See* and *The Legend of Jesse Smoke*. He was born in Georgia and raised around Washington, D.C., and received a BA, MA, and MFA from George Mason University. He's been awarded the Fellowship of Southern Writers Hillsdale Award and the John Dos Passos Prize, both for sustained achievement in literature. He lives in Virginia.